The Blind Season

OTHER WORKS BY RONALD L. DONAGHE

From the series: Common Threads in the Life

Common Sons, a novel (1989, 1997, 2000)

The Blind Season, a novel (2001)

The Salvation Mongers, a novel (2000)

The Gathering, a novel (scheduled publication 2003)

From the series: The Continuing Journals of Will Barnett

Uncle Sean, a novel (2001)

Lance, a novel (2002)

All Over Him, a novel (2003)

From the fantasy trilogy: Twilight of the Gods

Cinátis, Volume I (Renaissance Alliance Publishers, Silver Dragon Books, 2002)

Cinátis, Volume II (coming)

Gwi's War (coming)

War Among the Gods (coming)

Autobiography

My Year of Living Heterosexually and Other Adventures in Hell (2000)

Letters in Search of Love and Other Essays (1998)

Work appearing in other anthologies and novels

"Deming, New Mexico" in John Preston's *Hometowns: Gay Men Write About Where They Belong* (Dutton/Penguin, 1991)

"My Sister and I" in John Preston's *A Member of the Family: Gay Men Write About Their Families* (Dutton/Penguin, 1992)

"AIDS in Paradise" in Dallas Lemmon's *The Deming Six: Voices of the Chihuahuan Desert* (The Winesburg Press, 1995)

"Foreword" in Alfred Lees'/Ronald Nelson's *Longtime Companions: Autobiographies of Gay Male Fidelity* (Haworth Press, 1999)

"Foreword" in Mark Roeder's *A Better Place* (Writer's Club Press, 2001)

"Foreword" in Andrew Barriger's *Finding Faith* (iUniverse, 2003)

The Blind Season

Common Threads in the Life

Ronald L. Donaghe

Writers Club Press
New York Lincoln Shanghai

The Blind Season
Common Threads in the Life

Writers Club Press
an imprint of iUniverse, Inc.

For information address:
iUniverse
2021 Pine Lake Road, Suite 100
Lincoln, NE 68512
www.iuniverse.com

ISBN: 0-595-18976-8

Printed in the United States of America

This book is lovingly dedicated to Cliff, my life mate. The story-line was largely his idea. I have simply written the words to bring it to life. Without him, it is doubtful that my characters would have grown as much as they have, and for that, I am eternally grateful.

Common Threads in the Life

"You kids watch out now. It's the blind season. Them rattlesnakes are sheddin' their skins, kind'a rebirthin' themselves. So they's blind. They's scared. They'll strike without warning."

—Henry Stroud, Sr

CONTENTS

ACKNOWLEDGEMENTS

It has taken me since 1989 to complete the sequel to my novel *Common Sons*. The original *Blind Season* that was to be the sequel just never clicked, even though I spent eleven years writing and revising and reworking it. So in 2000, I put that doomed work aside and began the whole thing from scratch. I've worked at a fever pitch to get this novel to my readers who, over the years, have called me up in the middle of the night wondering when the sequel would be published, sent emails, and otherwise reminded me that they wanted to read more about the characters in *Common Sons*.

So I involved some of my readers in this project, and they graciously put aside time from their own busy schedules to read the various iterations I sent to them for comment. Besides all the readers who have read snippets of this work, I would like to thank Ken Clark for his most valuable input, and my writing colleague Mark Roeder, whose own work is coming along well, for also reading this work-in-progress. I would like to thank Duane Simolke for his excellent and comprehensive edits, as well as his incisive comments. I would also like to thank my friend, Christina Howard; she took much of her valuable time to give this work a critical read; and I would like to thank Ken Burchett for agreeing to allow his name to be used in a photo that was to be part of the cover design, and his gracious sister who likewise agreed to allow her newborn's picture (of Joshua) to be used, as well—even though the eventual cover morphed into something entirely different. If I have left anyone out of this list, it was not intentional, and I hope I am forgiven.

—Ronald L. Donaghe, Las Cruces, New Mexico
rondonaghe@rondonaghe.com • http://www.rondonaghe.com

PART ONE

ACTS

CHAPTER I

THE CONCEPTION

Neuvo Casas Grandes, Chihuahua, Mexico, June 1970

Tom Allen-Reece never thought it would really happen, even with all the talk Joel had done for the past few years. Yet they were waiting for him in the bedroom, right now. Tonight. But dread lay in his stomach; tears brimmed on his lower eyelids threatening to spill out. Although he was trying to work up the courage to join Joel and Sharon, he didn't want to.

On the talavera tiled table next to the leather couch where he sat, the yellow light cast by the small lamp gave his naked skin the same beautiful glow it had earlier given all three of them. All three were tanned in places and white in others, all three used to working outdoors. A few minutes before, in the stupor from two shots of tequila, Tom had thought how beautiful they were—him and Joel and Sharon—all three sitting together on the couch, taking shots of tequila and talking about what this night would mean.

This night, however, was never supposed to have happened—that is, if Tom had had his way, if he had actually voiced his deepest fears when Joel talked about having a child of their own. "Just think, honey, a gay family. You and me and our kid." Yes, those were hopeful words that rang of romance—*domestic* romance—the stability of a "family." Tom liked the idea of being a family, but they didn't need a "kid of our own" as Joel liked to say.

The idea had thrilled Joel as the months passed and he and Tom resolved themselves into a comfortable life in the small town of Common, New Mexico, a town they'd once scandalized, a town that Tom figured would always be their home. That's where Joel had always thought he'd raise a family of his own. But when that proved unlikely since he had fallen in love with Tom, Joel still tried to think of a way they could have a child. For months it had been, "let's adopt a kid, honey, like Mom and Dad adopted the twins and Henry and Sally."

At first, he had not talked about having their own flesh and blood child, but soon enough he had come up with that solution when he realized that two men would never be allowed to adopt.

Even though he was drunk, which he was not used to, Tom smiled, thinking of the way Joel lit up when children came into his life. He was always ogling the babies in the grocery store and on the sidewalks of Common on a Saturday afternoon.

The sitting room in the hotel suite was garish with Mexican paintings on velvet canvases and tiled windowsills recessed at least a foot into the adobe walls. The walls were Pepto-Bismol pink, Tom noted, with equally unnatural green palm leaves painted from floor to ceiling. Next to the lamp was a bottle of tequila, and next to the bottle were three shot glasses and a pile of squeezed and flattened limes.

Drinking to get drunk enough to do the deed seemed sordid in itself, but the thought of actually *doing the deed* with Sharon left Tom feeling numb. What right did he and Joel have to *both* have sex with her—or for that matter, either of them? Neither was married to her. Nor would they ever be. Yet she had agreed to carry their child—in fact had suggested it herself—though he could not imagine just how desperate she must have been to make the offer. She had known they wanted a child, and she knew they were looking for "some woman" who would be willing to carry it, but neither he nor Joel had even thought of asking Sharon. She also knew that their only stipulation was that they both had to sleep with this as yet unfound woman—together. Which one of them was the child's real blood father *had* to be left unanswered—at least that's what Joel had wanted. And knowing that, Sharon had still offered to be that woman.

Tom had agreed after Sharon had called them from Mexico with the offer, but he and Joel had argued about it before he relented, unable to put into words for Joel the underlying sense of wrongness the scheme had. Until the moment of Sharon's call, the whole thing had been theoretical to Tom, but to Joel it was one of those obsessions one got occasionally, and with Sharon's offer to carry their baby hanging between them, Joel had said, "but if Sharon wants to, considering her religious background, honey, what *wrong* is it?" Although Joel's logic escaped Tom, he tired of arguing with him, since for months and even years the whole thing *was* theoretical.

He listened to the silence coming from the bedroom. An arched doorway divided the sitting room from the bedroom. A heavy, red curtain hung on large rings in the arch, glowing with rosy light. They were waiting on him on the other side of that light.

But Tom wanted to bolt from the hotel, rather than walk in there; and he would have run, had this child not been so important to Joel, and if he didn't think Joel would actually do it with Sharon, without him, having come this far. Yet, to bring a woman into their bed made Tom feel odd, if not ashamed. If a heterosexual couple could not have a child of their own, they adopted one. Biblical examples aside, would any couple *really* ask another woman to carry a child if the wife could not? Or would a heterosexual couple *ever* ask another man into the bed with the wife, because the husband was sterile or impotent? Despite the moral questions that came to Tom's inebriated mind, the strongest, most cloying thought was that Joel might carry through without him, and it was this thought that finally gave him a reason to stand.

He was naked.

He took a slug of tequila straight from the bottle then looked down on himself as he stood in the middle of the room. He was beginning to stir. It was time to finish the thing that had begun so many months before. He made his way through the curtained arch into the bedroom, knowing his body could perform the dreaded act, even when his mind screamed at him not to.

Sharon had lit candles throughout the room, and the scattered lights gave the room an unreal glow as he looked toward the bed. Joel was lying on one side smiling at him. Sharon was lying on the other side, also smiling at him. Tom was relieved they were not entwined—as he had been afraid they might be.

"We're ready for you, baby," Joel said.

Tom noticed a slight edge of sadness in Joel's voice. He returned Joel's brave smile with his own. "Have you—uh—?"

"Not without you," Sharon whispered from the other side. "It is all right. Come." Her voice held a hint of reserve, as well, and Tom considered asking them, right then, if they really wanted to go through with it.

But he could not take time to think. If he didn't get this over with, he would run, and run far and long. Blood thumped in the veins of his neck as they made room for him between them. He lay down as close to Joel as he could get, spooning into him with his back against Joel's chest. Joel's warmth was familiar, yet strange this night in this room. He blinked back tears, then, and pulled Sharon to him.

*   *   *

It was done. But it was only the beginning. For all his dread and feeling heartsick at the thought of what they were going through to have their own child, and feeling as though they were violating Sharon in an unspeakable way, Tom fell in love with her that night as he never would another woman. It was a love borne of the knowledge that she would carry their baby, that she would go through the tearing pain of childbirth—but most of all he loved her because she was doing this out of love for him and Joel. What they had done would not end once the sun rose the next day, or the next. Time would not erase their act, either. It would last a lifetime, and that's what frightened him. Sharon and their shared child would also be part of their lives from now on. But he didn't know how much of a change he wanted in his life with Joel.

*   *   *

They flew across the Chihuahuan desert of northern Mexico heading for the U. S. border, dust billowing behind the pickup. It was battered and scratched, with shiny spots of raw metal showing through where something in some load had rubbed the paint off. The once bright yellow paint of the pickup had faded to pastel and was covered with mud flecks and dirt. In the open bed, the brown powder billowing up from the road coated their luggage. There were very few of Sharon's belongings in the back, however. As she had told both men, she wanted to bring nothing with her from her life in Mexico.

In the cab of the pickup, Joel was driving, Sharon was sitting beside him and, on her right, Tom sat beside her. Joel's eyes roved over the hot desert in front of them. The gray in his irises with the slashes of blue flickered with the reflection of sunlight on the desert, or became shadowed as they passed beneath the occasional oases of cumulus clouds drifting in the heat overhead. He looked west and east, then north, again. Behind them, to the south, the last of the mountains near Nuevo Casas Grandes had begun fading into the background and the more lush grasslands gave way to large stretches of barren land, fields of cacti, shrub, and Spanish daggers. From the massive expanse of land rose mountains off in the distance, which grew closer, then receded into the background, as they continued northward.

There wasn't another vehicle in sight, but Joel felt as if they were being chased—or should have been—either by the Federales or by Sharon's relatives. She had assured him and Tom both, however that, once shunned, and once she had decided to leave her Mennonite clan, no one would come looking for her.

Although he was apprehensive, he was fairly confident he could get her across the Mexico/United States border at Palomas, Mexico, without having to show a visa. At this border crossing, the Mexican guards did not question people as they entered the United States and would not come out of the shade to look too closely at them. He also figured Sharon could pass as his sister, if necessary, since she was blonde as he was. In fact, if questioned, that is exactly what they would tell the U.S. border guards. Although they could have traveled more comfortably on pavement, by coming out of Mexico through the city of Juarez and into El Paso, Texas, they had decided to cross where Joel's face was known as a regular, where he was on friendly terms with the guards on both sides of the border. He had been crossing at Palomas regularly for the past year, taking the used equipment from their various farms down into Mexico to sell to the Mennonites in Nuevo Casas Grandes. This time, if asked, he would tell them he had been on a vacation.

He was happy, though feeling a little awkward. Tom had been too quiet, once they had been with Sharon. Even though Tom had agreed to go along with him in attempting to make a baby with her, Joel knew that his husband of five wonderful years was sad and feeling guilty. Although they hadn't had a chance to be alone since the night before in the hotel in Casas Grandes, he knew Tom was having second thoughts about what they had done. Joel could, in fact, list every argument Tom had made against the idea when he had first brought it up to him. Tom was going to be proved right in many of those arguments, too. Joel knew his parents Eva and Douglas Reece were not going to like it one bit. The best he could hope was to set Sharon up in Common in a motel, probably, until he could break the news to them. Further, as Tom had also pointed out, the people of the town of Common already knew that he and Tom were gay and living together. Once word got around about the woman they had got pregnant and brought home, the gossip would really get spicy. Although Tom might not realize it, Joel had guilt feelings of his own. In a way, deep down within, where many of his feelings lived, Joel knew that part of what they had done was wrong, any way you cut it.

Still, he could not help but feel complete—not for having slept with a woman (Joel could not express how unimportant that was). He felt complete knowing that he and Tom would have a child of their own. With a twinge of guilt, even as he smiled to himself, Joel hoped Sharon *had* gotten pregnant. He knew there would be no other attempts like this one.

Within his heart, Joel also knew their child would be lucky to have him and Tom as its fathers. Sharon would be its mother and would, he hoped, take an interest in her child's life, although when she had offered to carry it, she agreed to have the baby and to let it live with them. She wanted things, things she could not have had as a member of the Mennonites in Mexico, where she was expected to marry one of her own and to bear many children, anyway. That would not have been Sharon's choice. Agreeing to have their baby, however, was her choice. She had offered to have it but, like Tom, Joel could not say what had brought her to such a decision. When talking to her about themselves and their desire for a child, they had told her they would pay the woman well for what she did and, as it turned out, Sharon had mentioned a dream she had, of becoming an American citizen. She told them of a tourist she had met in Casas Grandes who had first given her the idea that women in the United States were not destined to become a man's wife, that they could become anything they wanted. So when she made the offer to be the woman they were looking for, they told her they would pay her way through college, and provide her an apartment while she attended school, if that was what she wanted. If she was pregnant, of course, they told her they would want her to live in Common to have the baby, but when she decided it was time to go, they would send her to college.

In the meantime, the three of them needed to continue getting to know one another. He smiled at that, too, because until now, he had imagined that the woman who would carry their child would simply go away, well paid.

He glanced across Sharon and let his eyes come to rest on his husband's face. Tom was as beautiful now at twenty-three years old as he had been at seventeen when Joel first laid eyes on him. His dark hair and eyes were almost liquid in the June heat of the desert. His clear face was beaded with sweat as was his own and Sharon's, but it only added to the beautiful glow Tom's face always had.

Tom glanced back, returning a thin smile, and Joel's heart beat more rapidly, feeling such love for him even after five years together, he almost could not restrain himself from saying "*I love you*" in front of Sharon. But he did not want to exclude Sharon and so, stayed silent.

Now that they were committed to their plans, Tom had put his bravest face on what they had done, and Joel knew Tom had done it for him. He also knew that, like himself, Tom would always want to know and to remember Sharon. Once Tom committed himself to an idea or an action, he had shown in the past that he stuck by his decisions and by Joel. That they both loved Sharon (even if it would eventually be more like a sister than the "wife" who was carrying their child) Joel did not doubt. Even in his depressed state, Tom's arm was lying across Sharon's shoulders and touching him on the neck, caressing it. By that simple act, he knew Tom would support him, even when this latest in their string of outrageous acts came to light.

And people would find out. They always did in a small town like Common. There would be no preparation to defend himself and his actions. He would just have to live through it, keeping in sight his love for Tom and the reasons he wanted a child to begin with.

*   *   *

The desert changed little as the hot sun made its leisurely way across the world, first burning into Tom's side of the pickup, where he had an arm out the open window. Even the wind was hot as it whipped through the cab of the pickup. Around noon, the sun hit the back window, burning the back of Sharon's head, causing her to wish subconsciously that she'd worn her bonnet. But she was dressed, now, in American clothes, which Tom and Joel had brought with them—a pair of Levi's and a man's shirt, which Tom had assured her would be all right. "Women dress like this all the time," he had told her that morning, when they had suggested she wear them. "We need to do it," he had also said, "since…well, people might figure you for a Mennonite." Although it made her feel uncomfortable to do it, Sharon knew they were right. Still she felt sticky and hot, and did not like the feel of the clothing on her skin.

As the trip continued, it was Joel's turn to be burnt by the sun as it blazed a hot trail toward the western horizon. Out here, everything was lit and burnt and sultry, and Sharon accepted it. This was the world, the only land she had ever known.

Because it was hot and the wind was noisy as it whipped through the pickup, conversation was difficult and, soon, the three young people had lapsed into silence. Sharon kept her eyes on the northern horizon as they raced across the land, feeling she would burst if the town of Palomas did not appear soon in the shimmering heat.

She thought she was probably the happiest of the three of them. They were such beautiful men and so in love with each other, she knew her place with them would be limited. Yet she did not mind. They were her saviors. She was free. At times she was tearful at the loss of her parents, but they were caught by the Mennonite way and could not see, in their blindness, that the world was much, *much* bigger than Mexico and the community of Mennonite brethren living on the farm outside Nuevo Casas Grandes.

She felt the heat of Joel's right side, where her shoulder met his; and she felt the heat from Tom's body. Her shoulder was touching under his arm, but it was unavoidable, and she had been unaware of touching it until now. Although she had taken them both inside her the night before, there was already a pulling away from that intimacy; but again, she did not mind. She accepted it, just as she had accepted the fact that Tom and Joel were "that kind" of men—like those from the Book, who gave up their natural affection for women. Inwardly, Sharon shook her head. Tom and Joel were as naturally mated as any two young people she had seen in the community. Their affection was not *un*natural, though it was unusual; homosexuality was simply one of those items in the Bible she had never been able to comprehend. One was supposed to encounter all sorts of wickedness in the world, if one left the community of Mennonites.

This affection between two men was supposed to be one form of that wickedness—but it certainly was not one of those things she thought she would ever
encounter even in the world. Yet Sharon felt them to be good men to the core
of her being the first time she met them, because they were not ashamed of
their love for each other, the way Joel had so casually talked about his life with
Tom. So she was not ashamed of being with these two homosexual men, either.
It was clear that they loved each other, and she saw nothing wrong with their
desire to be fathers.

The three of them had met in Casas Grandes almost two months after she
had stolen away from the farm twenty kilometers from the city, where she was
begging on the streets, and these two beautiful young men had approached
her. By then, she was especially suspicious of men, and had even thought of
running away, but she had not eaten anything in three days, and she hoped to
get a few pesos from them. It was Joel, the blond one, who spoke first, asking if
they could help her.

She thought she had hidden her desperation, but she saw in his eyes that she
had not.

Then they had asked her to walk with them, bought her lunch, and coaxed
her to tell her story. How had she come to be on the streets? Wasn't she
Mennonite? She thought the Mexican shawl a turista had given her would hide
the fact of her background. But it had not, and she saw the curiosity in Tom's
face, the dark-haired one, as well—and she felt both their compassion.

Yes. Mennonite, she told them, as she mopped her plate at the café with the
last tortilla from the stack that had been set on their table. No telling how long
it would be until the next meal. She would have been content to leave her
admission of her background at that, because she wanted to appear as a tourist
and wanted to beg enough money to buy a bus ticket—one way to *Norté*
America. But she had been so lonely, so *alone*, and they had been so kind in
buying her a meal that she was relieved to tell her story. She could not help
crying as she talked and they listened with tears in their eyes; so she told them
more about herself, finally admitting to having been shunned—that she had
been caught in a private act of self-pleasure, dancing naked by the lake on the
community farm in the moonlight. Some of her clan even accused her of devil
worship because of it. When the elders had met about the incident and
demanded a shunning, her mother Meira and her father Standish Minnenger
had gone along with it. If they had not, they too would have been outcasts.

Still, she told them in her broken English, that the shunning had hurt deeply.
She could not find the words to express what an innocent act it was to want, for
once in her life, to swim in the lake as the boys could, without the strictures of

clothing. But even in the heat of summer, the women of her clan were expected to dress in layers of clothing, to work in the fields in long-sleeves.

In her case, her shunning would have lasted until she had become cleansed of her sin, but Sharon knew that once shunned, one never could regain the simple innocence her people treasured so much. No man in the community would marry her—especially not a sensual woman like herself. It would have brought corruption on them.

And so, she told Tom and Joel about her past. Then they had so very casually talked about themselves. "We're gay," Joel had told her, just like that. Joel, especially, had been willing to talk about it. At first, she did not know what the "gay" was, and barely recognized the word "homosexual," but thought she must have heard it somewhere. When she fully understood what Joel was saying, it did not horribly shock her, though she could think of a few passages in the Book that might describe this thing they were. But like many other things in the Book, she did not readily wish to believe it was so literally true. Because people had so unfairly judged her and used the Book to justify their judgment, she was therefore reluctant to judge Tom and Joel. In fact, in the Mennonite way in the community at Nuevo Casas Grandes, it was so easy to fall and to be judged harshly, especially when times were hard. Sharon was certain that, had she not been shunned for her sensuality, she would eventually be shunned for some other thing. She did not know when doubts had begun to creep into her thoughts about many things her people believed, but they had. She recalled meeting Norté Americanos on the plaza in Casas Grandes to whom she sold cheese and dried meats and other produce from the community farm. And though the turistas marveled at the produce (and its cheap prices), she had marveled at them.

She recalled one beautiful woman who had befriended her on a very hot day, when her parents had left her to attend their area of the mercado by herself. And wanting to practice her English, she had asked the woman where she was from. "I'll do better than just tell you, honey," the woman said. She bought Sharon a cold drink from another vendor on the plaza and sat in the shade on Sharon's side of the table, which was groaning with produce, and pulled a stack of photographs from her purse. "I'm from San Francisco, California," the woman had told her, showing her pictures of the city, from its skyscrapers glinting brightly in the sun to night pictures of the lights from those same buildings reflecting in the dark waters of the bay.

Sharon could not believe that any city on earth could be as big and beautiful as this San Francisco, nor so filled with people as the woman described. But the woman had laughed brightly at Sharon's ignorance and gave her a photograph that Sharon had found especially breathtaking.

"I'm a photographer," the woman told her. "I travel all over the world for *National Geographic*, but I always yearn to return to my beautiful city on the bay."

"But how does your husband think on this?" Sharon had asked her. "And do not your children miss you when you make this travel and take photographs?"

Again the woman laughed brightly at her ignorance, though Sharon did not feel embarrassed. "Oh, honey, I couldn't be married and live as I do!"

"Then how is it," Sharon began, becoming confused. "How is it that you...um...pay the *dollares* for your travel?"

"If you mean do I make enough money to live on?" the woman asked, laying a bejeweled hand on Sharon's arm, "I am paid very well by my company!"

But Sharon had been too confused by words such as "company" to continue asking questions in her bad English. The woman, however, continued to talk to her and, when the cold drink had grown warm, she bought Sharon a frozen fruit, which Sharon ate, even though Mennonites did not indulge themselves in such frivolous luxuries.

She showed Sharon photographs of some of her friends—most of them women. When Sharon asked if they were married, yet again the woman had laughed. "Oh, no, honey! We enjoy being our own bosses. This one," the woman had said, tapping a picture of a lovely woman in clothing Sharon thought of as a man's suit, "is a high-powered attorney for a bank, and this one," the turista said, flipping through more photographs and showing her a woman dressed in a gown the likes of which Sharon had never seen, "is a clothing designer."

Then Sharon saw a very odd photograph of two men standing close together, and one man was kissing the other on the cheek. "And these two men?" she asked, then stopped. She did not know what she wanted to ask. The woman laughed softly, this time, as if to herself. "Just friends of mine, honey. San Francisco is...well, a very unique city."

That day, Sharon's eyes had been opened to a much wider world than that which she had been raised in, one in which women married or did not, depending upon what *they* decided, not upon what their elders or men folk said they must do. A world, too, where men could do as those two had in the photograph, though it was too out-of-context for her to understand.

In an act of secrecy, which would have been frowned upon had she been discovered, Sharon hid the photograph of San Francisco at night, reflecting its lights in the bay, beneath the folds of her heavy cotton dress.

Even before she had been shunned, Sharon had searched for a way to escape the life that had been planned for her, including marriage to another Mennonite. She had not, of course, decided to run away to Casas Grandes and become a beggar. She knew it was not the way to accomplish anything—yet in the end, it had been the only way out.

For as long as she could remember, she knew there had to be more to life than what the community offered her—and the kind woman with the stack of photographs had confirmed her ideas. On other trips to Casas Grandes, where they always sold their cheeses and clothing and vegetables, she had seen the turistas from America, with their fine cars and clothing. But rather than feeling ashamed for them for their worldly ways as other members of her community might, she admired the women, especially those who walked the plaza with their heads held high, with their cameras snapping, handing out dimes to the little Mexican children, and spending what to her were fortunes on the Tarahumara pottery, for which Casas Grandes was well known, as well as the leather and copper goods.

In years past, she had often lain awake many nights until the household had gone to sleep. Then, dressed in her nightgown and slippers, she would go down by the lake, across the fields, undressing and swimming, or just letting her feet dip into the cold water while the wind off the willows bathed her naked skin. As often as she had laughed at herself and what she was doing, she had also gone to the lake to cry and to pray for something that would happen to change her life.

So, as time passed at the community among the Brethren, try as she might, there were just things in the community and in the Book that rankled her and caused doubts and disbelief. Unlike most of the other girls her age, she could not accept the fate of her birth as *just* a female, a man's property, if the truth be known—not since she knew that women in Norté America were free to decide for themselves whether or not to marry. She could not so easily submit herself to all the strictures of her life without the occasional pleasures she tried to enjoy, like her times at the lake by herself.

But all her hopes and plans came abruptly to a halt when she was caught. She endured the public humiliation and, after her shunning, she endured the silence. No one would speak to her. No one. Not the girls she had giggled with in class before their lessons began, nor the men who might have asked her to marry them.

Begging for food and a little change from the turistas on the plaza had been much worse, however, than her life in the community. On the streets, she had felt shame, had almost wished that she was like the others in the community. Saving money for a bus ticket would be long and tedious, and might take months. Jobs were scarce in Casas Grandes. And even though the Mennonites and the Mexicans had long been friendly with one another in their dealings, it was quite different for a Mennonite to look for work outside the community.

Those she asked did not take her seriously or resented the idea of giving a job to a Mennonite rather than one of their own.

Many nights, when the evenings were warm, she would sit on the plaza during the *paseo*, where the Mexican girls, wearing their finest town clothes, walked around the plaza, and the Mexican boys sat in their cars and pickup trucks watching them. The *paseo* was, Sharon knew, a dating ritual, but one that brought her sadness as she watched, because she could not be a part of that, either. She had listened to the strains of Mariachis and the laughter and had held herself.

There were kind people who had given her American dollars and others who had given her pesos, the turistas who had fed her at the outdoor food vendors, and even those who gave her pretty things. But there were also the men who had whispered to her from the shadows and had offered her money if she would show them a good time.

And when she had been shunned and, afterwards, when she was living on the streets, hungry and frightened, she would study the photograph and dream, only to have her dreams shattered by hunger, or by mistreatment by shopkeepers who would not even allow her so much as a cool drink of water. But even more frightening were the men who tormented her with their whispering and evil looks, as if they wanted to eat her.

Then providence had brought these two homosexual men to her. They had spent every day of a week with her, once their business in the Mexican city had been conducted. Before they returned to the United States, they left her in comfort for the first time in many days in the hotel, paying for an entire month with a shrug of their shoulders. They also left her with enough money for food and for a bus ticket, and gave her a telephone number to contact them if she ever wanted to.

Knowing she was finally free, she had put off purchasing the bus ticket, now that she had the means, deciding that she would observe the tourists in the hotels and plazas, listen to the odd and clattering sound of the *Ingles*, the English, learning how to pronounce that most odd sounding "r" which required pulling the tongue toward the back of the mouth, rather than rolling it near the front. She had even purchased herself a Spanish-English dictionary, which she read aloud in the evenings in her hotel room. Since the two young men, her saviors, had paid a month's lodging for the room before they left, she had decided to stay there until the time ran out, practicing her speech, learning to walk with her head held erect as she had seen the turistas do, rather than keeping her eyes cast downward in crowds as the Mennonite women did.

But just a few days before the time was up on the hotel room where she had been staying, she was out on the plaza and saw that her people, the Mennonites, had returned to sell their produce, and now that she was clean from a bath at her hotel that morning and had even washed her clothes, she dressed herself in the traditional clothing of her clan and went in search of her family. Although she had been shunned, she had been away from them for more than two months and ached to see them one last time before she purchased her bus ticket.

When she found them and went up to them, calling their names, speaking German, so they would know it was her, her mother turned but, seeing that it was Sharon, turned her back—as did the rest of her family when they saw her, even her little brothers and sisters. She stood in the dusty street, only feet away from them, their names dying on her lips, and knew that they would not care to see her again, though she ached for just a single kind word of good-bye.

So she had run from the dusty street of the plaza and returned to her hotel room, deciding that she would not wait another day. She would purchase her bus ticket that very afternoon and travel north, into America, where people were not so cruel. Only there was one problem that frightened and dismayed her. When she reached into the drawer in the small table beside her bed and pulled out her dictionary, opening it for the money she had hidden there, the money was gone. She tore the room apart looking for it, but in the end, she realized she must have been robbed.

*   *   *

In the cab of the pickup, she glanced at Joel, smiling to herself, remembering how, when she had experienced the blackest moment of her life—that of being utterly rejected by her entire family on the streets of Casas Grandes, and then discovering that she had lost all her money—a thought had occurred to her, one that had dried her tears.

She had remembered Joel telling her: "We want a child." It had been the conversation where they were telling about themselves—he and Tom—explaining about their relationship, and even though they were both men, they wanted to be a family. Sharon had remembered that women in the United States could choose to marry or not, and so she realized that men there could also decide, she supposed, to marry each other, if they wanted. Although the very idea was foreign to her, she did not doubt that this was so.

"We're just looking for some woman to carry a child for us and, when the baby is born, to let us raise it, and we will give the woman anything she wants."

Although it went against everything she had been taught as a Mennonite, when her family had utterly rejected her, and all she had left was a life of desperation on the streets, she reached out for help to the only two people she felt she could trust. She called the number Joel and Tom had given her and was relieved when they came on the line.

"Sharon!" Joel said, sounding delighted and even laughing, then calling Tom to the telephone so he could say hello. Sharon closed her eyes, fighting back her tears and when she spoke, she simply said: "I would like to carry your child."

After a silence, in which she was afraid they would tell her no, it was Tom who said, "are you sure? Sharon, we didn't mean…We don't want you to think"—

"No," she said. "I will be glad to do this thing."

They had agreed after a long deliberation, which she could hear in the background as she listened from her end.

"Thank you, Sharon," Joel finally said. "But remember, even if you decide you don't want to do this, we'll still help you." And when she told him she had lost the money for the bus ticket, Joel simply said, "we'll come get you, and if you decide not to do this, it won't matter."

But Sharon knew it mattered to them both, very much, and if carrying a child outside of marriage would get her away from her life on the streets and far from her family who had shunned her, it seemed a worthy sacrifice. So again, she said, "I will carry your child. We shall do this thing as you wish."

Then Joel had said an odd thing before he hung up. He said, "We love you."

*   *   *

She glanced at Tom and Joel on either side of her in the pickup and again smiled to herself. Yes, she knew they loved her; but best of all, she loved them as well. She was glad to be carrying their child—if, indeed, the planting of their seed had taken.

CHAPTER 2

CROSSING THE BORDER

Just as she began to think that the dirt road continued forever, and that they would travel on through the night and into the next day, they hit pavement as the sun was turning golden and approaching the western horizon. Up ahead, still shimmering in the heat waves of the hot day, Sharon saw a small town, no different than any of the other small Mexican towns she was used to. She could make out the multi-colored buildings of pink and turquoise and green, and the inevitable bell tower of the town church.

"Is this the Palomas?" she asked.

Both Tom and Joel laughed at her question, though for a moment, she did not know why they laughed.

"Yes, it is the city of *the doves*," Tom said. "It won't be long, now."

Then Joel turned to her. "Remember, Sharon, when we go through the check point, when they ask for your citizenship, say 'United States.'"

"And don't embellish," Tom agreed.

"What is 'embellish'?" she asked. The strange sounding word frightened her.

Joel laughed. "Tom just means don't give them details. Just act like you do this all the time."

Sharon still did not know what they might mean, but they were not afraid, so she would not be afraid. "*Junited Estates*," she said.

This time, Tom looked worried. But he smiled. "*Yewnited Ssstates*," he said, emphasizing the pronunciation. "Try it, again."

Sharon listened, realizing that she had fallen into the habit of speaking with a Mexican accent on the words. "*Yewnited Ssstates*," she said. "United States."

"Good," Joel said, shifting gears downward as they entered the southern outskirts of the small border town of Palomas. Almost immediately the smooth pavement of the highway deteriorated into hard ground where a recent rain had stirred up the surface of the street, so that there were bumps and valleys, and jaw-rattling pot holes.

In the last couple of minutes all three of them had spoken more than they had for the last two hours. As Sharon found her voice, she wanted to ask a million questions. "You will help me with my accent?" she asked, turning to Tom.

He smiled in return. "Anything you want."

Then Joel shifted gears, again, and the pickup slowed even more, until they were heading down the middle of the town. Just ahead, she saw what must be the border checkpoint. She was frightened and repeated the words over and over, "United States" until Joel slowed to a crawl. They passed from sunlight into shade and then were driving through a gate; then they came to a stop on the other side. A uniformed man, obviously a *Norté* Americano, stepped away from the small building and peered inside: "Citizenship?"

In turn, Joel, then Sharon, then Tom said the two words required of them.

When the guard nodded and stepped back, Joel pulled forward onto the pavement, and Sharon looked around. "It is the same!" she said, involuntarily. "It is the same!" and for a moment she wanted to cry.

Outside, the desert continued, just as it had in Mexico, into forever, with mountains off in the distance. "Are we not in the United *Estates*?"

They told her they were, and that part of the same Chihuahuan desert that dominated northern Mexico also dominated southern New Mexico. Joel did most of the talking, explaining about the sudden changes in the terrain farther ahead. "But we won't see any of it. Where we live, Sharon, it's all desert. A day's drive will take us into forested mountains. We'll show you after you're settled in."

She sat back looking around, feeling foolish at her outburst. Then she sat forward, again, as they came into the small town of Columbus, New Mexico. Here, Joel pulled into a gas station, and Sharon realized she needed to stretch and relieve herself. She slid out on Tom's side and touched her feet to the ground of *Norté* America. She wanted to kneel and kiss the earth, but she would wait until she was alone. Perhaps it was better that the land was the same, she thought. If it had been much different than what she was used to, it might prove more difficult to adjust to.

*   *   *

Tom watched as Sharon made her way inside the gas station, saw with satisfaction that she found the restroom, although she had not asked. He was
relieved to see that, dressed in Levi's and one of his sports shirts, she was not
obviously Mennonite as she had appeared in Casas Grandes in the clothing she
had attempted to modify. She had cut the sleeves off just above the elbows and
had sewn cuffs of blue onto the gray material. At the collar of her dress, she had
sewn the same blue material. That she was quite good at sewing was obvious,
although her clothing had looked hopelessly out of date and out of place.
Dressed as she was, now, he thought she looked about as ordinary as anyone
from Common. Still, he felt a jolt of sympathy for her, as she disappeared into
the shadows of the gas station. Her shoes were not feminine, at all. Nor had the
trip done anything for her blonde hair. Now it was rather flat and, like him and
Joel, she needed a bath.

He joined Joel at the gas pump. "We've got to take her shopping, Joel, before
Eva meets her. Your mother is sharp as a tack. She gets one look at Sharon and
she's going to be suspicious."

Joel smiled at him. His blond hair was longish in the style the guys were
beginning to wear even in a small town like Common, New Mexico, and the
day's growth of beard made him look tough, Tom thought. He was wearing a
faded blue T-shirt and his muscular arms, tanned to a deep gold, rippled as he
placed the gas hose back in the rack and twisted the gas cap closed on the tank.
His Levi's and work boots fit in with the rest of the guys at the gas station as
did Tom's.

"You're right, honey," he said to Tom. "She's done the best she can with what
she's got, but you know as soon as we drive through the gates at home, Sally's
gonna come running, and it won't be five minutes before she's back at Mom's,
telling her about the woman we brought with us."

Tom laughed at that. But Joel's unadorned words made him frown. He
would encourage Joel to rent a hotel room for Sharon, to allow her time to
become accustomed to her surroundings; and *then* they could take her out to
the Reece farm and introduce her.

He judged the time to be close to five, by the slanting rays of the sun. It was
a Monday. "I think we better head on into Common, then," Tom said, "and see
if we can't get her some clothes. We can rent her a motel room, too."

"We might as well eat when we get there," Joel said. He reached into the back
of his Levi's and took out his wallet. "Let me pay and we'll be on our way."

Tom felt a little better, glad that Joel had seen the problem as he had laid it
out. It was one thing for them to bring a male friend home with them, as they
had done in the past. But not a woman, and one whose primary language was
not English. Even some of the young men he and Joel had brought home to

live with them for a week or more had raised Eva's eyebrows the first couple of times. When they explained that the boys had been thrown out of their homes, or had run away from abusive parents, she understood, although she still did not like it.

Discovering that there were so many runaways and homeless children these days had been heart-wrenching for Joel. It was equally disheartening for Tom to see the way suffering children affected him. The satisfaction that came from providing a few meals and a bed for the runaways was just another thing that had encouraged Joel to want a child.

It was amazing to Tom that so many teens were running away these days, getting themselves into trouble and heading for the coast. Even in Common and other small towns, it seemed that the seventies had brought with it a new kind of thinking among the youth. Or as if the sixties just past had caused a shift in the way children and their parents related to one another.

Even the twins, Patrick and Detrick, whom Eva and Douglas Reece had adopted after the death of their parents, had seemed to change with the times, going from the poor kids they had been as Stroud children, to being well off with the Reeces. As soon as they finished high school, however, both of them had been eager to get away to discover the rest of the world. Not that they were unhappy. Far from it. They were much happier than Tom had ever expected them to be coming from the background they had, having the ghost of their murderous dead brother Kenneth hanging over them and everyone in the small town knowing about him. But they were both eager to go on to college. Even though Douglas and Eva seemed to want to hang onto them, to continue protecting them from the harshness of the world, the twins had made remarkable strides in the way they looked at that same world.

Patrick had blossomed in high school, and had been champing at the bit, so to speak, to get into UC Berkeley, where things were happening he wanted to be part of. His twin brother, Detrick, on the other hand, had blossomed in an entirely different way, and had wanted to attend a small agriculture college down in west Texas. That he was home a lot as a result was a relief to Douglas and Eva; but they encouraged him to be as active as he could in college. "You have a little fun," Douglas had told him, when Detrick seemed unsure if he should leave the farm at all. You've got the rest of your life to become a farmer or a rancher, if that's what you want."

Tom thought of Sharon like the teens everywhere. Although she was eighteen and had already achieved womanhood, she was running away from her former life, too; and she was probably one of the least equipped to encounter this United States that she seemed to expect so much from. Her path had intersected with theirs in a way Tom never could have imagined when he first caught sight of her on the plaza in Casas Grandes and urged Joel to look at the beautiful girl with the colorful shawl, who was, despite appearances, in a desperate way and probably a runaway. After that meeting, their paths in life were now parallel with Sharon's, if not the same.

*   *   *

At the Mennonite community farm, there had been no indoor plumbing, and Sharon had only occasionally used public toilets on trips to town. She had quickly become accustomed to them, however, in the hotel in Nuevo Casas Grandes. But this one was different. It was an American toilet in an American petrol station. It was dingy and somewhat dirty, with no adornment whatsoever, and those who might have cared for it took no pride in it at all. Was this the American way?

She had been disappointed as soon as she crossed from Mexico into the United States that the land did not suddenly turn green and beautiful. And she was disappointed, now, that this *Ladies* was so stark. She could clean herself up a little. But there were no towels in the dispenser, no soap in the dish, and so she tore off bits of her undergarments and, though there was no hot water, either, as there had been in the hotel, she bathed herself and flushed the toilet.

She stood at the mirror studying herself. Her hair needed washing, and the best she could do was tie it to the back and pull the blonde strands away from her face. She wore no makeup—had never worn makeup—and saw no reason to. She cleansed her face with another piece of undergarment, satisfied when her skin was shiny and clean.

Hoping that she would be presentable to the family of Joel and Tom, she smoothed out the shirt, rolling the sleeves up past her elbows and returned to the pickup.

"I got you a cold drink," Joel said, as she came up to him and Tom. He handed her a Coca-Cola in a bottle. The cap had already been removed. She had never had a Coca-Cola and gripped the bottle indecisively, as if it was an alcoholic beverage. But it was cold and felt good in the palm of her hand. She was thirsty and tilted it to her lips and drank. She was appalled at the burning bubbling sensation as she swallowed and did not like the feel of the liquid on her throat, or the extreme sweetness, and it made her want to belch.

But she grinned, instead, as she saw both Tom's and Joel's smiles at her reaction. "You don't like it?" Joel asked, still grinning.

"It is, how you say, medicino?"

"Medicine?" Tom asked, also grinning. "Would you rather have a Sprite? A Dr. Pepper?"

In response, she did belch, from deep down in her throat, and felt much better, though now both of her friends howled with laughter.

"Oh, Sharon!" Joel said. "We love you. You're precious. I hope you'll like *something* here!"

"I am certain that I will," she said, not sure at all. But it was what she had dreamed of for many years, to come to the United States and to learn about the world.

"Besides," Tom said, "Columbus is practically a Mexican village, just like Palomas. I think you'll feel better about things when we get home."

*   *   *

It was another half-hour, however, before they entered the town of Common. Tom told her what he and Joel had been thinking and that they would rent a motel room for her for a few days. Sharon would have been hurt, had she not realized the importance of what they were saying. "If it is all right with you," Tom had said, by way of explaining what they intended, "we need to get you some clothes like the other women wear, so you won't look out of place, when we take you to meet our family."

"You wish that I will be…*presentation?*"

"Presentable?" Joel asked. He shook his head, smiling broadly at Sharon in the dimming light of the late afternoon. "No, you are beautiful and very presentable. We just want you to have a chance to rest and relax."

She understood. She had realized the same thing when she was living on the streets of Casas Grandes and had tried to hide the fact that she was Mennonite. But she had not been able to buy Mexican clothing, and certainly could not afford the American clothing sold there in Casas Grandes. But she had noticed the women's shoes and hoped she could find a pair similar to those she had seen. They took her into a dry-goods store in the town of Common, and it was grander and more well lit than most buildings she had seen in Casas Grandes. Even though it was a small town compared to Casas Grandes, Sharon thought it must be greatly more wealthy. The town was different from Columbus, New Mexico, too.

As she walked through the dry-goods store, smiling to herself, she was amazed at the amount of clothing there was to buy, and frightened by the prices she saw in American dollars. That is when she knew that her friends were, indeed, rich Americanos, because they helped her pick out several pairs of shoes, a pair for working in the garden, a pair for wearing to town, another pair for wearing when she wasn't wearing the others—all of it confused and frightened her at the amounts they were spending, pulling from their wallets what seemed to her an endless supply of money. More money than she had spent her entire life.

They bought her dresses and skirts and blouses, and man's pants (which said Levi's on the pockets), and undergarments—all with the help of a woman whose only apparent job was to attend her and to take her to a small room where she could remove her clothing and put on the new clothing, and remove that and put on more, all the time saying, "honey, you're as cute as a bug in that *outfit*," and "let's see how your figure goes with this."

Then they rented a hotel room for her, although the sign said it was a *motel*. This time they did not want to see her undress, and she smiled at their newly apparent shyness around her. That she was suddenly shy as well seemed funny to all of them, but she understood. Their time with her as husbands was over. So she undressed in the bathroom and took a bath in the clean tub. They had shown her the shampoos and the lotions provided by the motel, and with the help of her own things was able to become clean and nice smelling before she slipped into her new clothing. She chose from among the items a skirt and blouse, which Tom said brought out the blue in her eyes and *complemented* her hair. Dressed in blues and greens, her blonde hair seemed to radiate.

CHAPTER 3

THE RUNAWAY

She threw away every stitch of clothing she had brought with her. She was almost sorry about it, when she pulled on the silky, almost non-existent undergarments and the skirt, which came just below her knees. She felt so light, almost naked, she was afraid people could see through the clothing. But when she came out of the bathroom, both of her friends whistled and smiled and nodded.

Then they took her to eat at a place called the Red Rooster Café, where they introduced her to the owner, a woman by the name of Margaret Jost. It was obvious to Sharon that both Tom and Joel were good friends with this woman and that she knew they were in love with each other. She was even more surprised when Margaret sat down at the table with them and listened to the tale of their trip to Mexico, although they left out the part where they had slept with her, and for that Sharon was relieved.

*   *   *

Margaret Jost was the only lesbian that Joel and Tom knew—and just about the only person they could both think of to confide in about bringing Sharon Minninger illegally across the U.S. Border. Although she was eighteen, and their action would not qualify as a kidnapping, Joel had no idea what all might be illegal with what they had done. But he knew he could be frank with Margaret, because she had always been frank with them. She had let them know she was a lesbian when Joel's old boxing coach, Bill Hoffins, had introduced her at the Unitarian church they attended. "Bill has told me about you two," Margaret said, then proceeded to tell them about herself and her mate, Rose. She told them with tears in her eyes of their forty years together, already into her fifth year without her. She had them over for cake and coffee and showed them the mantle above the fireplace where she kept a fresh cut rose in a vase in Rose's memory. "We bought the Red Rooster in 1956 when we came from Montana," she told them. "We didn't much care for the name, you understand," Margaret said, chuckling, "but Rose decided that we should keep it. She had some wonderful ideas for making themes out of it."

The Red Rooster Café shared common walls with the buildings on either side of it—a Sears catalogue store on the west and the State Farm Insurance Company on the east. The walls of all three businesses were white, stuccoed adobe. Parallel parking was available in front, with additional parking around the corner. The Sears store boasted large-paned glass, while the only window in the insurance office was in the lacquered door. The café had French windows, dressed with red checkered curtains and sills large enough for seasonal displays. In spring, mother hens and baby chicks adorned the windowsills. In summer and fall, displays of fruits and fresh vegetables enticed customers in for salads, fruit salads, and pies; and around harvest time, during the county fair, pumpkins, pies, and arts and crafts filled the windows, and customers could purchase prize-winning pies like those at the fair. In winter, the windows were frosted over and, on gray days, Margaret kept the lights on, promising hot chocolate and a warm, cozy place out of the weather. Tonight, with the coming of darkness outside, the soft glow of the lights inside the café became brighter as the panes of glass in the French windows began to reflect the lights back into the interior of the room.

After introductions were out of the way, Joel broke the ice. "Sharon will be staying in Common for awhile," he said. Then Tom added the details about bringing her across the border without a passport or visa. He finished by saying, "so we need to help her get her citizenship, Marge. Do you have any ideas?"

*   *   *

That this owner of the café was so willing to listen and to not be frightened at what they had done relieved Sharon, because this woman seemed to know important things about papers and citizenship and how to get a birth certificate that "proved" she had been born in the United States—and all four of them agreed it would be easier to obtain a birth certificate than to go back to Mexico and begin the legalization process. Margaret mentioned a courthouse fire in a nearby county, and even though Sharon had only the vaguest concept of this important piece of paper, she wondered how one could get a birth certificate if all of them had been destroyed in the fire. Whatever the outcome, however, it was a secret Sharon would have to keep—a lie that she must never divulge. Even though she was nervous about it, she trusted in this woman's ability, and so she would keep the lie and hoped it would not bother her, for lying was a sin—a sin she did not want to commit.

Margaret Jost had listened attentively, her short-cropped salt and pepper hair shaking with each vigorous nod of her head. She looked steadily into the eyes of each of them, Sharon noticed, realizing why Tom and Joel had chosen her. She was like one of the Mennonite elders whom everybody loved and went to for advice. Only she was a woman, and it was this that made Sharon happy, that the wisest person her saviors knew was female and that, here, in the United States, one could be respected and adored as a woman.

"*Do you speak German, child?*" came through in clear German, though in a more soft accent than Sharon was used to. Margaret was smiling at her.

Sharon nodded and returned her answer in German. "*It is my first language. Spanish is my second language, and I speak English, though badly.*"

"Then I shall teach you, child, if you would like." Margaret said in English. Her eyes had begun to twinkle, and even Sharon who did not know this woman, saw that she was excited at the prospect of taking her under her wing.

*   *   *

"Joel, you said you have put this girl up in a motel? Alone, here in Common?"

Margaret's voice had a serious quality, but something in the way she asked the questions made Joel smile. He already knew what she wanted. "Come to think of it, Marge, it's a jungle out there on the mean streets of Common. What did you have in mind?"

Some of Margaret's seventy odd years showed in the way she snatched at the air. "Achh! You know what I'm thinking, Joel. I'm thinking I have a big old house that hasn't seen real life in almost 10 years." She turned to Sharon.

"How would you like to come stay with me while you're in town? I could help you with your English, though I fear I wouldn't be of much use with your clothes fashion."

Joel was glad to see that Sharon was as happy with Margaret's suggestion as Margaret was. Both women's smiles brightened and, soon, they were speaking in snippets of German, English, Spanish—and laughing in the universal language of two people who know they are destined to become great friends.

Sharon caught Joel's eye once or twice and smiled, then returned her attention to Margaret. He saw a mother-daughter kind of thing in the way they were getting along, like the relationship his mother and her adopted daughter Sally had with each other.

Later, Joel and Tom returned to the motel and retrieved Sharon's things. They dropped them by Margaret's house a few blocks from the Red Rooster Café. By then, almost every light was on in the house. It faced the street and threw angled light onto the lawn as they crossed the yard.

Margaret and Sharon met them at the door, accepted the items quickly and the four of them hugged all round, saying their good nights.

"Hunh!" Tom said, once he had slid into the cab of the pickup with Joel. It was just the two of them, and Tom moved to the middle and hugged Joel's neck with his left arm. "I think I'm jealous of Margaret."

Tom's old voice, with the clever joke hidden somewhere in it came as a relief to Joel.

"Why, honey?"

"Margaret gets to watch Sharon's face whenever she encounters something new. I've been watching Sharon learn all day. It's fascinating."

Joel smiled in the darkness, finding Tom's lips. After a moment he pulled away. "At least we can relax for a few days, now that Margaret has offered to take Sharon in."

"And then all hell's gonna break loose," Tom said. Again, Joel heard Tom's old voice, and not the one that sounded resigned as it had when they went back to Mexico to be with Sharon. He was relieved, but had to agree that all they had was a few days to relax, because there was no predicting how his mother's meeting with Sharon would go, what questions it would raise.

CHAPTER 4

How It Had Come to This

It was dark when they drove through the gates at the Reece farm. Tom could read the sign for a moment as the headlights of the pickup shined on it. It said: *Reece Farms, Inc.*, which had been Tom's idea—to put up a sign, marking the headquarters of the new corporation. The Reeces had decided to expand a couple of years before. Douglas wanted to include all his sons (his own as well as those he adopted) in the family business, as well as Tom, as Joel's mate— hence Reece Farms *incorporated* and the sign.

During the renovation, the Reeces had also built walls on either side of the entrance. The iron gates stood open most of the time, so Joel did not stop to close them. The driveway had been paved and ran past the Reece home where lights shone in several of the windows. In front of the house the lawn lay shadowed and dark. On the east side of the house the twins' vehicles—Patrick's '65 Mustang, and Detrick's '68 Chevrolet Pickup—were parked side by side.

"Looks like the twins made it home from college," he said.

Joel smiled in return. "I was just thinking that. We've been gone so much ourselves, lately, it's hard to keep up with the rest of the family."

True, Tom thought. They had been away from home a lot and, now, as they hit gravel and continued past the shop and barn and pens, Tom sat forward, anxious to get home.

A moment later, Joel pulled to a stop and switched off the engine.

The lights from the farmyard did not penetrate the darkness and, once they stepped out of the pickup, shutting the doors, silence and darkness came together causing every movement they made sound loud. They retrieved their luggage and Tom followed Joel through the gate to their house.

*   *   *

Both of them knew the yard by heart, knew where each flagstone step lay on the upward slope of ground. Tom had terraced the front yard since it sloped downward from their small house on top of the hill overlooking the Reece farm. Tom turned just before he stepped onto the porch and looked back toward the east. It was a moonless night, and above the Florida mountains in the eastern horizon, the sky was filled with stars.

"Somebody's been here," Joel said behind him. He had been opening the screen door when a piece of paper fluttered to the floor, glowing white against the porch's darker wooden planks. He opened the front door and reached inside, flicking on the porch light.

In the sudden glare, Tom saw the deep reddish-brown splotches on the paper. Whoever had left the note had been bleeding, he concluded, as he looked over Joel's shoulder at the hurriedly scribbled writing:

Beat up
Need help
Leo

"Wonder when he left that?" Tom asked, not liking it at all. It meant that Leo had been in trouble and they hadn't been there; it also meant that, first thing after getting home, hot and tired and needing baths, they would have to find out where Leo was and how he was doing.

Leo Johnson had been one of the men they had brought home to live with them for a few days at a time—not that he had run away from home. He was Joel and Tom's age, a former classmate, but where they had been in a continuous relationship with each other, Leo had been in numerous live-in situations with men from Common, Deming, and even Las Cruces. Although each relationship had not ended badly, this last one apparently had.

That Leo had been beat up was not, of itself, surprising. Leo's life was a series of crises, and when he hit the climax of each crisis and found himself out on the street, he came to them. At times, Tom resented that Leo could take a vacation from his own life to enjoy their hospitality, which included Tom's cooking for him.

He hoped this time was different and that Leo had already found a place to stay. He hoped the blood on the note was from a nose bleed and not some kind of cut or gash. "Guess we need to call Mom," Tom said, meaning Eva Reece, "and find out if she knows anything before we go running off to find him. Leo could have left that note three days ago."

Tom's words came out sounding mean, but Joel just nodded as he folded the paper, picked up the luggage, and shouldered his way into the living room where he flicked on another light. The living room was small, although it was one of the biggest rooms in their house. The new bedroom and bathroom they had added onto the house a couple of years before was more spacious. They had moved into the new addition, so guests could stay in the old part of the house and have their privacy, as could Tom and Joel. Leo's frequent visits would have been enough reason to build another bedroom and bathroom onto their house, but when they added the other boys from Common and those occasional runaways who landed like wounded birds at the truckstop, it seemed inevitable that they should make room in their house for them. It had astounded Tom that the waitresses at the truckstop (who no doubt knew that he and Joel were gay) had sent the troubled youth to them for a friendly place to stay for awhile. The house now had two bedrooms and two baths.

The living room was still the same as it had been when they moved into it in 1965. Five years had only seen it get a good coat of paint, carpeting, and real furniture. But because it was small, they had to keep it tidy, with a place for everything, like Tom's desk in a small alcove next the front door, where they had built some free-standing bookshelves that served as a kind of room divider. The telephone was plugged in at the desk. After setting down the luggage behind one of the two sofas that faced each other in the center of the room, Joel went into the alcove and picked up the receiver and dialed his mother's phone.

Tom could hear Joel's end of the conversation, but he did not stop to listen. He went through the house turning on lights, checking the food in the refrigerator, and generally reacquainting himself with the stuff of their daily life. As he passed through the living room, Joel was still talking.

"Two days ago? Have you heard from him since?

"Yeah we saw their cars. 'Til mid July? That's it?

"'Til August? Yeah, quite a dif—

"No. We won't have to go back for awhile.

"Good, Mom. Umhmmm. Dad, too. G'night."

When Joel got off the phone, Tom had just finished brewing a pot of coffee, and had filled the sink with dish water. Joel passed through the room in a pensive mood, but he stopped at the sink and pecked Tom on the cheek as he was pulling off his T-shirt. Then he headed through the kitchen and into the newer part of the house, where they had built the addition.

Tom continued washing dishes, occasionally catching glimpses of himself in the darkened window pane over the sink. At the moment, all thoughts about Sharon or Leo had subsided, and even he would not have been able to say what he'd been thinking about, until he turned around to Joel, who had come back into the kitchen, stark naked. He put his hands around Tom's waist and, for a moment, laid his head on Tom's back. Then he got himself a mug and poured himself some coffee.

"Leo was out two days ago," he said, as he sat at the table at one end, where he and Tom usually sat in the mornings before work.

"Did Eva know how badly he was hurt or who did it?"

"If she did know who, she didn't say, but she said that Dad took him to the hospital. He was treated for a couple of cracked ribs and a broken nose."

Tom's stomach churned at that. "Good, Lord, Joel! That one sounds serious, and your mother didn't know who did it? Or Douglas?"

Joel pulled out Tom's chair for him and patted the back. "Come on, honey, you're just making extra work for yourself. Where'd you find all those dirty dishes, anyway?"

"Cleaned out the fridge," Tom said, looking at Joel so casually naked in the bright light. It would do no good to remind him that one of the kids might still come knocking—except they wouldn't bother to knock, which is how they had eventually come to understand the grownup secret that their older brothers, the twins, had known for several years. Henry had been just eight or nine, when he actually caught them in bed together, and was standing in the doorway, staring at them, when Tom noticed him out of the corner of his eye. Luckily, he was rolling off Joel's chest when he saw Henry.

But Henry hadn't stuck around for an adult explanation after wrinkling his nose and declaring. "I know you guys are 'gay,' so don't go trying to explain. I already know."

Tom smiled, remembering that, then noticed Joel sitting there idly scratching his balls. That made him smile even wider.

Joel looked up, smiling wanly. "I'm relieved we got that over with. I was close to backing out last night. Hard to believe it was just last night we were there."

Tom's own smile softened, realizing Joel was wrestling with the same demons he was—about Sharon and them. But he shook off the urge to say so. Instead, he looked at the wall clock above the refrigerator. Ten-thirty. Late. "I would like to make love with just you tonight," he said, grinning again.

*   *   *

When they were finished and lay snuggled in each other's arms despite the warmth, with Tom's face buried into Joel's clean, hairless chest of familiar scents and memories, he wondered for the hundredth time how it had come to this. It was just the night before, he thought, that they had been with Sharon; yet it seemed never to have happened, or to have been only a dream. For a moment, he hoped it had been. Then Joel squeezed him. "Do you think it'll be a boy or a girl?"

Even though the room was dark, light still filtered in from somewhere, causing objects on the dresser to gleam. From the position of the dresser in the room, with its tilted down mirror, Tom could make out their shapes in the bed. Joel's question shattered the familiarity, bringing back the night before, and he recalled more clearly Sharon's scent and the odd, disquieting feel of her breasts against his chest.

Maybe she won't be pregnant, after all, Tom thought with a desperation that threatened to spill over into his response. "It could be twins, Joel—a boy *and* a girl."

Joel laughed, and Tom felt it in Joel's chest. "That'd be something I didn't count on," Joel said. "It's weird, isn't it? To think we could be parents—real parents—and have children of our own."

"Well, you better settle for what you get, this time," Tom said, beginning to feel angry. "I'm not going through that again."

Although Joel didn't pull away as he might when Tom was angry, Tom knew his remark had hurt Joel, feeling his arms relax, and his hands, which had been stroking his back, lift away from him. "I wouldn't want to go through it, again, either, babe. I almost couldn't carry through last night."

This time, no laughter lightened his voice as it had a moment before, and Tom closed his eyes against tears of frustration that burned. He pulled away from Joel and propped himself up on an elbow, stroking Joel's face in the dark. Then he leaned over and pressed his lips on Joel's. There was no answering pressure in return.

"It was awful," Tom said, looking blindly in the dark into Joel's face; yet against the white of the pillow he saw the way his hair feathered out around him. "But I knew it was important to you. I knew you'd never be happy unless we tried it."

Joel returned the stroking, moving his hands along Tom's side. "Is it because we're a gay couple," Joel said, after a moment, "that you think it's wrong to want a child?"

This question was a familiar one, and wasn't one Tom had ever been able to answer. But with the possibility that Sharon was pregnant, its context brought thoughts to his mind he'd been unable to quite see before.

"Let's say the child is a boy," Tom said, "and he has to go to school, here in Common. Don't you think he's going to feel strange when all the other kids are talking about their parents, and if he tries to talk about us, the other kids are going to laugh at him. Or let's say it's a girl, and when all the other girls are talking about what their mothers are doing with their Halloween costumes and shopping with them for pretty clothes, how do you think our little girl is going to feel? Which one of us is going to be her mother?"

Tom hadn't said these words out of anger, but he heard Joel swallow hard, as if he were choking back tears.

"I've thought about that a thousand times," Joel said. "I know it's complicated. I know you think I just plow straight ahead regardless of what the issue is. I know you think I sometimes block out everyone's feelings when I go after something I want. And you're right, I do block out a lot of stuff. Like I did when you and I were going through that awful first time, and you were freaking out, and my friends were turning away from me, and my parents were hurt and your own disowned you. But babe, if I hadn't been willing to fight against that back then, we most likely wouldn't be together right now. Of course, if you hadn't also been willing to fight your way out of your own self-doubts and seen that you loved me as much as I loved you, I wouldn't have won, and we would not have each other, now. So, whether it's a girl or a boy, honey, and even if we were a straight couple, our child would have problems of one sort or another. Every kid does—even the golden children everybody loves."

Joel's depth of thought and his passion surprised Tom. He settled back down beside Joel and took one of his hands, entwining their fingers. He squeezed them hard. "Don't stop, now. Tell me everything you've thought about this."

Joel freed his hand from Tom's and slid it between Tom's legs, cupping him for a moment, caressing. Then he hugged Tom to him, laughing softly. "Oh, honey, you're everything to me. Even if I never wanted a kid to be with us or wanted a family, you would be all I ever really needed. You're everything I ever dreamed of, even *before* I knew I was gay. But about our kid—girl or boy—she or he is going to be all right, because it'll have us. I've thought about the gay thing and how the other kids will react. Well, we're going to have our child for at least five years before it goes to school and, by that time, he will know we love him. He will love us and he won't be able to imagine a life without two fathers. We'll be both its mother and father. When he or she goes to school, our kid will be able to face those other kids. I believe that, or I would'a never considered bringing one into the world or adopting one. Okay, so its problems are going to mainly involve having two men for its parents. But every child has problems. And you know what?"

"What?" Tom said, quietly, not wanting to interrupt.

"Our kid's going to be one of those children who has the biggest heart and makes friends easily. I'll bet he'll be able to help the others who have bigger problems than he does."

"But what if the teachers are mean to him?" Tom asked, just thinking of that aspect, and the thought frightened him, for the little girl or boy they were bringing into the world.

"I've thought about that, too," Joel said, again surprising Tom. "I'm going to take care of that on the day we take our little kid to school. I'm going to come right out and tell the teachers, if I hear one incident of intentional, calculated remarks on their part to hurt our kid, I'll get them fired. I don't like to use our power as a Reece in this small town, but you better believe I will. I'm going to make the principal understand that the teachers will have to be on their toes not to make any unintentional remarks either or treat our kid different from the others, or I'll step in and step on them. We're going to make sure our kid enters school on an even keel with the rest of the kids. I know teachers can be cruel—intentional or not—because I saw the way they sometimes treated the Mexican kids who came up from Palomas to go to school. I saw the way they treated Leo Johnson sometimes, because he was a sissy. I won't stand for it, and they're gonna know it right off."

Tom was stunned, not only that Joel had such plans, but also because he *had* thought so deeply about the problems a child might face with gay parents. He tried to look into that future time when their child would be five years old, but he could only see the past, recalling his own first days in school. Dimly, though with some clarity in the center of his memories, he recalled that his own father had done something similar on his first day. All he wanted to do was run off with the other kids and get to the playground where the others were screaming and laughing. But his father had taken him straight to the principal's office and said things that must've angered the principal. "No child of mine will be subjected to cursing, nor foulness, nor—"

But he was not about to try to argue Joel out of his plans for their child's first day of school. It was a long way off, and who knew what the future would bring? As Joel continued to talk, Tom glanced at the clock on the night stand. It was well past midnight.

"—do you?"

Realizing he must have drifted off, Tom opened his eyes. "What?"

"You don't think we're going to ruin our kid's life just because we're gay, do you?" Joel repeated.

Tom struggled to become more alert, recalling his original thought: how had it come to this? It was irrelevant to Joel's question. But Tom knew the answer now. Joel was passionate about children and had been that way all his life. He had been the one to suggest that his own parents adopt the Stroud children, when Kenneth Stroud had killed their parents, a brother, and himself.

"Of course I don't think we'll ruin our child, Joel. I know you will help overcome any obstacles this world will throw his way. And I'll be right there with you."

"Then what did you mean about last night being so awful?"

This time, Tom felt himself beginning to lighten up, his depression and dismay dissipating at the way their lives were about to change. After all, it would always be just the two of them together in the night, now that they had done their deed and had attempted to father a child "Oh that," he said, sliding his own hands between them finding that Joel was erect, though not necessarily out of desire. It was just the way they both stayed much of the time before they drifted off to sleep. "It was awful having to share you with someone, something I thought I'd never have to do. That's all I meant."

"I agree with that, honey, but you know we decided there really wasn't any other way."

"No other way," Tom agreed, pressing himself against Joel's familiar body once more, as exciting and wonderful now as it had always been, and which he was sure it would be fifty years down the road.

CHAPTER 5

THE REECE FAMILY

Just as the sky was beginning to lighten from the coming sunrise, a knock at the front door and then the sound of footsteps across the living room brought both Tom and Joel awake and scrambling for their clothes. They were laughing.

"Bet it's Sally," Joel whispered.

"Bet she heard us drive by last night and had to be restrained," Tom whispered back.

But they were wrong. When they went into the living room, still rubbing sleep from their eyes, the twins, Patrick and Detrick, were sitting on one of the sofas, grinning from ear to ear and looking as different from each other as Joel had ever seen them. Patrick's sandy-blond hair was getting long, and he wore a tie-dyed T-shirt and bell-bottom pants. Detrick's somewhat darker hair was cut more severely than he'd worn it at home and he wore the usual western-cut shirt tucked into his Wrangler's. Both of them had on boots, however, which Joel recognized. Both of them rose together and came at him and Tom, first shaking their hands then hugging them. Because Joel and Tom were still in their bare feet, the twins' six-foot plus height made even Tom feel short. Joel, always much shorter, would have seemed positively little in comparison to his adoptive brothers, except that he was the huskiest of the four of them.

As they were putting on their shoes, Patrick said, "we wondered how long it'd take you to get dressed! We've been waitin' here for what...Dete? Ten seconds?"

"At least, man," his twin said. "Mom says to come eat with us."

"Gee," Joel said, "I thought college *dudes* slept in. You realize, don't you, now that you're up, Dad's gonna put you to work?"

They all moved together and headed out the door. Sally jumped from behind the oleander bush by the steps, where she had been hiding, almost knocking Joel over jumping into his arms. Henry ran through the gate and surrounded Tom and Joel in his limitless bounding around, tugging first on Tom's arm, then Joel's and settling down only when Detrick pulled him by the shoulder and clamped him next to him as they walked to the Reece house. Henry was almost thirteen, yet to Joel he still seemed like the little kid who had come to live with them in 1965. But there was evidence in his sometimes squeaky, sometimes shrill or hoarse voice, that he was about to experience a growth spurt. For now, however, the child in him still dominated, and it was still fun to tease him about girls, whom Henry contended were at least from a different species if not from a different planet.

"You'd think we were the ones coming home from college," Tom said to Joel, taking his turn holding Sally's hand as they passed the barn and made their way through Eva's garden. "You ready to be off for the summer?" he said, turning to the twins.

"Not really," Patrick said, with a wide grin. "But I sure miss Mom's cooking."

"I sure am," Detrick countered. "I ain't stickin' my nose in a book 'til this fall."

That was the way of it, Joel thought, recalling the twins' differences from the time they had come to live with the Reeces five years before. Patrick was more outgoing than his twin and more academic, often helping his twin through high school English and history, and endlessly trying to get him to read the books that inspired and challenged him. Detrick had been less ready to make the changes that being adopted had entailed, from calling Eva and Douglas "Mom" and "Dad," to asking for things he wanted, as if he were still from a poor family and not from one as well off as the Reeces. But he was more willing to spend the day out in the fields with Joel than his twin, who preferred the paperwork that Eva required for the farm ledgers. In the end, both of them had graduated from high school near the top of their classes and both had decided to go on to college, though Detrick had chosen what he considered a much more realistic curriculum, one that would get him back into farming when he graduated. Patrick had done his chores and worked in the fields, as well, but as the years passed, anyone could see his real interests lay outside the small farming community.

Luckily, his choice of the University of California at Berkeley was within his academic range, and the school had readily accepted him and would be glad to avail him of the scholarships he had been awarded in high school. His letters home were volumes to the whole family, which Eva read with pride at the dinner table in the evenings, unable at times, however, to keep from frowning at the anti-war rhetoric Patrick sprinkled through them. Detrick had dutifully sent single-page letters, saying that school was going well, then asking about the crops and the kids, and the livestock back home. At these more simple letters, Eva's eyes shone with tears, for it was through his letters that Detrick was best able to express his love of his family; whereas Patrick could best express his love for the family in person.

She kept both sets of letters somewhere in her office, and would respond to each twin in the way she thought each would appreciate.

When they walked into the house, Joel saw, now that the twins were home, Eva was beaming as she forked mounds of pancakes and strips of bacon onto platters. Sally helped set the table, pouring juice expertly for her nine years, as she pointed out the places at the table where she wanted everyone to sit. She sandwiched herself in a chair between the twins, while she put Henry between Tom and Joel. Douglas beamed from his end of the table, smiling as his family took their places. As yet, he had hardly spoken, waiting for the din to die down, so he would not have to raise his voice to be heard.

It took awhile, however, since everyone wanted to know everything about everyone else. Joel could only smile to himself as he settled in and filled his plate. *You'd think the family hadn't been together for years,* he thought, rather than just the twins being away for their first year of college. But it seemed to be a special occasion, nonetheless, as the news from the twins came spilling out.

Patrick spoke about the anti-war protests he'd witnessed, and looked sheepish when Eva wagged a finger at him. "Don't let the politics get in the way of your studies," she said, and Patrick smiled back at her saying he'd brought home straight A's. "And don't you dare do none of that pot business, either," Eva said.

"Or drink," she said, turning to Detrick. "I know those cowboys at Sul Ross think more about partying than studying."

Detrick looked hurt, Joel thought, at Eva's admonishment, and didn't think she realized how it sounded, considering that Henry Stroud, Sr., and their oldest brother Kenneth, just barely eighteen, had been alcoholics and abusive drunks.

"You won't catch me touching that poison to my lips," Detrick said with his head bowed and looking uneasy. Then he brightened. "Besides, I brought home straight A's too," he said, looking across Sally at his twin, "though a'course it's probly easier at Cow-pie Tech than Hippie-U."

It was a dig Patrick was ready for. "Peace and Love," Patrick said, grinning, digging into the pancakes. Then with his mouth full: "They were just freshman courses."

"Eat up, boys," Douglas finally said from his end of the table. "We'll see if your first year of school has softened either of you. "Think you can still drive a tractor, Dete? And you, Paddy, I think you'll like the new Deere. You're supposed to be able to calculate tractor hours and fuel better. My logs need to be brought up to date, or Eva's gonna fire me."

"Which reminds me, Joel," Eva said "I've got some things we need to discuss."

*   *   *

She wanted to know about the sale of the equipment down in Chihuahua, the mileage on the pickup, and other things Tom was familiar with, having helped Eva keep the books for the corporation. But this morning, his mind was far from the gathering at the table and the banter among all those he loved. There were changes coming, even though the twins seemed to be their old selves, moving away in different directions, yet tied as closely to Douglas and Eva Reece as he was. Changes he was not so certain could be absorbed as easily as the addition of the four Stroud children had been. Or even his addition to the family as Joel's mate, or even as easily, after that first year, of integrating into this family the undeniable fact of their own son's homosexuality and the strained friendships it had caused them.

For coming soon, it seemed to Tom, was the most outrageous of all the acts he and Joel had ever engaged in. So, as the family ate and planned for the day, Tom kept thinking about Sharon Minninger and how she was getting along with Margaret. Joel had probably not forgotten about her, either, but Leo Johnson was still on his mind. When Douglas took the twins and Henry outdoors to get started on the chores and Sally busied herself gathering up the dishes and carrying them in precarious stacks to the kitchen, Eva, Joel, and Tom sat at the table to discuss Leo.

Eva lowered her voice as she talked, glancing occasionally into the kitchen from where they sat, then looking back at them.

"He was beat up pretty bad, Joel."

"But you don't know who did it?"

"He wouldn't say, but at least I found out who he was dating."

Over the years, Tom had grown accustomed to Eva, and even thought of her as his mother at times—someone he loved just as surely as he had loved his own mother. In the end, of course, it was Eva who loved him back. He was familiar with the lines of her face as she entered her fifties and of the new lines that had appeared around her eyes—those that came from new worries and new hurts—as she absorbed her son's homosexuality and his mate into her life. Her hair was still red, but had softened in the last five years to a more subdued copper and gray, especially around the temples. He had seen her in action against those who would hurt her child, who had in turn hurt her; Kenneth Stroud, not the least of these, who by his own hand had brought her four more children to worry over.

Tom, realizing he'd been staring at Eva, glanced from her face to the china cabinet that had been hit in the shotgun blast Kenneth had sent through the dining room window. The cabinet stood in the same place along the northern wall. It's frosted glass panes of flowers had been replaced with plain glass, and the broken china within had also been replaced. As had the shattered window. Still, the room echoed with that violence, and it was no doubt here, under the bright light of the chandelier, where she had probably brought Leo the night he had come by after his beating.

"I found out he'd been dating this new police officer in town," Eva said, once she had assured herself that Sally was out of ear shot. "You know the one, Joel. Last name's Barela."

That Eva had come so far as to be able to say, quite nonchalantly, that some man had been *dating* another was not surprising; nor was it surprising that she had been able to find out whom Leo had been dating. In a small town like Common, where the Reeces were known to every family in the town, especially the business owners and their wives, the Reece name had not diminished in influence—though perhaps it had been tarnished by Joel's homosexuality. But Tom was continually surprised at Eva's resilience in the face of all the new information she absorbed and the enormous changes rippling through the country. Most surprising, however, was that she had even tried to find out more about Leo's attacker, rather than simply treating Leo with kindness and letting it go at that.

"Do you think this Barela could be the one who beat him up?" Joel asked. He glanced at Tom. They both knew perfectly well who Eugene Barela was. But apparently Joel did not want to worry his mother with that knowledge.

"That's what I think, honey. You've surely seen the man, strutting around like a damned peacock in heat; you'd think he became a police officer because he likes the costume!"

They all laughed at this, because it was a precise description of the officer in question. That Eva was able to see the same thing he and Joel did was particularly funny, Tom thought, though perhaps she did not realize just how true her observation was. Even Leo had called officer Barela a cop queen, apparently before they had begun to date. Tom hadn't liked the campy humor Leo attached to such things, but this morning he laughed as hard as Eva and Joel.

Then Eva got up from the table, suddenly, it seemed to Tom, as if dismayed at the discussion. "Go visit Leo, Joel. I told him you'd come by when you got home."

"But where is he staying?" Joel asked. The last they knew was that Leo had been living with a guy by the name of Frank Thurmon in the town of Deming a few miles west of Common.

"I think he's got a motel room at the Drifter. Said his parents wouldn't take him back in."

"It's no wonder," Joel said. "Leo's apparently not capable of working."

At that disparaging remark, Eva left the room and went into the kitchen, cooing as she went at the work Sally had done rinsing and stacking the breakfast dishes.

They left by the dining room door that led into the garage.

The sunlight that now greeted them burst over the mountains to the east. The predawn had given way to another cloudless day, promising to be a scorcher. They made their way back through Eva's garden and found the rest of the guys at the equipment yard.

Douglas was instructing the twins and Henry on the day's work. In contrast to Eva, his face was less creased with worry lines than his wife's, and Tom thought how much like his father Joel was. Tom worried more over their own finances and what people thought of him and Joel. Like his father, Joel worried intensely for a time, came up with a solution, carried through, and forgot about it. Douglas had already started up the new John Deere tractor and was giving the twins turns at driving it around. He was squinting and smiling. Unlike the old poppin' Johnnie that had come from their purchase of the Hotchkiss farm, which Joel had taken into Mexico to sell to the Mennonites, this new one ran smoothly, seemed taller and more capable, as well, of handling the work the Reece farms demanded. Detrick was grinning from ear to ear as he maneuvered it around the equipment yard. Patrick was standing next to Douglas, taller than him by several inches, nodding at something Douglas was saying.

Douglas nodded toward Joel and Tom as they walked up, then turned back to Patrick. "See if you and Detrick can attach the cultivator to the new bar. Shouldn't be difficult, but you're likely to encounter kinks. Let me know if you need any supplies and I'll run into town."

When Patrick grinned and walked off, Douglas turned to them, still smiling. "Those two boys," Douglas said, as if that explained what he was smiling at. "Got in kind'a late, huh?" he said, turning his full attention to them. "I take it you found out about Leo?" Tom noted that, like Eva, Douglas' hair was more gray than when he'd first met the man, but he had changed less than Eva in the last few years. Perhaps it was no wonder since he'd gotten the large family Joel had said he'd always wanted. That was another attribute Joel shared with his father, his love of children, and it had made Douglas glow with pride, as he was doing now, watching Detrick on the tractor and Patrick strolling across the equipment yard.

Joel answered for them. "Yeah. If you don't need us for awhile. Guess I need to find out what happened."

At this, Douglas looked squarely at them. "Eva tell you how bad off Leo was?"

"Cracked ribs and a broken nose," Joel said.

Douglas nodded, still frowning. "He got off lucky, if you ask me, son. You boys had a run in, yet, with that Barela?"

"What d'you mean?" Tom asked.

Douglas squinted, glanced back toward the twins. They were both on the tractor and were pulling Henry up. He smiled then turned back toward Tom. "Eva says Leo and Barela were dating. I thought so myself, but I'll tell you, if you haven't had any personal dealings with the man, you ask me, he's some kind of nut. I've told that to Deputy Gray, myself. But the man just throws up his hands, saying how short the budget is and he's all we could afford."

There was surprise, rather than anger, in Douglas' voice, at the county's decision to hire someone like Barela, Tom thought. "Have you had personal dealings with him?" Tom asked, glancing at Joel. They had talked about telling both Eva and Douglas about the way Barela had managed, quite quickly, to zero in on them, showing up at places where they hung out in town, making it much more than coincidence. Now that Leo had apparently been *dating* Barela, even when he was supposed to be in a relationship with Frank Thurman, it was obvious that Leo had told the officer about him and Joel.

Douglas nodded at Tom's question, his frown deepening. "He pulled me over one afternoon about a week ago, lights flashing, right there on Main. I knew I hadn't been speeding or run a stop sign, then that ass comes up to my door, hitching his pants like he was Marshall Dillon, and grins at me. "'Quite a way to introduce myself to one of Common's most prestigious citizens,' he says, as if I appreciated looking like a common speeder," Douglas said, then he laughed. "Told him, too, how much I appreciated his ridiculous show. Told him how I pay his salary and don't appreciate kid games with our cruisers. Damn funny, though, what he said, then."

"What was that?" Joel asked. He glanced at Tom and the look in his eyes said they should keep it quiet what Barela had done to them.

"Said he wanted to meet the father of the two most famous boys in the town. I got his drift. Then I hear about him and Leo; then I see what that bastard's capable of. You boys stay clear of him. He may be gay, but that don't stop him from being a nut. Psycho is my opinion. You'll let me know if he pulls any stunts on the two of you?"

"Yes, Dad," Joel said.

When they were nearing their own house, Joel threw his arm around Tom's shoulders. "I almost told Dad about the way Barela seems like he's trailing us, you know? But I think we better not. I wouldn't want Dad to mess with police business. He's got enough to worry about, don't you think?"

No, Tom thought. He would have felt much better if he thought Douglas would try to get the man fired. Tom had almost managed to forget about Barela since leaving for Mexico, but the incident with Leo had brought it all back to the surface. He shuddered, not because he felt in any immediate danger, but Douglas was right. Barela had stopped them a few weeks before, far enough away from town that showed he had been trailing them, then pulling exactly the same flashing-light stunt Douglas had just told them about. Now, more than ever, Tom was leery of him.

So, as they made their way into town, his thoughts were scattered, first thinking about Sharon, then drifting to Leo, then stopping on thoughts about Barela.

CHAPTER 6

GAINING INFORMATION

It was close to eleven o'clock by the time they finally made it into town. They intended to visit Leo at the Drifter, but wanted to check on Sharon, first; no doubt she would be at the Red Rooster. It was coming up on the lunch hour at the café when they entered. It was predictably noisy, as well, as they surveyed the place to find a table. Joel spotted one, but hesitated, noting that Officer Eugene Barela, himself, was sitting in a nearby booth against the west wall, with his back to the door. Joel looked around, frowning to himself, and did not see Sharon. But he did see Margaret coming through the double swinging doors at the back of the café, carrying plates of food, which she set down on a table, nodding as the customers surveyed their meal and, apparently, approved.

She was wearing a one-piece shift of gray that matched her iron gray hair, which she kept clipped short and parted in the middle. Joel smiled to himself, wondering if the customers would know a lesbian if they saw one. Then she caught sight of him and Tom and wove her way around the tables. "Hello, boys," she said in her usual, but surprisingly high, feminine voice. "I've got Sharon in the kitchen. She says she knows some dishes people might like. She's teaching the cooks how to make them. I hope you'll stay to try them."

Joel glanced at Tom and back again. "Is Sharon getting used to things?"

Margaret smiled. "She's a quick student. She had never seen a television set before last night and was fascinated." Margaret barked a short, high laugh. "Reminds me of myself when I was a girl, as a matter of fact. But let's move out of the way," she instructed and took her accustomed place behind the cash register. Tom and Joel stayed on the customer side of it, just out of the doorway where another couple walked in, surveyed the crowd, and found their way to a small table. All three watched them go.

As she cashiered, Margaret told them about Sharon's fascination with the concept of television, and how she had tried to explain how the images were broadcast across the distance through the air, then waving a hand to dismiss her explanation. "But of course I have no idea what form of signal a TV uses," Margaret laughed. "And Sharon was as fascinated with my toaster and other gadgets. Can't say as I got much sleep last night, and that girl was up at four this morning!" Then a cloud passed over Margaret's face, which was gone in a second. "You'll have to tell me how the three of you met, Joel. Sharon tells a fascinating tale of being on her own." She lowered her voice as people passed by on their way out the door. "She calls you two her saviors."

Joel did not know how to respond or how much to tell her—especially why Sharon might call them her saviors. There was something about that which Margaret didn't like.

"We did kind of help her get off the streets, Marge," Joel said, after a moment. "You think she's doing all right?"

"She'll be fine, Joel. Would you two like something cold to drink?"

Joel glanced around the room as it was getting more crowded. "Maybe just a quick one. Looks like you're busy." Joel eyed a small table near the back, close to the booth where Barela sat. Although it made him nervous to think about striking up a conversation with the man, he wanted to find out if he was the one who had beaten Leo Johnson. How he would do that, he had no idea.

When Margaret turned her attention to a couple at the cash register, Joel led the way through the crowd to the small table. Tom followed, although Joel knew he had also seen the police officer and probably wouldn't like the idea of sitting so close to him. But Tom made no objection as they crossed the room. Joel positioned himself in the chair facing the officer. Barela was alone in the booth, looking off into some middle space between the cup of coffee he held to his lips and the back wall. The corner was rather dark, since there were no windows along the west wall, but the officer's accoutrements gleamed. The overhead light caught the top edge of his badge and made the brass buttons on his blouse chip light. Even the texture of his black sleeves and the silk ribbon running along the outside seam of his pants leg shone in the dull light. Barela wore no cap, and the almost blue-black of his hair, the dark and rather expressive irises of his eyes, seemed polished as well. Over all, from the top of the man's head to the black gleam of his boots, Barela was spit and polish—his appearance and demeanor was of quiet power contemplating itself; and because Joel knew Barela might have beaten on Leo, cracking his ribs, and breaking his nose, his appearance was rather intimidating.

When Joel sat down, Barela looked directly into his eyes and smirked. Joel's heart began to pound, his palms to sweat, but that made him more determined than ever to find out what he could; so he flashed the officer his brightest smile. "—doin' officer?" Joel managed to say in his best clipped local slang. "Hot'nuff for ya?"

He happened to glance at Tom, who had grabbed up a menu and was eyeing Joel over the top of it. Joel doubted that Barela could see Tom's face, except peripherally, and hoped he couldn't tell how nervous Tom was. For a moment, Joel regretted what he was doing, but he intended to finish what he'd begun.

Barela set his cup in the saucer, turning suddenly, facing Joel straight on; from this position, he could also see Tom clearly.

"Reece." Barela said, nodding at Joel, then looking at Tom, who began to study the menu with greater concentration. "Reece," he said, again, staring at Tom's profile.

Tom glanced at the officer, nodded, and turned back to the menu.

"Might say it's hot," Barela said, smirking again, picking up Joel's question.

In that short exchange, Joel knew two things—that he acknowledged their relationship as a couple, addressing both of them by the Reece family name; and his smirk said he thought it was funny and not something to be respected.

It had dismayed Joel over the years, especially when he and Tom had gone out to California to visit their friend Pete Thompson, that many of the gay men they met ridiculed gay relationships, as well, claiming it was not natural for men to pair off as though married, that it was some kind of affront for gay couples to close themselves off from the potential of having sex with those other than their partners. Pete, himself, who had been such a sweet and innocent kid when he lived in Common had taken on much of that attitude, although he and his trucker friend, Blue, had more or less been together ever since they met. "We've got an *open* relationship," he'd told them, insisting that it was best that way, saying that Blue shouldn't be restricted while he was on the road, nor should he be restricted there in San Francisco.

Barela had managed in that short exchange to remind Joel of all that.

"So…" Joel said, seeing that Barela was still facing him fully, as if he invited more conversation. "What d'you think of Common? You been here, what, about a year?"

"'Bout that," Barela said. He didn't move a muscle, and continued to stare directly into Joel's eyes, with an uncanny air that said he was reading Joel's mind. Joel supposed it was something they taught in the police academies— the art of quiet intimidation.

It worked. But Joel wanted to keep the conversation moving, until he could find out what he wanted to know. "How does it compare to where you came from?" he asked. Out of the corner of his eyes, he saw a waitress approaching with two glasses of what looked like lemonade, which Margaret must have sent over. He saw that Margaret was watching the exchange from the cash register. When the waitress set the drinks down, Tom thanked her and put the menu aside, taking up his drink with the same air of nervousness.

Barela stared a moment more. "Folks are more curious, here," he said. "Sometimes…people in small towns ask…too many questions. Talk too much. Know each other too intimately. Know what I mean?"

"Yeah, I surely do, officer Barela. Somebody gets knocked around, why the whole town knows about it. That what you mean?"

Tom kicked him under the table.

"Somethin' like that, Reece," the officer said, smiling. He kept his eyes on Joel, as if he wanted to eat his face, while he reached for his cap and placed it precisely on top of his head, managing to position it without touching the patent-leather bill. He got up, hitching up his pants, and in that one act revealed the outline of his penis, lying at an angle. "I come from Alabama," he said. "Just like that song."

Then he strutted off without a backward glance and walked out the door without acknowledging Margaret or her kindness in providing Common's finest with endless, free cups of coffee.

As soon as Officer Barela left, Tom expelled a long breath. "Damn it, Joel! What were you trying to do? Sometimes you make me so mad I could spit! You know that?"

He knew, but he'd had to do it. "I'm sorry, babe."

"But you can't say it won't happen, again. Right?"

"I can't."

This short exchange was followed by silence. Joel was not afraid that any officer in Common would hassle him unless he broke some law or held up the bank. The Reeces were well known in the small town, personal friends with the sheriff and his deputies. Joel was not afraid of the guy, but frustrated with the man's attempt to intimidate him with his uncanny stares. Barela definitely had a problem of some sort—if he was also gay—seeming to hate and ridicule it at the same time. He would be glad when he talked to Leo.

As soon as Barela was out the door and Margaret finished with a customer, she came to their table and sat down. Joel asked her about the officer. She smirked just as Barela had done. "Oh, him," she said, "It's cops like that—men like that—who give the rest of you males a bad name."

Joel was surprised at the bitter tone of her voice and said so. Tom kicked him under the table, again, but Margaret didn't seem to mind the question. "Bitter?" she said, looking toward the door, as if she could still see the police officer. "Honey, he's dangerous. Not that he's going to fly off the handle in the line of duty. He seems pretty well self-controlled, but he has me pegged, I'll bet, and the two of you. Your friend Leo was in here a week or so ago. Barela couldn't take his eyes off him."

"Yeah, according to Mom," Tom said, meaning Eva Reece, "Barela and Leo were dating. I guess they decided it would be too dangerous for Barela's reputation to sit together." It was the first words he'd spoken in a few minutes. "Guess you don't know that Leo was beat up a few days ago."

Margaret was not one to react too strongly, but a kind of fear brightened her eyes. "Then it just proves what I thought. Barela is dangerous—if he's the one who did it."

"But do you think Barela's the type to use his badge? You think he'd try something against Tom and me?"

Margaret sneered, again looking toward the door to the café. "Given the chance to do something, as long as it was in the line of duty, he might," Margaret said. "But I don't mean that he's dangerous as a police officer. I just wouldn't want to have him as a neighbor, as an off-duty friend—or enemy— might be a better way of putting it."

When Margaret left, Joel felt worse about having subjected Tom and himself to a face-to-face with the cop. Glancing at him, Joel realized he'd again made a big mistake. "Whyn't we go say hello to Sharon before we leave? If you want, honey, I can go see Leo by myself."

*   *   *

By the time they left the Red Rooster, it was nearing noon, and the bright June sunlight reflected off the whitewash of the adobe buildings along the main east-west street through town. They were heading west, getting close to the Drifter motel on the north side of the street. It was set back from the road and was surrounded by huge mulberry trees, shading its walls from the sun, though the pool near the parking lot was a burst of glassine brilliance that hurt Tom's eyes. They teared up and he wiped the tears from his face, smiling at once to himself about Sharon, who already seemed to be at home in Margaret's café among the cooks in the heat-stifled kitchen, and frowning a moment later at the thought of Officer Barela and Joel's insistence on engaging the man in dangerous conversation.

When he glanced at Joel, he realized that his thoughts had been evident. "You all right, babe?" Joel said. "You still angry at me? You look like you're about to cry or something."

Tom shook his head, forcing a smile over his frown. "The light hurts my eyes is all."

But it wasn't, as soon as they had parked on the heat-melted tar and gravel lot, and were heading to the door of a room facing the swimming pool, where Leo's car was parked, Tom realized he didn't want to see Leo at all, beat up and suffering or not.

He didn't like Leo sometimes. After all these years, from the time he and Joel had first gotten together, and through the years, as Leo came into their lives during one crisis after another, he resented that Leo was so out-of-control in his own life. Or he resented it that Joel always seemed to be rescuing him from himself. This latest episode with whomever had beaten him up caused a sense of sympathy in Tom's chest, where it was also partnered with a growing sense of resentment. But he tried to smooth away the evidence of his dislike as Joel knocked on the door.

The curtain in the window next to the door moved open, then they heard the chain being pulled off the door. A moment later, Leo opened the door a crack, pulling back into the shadows like a mole retreating from the noon sun.

"Oh, girl! You're finally here!" Leo said, pulling the door open wider and stepping back into the interior gloom.

You just knew we'd come, didn't you, Leo? Tom thought, feeling his resentment rise, then forcing it down. As his eyes adjusted to the room, his stomach lurched at the sight of Leo's face. Both eyes were swollen shut and were dark purple golf balls. A gash about six inches long ran from his left ear to just below his jaw.

"Shit, Leo!" Joel said, as he too caught sight of his friend. "You sure you shouldn't still be at the hospital?"

"No. M'okay. Think." Leo said, coughing. If it had not been for the sound of liquid in that cough, Tom would have thought Leo was seeking sympathy. But Tom doubted that this was an act.

Leo retreated to the bed, which dominated the small room. Joel and Tom sat in the two chairs on opposite sides of a small desk, below the window. The air conditioner was rattling ineffectively against the heat. Lukewarm air, with a wet feel to it, blew across the bare desk.

Tom could hardly look at Leo and clenched his teeth against his rising gorge at the hamburger look of his face. He was not wearing a shirt, and the ace bandage encircling his skinny chest barely hid other bruises and gashes. In contrast, Joel's face was blank, except for his eyes, which betrayed anger and sympathy, becoming a dark gray, pooling with tears.

"Who did this to you, Leo?" Joel said, his voice sounding stunned as he sat on the edge of the chair, forearms resting on his thighs, looking intently at Leo.

But Leo shook his head, pursing his lips, which were also swollen. "Can't tell you, girl."

"You mean you don't know?" Tom asked, trying to force calm into his voice, rather than the anger he felt. "Or you don't want to say who it was?"

Leo hugged his chest with his long, thin arms, rocking to and fro. "I can't tell you, Tom. I'm afraid, if you want to know the truth."

Joel apparently could stand it no longer and in one movement was sitting next to Leo on the bed, with his arm around his thin shoulders. "Aw, just look at you," he soothed, his eyes full of tears.

Tom forced down a jolt of jealousy at the tender way Joel held his old friend, reminding himself that it was just Joel's way, and nothing to be resentful of.

Leo began to cry, and the tears leaked out from the slits of his swollen lids. "It was awful. Thought I was going to get hurt bad."

Joel pulled him closer. "Aw, Leo, don't be afraid. We're not gonna let whoever did this hurt you again. Now tell me who it was."

It wasn't easy getting the information out of Leo. Between his reticence at revealing the name of his attacker, and his obvious desire to tell them about the attack, he cried and laughed, and lay against Joel's chest. Then he lit a cigarette and pushed Joel away with the drama of an actress in high camp snorting smoke out of his nostrils.

"If you want to analyze her," Leo said, finally, "I think she doesn't like being a faggot."

Joel laughed and gave Leo a small hug. Tom laughed, too, actually glad that Leo seemed to be coming out of his earlier funk.

"You been staying in bed, getting plenty of rest?" Joel asked.

It was irrelevant to what Leo had just said, and he looked at Joel, apparently rolling his eyes, though it was impossible to see them. "That's what got me in trouble in the first place," he retorted with a badly done laugh. He wheezed.

"What do you mean?" Joel asked. He got up from the bed and sat back down in his chair.

Leo continued with the details, punctuating his story with moments when he was lighting his cigarettes. He slumped into himself, as if suddenly very tired. His face looked like he'd bounced it against a brick wall. "I'll never forget it. He likes the dirty deed missionary style. I'm the woman. Well, sometimes, you know, I like to switch off. You two should know about switching off, right? I made the mistake of touching his national vault with my finger! And girls, that bitch sat up like I'd been trying to rob it! He began slapping me around, and I was so stunned I asked if I'd hurt him. Foolish me! It drove him nuts!"

Tom was disgusted with the images that Leo's description conveyed, and with Leo's more normal behavior—or rather, his uniquely nervous camp—

Tom grew slightly irritated, reminding himself that this was a friend. Leo's particular brand of story telling, however, embellished with disgusting words and graphic details, made Tom wonder at Leo's stupidity in having sex with someone like that (probably Barela) in the first place. Joel had often said that, of those he knew, except for James Gray the deputy sheriff, the men on the police force of Common, New Mexico, were badly trained, underpaid, and interested in the job because they got to carry weapons.

Everything sure pointed to Barela, considering Eva's remark earlier, knowing that Leo had been dating a homosexual cop and Margaret's saying Barela couldn't take his eyes off Leo in the café. *No*, he thought. Not homosexual, but a real pervert. It was obvious that Leo didn't have to say who it was; but his refusal to speak Barela's name was some sort of talisman against the danger the officer represented. Besides his sympathy, Tom was dismayed at Joel's growing anger, the more Leo talked. It made him worry.

But who am I trying to protect? Myself? Joel? Joel could take care of himself. He was becoming more confused, wondering, too, what he was wanting to protect himself from. In an effort to get over his uneasiness, he sat back in his chair with his arms folded across his own chest. "Can we get you anything?" he asked.

Leo turned and smiled a crooked, wrecked smile at him. "No, hon. I'll be all right. It's nice that you two came by. I was feeling rather lonely."

Then Leo got up. "You're right, Joel. I think I do need some rest. But hugs for coming by."

He waved to Tom with a limp wrist. "Thank you, too, darling!"

Tom sighed with relief as they made their way across the parking lot and got into the pickup. "It's Barela, isn't it?" he said to Joel.

"No doubt," Joel said, as he slid into the driver's side. "That fuck! Oh, babe, Leo looks bad!"

At that outburst, Tom felt all his fear returning, along with his anger. He would have to keep an eye on Joel, because he knew his husband intended to confront the officer.

CHAPTER 7

MARGARET JOST

Margaret didn't mind being in her seventies. If the truth be told, she often felt like she could live to be a hundred, and at other times wondered why she did not feel the aches and pains some of her friends did at that age. Coming from good German stock, with more than a dash of Swedish hadn't hurt, she supposed. Only, if the same truth were told, she was more than ready to follow Rose into the afterlife. Every night before she went to sleep, she spoke softly into Rose's pillow, giving her the news of the café, how the displays for that year's harvest season looked in the window of the Red Rooster, what events in the small town of Common had taken place. She talked, in fact, until she fell asleep and dreamed dreams of remembering, sometimes feeling Rose as solidly in the bed with her as she had when they were both girls, so many many years before.

And what changes the small town had seen in this first decade without her beloved. When Joel Reece and Tom Allen had come into her life, Margaret had not only whispered to Rose in their bed, but sat up many nights with the lights on, propped up on an elbow, talking to Rose's pillow and seeing Rose, instead, lying there smiling at all that she told of the two young men she had been introduced to at the Unitarian church: "by that nice young coach, Bill Hoffins, and his beautiful wife, JoAnna."

More than most, Margaret supposed, she had clung to every bit of news and scrap of gossip that had come into the café when word first hit the small town about the Reece kid, Joel. Words like homosexual, fag, fairy, and pervert had filled the café in the first few weeks when it came out that the Reece boy and the preacher's son were homosexual—and it was all so public and heart-wrenching and, yet, it was viscerally exciting, in a way. Margaret had to stop herself from banging plates over the heads of some of her best customers, the way they had carried on—especially when some of her women friends had tried to pull her into their conversations, inviting her to condemn the two young men.

"Oh, Rose…" she had lamented, while at the same time laughing, "Charlene Dyer…remember her? The one we thought was so beautiful? She says she felt dirty, having ever visited the Reeces, knowing what she knows, now. I was so disappointed to hear her talk like that, Rose. She having been our guest, remember, when that no account husband of hers ran off with the waitress from the truck stop?"

And so it had gone during the summer of 1965 and beyond.

Margaret remembered it all so clearly, had shared it all with Rose. How the Stroud boy had killed his parents and one of the little children and then himself. But no sooner had that part of the scandal blown over than she met the infamous Joel and his preacher's boy at the Unitarian church. She had cried with both sorrow and delight; they were so beautiful and so obviously in love with each other, she hadn't been able to help herself from confiding in them, without knowing whether they would be mature enough to keep secret the news of her own homosexuality—and not let it out into the public, as their own coming out had been. She had never divulged that truth outside a small group of people who made up part of the congregation of the Unitarians.

As the months passed further and further away from that terrible summer of 1965, Joel and Tom had become her friends, spending much of their time in town at the Red Rooster. Margaret would go to bed talking to Rose's pillow, keeping her up on the news, almost daily.

"Joel's one to watch out for," she had said to the pillow and laughed. "He's physically strong enough to take care of himself," she explained, "but if anything ever happens to Tom, honey, he may not be emotionally strong enough to get through it without a great tear in that beautiful heart of his."

She had seen the way Joel had once again riled up more than a few of the members of the town, when he insisted on buying wedding rings for himself and Tom from that jeweler, Thompson. It angered the man, not only because he was active in the Allen boy's church and had rekindled the scandal there, but because, like the preacher, he had disowned his own gay son, Pete, and didn't like being put into the position of refusing to do business with the Reece boy. "Well, it didn't matter," she confided to her sweet Rose, "they got'em, girl, got their rings, and old Thompson near had a fit over it!

"Oh, I know Thompson didn't have to sell the rings to the boys, but Joel didn't see the sense in having to go out of town, either. So, I hear they locked horns, Joel and Mr. Thompson—and Joel won!"

People noticed those rings, too, Margaret remembered, whenever the two boys came into the café. Tom was nervous, but bravely sat there, fiddling with things on the table, his wedding band seeming to pick up light from every corner in the room, drawing attention to it. Joel would call him babe, and talk loud enough for people to hear about those rings; and yet Margaret did not lose too many customers, even though several had warned her: "you need to tell those boys they're upsetting decent people coming in here." But Margaret hadn't even drawn a breath before she responded: "I couldn't possibly do that. If I allowed only those without sin to cross my threshold, I wouldn't have any customers." Then she took the news to Rose before drifting off to sleep, never once thinking how odd it might seem for an old woman to amuse herself by talking to the empty air in her old-lady's bedroom. She didn't think it was odd, because Rose was there and always would be.

It was one of the ways Margaret had made it through many years without her own mate, now that she was dead, to take the two boys under her wing. And then came a few more kids in the same pickle the Reece boy and the preacher's son were in. During the last five years, Tom and Joel had brought more of their friends by the café, boys like that poor effeminate Leo Johnson, who had later blossomed into what Margaret could only think of as a coquette. Like a pretty girl, Leo realized he was pretty in a way that could attract other gay men to him, with whom he played awhile then brushed off. One of them had been that nice man, Frank Thurmon, from Deming, from the next county over. Even though Leo had gone on to other men—namely that horrible cop, Barela, Frank came to the Red Rooster just to visit with her (as well as hoping to get a glimpse of Leo, she thought, sadly). And then there were the other boys Tom and Joel had brought with them, boys who were runaways, heading out to California like so many kids seemed to be doing these days, what with that *hippie* movement breaking out. Tom and Joel took runaways under their wings, invited them into their home, soothed their broken hearts, and reluctantly sent them on their way.

Then there was the heartache Tom had gone through, which Margaret had helped him get past when his own parents had finally left Common. She had waited on the preacher and his wife from time to time, and had been dying to sit down and tell them how ignorant and ultimately hateful they were for disowning Tom. But she hadn't, and when Tom came into the café by chance when his parents were there, she could see the hurt and confusion in his face, bravely sitting through his breakfast with Joel while, just a few feet away, his parents studiously ignored him. Then came the day when the boys had come into the café for Margaret's famous strudel. Tom had bought the newspaper, flipping through the few pages, only to discover the short article about his parents leaving town, under what must have been a hurtful headline: *Local Minister Takes Job in Arizona.* Tears had welled up in his eyes that glistened as brightly as the wedding band did when he brought his hand to his face to wipe the tears away. "I never thought they wouldn't at least say good-bye," Tom said.

That day, Joel was less restrained in public than he normally was, and had scandalized the other customers by throwing his arms around Tom, right there in the café, kissing him on the cheek and soothing him.

She had seen those two boys grow up in her café—witnessing their adjustments to each other, like the times they came in looking upset with each other, talking in low whispers, leaving their breakfasts untouched as they worked through each others' pain or misunderstanding. During such times, after saying hello and bringing them drinks or breakfast, Margaret held back, rather than sitting with them for a few minutes as she usually did. It finally came to light that one of their longest-running disagreements was that Joel wanted a child and Tom didn't like the idea; so they brought Margaret into the conversations about it.

Margaret relayed the problem in detail to Rose's pillow what the boys had told her. They had volunteered at the children's hospice where Bill and JoAnna Hoffins' autistic child was, and Joel had seen all those children in there, either the ones with cancer who were dying, or the ones who had been hospitalized with unexplained broken bones and lacerations—the abused kids. Joel had apparently been so hurt by what he saw that the idea came to him that he and Tom should adopt a child. As usual, Joel was adamant and could not help himself, once the idea took hold, to examine the possibility from all angles, over and over, until Tom relented and they both asked Margaret what her opinion was.

Even though she had felt sorry for Tom and said so, she and Rose had always dreamed of raising children of their own, too. So, in explaining to Tom and Joel how much more impossible had been their dream of children, since they were of child-rearing age in the 1920s, she took Joel's side in what was a painful argument between the two boys. "I'd do it, Tom," she had said, careful to pat Tom's hand, the way a mother might, speaking softly and soothingly, realizing that she might upset him. Over the years, it seemed that Tom had eventually come to support Joel in this, as he had in getting the wedding bands.

Nothing had come of Joel's desire to adopt. But, who knew? It was the 1970s, after all, and things did seem to be changing. Although the boys no longer seemed to be fretting over the idea, she didn't doubt that Joel was still adamant about having a child of his own.

Then came the day when they had brought Sharon Minninger to meet her. Another broken wing, another runaway, whom they had apparently rescued right off the streets in that small town south of the border, known widely for its pottery. That first evening, she had been delighted at meeting such a beautiful young woman, glad that, once again, Tom and Joel had extended their hearts and brought her into their sheltering world. But there was something disturbing about this time, she thought. Something that even the young woman was not divulging.

*   *   *

Margaret came out of her reverie. It was near closing time. She was cleaning out the cash register, quickly counting her take for the day, and making out the deposit slips. Sharon was running the vacuum cleaner. She had already restocked the salt and pepper shakers, refilled the napkin dispensers, and had washed down the tables.

Margaret's thoughts had been running over and over the last few years that day, as she watched the exchange between Barela and Joel, and then talked with the two young men after the officer had left. All day, in fact, she had been wondering just what it was between Tom, Joel, and Sharon. Sharon's face certainly lit up whenever she mentioned the two young men. When they had left after visiting with her in the kitchen, their own faces betrayed a kind of happiness, too, even though they were on their way to visit Leo Johnson.

When Sharon killed the vacuum cleaner and was rolling up the cord, something in the way Sharon placed her hands in the small of her back and arched to get a kink of tired muscles out reminded Margaret of a pregnant woman, full with child. Margaret was struck with a thought so odd, yet oddly forceful in its way that, as she dimmed the lights and began locking up the café, she couldn't shake the thought. Sharon smoothed her hair and wove her way through the tables, ready to join Margaret in their walk home. Margaret looked more closely at her. Sharon was, if anything, too thin, though well muscled, to be even remotely with child, and Margaret attributed her sore back to the work she had been doing all day.

Yet, still, the image remained in her mind, as she and Sharon walked home.

CHAPTER 8

DOUGLAS REECE

June slipped into July as the temperatures continued to soar, now staying in the triple digits, and everyone began looking toward the skies for the monsoon season. Douglas noted with a sense of pride that the twins slipped back easily into their role on the farm, neither Detrick nor Patrick complaining about the dirty work it required, even though they were now college students. There was a lot of work to be done, and both boys got up early when the day was as cool as it was likely to be—usually up and waiting for him in the breakfast room, already drinking coffee when he wandered in.

It reminded him of when they had first been adopted. During that first year, they were both still shy and hesitant about calling him "Dad." Even when they got used it, as often as not they called him "Sir." Edna Stroud would have been proud of her two sons in the respect they showed others. Something in the way they said "Sir" made Douglas always conscious of the esteem in which they held him. Even though he was a good man and tried to think through problems and situations, whenever they called him "Sir," he was conscious of his role as their mentor and therefore tried to return their respect, teaching them that mutual respect was something valuable and to be cherished.

But those few short years had flown by, and now they were only home for the summer, and Patrick not even that, since he had decided to the attend the second summer session at UC Berkeley; and so every day with these two boys was precious, because it was so fleeting.

As he worked with the twins, Douglas grieved a little at the short time he had had them in his life, the short time he could be a real father to them, before they went out into the world.

Were they ready? He wondered, considering that their childhood and part of their teen years had been influenced by old Henry Stroud, Sr., that drunken, no good; and part of their formative years had been made a nightmare by that no-count older brother of theirs. Yet nothing in their demeanor, other than an almost too-painful-to-watch hunger for the love they found at the Reece home indicated that they were permanently damaged by their previous upbringing.

Nor did their first year in college seem to have spoiled them for something more appealing than farm work. Both boys did the farm work, the mechanic work, and the bookwork Eva required of them with good humor, most of the time. There were already differences, however, in the way each perceived the wider world they had discovered away from Common. They had good-natured arguments about their respective schools. But Douglas knew that, with each passing year, these differences would become larger, and he hoped they would never differ so much that their love for each other would not prevail. He had worried more about Patrick's choice of schools than he did Detrick's, because UC Berkeley was a hotbed of dissent against the Vietnam war, and just the year before, the National Guard had killed students at Kent State. At Berkeley, there had been the takeover of the administration building. How much this kind of activity would affect Patrick worried him and Eva.

Still, Douglas had stayed silent when Patrick announced that his scholarships awarded to him at Common High would be accepted at UC Berkeley. He had stayed quiet, as well, this first summer when the twins argued about the Vietnam war. Detrick took the side of the patriots and those who were serving their country in uniform; Patrick took the side of the people protesting in the streets. Douglas only voiced his opinions when the boys asked for it, which they did often enough. Neither of them liked violence, and it was Patrick himself who had allayed much of Douglas' concern about whether the student activism at Berkeley would have too much influence on him and possibly cause him to prefer the protests to hitting the books.

"I've seen too many arguments break out among those on the quad who disagree with each other, so I don't join in the groups, because I know going to college is a chance for me to better myself. I want Ma (meaning his mother Edna) to look down and see I'm makin' something of myself."

And so the days flew by, and Douglas began to count off until the end of July, hating to see Patrick leave, but not wanting to hold him back. He was a level-headed boy and seemed to be focused where it counted.

On a whole other issue, however, the twins were like the two young teens he had adopted, and that was how they thought of Joel and, by association, Tom. It was coming up on Joel's twenty third birthday, July fourth, and the twins had taken over planning a surprise party for him.

As the temperatures rose, so did the twins' anticipation for Joel's party. They shared their plans with Douglas, Eva, and Tom, swearing them to secrecy. It was Douglas' responsibility to contact Joel's friends in town, since Tom felt that Joel's suspicions would be raised if he tried to do it under Joel's nose, and on this hot July day, Douglas was driving the family Caddie, carrying a list of names he hadn't been able to reach by telephone.

He had already contacted Joel's old boxing coach, Bill Hoffins and his wife JoAnna, who had said they would come as well as contact other members of the Unitarian church, where Tom and Joel had been going since 1965. "I know Joel will be delighted if Rev. Suskine would show up."

Then it was off to the Red Rooster Café, run by Margaret Jost. Douglas had always been tickled with Joel's apparent close friendship with the old lady. Douglas had been introduced to her several years before when he joined Tom and Joel for breakfast. Then many times thereafter, when he and Eva were in town together, they made a point of stopping by for an afternoon lemonade and visiting with Margaret. Neither of the boys had ever divulged the fact that Margaret was a homosexual, like them, but Douglas had always suspected that she might be. This fact did not bother him, nor did Eva let it bother her. He again thought of role models, as he had tried to be to the twins. Margaret Jost, if she was indeed a female homosexual, was a good role model, Douglas thought, almost a little sorry that he could never quite feel comfortable to ask her about herself, since in a way she reminded him of his two elderly aunts who had befriended him when he was a child. Their own homosexuality had come to light only after their deaths; yet Douglas had thought that his own less hysterical view of what it meant for his own son to be homosexual was a direct result of his realization that his two aunts (one of them not really his aunt) were kind and decent.

In fact, both he and Eva liked the woman. Margaret Jost had turned out to be quite a fascinating character, active in the schools when it came to supporting kids and their arts and crafts, active on the city council when it came to attracting businesses to the county. Douglas had found her to be a tough-minded old lady and reasonable when it came to the kinds of business she thought the town needed. She had been largely responsible for the chile plant that had gone in, near the old airport. Her support for such a plant hadn't hurt Douglas any, either, he reflected, since Reece Farms, Inc., owned a fifty-one percent share in the plant. Just as it did, now, in the two cotton gins, which had been threatened with closure, when the gins over in Deming had consolidated and had put in the pima gin, attempting to draw all the ginning business away from Common.

It was a quiet afternoon when Douglas maneuvered the Caddie into one of the parallel spaces in front of the café. Down the street to the east, where the cross street led through the heart of downtown Common, there were a few people on the sidewalks. The heat seemed to be keeping most people indoors, however. In fact, when he opened the door to the café, he was momentarily surprised at the bustle for a Thursday. He looked around the room, nodding at a few of the business owners who had sought relief from the heat or were having a late lunch.

Because Douglas was one of the town's most important farmers, his business was almost essential to the survival of some of the local enterprises. Having bought up numerous family farms over the years that were struggling, then hiring those same people or other families to work their farms but taking on all the expenses himself, Reece Farms, Inc., was able to keep local families working and the farms in operation, rather than allowing outsiders to come in and slice up the land as they had done in Deming. There, some of the best farm land had been subdivided into "ranchettes," which had lain fallow for a decade. For these reasons, farm production had actually increased in Common, while farming in some of the neighboring counties had decreased.

Douglas stood for only a moment before Margaret Jost saw him as she came through the double doors to the kitchen. She waved and indicated a table next to the swinging doors. He nodded and made his way to the table. When he sat down, Margaret smiled and said she'd be back in a moment. "There's someone I want you to meet."

Douglas took this opportunity to scan the room, noting that Claud Benson, the owner of the Ford Tractor and Equipment Sales was with some obvious out-of-towner (no doubt a salesman) and was poring over some brochures. Douglas chuckled to himself. Then he saw Bill and Cliff Crawford. Their parents had sold their farm and moved into town, where a lot of the retired farmers moved, once they sold out—at least those who did not go directly to the nursing home, having ruined their health after battling the elements and the banks for most of their farming careers. The Crawford boys were now co-owners of one of the gins that Reece Farms, Inc., controlled and, on a whim, Douglas decided to test the waters with them, knowing that, at one time, they had been good friends with Joel, until they found out he was homosexual.

Although Joel never talked about them, except in passing when it involved business with the gins, Douglas knew he'd been hurt that his childhood friends had turned against him. When Bill Crawford looked up to see him coming his way, Douglas could not read the look on the boy's face, except that he did not smile. The younger brother, Cliff, did smile, however, and nodded when Douglas sat at their table.

"Hot 'nuff for 'ya, Mr. Reece?" Cliff said, eyeing him.

"Not as bad as some years," Douglas said. "but the weather's good for cotton."

"Yep, it shore is, Douglas," Bill said. "You have a chance to look at last year's numbers on Gin A?"

"I did, as a matter of fact," Douglas said, looking into Bill's face, seeing something in his eyes that could be a little fear, a little hope, and he knew Bill did not like him, though he doubted it had less to do with Joel and more to do with the fact that he was Bill's boss in a way. But he decided to allay the boy's fears, if it had to do with the operation of the gin. "Not the best numbers I've seen, you understand, Bill. But better than recent years."

The fear subsided in Crawford's face and a slight, but nasty smile took up residence. "How's Joel and, what d'ya call him…his husband?"

Douglas surprised them both by laughing loudly, and when he knew he'd made a few heads turn toward the table, he spoke in a normal if somewhat gruff voice: "Yeah, Joel does call Tom his husband, as a matter of fact, there, Bill. And we consider Tom our son—or maybe son-in-law. Seems they've been with each other through, what is it…two of your wives? And you've fathered how many children? Three? As I hear it told, both your wives have left you and took your children with them. You keeping up with their child support?"

The fear pushed away any remnants of a smile, and invited a bit of hatred to enter Bill's eyes, as well. Cliff, meanwhile, was looking around, then ducking his head, as several of the business owners continued to look.

Douglas took note, not only of the two boys' discomfort, but the idiot grins on some of the faces of the men he helped stay in business. But he was enjoying this moment in a grim sort of way and would store it away with all the other insults people had tried to heap on him because of Joel. "Do you?" he said.

"Do I what?" Bill asked, obviously having no idea what Douglas' question referred to.

"Keep up with your child support."

When Bill didn't answer, Douglas got up and slapped Bill on the back. "I thought not. Seems to me, son, you should worry less about other people's personal business—if you get my drift—and concentrate on your own. Nice seein' you, though." With that, he turned and walked back to his table, glancing around at the others and smiled, nodding. It was all a matter of perspective, he thought, concerning Joel and Tom. He knew about the sordid personal lives of many of the men in the café and he returned the grins of those he knew the most unsavory things about. There was more than mere money involved in the currency of business, and if anyone thought they'd embarrass him publicly, they would be disappointed.

Margaret returned with a beautiful young lady by her side, and when Margaret sat down at the table, she pulled out a chair for the young woman. "Sharon, I'd like you to meet Joel's father, Douglas Reece." The young woman's face lit up so much that Douglas was confused. But he nodded to her. "Sharon? It's good to meet you."

"It is good in meeting the father of Joel, too," she said. "He has told me of you and your wife, as well as all your children."

Still confused, Douglas tried not to let it show. "Are you visiting from out of town? How is it that you know my son?"

"Oh, yes!" Sharon said, smiling widely. "I have met both him and Tom. I came from out of town as you say, but I am now to be living here. I am to be working for Margaret."

At this, Douglas could only nod. The girl was blonde and beautiful, but something in her speech patterns seemed forced and awkward. He could not put his finger on just what it was, however, and shrugged it off, noting the time on his watch. "I need to run along, Margaret," he said, turning from Sharon's captivating face—odd that such a beautiful woman did not wear makeup. "I, ah, came to invite you to Joel's birthday party on the fourth. It's supposed to be a surprise. Tom suggested that I invite you."

Margaret, who had been watching the exchange between Douglas and Sharon, smiled now. "I would love that, Douglas. Only I wonder if it would be all right to bring Sharon. As she says, she is from out of town, and I would not want to leave her to her own devices. If that is all right."

"Certainly. Were you going to be open for the fourth?"

"Indeed. Saturday is a busy day. But I think I will close early. We both need a rest, don't we, honey?"

"We're going to have a barbecue toward sundown, then fireworks," Douglas said, nodding at Sharon as well. She smiled brightly.

"Ah! Yes. The fourth of July fireworks! I have never seen these things."

Also odd, Douglas thought. "They won't be too spectacular, I'm afraid." Then he got up from the table. Margaret extended her hand and Douglas shook it. Then Sharon extended her hand, and Douglas took it a little more gently, smiling at her. "I am sure that Joel will be pleasantly surprised for you two to show up. I don't think he's even aware that his birthday is going to be anything special, this year."

CHAPTER 9

BIRTHDAY CONFESSIONS

On Saturday morning, Margaret awoke to the smell of rain. As was her habit, she slept with the window open. She got out of bed, feeling a little stiff and thought, yes, today would be a good day to close early. She looked out the window. Although the sun was not yet up, it was light enough to see that heavy rain clouds had moved in during the night. A glance at the clock beside her bed told her it was 6:30, and for a moment she felt anxious, realizing that she and Sharon only had a half-hour to open the café and that breakfast would be delayed if any customers expected a batch of pancakes or waffles this early. Luckily she had made the biscuit dough the night before, a recipe Sharon had showed her. "We make this at night," she explained, "because the men are up and hungry so early, and this dough rises more slowly, so it won't be too…um…how you say, fluffy."

Margaret noted that Sharon's memories came from her farm life, and all she knew were such memories. She had only been in Common for about three weeks.

Then she heard Sharon down the hall in the other bathroom. It sounded as though she were sick, and for a moment, it reminded her of Rose in her last days, sick from the heavy drugs that she had been given.

Poor child! Margaret thought, putting on a robe, sliding her feet into the slippers by her bed, and padding down the hall, listening at the bathroom door. Sure enough, the child was sick. She knocked gently.

"Sharon? Honey? Are you all right?"

A moment later, Sharon opened the door. Her face was pale, but the color was already returning to her cheeks. "I think I'll be fine. For the last couple of mornings, though, I've been *nauseation.*"

"Nauseated?"

"Yes! But I am thinking it is nothing. Something I eat."

Suddenly, Margaret did not think so. A memory came to her of the way Sharon had placed her fists in the small of her back and stretched to get the kinks out the other night in the café, like a woman, pregnant with child.

*   *   *

It rained all afternoon, thoroughly wetting down the farmyard. As Joel and Tom made their way to the Reece house (on Tom's insistence that they were going to have a birthday supper for him), water was pouring from the downspouts on the barn, causing areas within the fence to puddle. Water was splashing onto the concrete slab outside the workshop, and bright slicks of oil made rainbow colored puddles. The sunlight had returned, but the rain had lowered the temperature.

Joel was surprised when, as they neared the Reece house, there were at least a dozen cars pulled up on the east side of the house. He recognized the Hoffins' MG and the old clunker that Margaret Jost drove; but there was also a new pickup he did not recognize, and others that looked only vaguely familiar.

"Tom. What have you done?" he asked, smiling at Tom.

"What?" Tom said, his face a blank.

"You know, buddy!"

"I guess Mom and Dad are having over a few guests," was all that Tom would say.

But Joel knew something was up, for sure, when Sally stuck her head around the corner of the front porch of the Reece home and ducked back instead of running out to meet them as she normally would.

So when they entered the house by way of the living room, instead of the garage, it was no surprise to Joel when almost two dozen people, cried "Surprise!"

It took a moment for him to recognize some of the people in the crowded room. He immediately saw Sharon, smiling brightly at him. She was wearing what appeared now to be her favorite color of bright yellow—one of the dresses that he and Tom had helped her pick out. Beside her, Margaret Jost was wearing a soft blue pantsuit and, unlike Sharon, she was wearing a bit of makeup.

Beside her were Bill and JoAnna Hoffins and the Rev. David Suskine, whom Joel and Tom had gotten to know well since first meeting him five years before. Next to David, but somewhat shorter than David's six-foot, four inches, was a man Joel did not recognize, although when Joel's eyes came to rest on him, the guy smiled. It was an odd kind of smile, Joel thought, observing the man for just a second more, noting his rather formal dress of white shirt and tie, black slacks, and black shoes. Joel imagined that, in the den off the living room, would be the guy's jacket. Next to him, Joel was very surprised to see Frank Thurmon, and he wondered who had made up the invitation list. Frank was smartly dressed in a knit shirt and slacks and penny loafers, a style Frank always wore when he came to Common from Deming. His construction business there had provided him with a good living, as well as kept him well toned, and Joel wondered yet again why Leo was so flighty as to let Frank get away. Frank nodded at Joel, smiling slightly, though looking ill-at-ease in the crowded room.

People had already begun to break up and cluster in groups. Off to one side of the living room, where Eva and Sally had set up a punch bowl and a line of chips and snacks, were Patrick and Detrick and their friends from high school, whom Joel recognized but whose names he could not recall, except for Patrick's best friend Terrance Lawton. Terry had convinced Patrick to go to Berkeley with him. It was a good thing, Joel thought, that Patrick had been influenced by Terry, whose father owned the major bank in town. Like Patrick, Terry had also let his hair grow longish, but today, neither he nor Patrick wore their tie-died shirts, as Patrick had the other morning. They were casually dressed, as was Detrick in new Wranglers and their old boots, and for just a moment, Joel was reminded of the very first time he had given the twins pairs of his own pants, helping them change out of the rags they had worn that day when they were going to work for Douglas. It was that very morning when Kenneth had killed their parents, one of their younger brothers, and himself.

That day, the twins had looked lost, their faces blank; now, they were playful and boisterous, laughing and talking as they and their friends huddled at the snack table. Two of Detrick's friends from high school had dressed up a little, but they had already pulled their ties loose, letting them hang from the open collars of their shirts. The twins and their friends had briefly smiled at Joel, when everyone had said happy birthday, but they were now lost in their own conversation.

He saw Sally, wearing one of Eva's dresses, and two other girls about her age, slipping from the dining room, through the living room, and into the hallway that led to the bedrooms. They were also dressed up, including pinned up hair, slight bits of makeup, and what were also Eva's dresses. Joel's eyebrows went up at this, and he wondered if it was with his mother's blessing. He cringed at the thought of what her dressing room might look like, if the three girls had been given free reign.

He looked around, noting that Eva and Douglas were visiting with the Bensons, and Joel's face turned red, recalling one time when he had been in their home to pick up their daughter Melissa for a date. No doubt, as he had heard Douglas relate a couple of stories, Claud Benson was well aware that Joel was gay, and he didn't doubt that his wife knew, as well.

In all, including the family, at least twenty people had greeted Joel's wide grin with smiles, and he felt lucky to have so many friends. He noted that everyone of them, except for Frank and Margaret, were straight—at least the ones he knew. This also made him continue smiling.

Once the little surprise party had made their greetings to Joel and wished him a happy birthday, he went up to Sharon and Margaret and thanked them for coming. There was something subdued in the way Margaret greeted him. Although she smiled and her voice sounded the same, something in her eyes showed a bit of sadness.

"Have you met my family, yet?" he asked Sharon.

"We have only been being here for a few moments before you came into the house," she said. "It is a palacio, Joel! I would never dreamed to have become the friends of a..." she trailed off, her words failing her. This time, Margaret did not offer her an English equivalent, leaving Sharon speechless.

Joel smiled at Sharon and Margaret, turning to Tom. "Would you visit with them for a minute, babe? I want to get Mom and Dad and introduce them."

Joel was a little surprised that Tom frowned slightly, doing a bad job of trying to cover it over with a smile.

*   *   *

As he looked through the dining room window on his way to find his parents, Joel saw Henry and a couple of his friends on the front lawn. Tables and chairs had been set up for the barbecue, but the rain had wet everything, and the meal would be eaten indoors. Henry was wiping down the folding chairs and his friends were stacking them on the front porch.

In the dining room he found his parents, now visiting with the Hoffins. His father was listening to something Coach was saying, and Joel smiled at his father's face and his eternally playful smile. Joel hugged Bill and JoAnna and shook hands with Rev. Suskine. "Glad to see you, Mr. Suskine."

"I wouldn't miss it, Joel," Suskine said. Then he nodded at the man beside him. "I brought along a friend especially to meet you and Tom."

The guy was not much older than they were, Joel thought, though his face was lined in ways that made Joel think he worried a great deal.

David introduced him as a cousin. "Martin is working on his master's at the university," he said.

Martin shook Joel's hand in a grip that surprised him. "David told me about you and Tom," he said. Although he smiled, it disappeared almost instantly. "I've been looking forward to meeting you—you know?" Martin's greeting ended in a question. It was obvious that he was gay and had been brought here to meet them because of it.

Joel clapped the guy on the shoulder, feeling beneath it a boniness that was almost repulsive, but he smiled. "That's great, man," he said, trying to smile as brightly as he could. Martin had Suskine's angular features and there was a family resemblance. He felt sorry for Martin, however. Although he smiled at Joel, the deep lines in his face hinted at a youth spent in worry or sadness, some kind of agony, anyway, that scarred Martin's otherwise handsome face.

*　　　　　*　　　　　*

When Joel left to bring Douglas and Eva back to meet Sharon, Tom was suddenly apprehensive, and it dawned on him, now, that he had unwittingly caused this too-soon meeting, by agreeing to the surprise party for Joel and suggesting to Douglas that he should be the one to invite Joel's friends. Tom was unsure if Sharon would be able to pass as anything but a runaway. If her accent was still too heavy with a Mexican influence, Douglas wouldn't be too hard put to connect Sharon's Mennonite background from the midst of a Hispanic culture. Where else would a blonde person with a strange Mexican-Germanic accent come from? Tom was afraid that once Douglas and Eva saw her, Sharon would be wearing a sign that said "runaway from Mexico." So Douglas surprised Tom, when he came up to Sharon and Margaret and called Sharon by her name. And it was he who introduced Sharon to Eva.

"She's working for Marge, honey," he said.

Eva, obviously unaware of the connection between Sharon and her son and Tom, was gracious and therefore not suspicious of Sharon's strange accent.

"I detect...what is it...German?" she asked, smiling at Sharon.

"That's right," Margaret offered. "Sharon's relatives in Montana are recent immigrants."

Eva nodded. "What brings you to such an out-of-the-way place as Common?"

Tom's heart caught in his throat, and he exchanged glances with Joel. But there was nothing either of them could say.

Sharon only smiled. "It is strange. This is true. But I was born in Lordsburg, and though I was only a small child, I remember the desert and the farms."

"I see," Eva said, apparently satisfied. Then she excused herself. "I have to set out dinner."

"Then I should like to help," Sharon said. "I am working for Margaret in the Red Rooster, and I am learning many things."

*　　　　　*　　　　　*

Douglas had listened to the brief conversation and had been more confused than he had been at the café. There was something off-kilter about Sharon and her story of coming from Montana. Something that even Margaret was hiding. He recalled Sharon's enthusiasm for meeting him the other day as well, and the way she had immediately connected him with Joel as his father.

So Douglas had also watched his son's and Tom's reaction to the conversation between Eva and Sharon, and it was then that he became even more suspicious. Not something that felt bad, necessarily, but something just plain off-kilter.

*　　　　　*　　　　　*

After Sharon and Margaret followed Eva out of the room, Joel introduced Tom to Martin Suskine and, since David and Tom had religion in common, he left Tom alone with them while he sought out Frank Thurmon. Frank had been looking both uncomfortable and alone in the midst of the rest of the crowd. Frank was standing by the punch bowl listening, though not joining into the conversation, among the twins and their friends.

"I guess you heard what happened to Leo," Joel said, as he came up beside Frank.

Frank nodded, frowning. "Ah, I'd like to have a smoke, if you don't mind, Joel…only I don't see any ashtrays."

"Let's go out on the porch," Joel said, and led the way.

The air was still cool as the sun began its final descent toward the western horizon. Clouds had gathered over the distant mountains, however, and the sunset would be hidden. It felt wet, as well, when Joel and Frank stepped out onto the front porch.

"I've wanted to see him, Joel," Frank said, pulling a pack of Marlboro's from his shirt pocket, flicking open the silver lighter he produced from a pants pocket. He flicked the lighter and cupped his hands around the end of the cigarette. When he drew in the first puff of smoke, he rolled his eyes as if it were a savory drug, rather than the stench Joel caught a whiff of.

"Well, you should go then," Joel said. "I don't know why he ever broke up with you in the first place."

Frank blew the smoke out. "He told me he'd met someone else! And I can't help thinking that, whoever it was is the one who beat him up."

"That's what I think, too, Frank. But Leo won't tell me who it is."

For a moment, Frank puffed quickly on his cigarette, thinking. "Was it bad?"

"Pretty damn bad, Frank. I'm sorry."

"I'd like to say it serves him right, but I can't. It breaks my heart."

Joel watched Frank finish the cigarette, amazed that anyone could breathe in so much smoke without coughing his head off. The cigarette glowed dully in the gray of the darkening afternoon.

"How does he do it?" Frank asked, when he came up for air. He dropped the cigarette onto the concrete porch, smashed the butt with the toe of his shoe, then picked up the flattened butt and stuck it into the Marlboro box.

"How does Leo do what?" Joel said.

"Meet so many men. Shit, there ain't five thousand people in this whole town—much less a lot of faggots. *Why* does he do it? I want to know that, too!"

In the year or so that he had known the man, Joel liked Frank Thurmon. He hoped that they could remain friends. He seemed to be a down-to-earth sort.

"We always thought Leo would begin to settle down," Joel said. "We thought that, after he met you, he would for sure. You're the most stable man Leo has ever been with, but I guess he's not ready."

Frank's anger was giving way to a quiet struggle to breathe. Joel saw that he was about to cry. It made Joel uneasy, thinking Frank would break down, here, just when dinner was about to be served.

But he took a deep breath and squared his shoulders. "Is it that simple?" Frank asked. A husky sob seemed to smother him. He took another breath. "Is this what this fucking *gay* business is all about? They tell you how much they love you and how they never want to lose you. And you believe them enough to turn your life upside down, and then they just drift off with a new dick! What happened, Joel? I tried to build my life around Leo after I divorced my wife. Hell, I divorced her *because* of him. He seemed so damned right for me! And it was better with him than with Jennifer. She and I stood each other for ten years, and we stayed married, trying to do right, trying to make things work. But it's like a game to Leo!" He sighed. "I'm too old for this. You know I would never lay a hand on him like his latest fling!"

Despite his efforts, tears brimmed on Frank's lower lids, but Joel didn't attempt to hold the man as he might have, as Frank seemed to need.

"Frank, I know you must be feeling terrible, and all you probably want to do is stay home and throw a big drunk or something."

"You're right about that. I could pull a drunk."

"But would you consider coming back here to Common to visit us? Leo's my friend, you know, but I was kind of hoping just Tom and I could get together with you sometime. There's no reason why you can't make this a regular thing, you know? You've never even seen our house. We'd enjoy having your company."

Frank managed something like a smile. "Thanks, Joel. I'll tell you, I always felt things, you know, for men. But I didn't know how complicated it is, being *gay*."

The emphasis was bitter, Joel thought. "Yeah. It is. It seems like some of us are lucky, considering me and Tom, I mean."

Frank nodded. "You know, most of the men I've met down there in El Paso at them gay bars, they're…" He waved a hand. "You go to those places to drink and dance, but I'll bet half the guys there spend the whole night talking about being homosexual. It seems like it's the only topic they like to discuss. And you know what they talk about the most?"

"No."

"How they got to be that way!"

"Oh," Joel said. "Who cares?" Then, realizing that he had no advice for Frank, said, "Well, listen, about Leo…I'll go with you, if you want to see him. He's staying at the Drifter, down on Pine. Maybe, you know, he'll be glad to see you."

"That may be," Frank said. "But I ain't getting my hopes up."

*   *   *

By the time dusk came, the rain clouds had cleared out and the sunset was just a glow in the western sky. But the air was fresh and cold, and those at the birthday party moved outdoors for the fireworks. Douglas sat near Sharon and brought Eva with him. As the twins set off each of the various fireworks, Douglas watched the young lady's reactions. How could anyone reach adulthood and not have seen fireworks? Yet that's what Sharon had said a few days before; and now, she could not contain her astonishment.

By then, Joel and Tom were also sitting next to her and Margaret on the other side, and Douglas noticed that when the air grew colder, Joel put his arms around both Tom's and Sharon's shoulders, and she laid her head on his shoulder—a gesture Douglas might have expected from one of the twin's girlfriends, but not with his son. Again, it was off kilter to Douglas.

Was this something deeper than mere friendship? Douglas wondered, although it seemed too odd, and that was ironic. These days, it was just as difficult to imagine Joel as heterosexual as it had been a few years ago to think of him as "gay." Yet there it was, and Douglas was more confused than ever. Who was this girl, and where did she come from? Certainly not Montana. That's where Margaret was from. Margaret did not say that Sharon was a relative; so what were the odds that some Germanic speaking girl claimed to be from Montana where Margaret was from? It was too much of a coincidence.

Chapter 10

With Child

After the dinner, the fireworks, and bringing out a birthday cake with 23 candles and Joel opening his gifts, the number of guests at the Reeces' dwindled to Sharon and Margaret, Martin Suskine and Frank Thurmon. Frank had offered to give Martin a ride to his cousin's house later in the evening, so David Suskine had gone home.

In this more intimate setting in the Reeces' living room, Joel returned his attention to Margaret and tried to carry on a normal conversation. But Margaret still seemed displeased with something, although as before, her voice sounded the same, and she smiled at appropriate places in the conversation.

But Tom was also subdued and sat in a chair somewhat off to the side and did not contribute his voice to the after-party talk.

The conversation was, in fact, stilted, reminding Joel of the few times in high school when he had agreed to visit a girl's family before taking her on a date.

The same small talk.

Only Sharon seemed not to be subdued, and she was actually carrying the conversation at the moment. "I have been being lucky," she said smiling her pretty smile, her eyes twinkling, and captivating Joel with her beauty. "Since being here, I have a good job, and I wish to thank Joel and Tom for meeting me to Margaret."

Frank was smiling at Sharon, though Joel could tell that even he seemed a little confused with her and her strange speech patterns.

Then Joel caught Margaret's eye. He smiled, but the corners of her mouth barely moved from their downward slant. Something was definitely wrong and before he knew he was going to, he stood up from the couch, where he'd been sitting next to Sharon. "Marge, I need to ask your opinion about something. Could we go into the dining room?"

When Margaret nodded and stood up without hesitation, her eyes narrowed a little, reminding Joel of times in her restaurant, when they were talking about some bit of bad news. With that, Joel's heart began to beat a little faster as he waited for Margaret to pass in front of him.

A moment later, Joel pulled out a chair at the dining room table for her, and Margaret sat down.

"You look a little tired, Marge." Joel said. "Would you like some coffee...or hot tea?"

She agreed to tea and when Joel brought it back and set the cup and saucer in front of her, she nodded. "Thanks, honey. I think this will do the trick. Now...what is it you wanted to see me about?"

This time there was a genuine smile on Margaret's face and Joel almost decided that he'd misread her earlier expressions.

He sat down next to her, pulling his chair out and resting one arm on the table and the other cocked at the elbow on the chair back. "I'm not sure, now," he said. "But I'll give it a try..." His heart was beating faster and it was loud enough that he could almost believe Margaret could hear it. "You have been looking sad, or something, Marge, all evening. Is there something the matter? Something you need to talk about?"

Margaret nodded. "You're unusually perceptive, Joel. You surprise me. Tom's usually the first to notice such things." Again, there was the smile, but the sad tone was back.

"Yeah," Joel said, "I don't usually take notice..."

Margaret took a sip of tea and placed the cup in the saucer, then folded her hands beneath her chin. "How well do you know Sharon, Joel? I mean how long did you know her before you decided to bring her across the border?"

At the direction Margaret suddenly turned the conversation, a kind of embarrassment dropped into his chest as counterpoint to the thudding of his heart. "We first met Sharon in May of this year, early on."

"Walking the streets in Casas Grandes? Or when you went to her community to sell your equipment?"

"In Casas Grandes. Tom was the one who noticed her. But anybody could see she was not where she belonged. Marge, you should have seen her clothing. You could tell she was from the Mennonite community, but she had tried to disguise it by the way she altered her clothing. I don't have that much experience, you know, with things inside their community, but Tom was right when he pointed her out as a runaway."

Margaret nodded. "Yes, Sharon does tell the same thing. I also know, now, why she calls you her saviors, because she has told me about your offer to send her to school. But you might as well realize that since she has no real records, it will be difficult to build up a resume, of sorts, to verify that she is ready for college. Quite frankly, I don't think she is ready. I believe that she should enroll in night school and get her diploma. She could probably challenge much of the curriculum, but she's lacking in certain areas and, besides, she needs that diploma before she can apply to any college. She has big dreams and she is putting a lot of trust in what you have promised."

"Is that what's bothering you?" Joel asked, almost relieved that it was this. "I can promise you, Marge, Tom and I intend to keep our promise to her."

Margaret nodded, again, more firmly. Joel saw that she had suddenly gained enough information to proceed with something, the way she lay her hands on the table, cupping them around her tea. "Then, if this is the case, Joel, there is a missing piece to a puzzle I find myself unable to complete. To use a phrase I've been hearing lately, exactly what's in this for you? You are talking about thousands of dollars, you know, and several years. I don't doubt that you and Tom have the means to do this, but it's puzzling as to why you would."

Joel nodded in return, realizing that Margaret suspected something. He took a deep breath and slowly let it out. He suddenly wished that Tom was with him, because he was in too deep by himself. He wanted to tell Margaret everything, but it was not his decision to make. Tom should also agree that they should tell Margaret. But most of all, it was Sharon's decision and, apparently, she hadn't told Margaret much else than when they'd first met.

Joel simply could not respond, and again Margaret nodded, her eyes narrowed, and even though she smiled, Joel knew what was coming.

"Joel, I think Sharon is pregnant."

Joel still couldn't say anything.

"Honey," Margaret said, "I can see that you are not surprised, and that tells me about all I need to know. What I don't understand is…how could you do this? You have taken advantage of an innocent young girl. And even though she might have agreed to this, which apparently she did, having a child is not as simple, say, as you and Tom buying wedding rings. You have taken an irrevocable step, one that will change your life. But even more important, whether Sharon thinks so or not, it will change her life, too."

Joel decided that telling Margaret that Sharon offered to carry their child (and that they hadn't even thought of asking her) was a petty point—and not his decision to make, alone. He looked around the dining room, recalling the time he came out to his parents, right after they had returned home from a vacation. Tonight, he had inadvertently come out to Margaret about his relationship with Sharon, but he had not said so; nor had he mentioned Tom. Margaret might assume that only he was involved.

"Does Tom know?" Margaret asked.

Again, Joel was caught. If he said yes, she could still assume that he was the only one who had gotten Sharon pregnant; but that would be a lie, allowing her to come to that conclusion. If he said no, then Margaret might assume he was hiding things from Tom, and he didn't want her thinking that, either.

He was nervous, but it was different discussing something with Margaret than it was with his parents. Although she was a dear friend and it would hurt to hurt her, Joel felt he could lay things straight out, without really alarming and hurting her as deeply as he might his parents.

He sat up in the chair and touched her arm. "The truth is Tom knows—at least that Sharon might be pregnant. But I would really rather not continue without Tom and Sharon being with me."

This time there was no reservation, no hint of sadness, nor disapproval in Margaret's smile. "Of course, honey. I understand. But let us make this soon…say, tomorrow morning at the Red Rooster?"

Shortly thereafter, Margaret and Sharon said goodnight.

When they were at the front door, Joel hugged Sharon. "Tom and I will be by tomorrow morning."

And Margaret nodded.

"What was that about us going in tomorrow?" Tom asked, as Joel was closing the front door.

Joel did not want to get involved in a discussion while Frank and Martin were still there. "I'll tell you later." Then he turned toward the two men on the couch and invited them to end the evening with him and Tom at their house.

∗   ∗   ∗

Tom awoke at six o'clock the next morning. It was still dark in their bedroom, since it was on the west end of the house, but when he entered the kitchen, he saw the faintest light in the living room where the sun shone as it came up over the Florida mountains to the east. Whether or not there were clouds, he didn't know and didn't look.

He put on a pot of coffee, got out a pan and began cracking eggs and otherwise busied himself with breakfast until Joel came in. His blond hair was tousled and he had a stunned look on his face. Tom smiled. "Coffee's almost ready, honey. You look tired."

Joel was not wearing a shirt or shoes and his Levi's rode low enough on his hips that Tom saw he wasn't wearing underwear.

Joel came up to him, then, and wrapped his arms around Tom, kissing him on the cheek. "I'm not used to staying up 'til two in the morning. Thank goodness today's Sunday and we don't have to work."

"What time did you want to go see Margaret and Sharon?" Tom asked. The night before, when they were finally getting to bed, Joel had told him that Margaret thought Sharon was pregnant, and he had relayed their conversation. "We have to tell her the rest of the truth," Joel had said. "Looks like people are gonna find out a lot sooner than I thought."

"We probably should skip church and get in there before the church crowd, don't you think?" Joel said, now.

Tom agreed that it was fine. They had their coffee and eggs in silence. This was not unusual, and Tom enjoyed the familiar intimacy with Joel—just the two of them, the way it had been for five years. That was about to change—if Sharon was pregnant, which she probably was, he thought. At some time in the near future, they would have a baby in the house. He could not yet conceive of what that would be like, and he still did not know if he liked the idea. But he knew Joel did, and Tom was happy about that.

Like Joel, he realized that people were going to find out about Sharon a lot sooner than he thought; and he was disturbed at that prospect, because they would wonder who the father was; he was also worried that she had not had enough time to work on her accent. He was certain that Sharon's appearance at the Reeces, yesterday, had at least raised eyebrows. Douglas, rather than Eva, appeared to be the most inquisitive. He had not wanted Sharon to meet the Reeces for a while, but it was too late, now. How much, how soon Douglas would want to know Sharon's story would determine how easily he and Joel could break the news to him and Eva—especially the news that they were going to be grandparents.

So he greeted the day, during this quiet time with Joel, with a bit of apprehension. Joel had also said that Margaret was not pleased at all with Sharon's pregnancy, saying that he had taken advantage of her innocence. They would have to set that straight, Tom thought—both of them had taken advantage of the runaway. With Margaret's reaction to the news, their whole affair was cast in an ugly light, and Tom was certain it would also appear ugly to others.

*   *   *

They went into town just as the sun was fully above the Floridas, and on the morning after the rain, everything in the desert appeared to be refreshed. The bare patches of ground were a darker, richer brown. The crops on both sides of the highway looked greener and more vibrant, and what cars and pickups were moving up and down the streets of Common did not look so dusty and hot. The day would eventually turn hot and muggy, Tom thought. He felt the moisture in the air as they drove through town with their windows down.

The street in front of the Red Rooster was deserted, and Joel maneuvered the pickup into a parallel space along the sidewalk. When they pushed open the door to the café, a cheerful bell sounded. Usually, it was so noisy that you couldn't hear the bell. And as soon as they stepped over the threshold and were standing by the cash register, Margaret came through the double doors at the back of the café.

"We'll be just a moment, boys. Help yourself to some coffee." Then she disappeared, again.

The restaurant was empty, since it was just barely after seven, but as soon as they had helped themselves to their coffee at the waitress station near the back, the bell tinkled, again, and in walked Officer Barela.

Tom pretended not to have seen, but Joel set his coffee on a nearby table and greeted the cop from across the room. "Mornin' Officer Barela. A little early for a coffee break, idn't it?"

Tom was mortified at the challenge of Joel's greeting, which left the officer to defend himself.

"Not since I was on duty all night, it ain't," Barela replied. He sauntered over to the waitress' station and prepared his own cup of coffee. By then Tom had seated himself at the table, but Joel remained standing.

"Any crimes on the mean streets of Common?" Joel asked. He pulled out a chair and sat down next to Tom; then he threw his arm over Tom's shoulders, which made Tom almost choke on his coffee.

The officer grinned, and there it was, a glint of meanness in his eyes, Tom thought. Barela was homosexual, but he didn't like it that Joel was being so open about their own relationship.

"You know this town, Reece. It's quiet most times. All people have to worry about is other people's business." Barela made his way to the same booth where he had sat the other day, seated himself on the same side, with his back to the front door and his face to the back of the café.

Joel did not respond to the officer's last remark, for which Tom was grateful. He did not want a repeat of the other day.

*   *   *

Barcla's presence would make an awkward meeting even more awkward, Joel thought. He did not want to talk about Sharon if the cop could hear. No telling what he would make of the conversation, or even what he might do with it. So Joel felt anxious when Margaret and Sharon finally came out of the back. Today, Sharon was wearing green of a shade that contrasted brightly with her blonde hair. Margaret was wearing the powder blue pantsuit of the day before, and in the subdued light of the café, she looked a few years younger, her face, therefore more set—something anyway that made Joel feel he was in for it, considering how she had put things the night before, saying outright that he, Joel, had taken advantage of an innocent girl. You could add destitute and desperate, Joel thought.

Even though Margaret knew they were going to send Sharon to college, she still didn't like it that Sharon was pregnant, and her perspective cast their deeds, their actions, in a bad light. Like Tom, Joel saw the ugliness in it; but he also saw a kind of romance. If Sharon had made an independent choice and still offered to have their child, where was the wrong?

It was conceiving a child out of wedlock, making the child a bastard—that's where, he thought, taking a sip of coffee.

*   *   *

Fortunately, or maybe not, the Red Rooster was hit earlier than usual with a table of travelers who came in asking directions and ended up staying for breakfast, as soon as they breathed the aroma of freshly baked rolls coming out of the kitchen. So for a while, Joel had to wait to finish the discussion with Margaret.

Sharon left the table where she had been sitting with them to take care of the customers.

Joel watched Sharon's quick efficiency in waitressing, and watched Margaret's approval of the way she handled the customers. Margaret turned to Joel.

"Sharon catches on quick, doesn't she?"

"She does," Joel agreed. "We knew she was resourceful when we saw her in Casas Grandes, the way she had altered her clothing to avoid being spotted as a Mennonite."

Once the customers were taken care of and Sharon returned to the table, Margaret said, "I think we should talk about certain arrangements the three of you have apparently made." She rested her chin on folded hands, ready to listen.

"I told Margaret what we have done," Sharon said, smiling. "I could not keep from her this idea."

Tom glanced at him, and Joel saw that the frown from yesterday was back, though now it was tempered with the same sadness Margaret had shown at the birthday party.

Joel felt as though Tom and Margaret were accusing him, and he knew they were right. It was the culmination of a dream that had begun early in his life, which had taken a strange detour because of Tom, rather than a wife.

"I cannot believe the folly of youth," Margaret said, finally, looking at all three of them and smiling sadly. "What you three have done is commit yourselves to responsibilities and consequences you could have avoided. Yet, except for Sharon, I would say you are at least capable of handling them."

"But why do you say that Sharon isn't capable of handling these same responsibilities?" Joel asked. He glanced across the room at Barela, but could not read the man's face and decided that he probably couldn't hear them.

"Because Sharon is having to deal with being a castaway from her family, her home, her people, and her country, Joel. That is enough for anyone to deal with, without adding the burden of carrying a child. Perhaps what you should have done, if you were intent on this course of action was to first get Sharon settled, here, arrange her citizenship, and give her time to adjust to her new life."

Margaret was right, Joel thought, and said so.

"But what's done is done," Margaret said, then. "It is as useless to dwell on the 'should-haves' as it is to mourn the passing of one's youth."

Tom, who had been silent, finally sat up, looking first at Joel, then smiling at Sharon, then Margaret. "You do know that Joel may not be the one responsible for Sharon being pregnant?"

A strange look crossed Margaret's face. Then she nodded. "Yes, honey, Sharon told me that the three of you…participated, and even though I think you were crazy to do it, I do understand your reasoning."

"But you're holding Joel as more responsible than the rest of us," Tom said. This time his face was set in a serious manner that made Joel smile to himself. This was his husband defending his husband the way he always had in the past, and for that Joel was grateful.

Margaret smiled, with a bit of a twinkle in her eye. "Yes, Tom, it may seem so, and in a way I do. Because I know how much he pushed you to have children. I never dreamed you would even think of doing it this way, and it is this that bothers me the most—involving an innocent and desperate girl."

For a moment there was silence among the four of them. Joel appreciated Margaret's forthright statements. It showed him what he must do in the future to regain her confidence. He and Tom would not abandon Sharon, and they would help her with all the paperwork that would make her a citizen, would make certain she was never without the necessities, nor the means to reach her goals. But he did not feel daunted by the challenge of Margaret's words, only inspired to show her that he had never meant to take advantage of Sharon or her innocence.

By the time they said good-bye and left the café, it was becoming busy. Margaret had to stand behind the cash register while Sharon and the other morning waitress moved between the tables taking care of the customers.

When they stepped outside into the now muggy mid-morning, they were both surprised to see Officer Barela leaning against the hood of their pickup, arms folded, and smirking at them. His black uniform adding a note of menace to his appearance.

Joel was stunned and could not imagine what Barela might want. So he proceeded to open the driver's side door, and Tom went around to the passenger side.

Joel stepped inside and was about to pull the door shut, when Barela grabbed it, looking sternly at Joel as he did so.

Joel let go of the door. "Sorry, Officer. You want something?"

Beads of sweat lined the officer's upper lip. "Town gossip, Reece. I wouldn't think of spreading any, if I was you."

Aside from not knowing exactly what Barela meant, the threat in the cop's voice angered Joel. "Sorry, Officer. I don't follow you."

Barela grinned. "Rumors. About how someone got beat on…isn't that the way you put it the other day?"

Joel held his anger in check. He took hold of the door and pulled it out of Barela's grasp, slamming it shut. "I've got too much on my mind, Officer, to listen to or spread rumors. Like farming, insects move in and threaten your crops, you spray pesticide. You don't spray pesticide just because the bugs might move in."

When Barela touched the bill of his cap, his smirk was back and, without another word, he turned on his heel and sauntered down the sidewalk.

That was when Joel knew with a certainty that the cop was the one. Further, he seemed to think his intimidation had worked and he had nothing to fear.

And for a time, that's exactly what Joel wanted him to think.

Chapter 11

The Blind Season

As July came to a close, Patrick loaded up his Mustang and headed back to California. Then, toward the middle of August, Detrick did the same, tying down a tarpaulin over the suitcases and boxes in the bed of his pickup and also left home, heading southwest into Texas.

Joel regretted that he had not spent as much time with his adoptive brothers as he would have liked this summer. Like Douglas and Eva, he felt that they had been in the family such a short time before they were gone, and he worried that Patrick was growing away from the family and the farm a lot quicker than Detrick.

And so, as the dog days of summer were coming to a close, it was just him, Tom, Douglas, and when he wasn't in school, Henry—all preparing for the harvest season on the home farm. On the rest of the farms of the Reece corporation, the families living on them were responsible for the harvest. The Reeces owned close to two sections of farmland in the county. Fortunately, the land was adjacent to the Reece home farm or close enough that Douglas could oversee the other farms about once a month, unless emergencies required his attention, like a well pump going out, or major repairs needed on a tractor. The corporation covered such expenses but took the difference out in operating costs at the end of the season. Douglas' goal, of course, was to eventually wean the farms off the corporation and to sell them back to the families that proved to be most able to run them.

But with the twins gone, Douglas, Joel, Tom, and Henry had to work harder to complete all the tasks the home farm required.

There was little difference between the temperatures of August and those of September, but it seemed to Joel that the maturing crops in the fields, Eva's garden, and even the trees around the Reece home had begun to look tired, ready to turn yellow or drop their leaves. It was the last month of summer and a kind of endlessness to the days took hold.

But the end of summer did bring something new. Sharon was beginning to show her condition, and according to Margaret, customers in the café were beginning to ask questions, or speculate aloud. If some biddy came right out and asked who the father was, Sharon just alluded to someone "away for awhile." But she did not use the word "husband." Instead, she said "*he's* not in town, right now." But being with child out of wedlock was not as surprising in 1970 as it might have been in 1960—even to the busybodies who raised their eyebrows the highest. Those who took the greatest interest in her pregnancy, of course, were Margaret, Tom, Joel, and Eva and Douglas Reece.

It was, in fact, this interest that finally forced Joel to decide to talk to his parents. He took advantage one Saturday morning to broach the subject with Douglas when they were touring the other farms to see how the families were coming along preparing for the harvest.

Tom was helping Eva ready the books and ledgers they would need to keep during the harvest. They would also keep the paperwork from the other farms. So Joel and his father were alone in the pickup as they drove east toward the old Mulligan pecan orchard, which the Reece corporation now owned and the Marquez family operated.

They had their windows down and the breeze coming through the pickup was cooler than mornings had been a few weeks before; but even now, it would turn hot and sultry by mid-afternoon. Douglas was driving. They were passing grain fields on either side of the gravel road, where the golden heads of grain were radiant against a turquoise-blue sky. Occasionally, a flock of black birds splattered against the blue as they burst into flight at the sound of the pickup passing by.

Such days with his father were still frequent, and Joel always enjoyed them—just him and Douglas together, like it had been for so many years, as he grew into manhood and before he met Tom.

It was on this particular morning that Joel said, "I've got something very important to tell you, Dad."

Douglas didn't turn to look at him, but his eyes crinkled around the edges in a characteristic smile, the profile of which he presented to Joel. "I suspect that you might, Joel. I've been wondering how long it was going to take you to tell me."

Joel wasn't really surprised that he already suspected something, but he doubted that his father could possibly have guessed as much as there was to tell. Even though he was not afraid of his father in the least, his heart beat a little faster as he tried to form the words that would best broach the subject.

"If you suspect it might be about Sharon, Dad, you're right."

This time Douglas did look at him, and the smile was still there. But there was something else. There was the same sadness in Douglas' eyes as there had been in Margaret's. It was the older and wiser adult's perspective that Joel felt he still lacked. Things could make him sad, but he was as yet unable to see how the older adults around him could also smile when they were sad. His father's smile was always present, even during times of great stress. "Well, I won't play games with you, Son," Douglas said, finally. He turned back to driving. You gave both your mother and me gray hairs over you and Tom; but you've proven yourself with me on that score. So I won't try to guess what you have to tell me. Just spit it out."

Joel took a deep breath. "You and Mom are going to be grandparents. Sharon is going to have my baby. You suspected that much didn't you, Dad?"

Douglas shifted down and slowly applied the brake as they came to the cattle guard that divided the Reece home-farm from the old Mulligan place, then shifted down another gear and went smoothly over the cattle guard. "I suspected something like that. I admit that you seemed overly affectionate toward her the few times I've seen you with her. You stumped me for awhile, because I know you're gay. It wasn't to prove something to yourself, was it?"

"No, Dad." Beneath the pecan trees, still a dark green, but also looking tired, the air got even colder and Joel shivered as they ran beneath them. "Tom and I wanted a child of our own, and the truth is, Tom might also be the father."

At this, the smile did leave his father's face, and Douglas looked straight at him, the surprise there, evident. Then he laughed, but there was a sad tone in it, that wiser, older thing. "Now just how am I going to break this to your mother, Joel? How are you going to handle something as simple as a birth certificate? And one of you *will* be listed as the father. Needless to remind you, as well, you ought to marry her."

It was Joel's turn to be surprised. Down deep, where things hurt him, his father's suggestion to marry Sharon hurt a great deal.

"The whole reason Tom and I were with Sharon, Dad, was for us to be fathers. You don't have to worry about that. I will be putting my name on the birth certificate, or Tom will. I didn't think of those kinds of details, but you're right. But I can't marry Sharon, Dad. That would say that the last five years with Tom have not been a marriage, and it is."

Douglas chuckled, this time, shaking his head. He turned north and headed into the farmyard where the Marquez family now lived in the old Mulligan home. At one time the Mulligan's farmyard had been an inspiration to

Douglas. He had learned much of his own farming science from old man Mulligan. But as the years passed and the old man died and his sons took over, Douglas and his own son had surpassed the two brothers. But in the two years that the Reece corporation had run the old place, the Marquezes had refurbished the barn, razed the two wings of chicken houses and replaced the old horse stables with a workshop where the Reeces' older equipment was refurbished and sold down in Mexico. Now, newer equipment was out in the sunlight and the Marquez boys were working there.

Douglas merely honked and waved as he and Joel drove through. Farther down the road, they turned west and drove toward the old Hotchkiss place, which had been the first farm Douglas had bought when he had adopted the twins.

"At least you don't seem to have changed your mind about Tom, and I'm glad. But who's gonna raise the child? Or is Sharon moving in there with you two? You know it's gonna look a little like a Mormon household if that's what you're thinking. An upside down Mormon household at that."

Joel's nervousness subsided, again seeing that his father was even-tempered about what he had just told him. "We were thinking of having Sharon live with us, Dad, until she has the baby. But I think she and Margaret are really enjoying each other. Anyway, she's having this baby for me and Tom. We want her around as much as she wants to be near our child. But she's got dreams and plans of her own, too. We're going to send her to school. We can afford it, because we've been saving up for Tom to go to college. It just looks like Sharon's going to be the one to use that money."

Douglas was silent at this last, but he glanced at Joel, chuckling, as he maneuvered the pickup through gates and around corners.

Finally, as they were driving past the old Hotchkiss place, where Douglas was experimenting with a grape vineyard, whose care he left in the hands of the Donegal family, he hit the steering wheel with the open palms of both hands. "Well, Joel, I can see that you *have* thought through some of what it takes to be a father. I also know you love kids and have always wanted a family like I did. But you should realize that your relationship with Tom might prevent you from having the kind of family you want. No matter how well off you and Tom might be, or how committed and stable you are, people will not like having homosexuals being parents. Have you thought about the way they will treat your child?"

*   *   *

Douglas listened to Joel's answers and he was impressed with the depth of thought Joel seemed to have given the matter—but he wasn't about to let Joel know that he was impressed. He could see Tom's influence in Joel's thinking, because he admitted to the things that were wrong with the way they had fathered the child—a sign of maturity, Douglas thought. Joel could still strongly justify his ability to raise a child and, yet, admit that mistakes had been made.

He could accept his son raising a child with Tom; but he knew Eva wasn't going to like it. Further, he knew that if any moral busybody managed to contest the child's custody in court, it would be next to impossible for Joel to win—unless, perhaps, if he married Sharon and gave up Tom.

But that was as unthinkable to Douglas as it was to Joel. This whole affair was going to be another series of hard knocks for the two boys, and still later hard knocks for their child and Sharon.

By the time they pulled up at the Reece home and Joel finished talking, Douglas said, "Son. I agree with what you say. You've done a good job of thinking through some of the issues of raising a child. But it isn't good enough to assure that you will be able to keep it. Be aware, and be prepared. Now, I wish you could tell me what I'm going to tell your mother."

"I can do it, Dad. I was planning to."

But Douglas shook his head, laughing softly. "No. I think she'll be less likely to hit me than she would you. We'll talk more, later."

Joel slid into the driver's side of the pickup and started the engine, then leaned out the window. "Just tell her the truth." His blond hair was a metallic sheen in the morning sunlight, and his youthful and radiant smile was still that of the son who had confessed to being homosexual a few years before—at once secure that his feelings were as good as anyone else's and that it was his right to be *gay.*

Douglas could not help but smile inwardly as he stepped up onto the porch. *Joel's giving us a grandchild.*

*   *   *

Eva's reaction was surprising, even though he could have predicted much of it. As predicted, she was shocked and dismayed and confused, but with enough presence of mind to send Sally on an errand that would keep her out of earshot. Then she burst into tears, hit the ceiling, over-reacted, and poured coffee she didn't drink.

And then she began laughing.

"My goodness, Douglas! A grandchild by Joel. I thought I'd never see it! If it's a son, he'll carry on the family name. And just what am I going to tell our kinfolks?"

By this time, Douglas was having difficulty not bursting into laughter at his wife's reactions, which were nothing at all like those when she found out her son was gay. This time, she got her shock and horror out of the way, quickly, and actually seemed to be happy at the prospect that she was going to be a grandmother; never mind that Joel had got a girl pregnant out of wedlock. She hadn't even stopped to wonder about the birth certificate; and when Douglas said the child might also be Tom's, she had ignored it (after appropriate surprise and dismay) in favor of Joel's fatherhood.

Now she was sitting at the breakfast room table in the kitchen with Douglas, sipping on cold coffee—and beaming. "I'll have to call Kate and Trish this afternoon, you know," she said, staring out the window, smiling and turning back to Douglas long enough to clack her tongue. "I knew there was something odd about that girl, Douglas, but I couldn't put my finger on just what it was." She grinned.

"Eva?" Douglas said, suppressing a grin, himself. "Doesn't this bother you? I thought you'd be devastated. You seem positively radiant. Have I missed something?"

She was grinning, then she burst into tears, but smiled through them. "It's just about the most awful thing Joel has ever done, Douglas. It's as though I don't even know him sometimes. I would never have thought..." She threw up her hands. "But what's done is done, and it's up to me to make sure that Sharon is taken care of. What were they thinking?!"

Up to her? Douglas thought. *Uh-oh.* Although he *had* expected that, he doubted that Joel would be prepared to relinquish control to her and just might consider it meddling. But he wasn't about to mention any of this to Eva. She would settle down in a little while and some of the more practical matters would present themselves to her, but he doubted she would lose her enthusiasm. She had that look in her eye.

He had to admit that, this time, he had been wrong in what he had predicted would be his wife's reaction.

But as he thought about it, it was logical. She had lost two children, herself, and even though her life was full with the twins and Sally and Henry, and even though her two daughters each had two children, it was, in its own way, an undoing of her long sadness about Joel.

That would settle out in time, as well, Douglas thought. He had work to do, but he was reluctant to leave Eva to her own devices.

In a moment of silence, Eva said, "shouldn't you be repairing something, honey?"

"Meaning you want me to leave you alone?"

She smiled. "Well, not at all. But I think I need to run into town. I'll just bet Joel hasn't even thought about getting that girl a doctor, has he? She's going to need a regimen of diet and vitamins; and she'll need maternity clothes. You know Margaret's not going to think of all that, honey, being…old and never having been…well, it's just too much for her to handle, I'm afraid."

"Eva," Douglas said, carefully, "I think you're assuming a little too much, here."

She looked at him, her eyes crinkling. "Assuming what? You just told me that Sharon is pregnant, probably with Joel's child, although it could be Tom's. Either way, I'm going to be a grandmother. I have to think about what needs to be done. I've had experience."

Douglas chuckled at his wife. "You're assuming too much responsibility, honey. You've got your hands full, here."

She only nodded. Then she got up and left the room, leaving Douglas sitting at the breakfast table not knowing whether he should even try to stop his wife from taking over—assuming that Tom and Joel would even want her to. But he hadn't mentioned as much to Eva. Maybe she was right. Maybe the boys would appreciate her help.

He got up finally and headed out of the house through the garage. He hoped they would, anyway, because he knew Eva would be in town within a half-hour, if not sooner.

*   *   *

As it was, Eva didn't know where to begin. She was still in her work clothes and needed a shower, but her heart was pounding in her excitement, so she stood in her dressing room, her hand on her chest feeling her heart thudding. Her boots were caked with mud from her work in the garden earlier that morning, and she wrenched them off, barely noticing the cakes of mud falling on the gray carpet.

Shower, Eva, she said to herself, catching her reflection in the mirror. Her eyes were red from crying and when her mouth turned up in a grin she looked so funny to herself, she started laughing, again.

And calm down! She chided herself.

In the shower, with the hot water working the kinks out of her knotted shoulders she didn't know if she was happy or intensely sad. She thought of Joel and Tom, both of whom had apparently slept with the girl, but all she could see was Joel and Tom, together. Two boys becoming men, and so in love with each other, she often cried. It had taken her much longer than it had Douglas to accept that their love was genuine.

So what in the world was this newest thing? She didn't even finish the question before she nodded to herself. Joel always wanted kids, even though he never bothered to get a wife. She whipped the towel off the rack outside the shower and stepped beneath the heat lamp. Fresh sweat popped out on her skin and she rubbed herself down vigorously drying and massaging her skin until it turned red from the heat and the rubbing.

That's what this newest thing was. Joel had apparently convinced Tom and this girl, Sharon, and they had agreed!

It dismayed Eva that young people now days thought so little of the conventions of marriage that they shared their bodies, apparently intentionally, trying to make a child.

So many questions, she thought.

She pulled a lightweight pantsuit from her closet and slid it on, then brushed her hair back. She kept it short so she wouldn't have to bother with it, and by the time she was retrieving her keys from her purse and stepping into the garage, her hair was almost dry. In the Caddie, she tilted the rearview mirror down to apply just a touch of lipstick, since she hadn't bothered with the makeup she normally would have applied before heading into Common.

Then she backed out, slamming on the brake when she realized she hadn't told Sally where she was going. Luckily, Sally was running up to the car from the direction of the boys' house and Eva waited, letting the window down on her side and leaning out when Sally was almost to the car.

"Honey, I'm running into town on some errands," she said. "Find Douglas and make him fix you a sandwich, okay?"

"I can *do-oo* it," Sally said.

Eva nodded. "Then fix one for Henry, too."

Then Sally was gone and Eva maneuvered the car around the house and out the gate. She pressed the accelerator up to sixty, then at the intersection, pressed on it again, letting the wind into the car as she picked up speed. She felt like singing and crying at the same time, realizing that she was happy at the prospect that Joel, whom she'd felt she'd lost somehow, had managed yet another surprise. But she was also sad in a way she could not put her finger on or get her thoughts around.

The sadness was the *why*. Had he discovered that being in a relationship with another man was simply not enough? If that were so, then was there something missing in such relationships that even a child would not mend?

She knew Joel would argue with her about that.

She shook her head, veered the car north onto Eighth Street and once more brought it up to speed.

She passed by the Richie farm, where she had learned not too many months ago that their oldest son was gay, passed the Donnelly farm a mile up the road, where the husband had been killed about a week before when he'd driven the tractor over a septic tank that gave way and fell in with the tractor on top of him. Cars were still lined up outside the farmhouse, and she figured that theirs must be a large family.

It was a bright day for early September, and she still had to run the air conditioner since summer lingered well into September most years. This one was no different. The farms gave way to settlements of trailer houses, where the poor of Common were looking for their own plots of land, where their children could play outdoors and a cheap trailer house promised home ownership to the parents who were tired of paying rent down the drain every month. But Eva shivered at the effect of their choice, since the living conditions in the trailers did not seem to have improved their lives. Yards were full of broken down cars, weeds, and puddles of stagnant wash water.

She thought of Edna Stroud quite often when she passed along this stretch of road, not because it was where the Stroud family had lived, but because the poverty was so nakedly obvious. She shivered again, thinking that the childhood of the four children she and Douglas had adopted from the Strouds could have been even worse than children had it here.

Then she thought of that young woman, Sharon...what was her last name? *Minninger*? Where on earth had Joel and Tom met her? She did not recall having ever seen the girl at the Red Rooster before. Then all of a sudden she was in town. From where? Montana? My but she had a strange accent and seemed so backward in ways. And she was pregnant with Joel's child!

A smile crept onto her face, but she shook her head in consternation. Of all the—

She could not even think of Joel sleeping with some woman. It was so very odd. It had taken her five years to get used to the idea that her son was a homosexual—*gay*, as Joel insisted on calling it. Now he pulls this, she thought.

As she approached Common, the Saturday traffic forced her to slow down. But it still took only ten minutes from the time she had left the farm until she pulled around to the west side of the café in front of the Sears store where she could park at an angle.

My goodness! How am I going to approach this? She wondered as she stepped out of the Caddie and let the heavy door shut. She shouldered her purse and made her way directly around the corner, where she stopped. Nodding to herself that the direct approach would be best, she pushed open the door to the café.

Margaret was at the cash register. "Eva! What a pleasant surprise. Are you here for lunch? I've got a great fruit salad. On a day like tod"—

Eva shook her head, trying to smile. "I need to talk to you—and Sharon—if you've got a minute."

Understanding revealed itself in the old woman's face, but she smiled. "Let me get Linda to the register and call Sharon."

Sharon was taking an order when Margaret waived to her. She nodded and finished writing on the pad; then she disappeared through the swinging doors and came out a moment later.

Eva watched her, noticing that she was definitely showing, now. Her face was radiant, she thought, wondering at the same time if the child would be Joel's or Tom's.

She had not looked around the café and agreed to the table that Margaret suggested; had she paid a little more attention, however, she might not have agreed to the choice, for well within earshot of the table with his back to them was Bill Crawford.

He had seen Eva Reece come through the door and had seen that look on her face. It wasn't too noticeable, but Bill knew something was wrong. Eva was usually more...well, *still*, but she looked a little on edge. When he saw her and that dyke Margaret approaching, he turned around, hoping that Mrs. Reece wasn't going to strike up a conversation with him like Douglas always did, ending up making him feel angry and embarrassed. Eva usually didn't bother to acknowledge him, Bill thought. Today he was glad of it, since in preparation for ginning season this year, one of his maintenance men had stripped a very large, very expensive gear when they were cranking up the machinery, causing considerable damage to a blower. It would take several bales of cotton to recoup the expenses, and for a moment, Bill thought about getting up and leaving, since he was sure his troubles showed on his face.

A few minutes later, he was smiling to himself as he eavesdropped on the conversation Eva was having with that hot babe, Sharon, and the old dyke.

"...don't know whether it's Joel's or Tom's," Eva Reece was saying, and for a moment, Bill didn't know what they were talking about. Then it hit him. Sharon was obviously pregnant. Bill had seen it a few weeks before when he had come in to get another look at her. In fact, he had been coming into the café more and more as his infatuation with the good-looking blonde grew. He had purposefully struck up conversations with her whenever he was lucky enough to get her as his waitress. He knew she wasn't wearing a wedding band.

He'd looked on purpose, when he realized she was pregnant. He had even entertained notions of asking her out, pregnant or not.

"Have you been to a doctor, yet?" Eva asked, discovering that she was relieved with how willing both Margaret and Sharon were to talk about things. Sharon, bless her heart, because she knew Eva was going to be a grandmother. Margaret, because the old lady seemed relieved that someone with Eva's experience in such matters finally knew the story.

"She has, as a matter of fact," Margaret said. "Joel insisted as soon as we were certain."

Eva was glad to hear it and relieved, too, that Hossley would be the doctor.

"Did he put you on a regimen of vitamins?"

Sharon smiled. "I am taking them every morning and evening, Mrs. Reece," Sharon said, smiling.

As their conversation continued, Eva was beginning to like the young woman, realizing Sharon was the kind of girl she would have wanted Joel to marry, though she did not allow herself the pleasure of delving too deeply into that fantasy. Only a few minutes before, Sharon had made it clear that she had no intention of marrying either Joel or Tom.

"It was for them that I did this, Mrs. Reece," she said. "I know they are for each other and want a child."

Eva understood, but she didn't like it. She was saddened that Joel would even think to involve someone in such a scheme. It was wrong and it disappointed her that her son could be so thick headed and insensitive. She was disappointed in Tom, as well, for going along with it, and still in mild shock over the fact that they had even considered such a notion, much less carried through with it. In a way, it was more difficult to accept than their being homosexuals.

She patted Sharon's hands. She felt tears start and had to take a breath, hold it, and let it out slowly to avoid crying.

But aside from her objections to the way in which the three young people had given each other their bodies for this hair-brained plan, she was practical enough to know that fretting over it now would be useless.

The café was becoming more busy, and Eva noticed that Margaret was beginning to appear anxious, though being quite gracious about it.

"I see that you need to get back to business," Eva said. "I'm sorry I took up your time, but Douglas just told me this morning."

"That is all right," Margaret said. "I do need to get back to work, but as soon as this rush is over, if you'd like, Sharon can take off the afternoon and the two of you can visit."

"Oh! I can not leave you to all the work!" Sharon said, but Eva knew by the look on her face that she wanted to.

Margaret stood up. "I insist, child." Then she smiled at Eva. "Have you got other plans?"

"No. Nothing that can't wait. I'll be back around two?"

Bill had long since finished his lunch, but he stayed until Eva left. His troubles at the gin forgotten, he waited until Sharon passed by then caught her attention.

"Coffee, sir?" she asked.

Bill gave her his best smile. "That'd be real good. Your name's Sharon, ain't it?"

She returned his smile. "Yes. Sharon."

"I don't mean to keep you," Bill said, trying to lock eyes with her, but I was just wondering...I thought I saw Eva Reece in here a few minutes ago. I'm a friend of the family."

Her face lit up. "I recognize you, as they say...your are...um...a regular? You come in almost every day, and no one has told me you are friends. It was Mrs. Reece, yes."

Bill felt himself stir at Sharon's smile. "I thought so. I should'a said hello, but I didn't want to interrupt." Then he pulled out his wallet and laid a dollar bill on the table. "Nice meeting you," he said.

A moment later she moved off, and Bill sipped thoughtfully on his coffee. *Damned if Joel Reece didn't have a few surprises left in him after all,* he thought. And that preacher's boy, too—Joel's *husband.* The best he could get from the conversation was that they must have pulled a three-way, and he shook his head, stirring a little more. He'd never tried that before, but he sure as hell wouldn't do it with another man in the bed. At that thought, he felt himself deflate. It was time to get back to the gin. Time to take another look at the blower and see if he couldn't maybe get a few used parts. He would present the invoice to old man Reece when he stopped in at the end of the month.

This time, he wouldn't let the son-of-a-bitch embarrass him with one of his high-minded, know-it-all digs. On his way into the Farmer's Association, he ran into Jeannie Lynn, checking groceries. He tossed a pack of cigarettes onto the counter. "You ain't gonna believe this," Bill said.

Chapter 12

The Secret Gets Out

By mid-November, Sharon could feel the baby moving inside, turning, kicking, stretching; and she could feel herself giving energy to this child, this being inside her. Work at the café continued, but some of the customers who had been friendly, now seemed to withdraw more and more. Though many of the women were still polite and even inquired about the child, they no longer made reference to "your husband."

She knew it was because people had heard, and she had even heard customers saying the names of her saviors as she passed their tables.

But she didn't care. She was happy in a way she could not explain. The child inside her filled an emptiness that had haunted her in the Mennonite community, feeling as though she had never belonged, and never would. Here in this strange little North American town, where the customers sometimes shook their heads or clacked their tongues at her, others did not. Others talked to her, left her bigger than usual tips, smiled.

Like Mennonites, some rejected her, but others offered her casual friendships, so that her face lit up when they entered the café.

She did not mind the work. In fact, she enjoyed it, realizing a side of herself that could converse well with others. She learned from them the peculiar things that seemed to make them *Americanos*. It was a pride and a sense of comfort with their lives that seemed so different from people in Casas Grandes or the community of Brethren.

A copy of her birth certificate "lost in the fire at the county courthouse in Lordsburg" came in the mail one day, and with it, Margaret was able to obtain other records, or at least make claims to school enrollment, which she doubted the Common school system would ever follow through on obtaining, thanks to her friendship with JoAnna Hoffins who worked within the high school counselor's office and, conveniently, whose job it was to help dropout students obtain their high school equivalency diplomas. By her knowledge, JoAnna was also helpful in enrolling Sharon in night school to prepare for her college entrance examinations.

She would be entering night school next August. By then, her child would be almost five months old. But she could not look that far ahead. Instead, she did as she was told by Margaret at work and in the evenings at home. She also did as Eva Reece asked. She took her medicine (even though Eva said it was not medicine, but a *regimen*), Sharon decided it was still medicine. She also listened to Dr. Hossley, a kind old man with a large, scary mouth, who nevertheless soon made Sharon feel comfortable as he asked her questions and poked and prodded and put a cold stethoscope against her chest and against her stomach where the baby was forming.

Sharon saw the life of Common through her work at the café. Eventually, Margaret said, the whole town would make it through her doors, "many of them just to get a gander at you, honey."

"Because there are the rumors?" Sharon had asked.

She met the rich banker in town, Mr. Lawton, who was so nice, Sharon compared him with Douglas Reece and felt similarly toward the banker as she did toward Douglas. She learned of Mr. Lawton's son, Terry, who was best friends with Joel's adoptive brother, Patrick. She met other waitresses from other cafés in town, who said she had it lucky to have a boss like Margaret. "Girls don't like to leave, once they go to work for Margaret," they told her, as they sat at the tables in the Red Rooster, with their legs crossed, wearing their short skirts and lighting up their cigarettes, getting lipstick on the butts. "You let me know when you're ready to take off for the baby," a waitress by the name of Cindy Coleman had said. "I'll come in and sub for you. I know what it's like when your husband's gone all the time. Mine's a truck driver. I know what it's like to work when you're pregnant, too. I've done it three times."

Sharon also met Joel's teacher, whom Joel called *Coach*, even though he introduced him as Bill. He was JoAnna Hoffins' husband, and he also knew about JoAnna's help getting Sharon enrolled in night school.

"Glad to hear you're doing that, so you can go on to college," Bill Hoffins said, one day. "I never could get Joel to leave Common and find out about the world. All he ever wanted to do was be a farmer."

Sharon was surprised that someone did not think Joel knew about the world. But she could not tell this teacher this. She liked him and listened as he talked of her own future schooling.

The other Bill—the one who was a friend of Joel's, was not so nice, however, and she avoided his table when he came in, once she realized that he must have been the one to begin these rumors, which caused people in the café to draw away little by little.

Of the women who drew away and those who were nice to her and smiled as they asked about the baby, there was one woman who was worse than all the others, because she was like a woman at the Mennonite community, responsible more than the rest in stirring the cauldron about Sharon's shunning. She was also the only woman in the community to speak to Sharon once she had been shunned, smiling to her face, even while taking words Sharon had spoken about her midnights down by the lake and twisting them into something unpleasant.

This woman, here in Common, by the name of Jeannie Lynn, was the same; and it was she who came into the café one day and asked Sharon to sit down with her.

From the cash register, Margaret nodded for Sharon to go ahead and sit for a few minutes; but Margaret also frowned before she turned to a customer at the counter.

"I went to school with Joel Reece, you know," Jeannie Lynn said to Sharon.

"That is nice," Sharon said, uncomfortable with Margaret's frown. But Sharon usually did what people asked of her. Being a waitress in an American restaurant had taught her to accommodate people, even when she was afraid of them, or did not feel that some people had good intentions toward her.

"Yes! My yes, I had a kid's crush on Joel way back when," Jeannie said. Her eyes lit up for a moment, and Sharon wondered if she had been wrong about this one.

"But when he turned out to be a *faggot*," Jeannie continued, "it gave me the creeps! Now I've heard that Joel, or Tom, is the father of your baby."

And there it was, Sharon thought, the smile like the woman in the community, Sister Leah, and the hateful words.

"It seems everyone has heard the same thing," Sharon said. She did not want to be with this woman, so she chose her words carefully. "But I do not believe it is everyone's business."

"Then it's true?" Jeannie asked. "Which one is the father?" She accented her smile with pouty lips, which Sharon found annoying—and even funny, for children among the Mennonites who expressed themselves so childishly soon learned such behavior was not tolerated.

Sharon could not help from laughing, even as Jeannie frowned, her eyes gleaming. "I suggest you believe what you might, because you will anyway," Sharon said.

Jeannie clapped her hands together, laughing, causing people's heads to turn in their direction. "You speak so differently, Sharon. You sound like a foreigner." Jeannie's voice was raised as she said this.

"I was born in Lordsburg," Sharon said in return, her voice still normal. "But I have lived up north among my people. This is true."

Jeannie shrugged, digging in her purse until she pulled out a tube of lipstick. Then painting her lips, she looked straight at Sharon with her eyes open wide. "You avoid too much personal detail, kid. It makes people suspicious. But look, I've gotta run. I really hope you can make it here in our town—being pregnant *and* without a husband, that is. You get labeled, hon, labeled *loose*. So, here's some advice. Don't give yourself to a man just because he's nice to you. I'm talkin' the truth, now."

With that Jeannie Lynn was gone and Sharon returned to work. In the pit of her stomach, just above the kicking baby inside her, she felt fear, the same sort of knot that had formed in the days before she was shunned, knowing there was talk, knowing she could not defend herself, as she was not permitted to speak.

Still she was happy more than afraid, and she was learning to hold her head high, as she had seen the American turistas do in Casas Grandes.

I have not followed the ways of my people, she thought, watching the afternoon come to a close, as light began to slant across the welcome mat in front of the door to the Red Rooster. The sun would go down toward the northwest, shining against the French windows and, for awhile longer, the interior of the café would be lit. People's faces looked feathered and golden in the light, as did that policeman's in the corner, whose cap glinted the light, where the glare of the sun lit up his brass epaulets, while the black color of the uniform caused shadows around him.

Here, in Common, New Mexico, Sharon could hold her head high and look toward the people's faces and take their orders and even withstand their comments, like Jeannie Lynn's. Had she done so in the community, looking into her shunner's faces, rather than walking with her head bowed, those who shunned her would forever ban her from the community. So she had turned from her people's ways.

She knew it was a sin to have conceived this child out of wedlock, but she did not regret what she had done. Joel and Tom would make this child good fathers and the child would be loved. Margaret had come to support her, rather than looking sad. It was as it had been when Margaret had first taken her in.

Joel's parents, Eva and Douglas, had also looked sad for a time, but then that had disappeared from their faces, too. "How's our grandchild, today?" Douglas asked, each time he came into the café. Sharon always felt her cheeks burn with delight. It made her happy to tell him how the baby kicked and moved.

* * *

At the Reece farm, Douglas and Eva were growing daily more anxious for the birth of their grandchild. It didn't matter to Eva, either, that the child may be Tom's—she would not allow herself to picture the act of conception among the three young people, the way they must have mingled themselves to deliberately mask the paternity. So it was irrelevant to wonder which was the biological father; and therefore, it was irrelevant that the blood line might not be directly from the Reece side of the family. Eva was convinced beyond all doubt that her son and Tom would stay together until the end of their days.

So she busied herself with the purchases for the baby, urging the boys to plan for its arrival in their house. "You simply have no idea, Joel," she had said, "how much stuff a baby needs."

"I know, Mom," Joel said. "It'll need diapers and powder."

Eva had laughed until the tears rolled down her cheeks, while Tom and Joel looked on confused and no doubt thinking she was as hysterical as she looked, talked, and acted. But inside, where she could not possibly show them, she was the only one who was really prepared for the baby's arrival.

"*Lots* of diapers and powder," she had said, once she stopped laughing, "and infant clothes, which you'll need to change every time the baby pees or spits up which, for a few months, will be a dozen or so times a day if not more."

When their eyes became wide with realization, she continued: "You'll need almost as many blankets, and towels, and wash cloths. You'll need furniture to put these things in, too. And a bassinet and a crib."

"We've thought of those!" Joel said, sounding triumphant, with Tom beside him at their kitchen table, smiling at Eva.

"But if you want to help us pick them out," Tom said, "we'd be relieved."

Then they showed her the work they had been doing in what had been the spare bedroom, where they had let runaways and house guests stay. They made her cover her eyes as they led her into the bedroom. Then when Joel kissed her cheek and told her to open her eyes, Eva took a breath and looked around her.

At first, she was stunned at the amount of detail the boys had gone to in creating a space for their baby; then tears burned her eyes at the thought that everything was perfect, simply perfect—to think that her son, who had never shown much interest in keeping his own room clean had created such a lovely place. Tom's influence was, no doubt, evident everywhere she looked.

They had papered the room with a child's wall paper of rocking horses and dolls and brightly painted balls. "We're hedging," Tom said, "that either a little boy or little girl will be living in here."

They had hung curtains and blinds on the windows on the room's east and south walls and, at this time of late afternoon, the sun was no longer shining in the windows, but the room was softly lit. They had also covered the floor with a soft blue carpet, so that their steps into and out of the room were quiet.

The very next day, Eva did as they had asked and began buying all the things for the baby they had talked about, honking the horn on the Caddie and got them to carry the packages and bundles from the trunk of the car into their house.

It looked like Christmas had come in an afternoon, until every surface area in the living room, the kitchen, and what had now become the baby's room was covered.

Then the next day she had ridden into town with them, picked up Sharon, and the four of them went into the Sears and Roebuck catalog store to order the baby furniture.

Once it arrived, Sharon and Margaret, Douglas and Eva, Sally and Henry, and Joel and Tom spent an afternoon and long into the evening taking out the old furniture and setting up the furniture in the baby's room, and packing everything into the room, until it was overflowing. Besides the bassinet and crib, and a chest of drawers, and a changing table, Tom and Joel had also bought a futon, which they figured Sharon would be using, as well as anyone else who might be staying with the baby in the middle of the night.

When everyone had left the room or gone home, Eva sat in the baby's room, with just a night light burning near the closed bedroom door, rocking gently in the bent-wood rocker they had purchased, listening to the sounds of its creaking and wondering if the baby would be a boy or girl.

No matter which. It was going to have many grandparents, and any one of them could almost claim a biological lineage. There were Sharon's parents, and for the first time, she wondered where they might be. Sharon had never mentioned them to her. She and Douglas could also claim to be the baby's grandparents, and so could Tom's parents, if they ever relented about disowning him. Yes, so many grandparents, and yet…

The light seemed suddenly gloomy washing her in sadness. This was not the sort of family the baby needed. The paternity of the father being in doubt, the child born out of wedlock, and the fact that Sharon was giving up the child to her son and Tom seemed suddenly so wrong, she began to cry.

The issues that now presented themselves made her mourn for the baby coming into the world.

A knocking at the door caused her to jump. She got up from the rocking chair, wiping her eyes. A moment later, putting on her best smile she opened the door.

It was Joel.

"We were wondering what you could be doing in here," her son said, smiling, then frowning. "Mom? Have you been crying?"

Eva touched his cheek, his beautiful cheek. "As a matter of fact, Joel, I have been. But it's nothing."

"Nothing? Are you sure?" Joel asked, his face showing his concern. He was the same, ever beautiful, young man he had always been, who had seemed ruined when she learned that he was gay. Now, even though he was still that young man, he seemed ruined in a different way.

"Oh, Joel, I can't explain it. I was just thinking about your baby."

"There's nothing to be sad about, Mom." He turned away from her, then. "We've made some hot chocolate and thought you might like it. It's a little nippy out."

"Is it? It's warm in here."

"So you'll sit with us? I'll drive you home after."

She agreed.

When they went into the kitchen, Tom was just pouring three mugs and set them on the table. "You think we've got everything ready for the baby?" he asked, smiling. Then he frowned, but with more subtlety than Joel, and did not ask what she had been crying about.

"It's a start. But remember we haven't even discussed the feeding regimen we need to consider. If Sharon's going to nurse, we won't have to worry about bottle feeding for awhile. But when we start the baby on solid food, well…" she trailed off for a moment. "We'll talk about that later."

The light in the kitchen was bright as the three of them sat down. For a moment there was silence as they each sipped on their drinks.

Then Eva set her mug down. "Listen to me, boys. I think it's important that I tell you a few things, things you might not want to hear. The way you went about this…this having a baby of your own, it's"—

Joel and Tom both looked at her but said nothing. Joel, of course, did not bow his head, but Tom did, and Eva knew that he was probably more troubled about the issues than Joel was. Eva did not criticize Joel's lack of sensitivity—if you could call it that. It was just the way he was. Still, she needed to tell them things.

They still didn't speak, but were ready to listen.

She told them why she had been crying. Then she told them that she was disappointed in both of them for involving an innocent young girl, just so they could have a child. She talked about the baby's being born into a broken family.

At this, Joel objected, saying that he and Tom were as stable, if not more so, than most heterosexual couples their age.

"I'm not talking about that, Joel," Eva said. She smiled, feeling her earlier depression dissipate somewhat. "I have no doubt that you and Tom love each other as deeply as any man and woman, and you're right. You are involved in a stable relationship. I'm proud of you for that. Still…"

She told them of her thoughts about the baby's grandparents. "Some time, and it won't be long as things go, your child is going to start asking questions about where it came from. He's going to know very quickly that his parents are different than everyone else's. When he learns to call us his grandmother and grandfather, are you going to tell him about his other grandparents? Is Sharon going to be around for him? Do you really think that she will want to just carry this child of yours, then give it up?"

There were so many things Eva wanted to say, so many questions to ask, but at these few, both Tom and Joel looked thoughtful.

Joel drained his mug and rinsed it out at the sink. Instead of sitting down, he moved behind her and hugged her from behind. "We don't know the answer to all your questions. Sharon has agreed to give up her child, but we don't want her to just disappear, and I don't think she will. But she wants things, Mom, things she would never have had living there in…Montana with her clan. From what we understand, they're a backward people. Religious and strict."

Eva caught something in what Joel was saying. Some lie, but she did not call him on it.

"We'll try to explain things to our little boy, or girl," Joel said, sitting back down and looking at Tom. "We have thought about this, Mom. We know our child's going to have questions, and we're not going to hide anything from him. We hope that Sharon will want to involve herself in his life as his mother, but she also wants to go to college. She'll be here for at least a year before she goes away. Then before our kid goes to school, she'll probably be back. She might even choose to live right here in Common. And that'll be just fine with us."

"But even if she doesn't," Tom said, speaking up for the first time, "we'll make sure that our child knows her. When he gets to be old enough, if he wants, and if Sharon wants, he can visit her. But as to what you said about the child being born into a broken family, we don't see it like that. If anything, he's going to have a large family."

CHAPTER 13

SHARE US

Her life and circumstances had changed so much in so short a time that Sharon could almost believe the story she told people, about being born in Lordsburg and raised in Montana. She might as well have been, she thought, since her real past also seemed unreal.

It was as though she had awakened after a long dream and was now living her real life. Still, she wondered about her mother and father and her little brothers and sisters. They would grow up remembering very little of their older sister, and this made her sad.

Sometimes, when she was in bed and was feeling the baby kick or turn, she cried for her lost family, thinking of how in different circumstances her mother would have rejoiced over a grandchild—but not this one born out of wedlock. By morning, however, she would awaken into near darkness, whisper to the growing child within her and think of Margaret and Joel and Tom and Douglas and Eva and the other friendly people in the town, and she would be happy again, ready to meet the day.

Best of all, each day brought the possibility that Joel and Tom would stop by to visit; and each day brought the eventual birth of her child closer. She wondered if it would be a boy or girl, what it would look like and, most importantly, if it would be possible to tell whether it was Joel's or Tom's.

When winter came to Common, and the skies stayed gray for days at a time, Sharon found herself feeling less able to hurry from table to table waiting on customers. The baby was heavy and large enough, now, that it shifted as she walked, sometimes pulling her off-balance. Turning in the bed was also difficult.

Margaret was more like a mother by then, rather than the wonderful friend she had come to be. But, when the snows fell after the American Thanksgiving, which she and Margaret spent with the Reeces, Sharon felt homesick in a way she could not explain. The holiday of Christmas spent among her people seemed long ago and far away, rather than just one year ago. Instead, Christmas at the Reece home swam like a dream, and she could not quite believe it was not a dream as gifts for her and the baby mounted around her, and gifts for the children Sally Ann and Henry were opened and piled next to those of the twins, Patrick and Detrick. Although Sharon was the twins' age, she felt more like the adults at the Christmas in the Reece home. Joel and Tom shared gifts with the rest of the family, as did Eva and Douglas.

So it felt odd to Sharon, that while she was the twins' age and wanted to go off to college like they were doing, she had to first have her baby, attend night school, and then, with her high school diploma in hand, she would go away. By then, the baby would be well over a year old.

Still, Sharon wanted to get to know the twins; but Sharon thought there was something unreachable about them. Patrick, the one who was attending the school in Berkeley, made her the most nervous; yet she wanted to talk with him about the school in California. Although he was polite to her, she felt herself breaking out into a sweat under her arms as he hugged her and asked about the baby, and winked. She was afraid to ask about his college. Detrick, on the other hand was more down to earth, like Joel; when he hugged her, he was the one who seemed nervous and she whispered in his ear not to be afraid of her— again feeling like an adult, rather than his age.

So it was with some surprise, during the days following Christmas that Patrick and Detrick invited her to go out with them and their friend, Terrance Lawton. Sharon was visiting with Joel and Tom when the twins came by on a bright and sunny afternoon a few days after Christmas.

Sharon was in the baby's room sitting and contemplating the birth when she heard a commotion in the living room.

When she ran into the room holding her extended abdomen with both hands, she realized that the sound of laughter and good-natured shouting between the twins and Joel and Tom had fooled her into thinking something was wrong.

But when she stood a few feet away from them with her hand to her mouth, not knowing whether to laugh or cry out to them, they all turned to look at her with smiles.

Patrick said, "Hey, Sharon! Dete and I were just asking about you. We told these guys we wanted to take you out to dinner with us."

Sharon was stunned as she looked into Patrick's smiling eyes, then looking to Tom and Joel. "Do you think your brothers would want a pregnant woman with them?"

Everyone laughed. But it was Patrick who answered for them. "Of course we do, Sharon. My best friend, Terry, wants to take you to dinner for a change. Says you've served his father a lot at the Red Rooster, and his father has told him how beautiful you are."

"Besides," Detrick said, standing next to his twin (both of them with teasing smiles), "we're gonna be uncles, and this is the only time we'll be home before the baby's born. What d'ya say?"

Again she looked at Joel and Tom. "Do you think I should do this? Since I have been here, I have not gone out with people my age."

"It's about time, then," Tom said. "Maybe they'll tell you about their schools. Since neither Joel nor I have gone to school, we wouldn't be able to tell you as much."

"Enjoy it, Sharon." Joel said, his smile radiant, which made Sharon feel suddenly enthused with the idea.

"Can you take me to Margaret's so I may change?"

So it was decided, and she went into town with Patrick and Detrick in Patrick's Mustang. She sat in front with Patrick, laughing as she got to know them a little better. By the time she had rushed through Margaret's house getting dressed and they rolled into the entrance of the Lawton house, she was alternately knotted with excitement and queasy with dread. The Lawton house was even bigger than the Reece home. It was a two-story home with rounded walls, which she recognized to be adobe, built much in the style of a hacienda she had once seen near Nuevo Casas Grandes.

She had expected them to eat at the Red Rooster, but the three boys had other plans and drove west out of Common to a steak house on the top of a hill that overlooked the Mimbres valley. Again she had sat in the front seat, and Terry Lawton had sat behind Patrick, but had leaned between the two bucket seats, close enough that Sharon felt his breath on her neck, close enough, too, that she could smell him, and she breathed deeply, feeling something else in the pit of her stomach, a feeling that until now, she had felt only for Tom and Joel. But this time, it was more intense.

When she stepped out at the steak house and Patrick was helping her out of the car, her knees felt weak.

The three boys surrounded her as they walked across the lot to the entrance of The Angus Iron. Even though the night was nippy and Sharon pulled her light jacket tighter about her shoulders, her face felt flushed, and she didn't know if it was from embarrassment or enjoyment.

The waitress who seated them was one Sharon recognized as Cindy Coleman—one of those who had been nice to her when she introduced herself at the Red Rooster.

"I remember you!" Cindy said, smiling. "Oh, hon, you're really showing, now." Then she led the way to a table in the middle of a large room, glancing over her shoulder. "I know you three guys as well," Cindy said. "You might've met my husband, Nicky?" Her voice went up in a question.

"I have," Patrick said. But he was frowning, and Sharon wondered why. She glanced at Detrick and felt a little better, seeing that Detrick was not frowning, though his smile had faded.

"Didn't Nicky give Joel and Tom a hard time back in '65?" Patrick continued, "when everyone found out about them?"

Cindy stopped at a round table with four chairs and turned around. She was still smiling. "Lots of people did, Patrick. You *are* Patrick aren't you?"

Patrick nodded.

"Well, I for one have grown up a little, though Nicky might still be a creep. All right?"

Terry slugged Patrick on the arm. "Never mind him, Cindy," he said. "Patrick's just over-protective of Joel."

When they were seated and Cindy had disappeared after taking their orders for four T-bones, baked potatoes, and salads, a moment of silence fell at the table and Sharon looked around.

She was surprised to recognize so many faces, and she realized that Margaret had been right that, eventually, the whole town would make it through the Red Rooster. She had seen most of them in the café over the few months that she had worked there.

People also noticed her and, as though the good ones and the bad ones were all gathered into one place, she saw many people looking back at her and either smiling before they turned back to their own business, or leering and, quite obviously, saying something about her to those at their tables.

During the meal, Sharon looked around the large room, watching the waitresses scurrying from table to table, and she sympathized with them and could not quite take in the enormity of the place. She picked at her steak, while the three boys ate theirs to the bones and talked about college. She listened intently, barely understanding what they meant by "the antiwar movement." Patrick and Terry were more intense with each other when they talked about that, nodding occasionally at Sharon to include her in the conversation.

Detrick remained quiet during this discussion, but he came back to life when they began comparing their school with his.

At times, Sharon thought the boys were arguing, but they continued laughing, and she glanced from face to face, wondering what it would be like to see the "hippies" Patrick and Terry talked about, though she knew what Detrick meant when he talked about the rodeos at Sul Ross. She had, herself, seen these events and informed the three of them, forgetting for a moment that she was not to mention her own background.

"You mean there in Wyoming?" Terry asked. "Is that where you saw the 'vaqueros'?"

"Montana," Sharon said. "Yes, some were called vaqueros. They traveled all the way up from Mexico, where...I once went."

The Angus was crowded with all types of people who sat at the rustic tables with the checkered tablecloths. She saw some people clearly, but others were obscured by the timbers throughout the room that held up the open-beam ceiling, where large wrought-iron chandeliers hung heavily over the tables casting pools of light onto the customers.

"Ain't you s'posed to be eating for two?" Detrick asked when Sharon set down her fork and wiped her mouth with a napkin.

"I do not see how you can eat such a large hunk of meat!" Sharon said. She wanted to laugh but merely smiled across the table at him.

Patrick and Terry laughed, but Terry, who was sitting on her left, leaned in close enough that she could smell his cologne. Again, there was that funny feeling in her stomach. "You know how farm boys are, Sharon. I've seen Dete put away a calf by himself."

Again, Sharon did not know whether she should laugh, and did not know what response was required of her, though she knew they were all teasing each other.

By the time dessert came, Sharon felt warm and even comfortable with her friends, and she was laughing and smiling when she glanced at a table not far away. There sat Jeannie Lynn, the blonde woman who called Joel "faggot," and Bill Crawford. They were staring at her and leering. She felt her smile disappear and looked down at her plate. None of the boys at her own table noticed her reaction, until Jeannie Lynn made her way over to them and stood behind Sharon.

No one smiled, but the twins and Terry looked up at Jeannie.

"What do *you* want?" Patrick said, his frown returning from earlier in the evening.

Sharon felt the heat of Jeannie's chest against her back, though she refused to sit forward.

There was a moment of silence, then Jeannie placed a hand on Sharon's right shoulder. "It just amazes me," Jeannie said, her voice loud, "how quaint you boys still are, considering your background and all, how you could bring this innocent girl in a place like this. You just know people are talking and asking, who's the baby's father?"

"That's enough, Jeannie," Terry said. "We know who's talking. You and all the rednecks in the town who've stayed in Common rather than trying to better yourselves. You have room to talk, you know?"

Jeannie just laughed, but Sharon heard the intake of her breath, and the laugh sounded forced. She glanced at the painted nails on Jeannie's fingers. The nail polish was chipped and one color had been painted over another. "Well, there's more of us rednecks than freaks like you, Terry, if that's what you choose to call decent people who slave in the stores and on the farms your fathers own. Money can't buy happiness, and I can't see how any of you can value decent things when you hang out with trash."

Detrick stood up so fast, Jeannie didn't have time to move, when he slapped her across the face. "Shut up! No one invited you to come over here!"

In a moment, the noise in the room came to a dead halt, and all eyes were turned to the table. Bill Crawford ran over in that same instant and dived into Detrick, and both fell to the floor, knocking over chairs and causing other people to move away. Patrick and Terry jumped up and were pulling Bill off Detrick, when Jeannie grabbed a handful of Sharon's hair, pulling her head back.

"You brought all this on, you know," Jeannie growled. But no sooner had she said that when Cindy Coleman and the manager of the restaurant were pulling her backwards, knocking her hands away from Sharon.

When the fighting had suddenly come to a stop, others in the restaurant tried to resume their meals, seeing that the manager had things under control. Sharon was shaking badly as Terry helped her up from the table. She could not look at him or anyone, but she heard the manager saying, "Don't come back or I'll call the cops. You want to brawl, go to a bar."

Thinking he was speaking to them, Sharon began to cry, but Terry wrapped his arms around her and pulled her close, kissing her cheek. "Aw, don't cry Sharon," he said. "He's not talking about us, see?"

She glanced up and saw that both Bill and Jeannie were being led out of the restaurant by a couple of men she had also seen at the Red Rooster.

"Dinner's on us," the manager said, when he returned to the table, speaking directly to Patrick who had his wallet out and was throwing bills onto the table, next to the check.

"No. No, that's fine Mr. Keller. There's no cause for you to treat us. I'm just sorry this had to happen. We had no idea what that Lynn girl was up to when she came over."

The manager picked up the money and the check and handed the bills back to Patrick. "I insist, son. I know your father, Douglas. You're good boys."

*   *   *

After they dropped Terry off, and were on the way to Margaret's to let Sharon out, Patrick glanced at her as he turned a corner. "I can't apologize enough for what happened, Sharon. Are you going to be all right? It didn't hurt the baby, did it?"

Her eyes were spent of tears, but she found that her voice shook. "No, Patrick. It did not hurt the baby, though I cannot understand this. Why some people are so...hateful."

"It's about Joel and Tom, mostly," Detrick put in from the back seat. "That's where it started. Then there's us, you know, our own background."

"I know of that. Joel has told me. But was it not a tragedy? Why then should people be less kind to you?"

Patrick pulled to a stop in front of Margaret's house. The porch light was burning. "We've often wondered that ourselves, Sharon. At first it hurt us to know that people hated us—not just for what our older brother did, but because someone like the Reeces would adopt us."

"But why is this so?" Sharon said. She did not reach for the door handle. "Eva and Douglas are so kind to everyone, as are my Joel and Tom. They rescued me from a very different life, you know?"

There was silence a moment, as Sharon's words hung in the air of the Mustang. Patrick cleared his throat. "We...ah...haven't been told much about that, Sharon. Your background, where you came from. But I sense that it is really none of our business. We're just glad you're here with us, now. You add so much to the family."

"Even though I am pregnant and have caused such a scandal? And even though so many people of this town, like that Jeannie, consider me...what did she say? Trash?"

"No!" Detrick said from the back seat. He leaned between the two front seats. "There are not so many people who think that, Sharon. Truth is, Jeannie Lynn and Bill Crawford, and a few other people are the trash, if you want to know. Don't go thinking that, okay?"

Sharon felt the tears coming again. She nodded her head. "Okay, as you say. All right. I will not."

*   *   *

When Sharon let herself into the house, she saw that Margaret had not waited up. Although it was still early, Margaret had already gone to bed and, for that, Sharon was relieved, because she did not want Margaret to see that she had been crying.

It was all right to cry for her lost family, she thought, and she had done it in front of Margaret. It was all right to cry because you were happy and could not help it. But Sharon decided that night that it was not all right to cry when cruel people were unkind. You do not show such people as these your tears, she thought; nor do you let those who worry about you see such tears, either.

CHAPTER 14

WITHOUT WARNING

When the phone rang, and Joel heard Leo's voice on the other end, he was relieved that Tom was not in the house. Thinking that he was probably still with Eva going over the last of the harvest records, Joel sat in the desk chair, ready for a long talk with his friend.

"How've you been, Leo?" Joel said, smiling unconsciously. "Sorry I haven't had time to visit with you since, you know, your troubles."

He couldn't be sure, but he thought he heard Leo crying on the other end. "You are all right aren't you?"

Leo cleared his throat. "Yes, hon, I'm fine. But I've got news."

The house was cold, and Joel wished he'd had time to turn the thermostat. Already the last rays of sunlight were disappearing from the room, and Tom would be coming along soon. "What news? Good I hope."

"No. It's bad, I'm afraid."

"You haven't been beat up, again, have you? You did break off with Ba…the guy who did it, didn't you?"

"Of course, I did, hon," Leo said. "I'm not a pain queen."

"Well, of course you're not, Leo."

"But I think I've done something really bad, this time."

Joel felt his stomach lurch. It always made him nervous for Leo to call out of the blue. It was usually something bad. "Well, what did you do?"

"I got back together with Frank. You remember that hot number from Deming?"

"Well, hey," Joel said. "That's great. You know Frank really loves you, don't you?"

"I know he does, Joel. I love him, too, I think."

"I hope you do, Leo. Frank's a great guy. So what could you have done that was so bad, then? You've probably made Frank the happiest man on earth."

"Uh-huh," Leo said, as if distracted. "I'd hoped so, but he kept after me to tell him who…you know…beat on me."

"And did you?"

"I did, Joel, about a week ago. I haven't seen Frank, since."

Again, Joel's stomach lurched. "Have you called him, at least?"

"Of course I called him! Joel, he hasn't been in Deming. I even called his secretary, and she hasn't seen him either. I'm really worried, now. He didn't seem so upset when he left that night. The night I told him about Barela."

"So it *was* him. I thought so. You don't think Frank went to confront him, do you?"

"I'm afraid he did, only I can't just call up Eugene and ask him. I never want to see that bitch, again."

Like Tom, Joel was sometimes disgusted with the way Leo put things. But he laughed at Leo's use of 'bitch' for the butch cop. "Well, look, Leo, don't you dare call him. Maybe Frank had to go out of town on business. Where are you staying, anyway?"

"I'm back home, believe it or not. I told my mother I needed a job and my father said if I didn't mind gettin' my hands dirty, I could drive a tractor for harvest. So I'm living with the hired help in the old house. It's been a real trip decorating the place."

Joel laughed about that, though part of his mind was churning. "Okay, Leo, good. So, anyway, you have no idea, at *all*, where Frank might be? He didn't call you after he left that night?"

"He did not. Not a word, hon, and I'm scared."

"Well, don't go too crazy, all right? I'll see if I can't find out something myself."

"Don't you go near Eugene, either, Joel. She's a real tough bitch. Besides, maybe you're right. Maybe Frank's on business somewhere."

"Maybe so," Joel said. "Look, I've gotta bathe, I just came in from the fields, and Tom's going to want to clean up when he gets in."

"I understand, Joel. Thanks for being there. You always are, you know?"

"I know, Leo," Joel said, and set the receiver into the cradle.

By then, the sun had gone down and the whole house was gloomy. He flicked on the light in the living room, adjusted the thermostat and went through the kitchen into their part of the house. His face revealed his worry, and his stomach churned, imagining things he could not quite focus on. What if Frank did confront Barela, he thought, as he turned on the water in the tub.

He ran it hot and only added cold water at the end. By then the mirror over the sink was clouded up and, as he sank into the hot water, the steam rising from it blurred his vision. He did not like violence, but he knew the cop was capable of it, and if Frank had confronted him, there was no telling what might have happened. He decided that he had to find out…this time without Tom's knowledge and, again, he was relieved that Tom had not been there when Leo called.

*   *   *

Tom left Eva's office shortly after sunset. They had finished the tallies on the harvest for most of the farms, including their own. In January, they would begin disking under the cotton stalks and the stalks for the grain and corn. Five years on the Reece farm had taught Tom that every season brought it's own kind of work. Winter saw the end of the harvest season and was the slackest time of the year. But with almost two sections of farmland to oversee and work, the Reeces had very little time, even then, for relaxation or vacations. Winter was also the time for major repairs on all the equipment, and for the next couple of weeks that's precisely what each of the farm families would be doing, with Douglas going to each farm and assessing the costs for the work.

It was surprisingly nippy out as Tom walked from the Reece home past the garden and equipment yard, past the barn where the livestock had already been put to rest for the night. The day had been beautiful, however, so Tom did not mind the cold.

He had been happy for Sharon, that Patrick and Detrick had taken it upon themselves to take her out to dinner the night before, but when he had asked Patrick about the dinner this afternoon, Patrick said there had been a little trouble at the end, though he was quick to add that up until then, they had enjoyed themselves.

"You know that Lynn girl?" Patrick said, frowning. "The one who works at the Farmer's Association as a checker and usually cats off to Mom?"

Tom knew her, though over the years when he and Joel went grocery shopping, her tired comments and mean jokes about them usually rolled off them. There was no longer any shock value in her remarks, and even the other customers had heard it so often, they just rolled their eyes. Jeannie was a tiresome person, who didn't realize that her own reputation had suffered over the years as a result of trying to ruin someone else's. "You saw her?" Tom asked. "Did she say something to you?"

"Worse," Patrick said. "She came up to our table and got behind Sharon, you know? And made a scene. Detrick slapped her! And that got Bill Crawford on him in a flash. The manager and his waitress Cindy broke it up and threw Jeannie and Bill out. It made Sharon cry."

That was troubling, Tom thought, as he went through the gate and up the flagstones. He would suggest to Joel that they visit her this evening.

The light in the living room was on as Tom entered the house, as well as the kitchen lights, and when he stood in the kitchen, he heard Joel splashing in the tub.

A moment later he walked in. Joel was lying in the tub, his skin red from the heat of it, and steam had filled the room. Here, it was warm, and Tom would have liked to undress and join his husband in the big roomy tub. That is precisely what he had done often enough, with them ending up making wet, soapy love. But tonight that option was out.

He leaned over Joel, removing the wash cloth from his face and kissed his soft, wet lips, running his tongue into Joel's mouth.

"Ummm," Joel said, not opening his eyes. "I hope you're my husband and not some stranger!"

Tom laughed. "You better be able to tell by now."

Tom sat on the dressing chair next to the sink and waited for Joel to dry off and dress; then when Joel followed him into the kitchen Tom poured him a cup of coffee and poured one for himself. They sat at the corner of the table holding hands.

"Hard day?" Tom asked.

Joel took a sip of coffee, set his cup down. "The usual, running the disks until it got too dark to see well. But we made acreage since the twins are here. I'm gonna hate to see them go. It's always so empty when they're gone."

"I will too," Tom said. "Listen, though. Patrick said that Jeannie Lynn caused trouble at the restaurant. I wasn't real clear on exactly what happened, but I think we need to go visit Sharon tonight, unless you've got other plans...okay?"

A troubled look crossed Joel's face. "That would be fine, honey. Only, I got a call from Leo Johnson when I got home, and I think I need to go see him."

Tom was immediately bothered. "What did he want this time, Joel?"

Joel's face remained troubled. "He and Frank got back together, which ordinarily would be a good thing. Only he says Frank's missing. He hasn't seen him in over a week. Says he's even called his secretary in Deming, but she doesn't know where he is, either. I thought I'd go visit Leo and see if I can't figure out maybe something he hasn't thought of, you know, since Leo's so scatterbrained."

Tom sighed, trying to keep the anger out of his face. "I honestly don't know what visiting Leo's going to do. Why don't you call up Gray and see if the police have a better notion of how to go about finding someone. Surely there's a good explanation, something Leo forgot. But does it have to be tonight, honey?"

Joel smiled wanly. "I guess not. Our girl sounds like she needs our attention."

*   *   *

Joel had left out a large chunk of his conversation with Leo, of course, because if Tom knew Frank had gone to confront Barela, he would know that Joel would go to the cop, himself. But Joel didn't have a better idea of how to proceed, anyway, so he tried to put Frank out of his mind as they entered Margaret's house.

Both women were delighted at the company, even though they were apparently tired from their day at the Red Rooster. Margaret greeted them both with hugs, as did Sharon, but they were both dressed in their night clothes, and Joel decided that he would try to cut their visit short.

When he suggested that they only stay a few minutes, Margaret laughed. "Oh, no, honey, we always change early. Besides, I know why you're here. Sharon was so upset with what happened. I think she needs to talk."

Sharon was more subdued than Margaret, though she also smiled and seemed happy that they had come to visit. But she allowed Margaret and Tom to make hot chocolate, while she sat on the couch with Joel.

She had bought herself a luxurious yellow robe of a kind of silk material that shone in the bright lights of the living room. Beneath the hem of the robe, Joel saw that she was also wearing matching yellow pajamas, and he complimented her on her choice of color. "You look so good in yellow, Sharon. It really sets off your hair and your skin."

Small talk, Joel thought, was a good way to get started. He felt awkward around Sharon by himself, and he was surprised at himself for that. He noted how much weight she had gained and how she held her stomach.

Sharon smiled. "The baby moves all the time, Joel. It is so…mirac…miraculous. Feel him?"

Joel placed his hands palm down on Sharon's stomach and was surprised to feel the baby so close to the surface. "Does it hurt for me to touch you, there?"

She laughed at that. "Oh, no. Press more firmly. Do you not feel his head?" She placed her small hands on top of his and moved them down a little. "There!"

Joel's heart pounded feeling his child's body inside Sharon. It brought tears to his eyes as he felt its little head not much bigger than a baseball, and then he moved his hands higher, feeling what must be a foot. "It is miraculous," he whispered.

When Tom and Margaret returned from the kitchen carrying their drinks and cookies, Joel exchanged places with Tom and placed Tom's hands where his had been. "Do you feel it, honey?" he asked, smiling first at Sharon and then at Tom, then watched the surprise and delight on Tom's face as he felt of Sharon's belly.

Margaret laughed from her chair, looking on. She winked at Joel. "It's fascinating, isn't it? To know that the child is continuing to grow and move, and it makes me feel like a grandmother, you know?"

"We do," Joel said. He was now sitting on the floor by the couch, and he would have been completely content had it not been for thoughts of Frank. The last time he'd seen him was in July, and it surprised him that he could be so far out of touch with someone like that, that not only had he and Leo gotten back together, but their lives had suddenly taken such a weird turn. *Frank is missing.* He held that thought and tried to remember what his pickup looked like. Or did he drive a car when he came to Common? License plate! He thought, suddenly, and knew that as soon as he could, he would call the police department, giving them a description of Frank's vehicles, which he would get from the construction company—

"—miles away, Joel."

"Huh?" Joel said looking at Tom. "What did you say?"

"I said you look like you're a thousand miles away. What were you thinking about?"

He told him. Then he tried to concentrate on their visit, soon becoming absorbed in Sharon's tale of what had happened at the restaurant.

"We were having such a good time," Sharon said, finally, working up to the scene that had ruined her evening. "Your brothers are very kind, you know, to have taken me out. I did not know if they were embarrassed to have a pregnant woman with them. They are all so young, the twins and their friend Terry."

"Nothing to be embarrassed about," Joel said.

"Except that people think they know who the father is," Tom said. He was still sitting beside Sharon, with his arm on the back of the couch and looking down at Joel next to him on the floor. "So it was potentially embarrassing for them, I would think. But they've had a few years to get used to how mean some people can be."

"Still, it's hard to know that people like that Lynn girl and that creep of a friend she has in Bill Crawford would be so blatant," Margaret said. Her eyes were burning with a kind of anger that made Joel uncomfortable to see. He hoped that she was not as deeply upset as she appeared to be.

Sharon laughed a little, which caused everyone to look at her. "It is not so bad, Margaret, as it was to be shunned by everyone in the Brethren. For I had no friends, there. Not even my mother and father. At least here I have so many friends; and there were even people at the Angus who did not like to see how this Jeannie and Bill treated us. We must all be brave, for I think we have not seen the last of such things."

At that, no one spoke, and Joel felt a kind of anxiety steal upon him. Five years was a long time to be the town freaks, he thought, and now he and Tom had brought another person into their lives—two other people, when the baby was born—and he did not know if he could protect Sharon and the baby from all the trouble that apparently awaited them from the people of Common. Maybe Coach was right, he thought. Common was too small. Everyone knew too many things about each other. You couldn't hide anything.

                *   *   *

Margaret's house was a Victorian in what had to be the oldest neighborhood in the small town. The streets, here, were divided in the middle with trees, so that when Tom and Joel left Sharon and Margaret at the front door and it was shut behind them, it was almost too dark to make out the cars on the other side of the trees. But just as Joel opened the driver's side of the pickup and was sliding into the seat, someone lighting a cigarette across the way caught his attention. He could not see clearly, but almost felt the eyes of the man in the shadows looking intently his way.

Then he noticed the pickup, almost hidden in the darkness, but glinting darkly from the light shed by the street light farther away. When he had the pickup running, with Tom sitting next to him, his arm around Joel's shoulder, Joel said, "hang on," then he headed down the street, made a quick U-turn, and raced toward the dark pickup truck. At that moment, he switched on the high beams, catching the man by surprise. In the second or two that the lights shined on him, Joel was certain it was Officer Eugene Barela, dressed in dark clothing and standing by a black or dark blue pickup.

And that did it. He knew the cop was stalking them, apparently very closely for him to know that they had been at Margaret's.

"What was that all about?" Tom asked, as Joel slowed at the next corner and headed out Eighth Street for the farm.

Joel didn't know how much to tell him.

So he kept it vague, telling Tom that he'd seen someone across the street from Margaret's lighting a cigarette. "I thought it was kind of odd that someone would be out so late when it's cold, and when I saw him light the cigarette,

I knew he was looking across the street at us. I just wanted to get a look at the guy."

"I wish you would have told me, Joel, because I could have seen who it was, too. Only I didn't. Did you?"

Joel was relieved that Tom didn't know. "Not really. It was too dark, honey. I guess it was just a neighbor. You know that whole neighborhood is full of old people, like Margaret. Maybe he was just curious or watching out for her."

"Maybe, so," Tom said. Joel listened for worry in his voice but heard none and, again, he was relieved.

*   *   *

Joel wanted Tom to sleep soundly that night, because he had a plan, of sorts—one that might be dangerous—and he could not think of a better time to carry it out.

So, when they got home it was nearly ten o'clock and Joel got undressed, deliberately leaving his clothes in the living room; then fully naked, he made Tom take off his clothes, kissing him on the mouth and neck and working his way down his chest with his tongue. By the time they were lying on the couch in the living room with just a few candles burning, Tom was worked up and, for awhile, Joel forgot himself, taking Tom inside of him, first lying beneath his husband's grinding hips, then rolling over and sitting astride Tom, grinding his own hips until Tom was deeply inside. Joel worked at it until he was glistening with sweat. But when Tom tried to grasp him to help him along, Joel held back. When Tom had poured himself into Joel, Joel switched and entered him, taking it slowly, working himself deeply inside, holding off, working Tom into a sweat. By the time he had also been drained, Joel lay with Tom on the couch stroking his body, kissing him deeply. When they were both spent, it was almost midnight, and Joel led Tom into the bathroom and ran a hot bath for him.

While Tom was soaking, Joel massaged his shoulders, his neck, his arms and legs. Later, they made their way to the bedroom, and Joel lay awake with Tom beside him, until he was sure that Tom was sleeping deeply. Even though Joel was tired, himself, he fought to stay awake, glad that Tom had made love to him so vigorously. He doubted he would awaken too readily.

He lay still, listening to the ticking of the clock on the dresser, listening to the soft sweet rhythm of Tom's breath, thinking of how he should proceed.

It was obvious he would not be able to find out Frank's license plate numbers tonight, but he could at least find out where Barela lived. Although he did not know precisely what he would do, he slowly rose from the bed, listening for a change in Tom's breathing, then made his way into the living room, where he dressed quickly.

He switched on the lamp at Tom's desk and looked through the phone book until he had found Eugene's phone number and address. He was surprised to see he lived on the same street as Coach Hoffins. Then, without thinking too deeply, he slid on his jacket from the coat rack near the front door and stepped onto the porch.

He stood on the edge of the porch breathing in the cold air. It was around two-thirty, now, as best he could determine. He listened to the night. Nothing stirred, nothing cooed. He stepped off the porch and, in the darkness, looked toward the town of Common. There was the same string of lights he had always seen, but from up on the small hill, he saw the sprinkling of lights beyond Common to the north, where people had begun to move into the country and to install the outdoor lights that the Public Service Company had made available. They were supposed to reduce crime and to dissuade prowlers. Living this close to the Mexican border, however, people occasionally reported illegal aliens sleeping in barns, stealing vegetables from their gardens.

Somewhere among those lights, Joel thought with a stab of cold anger, that cop was probably sound asleep—after what he'd done to Leo and, now, probably Frank. He shook his head, fighting back the sting of tears for his old friend and fear for what might have happened to Frank. He could not imagine, did not want to.

That son-of-a-bitch cop thought he'd gotten away with it. Joel remembered how he stared openly at them at the Red Rooster, how he had met them outside one morning, trying to intimidate them. Joel had assumed the guy was interested in them because of their reputation, like everyone else who stared occasionally. He had watched the guy strut around, his ass reared out like a peacock, and Joel was even more determined that this was one of those times to stand up to that sicko. He only hoped it was not too late to find Frank. He dug into his pocket for the keys to the pickup.

*　　　　　*　　　　　*

He drove by the cop's house, and it was very near Bill Hoffins' in a section of town where the struggling middle class professionals lived. A teacher's salary, a cop's salary, made it possible to live comfortably, if not extravagantly. But this cop's house, come to think of it, was a little flashier than most. It had the self-conscious style of spit and polish, but with the added feature of bars on the windows. *That figures*, Joel thought, to enable the guy to bring home his prey and to make it difficult, if not impossible, for them to escape. He wondered about that as he slowed down, cruising past.

The pickup he'd seen on Margaret's street was not there as far as Joel could tell. There was no free-standing garage as at Bill's, so he knew Barela wasn't yet home. He debated with himself as he rolled to a stop on the edge of the property and killed the lights. Should he go looking for the guy, should he wait here for him to show up then step out of his pickup so Barela would recognize him? If he did that, Joel felt certain that the cop might think he was in for a little "fun." Or would he become suspicious?

His heart pounded in the darkness. No telling what Tom would think of all this. No doubt he would be freaked out. No doubt, like his mother, they would want to chastise him for acting without thinking, for bringing still more embarrassment to the family. Maybe he did have a blindness when it came to their feelings. But you couldn't let people get away with so much without acting. Who else would? Not Leo, not Tom, and maybe not even the other cops, if Joel went to them about Frank Thurmon being missing.

The guy could have killed Leo—a big, strong, macho fucker like the cop, beating up on Leo's wispy frame, smashing his poor pretty face to a pulp. Leo could have been killed, and no one would have been the wiser as to his attacker's identity. *Glad I know*, Joel thought, as he waited, listening to the engine pop and cool.

He had his window down, and his breath showed in the cold air. He was sitting up straight, his back barely resting on the seat as nervous as he was, checking his rearview mirror occasionally for headlights, still debating about staying or leaving. Finally, lights played off the trees, glanced brightly off the walls of the houses, and flashed in the mirror. His heart slamming against his ribcage, just as it had always done before a boxing match, he watched the approach of the vehicle. He sucked in his breath and let it out slowly, getting ready.

It was the pickup he'd seen across the street at Margaret's. It turned into the driveway, spraying Joel's pickup with light. Joel was cold, yet sweating as he pulled off his jacket and his shirt. He smiled to himself at the thought that his strong hairless chest would attract the guy. He stepped out of the pickup with no plan as to how things would proceed.

Barela was looking in his direction when he also stepped out of his pickup. He was a shadow, but leather shined dully on his belt and boots and cap. Likewise, with only a street lamp nearly a block away, Joel's naked chest was visible to him.

"Uh…howdy, officer Barela," Joel said, coming up to the fence, but not going inside.

The cop came closer. He was dressed all in black and, at first, Joel thought the guy had been on duty, after all. Then he saw it was not a uniform, but a self-conscious costume made to resemble one. There was also no gun belt strapped to the guy's waist, for which Joel was relieved. He'd not thought of the gun.

"Howdy, yourself, Joel Allen-Reece. How come you're hangin' out in my neighborhood this late at night—and half naked in this friggin' cold? Where's that cute *husband* of yours?"

Joel stepped away from the fence, to give the bastard a full view of his body. His heart was about to explode with anticipation. He touched his chest with both hands, running them down to the waist of his Levi's. He felt ridiculous. "Couldn't sleep, Eugene. Especially not lately. You saw me, tonight, at a friend of mine's, am I right?"

This close, Joel saw the smirk on Barela's face. "Yeah…so?"

In the boxing ring, before the bell signals the fight to begin, the point is to intimidate the opponent. In this case, it was to seduce and intimidate at the same time. "Leo told me all about you two. How you two been fucking and all."

"That right? You gonna believe a little faggot like that? Maybe he's just got the hots for me. You got the hots for me, too, you little faggot?"

Joel stepped up to the fence, stared at the guy. "Maybe. Leo says you're quite a stud. Are you?"

The opponent flinched. As close as they were now standing, with only the fence between them, Joel saw the cop's eyes glistening with interest. He wanted to puke. He waited for a response, his chest heaving.

"Aw fuck," Barela said, "I'll service your hot little ass. That faggot boyfriend of yours gettin' where he can't satisfy you?"

Joel didn't answer. He came around the side of the fence through the driveway. As in any boxing match, he walked right up to his opponent. But in this match, he reached out and cupped the man's crotch, feeling to his disgust that he was already stiff. He forced himself to squeeze.

Luckily, the cop didn't return the favor. Joel was soft. Pressing his body against the cop, he realized that, this time, he wasn't going after a bantam weight. Barela was nearly as tall as the twins, but with an extra twenty to thirty pounds on his frame.

Barela stepped back and grabbed Joel by the shoulders. His grip was strong. "You stupid faggot! You want people to see? You follow me indoors, or no sucky-fucky for you."

"Fine, you big stud," Joel said. When Barela turned away and led the way into the house, Joel reached into his Levi's and found his pocket knife. Its weight would make his punch harder. He needed all the advantage he could get.

*   *   *

"Get naked," Police Officer Barela commanded once they were inside with the door shut.

The living room was lit by recessed lighting. All the furniture was leather or lacquered black wood, trimmed in chrome. The walls were dark, with leather objects hanging all over them, like those in a dungeon. Joel's heart nearly stopped at the sight.

"You won't...won't hurt me too bad, will you?" Joel said, making his voice go higher.

The cop was too far away. He was undressing standing next to a leather couch. Or rather he was unzipping out of his clothes. In a moment, he was a naked ape with criss-crossed black-leather straps that came over his chest, disappearing over his back and reappearing between his legs. His cock was stiff, his balls were choked off with a leather ring. He looked even less vulnerable naked, the leather straps giving him a sinister, sick aspect. "I didn't have you figured, right, Joel. I never thought you were interested in me. Seems I've been wrong, though, eh?"

Joel didn't undress. He kept his hands behind his back, clinching the knife until it dug into his palm. "I'm interested all right, Eugene."

He waited just inside the door trying to make his eyes light up with desire, clenching his abdominal muscles for the effect of showing their rub-board hardness. The cop ran his tongue over his lips and came forward. "I'll rip those Levi's off your hot little ass! You want it bad, don't you?"

"Real bad," Joel said. "Just like Leo. Real bad."

The cop was within a foot of him when Joel struck without warning. All his pent-up anger came with it, slugging and slugging. With the element of surprise on Joel's side, the cop staggered back, and Joel flew at him, bringing to bear all of his strength and anger, striking out mercilessly, with a style uniquely his own—lightning quick, hard punches, with fists made solid by a lifetime of farm work. Leo's beat-up face propelled him at the cop, his boxing training kept him at an advantage.

Even when the big, bad, macho cop landed a couple of punches into Joel's ribs that knocked him back, it increased Joel's rage. It was all over within a matter of minutes. Barela was finally reduced to a heap, lying on the floor with his nose gushing, his jaw and eyes swelling.

"That was for Leo," Joel said, his chest heaving. He turned the cop over and, with his knee in his back, he opened the pocket knife, slicing the leather straps into two foot lengths. When Barela struggled and began to rise, Joel brought both fists down on the back of Barela's neck, knocking his face to the floor. Barela sighed and, for a moment Joel thought he had knocked him unconscious. But

Barela spoke with his face into the floor. "Kill me right now, bitch, or you're dead as"—

Joel slammed his fists into the back of his neck, again, then yanked both of the cop's arms behind him and tied the leather around his wrists.

He rolled the cop over and sat down on his chest with his knees on either side of him. Barela was breathing but, this time, he was unconscious. Joel slapped him until he opened his eyes. In the dull light from the black filled room, Joel saw where one of his punches had cut the guy. When Barela focused on him, Joel leaned into his face.

"Don't get any ideas about revenge, you bastard, or people will find out you got the shit beat out of you by a faggot."

Barela's eyes burned with hatred, and Joel slapped him with the back of his hand. "Now, tell me about Frank Thurmon. What have you done with him?"

"Nothing, you son of a bitch!"

Joel slapped him, again. "Wrong answer, Eugene."

"I don't know who you're talking about!"

Joel hit him, again. "Frank Thurmon, the guy Leo dumped for you. The guy who confronted you about beating Leo to a pulp and breaking his ribs—*that guy.*"

Barela spit into Joel's face. "You're dead, Reece," Barela said, then began to buck, pushing Joel up with his chest, beginning to roll. His weight alone was capable of gaining the advantage, as he rocked Joel sideways. Joel half stood, then slammed his butt into Barela's crotch.

A moment passed, then Barela sank back to the floor, groaning. Joel slammed his butt down on his crotch again, feeling his own anger rising. He remembered the night, years before, when he had fought against Kenneth Stroud, the night Kenneth had blown out the dining room window at the Reece home, how he had slammed Kenneth's face into the wall, over and over until Tom screamed that he would kill Kenneth if he didn't stop.

This time, Tom was not there to soothe his rage, and Joel fought to keep himself from pummeling Barela's face to mush. Realizing too that he was still gripping the pocket knife, Joel scrambled to his feet.

Straps of leather still hung from Barela's chest, which Joel cut into more strips and, working quickly, tied the cop's feet together, then looking around the living room, with one eye on Barela, he found a leather whip hanging on the wall. He ripped it down and cut it until he had several more strips, which he secured to Barela's wrists, then pulled his feet up to his hands and tied them all together, much like a rodeo cowboy ties up his steer in a roping contest.

His breath came in ragged gulps, and he was crying, trying to calm down. He had not realized all the pent-up rage inside, not only directed at the police officer, but maybe against the whole town and those who had teased him, those old friends of his who had turned their backs on him, those fellow boxers on the school team who had beat him up in the shower and left him there with cracked ribs.

He was crying, thinking that Tom would not understand this, nor his mother, nor his father. But then he thought of Leo, the last time he'd seen him, his face like raw hamburger, and of Frank who was still missing.

His hands shook as he searched for the phone and the phone book. He flicked on a light which shone on the room, shining off the black furniture and the chrome edges, and Barela's prone body in the middle of the floor.

Then he wandered out of the room into the kitchen, turning on lights as he went, until he found the phone hanging on a wall near the refrigerator, and the phone book, lying on the counter. He flipped through the pages in front of the book until he found the Common Police emergency number.

When someone came on the line, Joel took a deep breath. He identified himself. "May I speak with Deputy Gray, if he's on duty, please?"

Joel doubted that his father's friend would be there, considering it was in the middle of the night, but a moment later, Officer Gray identified himself.

"Joel? What's going on, son? Why are you calling?"

Joel told him where he was, gave him the address. "I've got Officer Eugene Barela tied up in the middle of his living room, sir. He's responsible for beating up Leo Johnson a few months ago. He's been following me and Tom, my…uh…husband, around town. He…"

Joel did not know how to continue and found his breath getting tighter in his throat. "Could you please come over? I also think Barela's killed someone."

"Be right there, Joel. Don't you dare leave the premises." Then the phone went dead.

*   *   *

Joel waited for what seemed like a half-hour, but as yet no sirens screamed in the night, no flashing lights indicated that the cops were on their way. He paced the floor, keeping his eyes on Barela, then flicked on more lights, wandered down the hallway, trying all the doors, looking into one small room, then another. The layout was similar to Coach's, but it seemed to be a little bigger. He flicked on a light in a room at the end of the short hall, and found himself staring directly into the face of Frank Thurmon, tied up and naked on a bed with a black leather-looking covering. There were things hanging off Frank's chest, and what looked like splotches of blood on his legs. But Frank was awake, staring wild-eyed at Joel. His mouth was bound with a gag, but when he realized who it was, he hung his head and began to weep.

Just then, Joel heard the sirens and saw the lights dancing off the walls of the bedroom.

Joel pulled the gag from Frank's mouth and began untying his friend. "You're all right, now, Frank. Geez, Leo just told me today that you were missing!"

"Water? Drink?"

His voice was raspy, but Joel understood. He untied his feet. "I'll be right back. Don't try to stand, okay?"

When Joel went into the living room, Deputy Gray was untying Barela. Two other officers were looking around the room and shaking their heads. Then Deputy Gray looked up at Joel.

"Joel, I don't know what went on here, but you damned well better have a good explanation. You've made some serious accusations and, from the look of it, you've beat the hell out of one of my officers."

"Frank Thurmon is back there," Joel said, indicating with a nod of his head. "He's alive, sir. But he needs some water. Barela had him hog-tied to a bed."

At that, the two other officers made their way down the hall, while Joel went into the kitchen, opening cabinet doors until he found the glasses, then filled one and took it down the hall.

By the time he re-entered the bedroom, Frank was sitting on the edge of the bed, and one of the officers had found a robe and put it around him. He was no longer crying, but when he took the glass from Joel, tears shown in his eyes, and he rasped. "Was using me, Joel. Sex slave."

The two officers looked embarrassed, but Joel barely registered their reaction as he put both arms around Frank and hugged him.

*   *   *

Joel didn't make it back home until dawn was beginning to show in the east. Even though he had put his shirt back on and had his jacket buttoned to the neck and the heater running in the pickup, he was cold and thought he would never warm up.

He had washed his face and chest at Barela's house and had gone to the police station following Gray's patrol car, where Frank was sitting in the back seat. Gray had questioned both of them, but mainly Frank, asking when he had been kidnapped, and asking where his own car was. It turned out that Barela had just parked it in a church parking lot near his house and hadn't even bothered to remove the license plates.

To his accusation that Eugene Barela had repeatedly raped him, Gray seemed embarrassed and had talked in a low voice to one of the other officers saying that Thurmon had been "unmanned" rather than calling it rape. Joel didn't think he liked that term, since it implied something about being gay. But to Joel, Gray had been his usual friendly self, once he had scolded him for taking the law into his own hands.

About that, Joel did not feel badly, could *not* feel badly, since he had found Frank.

But as he walked up to the house from the bottom of the hill and saw Tom standing on the porch with a cup of coffee in his hands and looking stricken, Joel felt deeply ashamed of himself. Here, again, he had acted without thinking, just slugging his way through and inviting whatever trouble might have resulted from it. When he stepped up on the porch, he saw tears in Tom's eyes.

"Where have you been, Joel? I woke up this morning about four o'clock and you were nowhere to be seen. I saw the pickup was gone, so I figured you might have gone down to the shop or something, but you weren't there."

"Can we go inside, honey?" Joel said, by way of an answer. "I have a lot to tell you, and you're not going to like any of it."

When they were inside, Joel went to the sink and washed his hands. It was then that Tom saw the blood and the bruising.

"What in the hell have you done?" Tom asked. "What?!"

Joel explained it, from the time Leo had been beat up, until the day before when Leo called telling him that Frank was missing. Then Joel told Tom that, the night before, as they were leaving Margaret's, he was sure it was Barela who had been standing across the street.

"That's what did it for me," Joel said. "I knew the guy was following us, and I didn't like it one bit. To think that he's pulled so many stunts on our family, and then stalking us wherever we went."

"So…you went to his house? You went there with what, exactly, in mind?"

"To make him tell me where Frank was, honey. As bad as he beat up on Leo, I figured he was capable of doing anything."

Tom had not smiled during their whole conversation, and the tears that had been there when Joel saw him on the porch were still in his eyes, and new ones pushed those down his cheeks. He shook his head sadly. "Go on. Finish it, Joel. Show me just how crazy you are, how reckless and stupid, and blind, and insensitive to everybody's feelings but your own."

Joel was stunned. But he knew Tom was right in a way. He didn't know where to begin.

PART TWO

COMPLICATIONS

CHAPTER 15

BIRTH DAY

March 15, 1971

Joel walked around on eggshells for weeks after the incident with Eugene Barela, and Tom didn't let him off the hook, either. That was how Joel described it to himself—eggshells and hooks. They got up in the mornings and when they kissed, he always met Tom's eyes with the sadness in them and the knots in his own stomach, knowing that what he had done was not going to be so easily forgotten.

It was as it should be, he supposed, and he would just have to live through it. Nor were his parents, but especially his father, any more sympathetic to his side of the story. They all told him the same thing: "You could have been killed, Joel. Don't you *ever* think about things like that? Can't you *ever* just let things slide, or let the right people handle things?"

But despite being chastised—and even in spite of the fact that Tom was hurt because it frightened him at what Joel had done—Joel saw that a lot of good had come from his confrontation with the cop. Most important, Barela was behind bars awaiting trial and was no longer a threat to Leo. Second—and something Joel would always be glad of—he had probably saved Frank's life. Barela had not only used him as a sex slave, but had been torturing him. The things that had been hanging from his chest the night Joel found him tied to the bed were electrical devices the cop had invented for his more ambitious sex sessions. Finally, Barela was no longer the shadowy threat he had been, always around the corner, across the street, or outside the café trailing him and Tom. That threat had been removed.

Joel did not justify his actions to Tom by explaining any of this, however; nor did he wait for Tom to discover them on his own. He decided that Tom was right in punishing him, though he did hope his iciness would fade and they could get back to the happy couple they had been.

New Year's came and went, as did the coldest part of the winter and, finally, Tom forgave him. When Leo and Frank came to visit one day in early March, it was Tom who seemed to enjoy their visit more than Joel. When they left, Tom was beaming.

"Can you believe how much Leo seems to have changed, honey? Did you see the way he was treating Frank?"

Joel was lying on the couch reading the new issue of *Time Magazine*, when Tom came in from saying good-bye to Leo and Frank. He sat up and tossed the magazine onto the coffee table. "What do you mean, the way he was treating Frank?"

Tom sat down beside him, and kissed him on the mouth. "Just the way one would hope Frank should be treated. Like the great husband he could be."

Joel looked at him and smiled. "Yeah, I did notice. It used to be Leo would pout and order him around, at least when they were first together, remember? But you're right. Leo treats him like a husband, now, and not some puppy-dog plaything."

"Exactly," Tom said. "And you know what, honey?" he smiled and kissed Joel, again.

"What?"

"It's the way you deserve to be treated. I've been treating you badly for quite a while. You know, since that night you beat up Barela and rescued Frank. Can you forgive me? I know that you meant well."

Without even realizing he was going to, Joel began crying. He didn't sob, nor feel the hurt of the last few months erupting from deep within himself, but his eyes stung with relief. "Thanks," he said. "I've missed us...the way we were, you know?"

Tears came to Tom's eyes, just then, as well. "I know. I've missed us, too," he said. "But will you please promise not to take such an awful chance again?"

Joel nodded and hugged Tom to his chest. "I will try, honey. I know you were right to punish me for the way I handled things. So I promise that, when I start getting a dangerous notion in my head, you'll be the first to know and you can talk me out of it, or we can discover a way to approach it that doesn't carry so much risk."

"The only thing I find wrong with that," Tom said, with one of his impish grins, "is how will you know it's a 'dangerous notion'?"

Joel laughed then, more deeply than he had in a long time.

*   *   *

When they got up the next morning from a night of love-making that left their lips bruised and both of them aching to keep it up, they shared a large breakfast at their kitchen table, kissing, and interrupting their breakfast to do it again.

Then Joel dressed and hugged Tom good-bye and headed out to the equipment yard. The mid-March sky was overcast and a cold wind blew dust around, but Joel was happy and barely noticed as he started the new John Deere that he'd helped Douglas hitch the deep plow to.

He sang at the top of his lungs as he lumbered along past the irrigation ditches and into the acreage where cotton had been planted the season before. The wind was blowing fiercely from the west across the fields that had already been plowed, and where he entered the field with the tractor and lowered the plow, a cloud of dust was churning. But he barely noticed. He could not stop thinking of Tom, as if they had made love for the very first time the night before. Over the roar of the engine and the howl of the wind, he shouted: "I LOVE YOU! Do you hear me you beautiful man?!" He became erect recalling the night before, and it ached so soon after making love in the kitchen. But it hurt, good. Tears of sheer love for Tom spilled out, mixing with those tears caused from the blowing sand, until his face was streaked with dirt.

As the morning wore on, he laughed and sang, feeling his youth and his love for Tom, knowing he was crazy in love with him and always would be. No one else could hurt him as Tom had; but no one else could make him feel as happy, either, and that, too, was as it should be, he thought.

*   *   *

Tom was barely out of the bath and still naked when the phone rang. Although he did not rush to answer it, he did not want to miss a call, so he toweled himself off at his desk as he picked up the receiver.

"Hello?"

"Tom? This is Margaret. Sharon's water broke. I've called Dr. Hossley, and we're heading to the hospital."

For a moment, Margaret's words did not penetrate his mind. Then it hit him. "Oh! Sharon's water broke! I'll have to get Joel out of the field. I'll call Eva. Is there anything else I need to do?"

Margaret was laughing. "Just get in here. Her contractions have started and, even though she's not concerned about making it, I am!"

The phone went dead. Tom closed his eyes, feeling his heart begin to pound. Then he dialed the Reeces and told Eva, and she hung up even quicker than Margaret had, leaving Tom stunned, still feeling sluggish.

Then he raced to the bathroom pulling on pants without underwear, grabbing a sweatshirt of Joel's off the towel rack, and forcing himself to slow down when he realized he was trying to pull on his boots without socks.

Ten minutes after Margaret had called he was running toward the equipment yard and jumping into the pickup. He was crying for both joy and sadness, but he pushed the sadness out of his mind, though he could not quite dislodge it from his heart and raced over the irrigation ditch and down the dirt road to the field where Joel was plowing.

Joel was heading in the opposite direction and would probably not turn and see him there, so he threw the pickup into gear and tore out, again, racing first toward the east, then turning the corner and throwing himself into a dangerous slide, his heart racing with the increase in speed and he then headed south.

He took the next corner more slowly, heading west, and remembered the first time Joel had ever brought him out to the farm and was driving him around the same field. He smiled to himself at how much had changed, and yet how the field was the same, then he pulled to a halt, and the dust he had churned up settled over the pickup, causing him to sneeze.

Jumping out of the pickup, he began running across the newly turned earth, his boots sinking into the loose, sandy soil and slowing him down. Out of breath, he stopped and bent over, then looked up and began waving his arms.

He was grinning from ear to ear when Joel finally noticed him, and he ran forward again, shouting, "We're going to be fathers! Sharon's water broke!" all against the blistering wind that raced from west to east, against the steady drone of the tractor's engine.

When Joel finally came to a halt, his face turned from worry to a knowing smile. He cut the engine, jumped down, and threw his arms around Tom. "It's Sharon, isn't it?"

"Yes!" Tom shouted, then caught himself. "She's having our baby, honey! We're going to be fathers!"

They hugged and danced in the field with the wind racing across the vast expanse of the desert all around them, falling in the dirt that stuck to their clothing, and laughing and hurrying to the pickup, oblivious to the cold or the dirt on their faces and in their hair, oblivious to the vast sky overhead full of storm clouds, oblivious to all but each other, oblivious that their lives were about to change forever.

*   *   *

They did not stop at the farm to change. They did not stop at the Reece home to see if Eva and Douglas or Henry and Sally were there. They assumed they were on their way to the hospital as well. They drove straight through the gate and onto the pavement. Tom was behind the wheel and, as he drove, Joel rummaged around in the glove compartment for rags, which he used to wipe the smudges of dirt off Tom's face and then his own. Tom kept the accelerator down and punched the old pickup up to 70, turning onto highway 490, then a mile later, turning north onto Eighth Street, pushing the accelerator back up to 70 and heading on into town, going straight for the hospital.

They talked little. Joel was too stunned to say much. Tom was too absorbed in keeping the pickup speeding through the traffic, until they came to a halt in the parking lot of the hospital. Joel had not been here since he and Tom had volunteered in the children's hospice wing, where the Hoffins' son, Linton, and other chronically ill children lived.

Joel thought, but did not say it, that their child was going to be happy and healthy and would never be abused, and would not have cancer. He did not want to tempt fate by saying it aloud, but he had made up his mind that their child was going to be healthy. He would protect their baby with his life if necessary.

Tom's thoughts were also racing, and got snagged on the idea that he would have liked to have his own mother with him, to present her with a grandchild—that was the sadness he felt and could not shake. But, again, he put that thought out of his mind as soon as it came, and did not skip a step as he and Joel walked arm-in-arm through the front door of the hospital. Neither of them noticed the disapproving looks they got from the nurses and staff, who knew full well who those two young men were, knowing precisely where they were headed, watching them walk toward the maternity ward, shamelessly holding each other.

*   *   *

Eva was appalled when she saw them coming down the hall, as well, but not because they were holding hands or because of what people might be thinking of her gay son and the young man he called his husband. She was appalled because they were filthy from head to foot.

She put up a restraining hand. "You cannot go in there like that," she said to their surprised faces. "Joel, you should have taken time to change clothes! What have you two been doing? Rolling around in the dirt like cats?!"

Douglas came out of the room behind her and laughed at the sight of his son and Tom. "Now, Eva, calm down. Dr. Hossley says they can be in the delivery room with Sharon; he's had the nurses bring in their gowns." He handed Joel a comb. There's a bathroom in the waiting room. Try to clean yourselves up a little."

He chuckled at the two boys and at Eva's frown. She did not see Douglas roll his eyes behind her back and smile at her excitement.

Margaret met them in the waiting room and hugged them both. "She's asking for you boys," she said, smiling. She handed them each a green gown, a cap, and a mask. "They've also put towels in there. They said you had to clean your hands, especially, really well."

"Thanks, Marge," Joel said, smiling at his old friend. He looked around and winked at Henry and Sally who were sitting side-by-side on one of the couches. Sally's feet were dangling in front of her, not tall enough yet to reach the floor. Henry jumped up and tugged on Joel's sleeve.

"Tell Sharon I want a boy, okay?"

Joel hugged Henry to him. "I'll tell her you put in your order, okay? But I can't promise anything. Let's just hope he has all his fingers and toes."

*   *   *

Dr. Hossley was a skinny man, whom Joel had known all his life. Taken to him for one ailment or another, and the last time, treated by him when he was beaten up by the boxing team in 1966, he hadn't changed a bit. He had always been a gray-haired man as well as Joel could remember, with kind wrinkly eyes and a grimace full of teeth, as if he were in pain. His shoulders were what gave him away as being unnaturally skinny, however, and it was those bony shoulders that Joel remembered, now, as the doctor came into the waiting room. He and Tom had dutifully changed into their hospital gowns and were laughing at each other, Joel, because Tom wasn't wearing underwear under his gown, discovering that he had forgot to put any on when he was rushing to get dressed, earlier; Tom, because Joel had been camping around, trying to act like a woman, and it was impossible for Joel to make it even remotely convincing. "You just look like Joel in a gown, honey," Tom had said a moment before the doctor had walked in. "Or maybe a hospitalized Roman soldier."

But the doctor was all business, and had splashed cold water on their laughter as soon as he spoke. "Let me see your fingernails," he said, putting on his mask. Tom held out his hands for inspection and the doctor nodded approval. "Joel?" Dr. Hossley said, a moment later. "Your hands?"

Joel held them out. Dr. Hossley took hold of them, turning them over, digging one of his nails under Joel's thumb nail. "Is this grease?"

Joel looked at the thumb nail of his left hand. "No, sir," he said, examining the nail. "It's discoloration. I think I banged my thumb with a wrench about three weeks ago."

The doctor let go of his hands. "Good. Now, Joel, I want you to understand that this is highly unusual for me to let the...ah...husband in the delivery room." He looked at both Tom and him. "But Miss Minninger, whom I've become quite fond of over this last several months has asked that you both be allowed into the delivery room. Neither of you are weak-kneed when it comes to blood, are you?"

Tom shrugged and looked a little sickly. "I don't know, Doctor. Cuts and things like that don't bother me. Why?"

Dr. Hossley looked at them both, his eyes shining above the face mask, his voice a little muffled behind it. "Because you're going to see a lot of blood, boys. Don't be concerned. It's natural with child birth. It's placental blood. It doesn't mean the baby or the mother is any danger. You understand?"

Tom and Joel both nodded.

The doctor turned to the others in the waiting room, looking at Eva and Douglas, then Margaret and the children. "I've been attending Sharon now for several months, as you know. She is as perfectly healthy as any young woman I've ever seen, so you folks just relax, and let's see if we can't make this birthing a celebration for the miracle it is."

Dr. Hossley's voice quality had always been reassuring to Joel, even when he was a child and was afraid. He remembered the time he had broken one of his toes, and the doctor said it wouldn't hurt; but when he jerked the toe back into place, Joel squealed in pain, crying out that it really hurt bad. Dr. Hossley had just laughed with his grimacing mouth full of teeth. "Now I don't remember feeling a thing, Joel. Are you sure it hurt?"

With that Joel had laughed, too. The next time he came in, this time with a dislocated shoulder from falling out of a tree on the playground at school, he told the doctor it was okay. "You won't feel a thing Dr. Hossley, so go ahead."

Now, the doctor looked him full in the eyes, his own crinkled with amusement and fondness for Joel. "I know what you and Tom have done," he said, as he walked with them from the waiting room to the delivery room. "Small town has this case sewed up, if you get my drift. I can't say that I like it, either, not because of what you might think, though. But I know you, son, and so I doubt you will abandon your responsibility. But the two of you are going to have to decide whose name is going on the birth certificate as the father. In the years to come, that will be about as binding a legal document as you can imagine."

A moment later, they entered a brightly lit room without windows, and there was Sharon lying in the bed smiling at them. She held out her hands and Tom went to one side and Joel to the other and they each took a hand. Joel kissed Sharon on the forehead, and Tom did the same. She was beaming and only stopped smiling as a contraction hit her.

"This is what you wanted, Joel?" she said, raising her voice into a question at the end. "I hope you will be pleased with your child."

Joel felt tears sting his eyes and he smiled at her. "We love you, Sharon. Don't ever forget or not believe it. This child will be all of ours."

Sweat beaded Sharon's forehead as she was hit with another wave of pain. The doctor took her pulse and looked at his watch, letting none of them know what he was doing. Then he pulled the covers down from Sharon's shoulders and helped her place her feet in the stirrups at the end of the bed.

"You have work to do, young lady. Now you boys watch and maybe learn what women have always known. They are the stronger sex. My nurse will be in momentarily, so do as she says. When she tells you to, you punch this buzzer, and I'll come running."

When the doctor was gone, Joel looked around the room. It was really nothing more than a regular hospital room with equipment he could not guess a use for. The buzzer was a beige button on one of the many thick plastic wires attached to the bed.

He was holding Sharon's left hand, and when another pain took her, she squeezed his hand. Tom was holding her other hand and squeezed back when he felt her strong pressure. He looked across the bed at Joel and smiled, then down at Sharon and felt the tears welling up in his eyes.

"It is all right, Tom," she said in a clear, strong voice. I have helped birth many babies. It is nothing, just my turn."

*   *   *

In the waiting room, morning gave way to noon, and Sally and Henry began to get restless. Eva dug into her purse and pulled out several coins. She handed them to Sally. "You and Henry go down the hall if you want and see if you can't find a soda machine."

"But no running and no noise," Douglas said.

Margaret watched the exchange and smiled to herself. She would have to be calling the café in a little while to make sure everything was under control, there. But she did not want to miss a moment of the waiting, here, almost as if something she had wanted for fifty years was about to come to fruition, and so a few more hours were nothing to her. She observed Douglas and Eva Reece as they also waited, neither of them really talking, except in short bursts with, "You think it will be a boy or a girl?" and the other smiling. "Doesn't matter to me."

Margaret hoped that Sharon would have a girl. She could not say why if someone had asked her, except that Rose had always thought a daughter would be the most fun to raise, and even when they had both passed child-bearing age, Rose had doted on the little girls who passed through their café. In fact, she had kept a candy jar behind the counter and when children were particularly restless and causing their parents grief and were getting cranky, she would ask the parents if she could show the children something. The children's faces would light up with curiosity, and in most cases, the parents would let them go with her. Rose would make a mystery out of the hidden treasure behind the counter, taking as much time as she could to settle the children down, then she would send them back to the table with a lolly-pop or a Tootsie Roll. But she really shined, when it was a little girl. She had dolls tucked away behind the counter, too, and would let them play with them and eat their candy and sit on the stool behind the register, until the parents were finished eating.

Oh, Rose, Margaret thought. *I feel like I'm going to be a grandmother! You would like Sharon, dear. She has lifted my heart a long way from where it was before she came to live with us.*

She smiled at Eva. "Would you like me to call the café and have something brought over? Or I could send Douglas, if he doesn't mind."

Eva was looking as restless as Sally Ann had been a few minutes before, flipping through the *Reader's Digests* and then studying the pictures on the walls, then digging in her purse. At Margaret's suggestion, Eva turned to Douglas. "Are you hungry? Would you mind going?"

Douglas stood up and stretched. "I think I could use a break."

Margaret nodded, then dug into her own purse and brought out a tablet, scribbling on it, then handing it to Douglas. "Just hand this to Julie Ann. She'll be the girl with the red hair. She knows where I am. Tell her to call the hospital if I'm needed."

When Douglas walked out of the room, it was just her and Eva. Margaret got up from the chair where she had been sitting, moving to the couch beside Eva.

Eva moved her purse and turned on the couch to face her. "You've never had children of your own, I take it?"

Margaret smiled at the question. Neither Eva nor Douglas had ever asked many personal questions, and she thought she knew why. Now it was her turn, she thought, to alleviate some of Eva Reece's curiosity.

"No, I haven't. You must realize, dear, that Rose was more than my business partner. I don't remember if you and Douglas had ever come into the Red Rooster when she was alive. She died about ten years ago."

Eva smiled in return, though her eyes darted from Margaret's face for a moment then back. "I can't recall if I did meet her. When I had the kids at home, I don't think Douglas and I ate out very often. We kind of changed that routine when we adopted all those children from the Strouds. You met the twins?"

Margaret nodded.

"We felt like we needed to be different with them than we were with our own three children. They had missed so much, you know, with the kind of life they had led. That's why we pushed ourselves to go out almost every Sunday. But it wasn't until Joel and Tom introduced us to you that we started making a regular stop out of the Red Rooster."

Margaret nodded, again. "Rose and I always wanted children, to get back to your question. But we lived in a very different age than it is now, I suppose."

Eva nodded, this time. She put her arm on the back of the couch and touched Margaret's shoulder for a moment. "It is different these days, or so it has been for Douglas and me. We rarely had it in our consciousness about homosexuality, you know. Not until Joel and Tom hit us over the head with it. But I'm no longer surprised when I happen to discover that someone's child is gay. I can sympathize with the parents, as you might imagine, but I have little tolerance for those who simply cannot get used to the idea."

Margaret was pleased with Eva's response and her frank way of stating things. But enough had been said, she thought, and didn't need to continue in that vein. "It has been a wonderful experience for me," she said, wanting to put her hand on Eva's shoulder, but deciding against it, "to have Sharon living with me. She is a bright girl and a quick learner. Have the boys said what their plans are regarding the living arrangements, now that the baby is almost here?"

Eva shook her head and a kind of distress crossed her face. "It dismays me to think, Margaret, that none of them—Joel, Tom, or Sharon—seem to have thought beyond this moment, right now. Has she indicated to you whether she really plans to just turn her baby over to the boys? I don't think I could do that."

This time, Margaret felt a little distressed herself. She folded her hands in her lap. "You do know that Sharon plans to attend university once she gets her high school diploma?"

Eva nodded.

"She'll be attending night school this August, but I doubt that it will take her but six months to test out of high school, considering that she's almost nineteen. So I'm afraid come August of the next year, when the baby is what…seventeen months old? She will be turning the baby over to your son."

"That concerned me," Eva said. "I don't think any of them realized what a responsibility having a helpless child can be, and I did not like the idea that Sharon was going to have this child. Not only because it was out of wedlock, but because she would be tied to it and could not, herself, have a chance to get an education."

"That's exactly what I felt," Margaret said, warming up to Eva. "The way things are these days, women need to be as self-sufficient and independent as any man. I was heartbroken to know she was pregnant, and more than a little disappointed in both Tom and Joel for being so fool hardy. Men just don't have any idea what single mothers go through."

Eva smiled and nodded vigorously. "That was my exact concern, Margaret. But we both know that there's no turning back, now. So if it is Sharon's desire to go away to school and to leave her child in our care, well, we've got room. I hope you will take an interest in the child, too."

Margaret felt tears sting her eyes. "I certainly will. I feel like a grandmother to that child, or maybe a better word is great-grandmother, since I'm old enough to be Sharon's grandmother."

When Sally and Henry came back with their sodas, they stood in front of Eva. "Has she had her baby, yet?"

They were disappointed to find out that nothing had changed; but when Douglas came in a few minutes later with a bag and began digging out fried chicken, they forgot about everything else and settled down in a corner of the waiting room with their paper plates and sodas, fried chicken and French fries.

Douglas set out the rest of the meal on the coffee table in front of the couch and pulled up a chair on the opposite side. "Do we know anything, yet?" he addressed his question to Margaret.

She smiled, having always liked him, having always seen a lot of him in Joel. "These things take time, Douglas," she teased. "But I hope it's not going to be one of those marathon labors."

Eva had placed a plate in her lap, but had not yet taken a bite. "I recall with Kathleen, that it was relatively short. About six hours, once the contractions started in earnest. But with Joel, I think I was in labor for at least ten hours. Of course I was older then and had lost a child between him and Patricia."

And so the hours passed, and it was not until the sun had begun to turn the hallway outside the waiting room golden that a nurse popped her head in the door. "Congratulations, folks. Miss Minninger has just given birth to an eight pound, three ounce baby!"

"Baby!" Eva laughed. "Do you mind telling us if it is a boy or a girl?"

The nurse came into the room. "I've been instructed by Joel, I believe he said his name was, to show you to the room where we've taken Miss Minninger. He and his...friend...want to introduce you to your grandchild."

"Can we come?!" Sally asked jumping up from the floor. "Can we?"

The nurse's smile turned into a serious expression. "Little newborns are very fragile, honey, and susceptible to all kinds of germs. When we put the baby in the nursery, you can look in through the glass."

Chapter 16

The Name

As they neared the door to Sharon's room, Douglas held Eva back, allowing Margaret to enter first, and then he gently nudged Eva into the room behind her. Margaret glanced toward the right side of the bed where Joel was standing, holding the baby, but made straight for Sharon who was sitting propped up on pillows. Her blonde hair was wet, she was sweating, but beaming when Margaret approached her and bent over her giving her a kiss.

Eva also noticed Tom on the left side of Sharon's bed holding her hand and smiling as they watched the family make their way into the room; but Eva could not help herself; after smiling at Sharon, she moved up next to her son, who was holding the baby in a bundle, looking both happy and stricken at the same time. He held the bundle tight against his chest and allowed Eva to raise the blanket off the baby's face.

"Mom. Dad. Margaret," he said, his voice sounding husky and teary, "I'd like you to meet your granddaughter, Shara Margaret."

A soft cry of surprise from Margaret as she awkwardly turned to Joel made the tears come to Eva's eyes, as well.

"Did you say 'Margaret'?" Margaret asked. She joined Eva in holding the blanket away from the baby's face. "Let me see you, sweet heart!"

Barely able to tear her eyes from the small child that Joel held so tightly, Eva went over to the bed and kissed Sharon on the forehead. "She is beautiful, honey."

"Thank you, Mrs. Reece," Sharon said, her voice a whisper. "I have helped many women with their own children, but no one can tell you what it is to feel like! It is wonderful and it hurts!"

"She really had a rough time," Tom said, speaking for the first time. He was still gripping Sharon's hand. He squeezed it. "Now we just have to get Sharon back on her feet. Dr. Hossley says she shouldn't have to stay too long, just a few days, until they run tests on the baby to make sure she's all right. We've already counted her fingers and toes."

Sharon laughed, her blonde hair shining wetly in the light from the lamp over the bed. "She is so tiny, so beautiful." Then she looked up at Douglas. "Come, Mr. Reece, have a look?"

Eva turned back to the baby, seeing that Joel was rigid, and still looking stricken. "Honey? May I hold her?"

Joel held the baby tighter, his smile wavering. On his right hand, his wedding ring caught a glint of light. For some reason, which Eva could not explain, it brought home so much, all at once. Her son, her *gay* son, was a father, he and Tom had slept with Sharon, and they had produced this child, and here he was afraid to relinquish the baby.

"It's all right, honey," Eva said, understanding Joel's fear. She brushed his cheek with the back of her hand. "Nobody's going to take your baby away. I just want to hold her for a moment."

Joel glanced across the bed at Tom. Tom nodded, his own face looking odd, Eva thought, and wondered why. But he stood up and came around the bed. He stood behind Joel and kissed him on the cheek. "It's all right, honey. Let your mother hold your baby."

For a moment, Joel seemed indecisive, but his arms relaxed, and he handed the baby gently to Eva. "Don't drop her, Mom. She's so delicate, don't you think? So tiny."

Eva knew she should not move away from Joel, even though she wanted to sit down, open the blanket, and get a better look at her granddaughter. But Joel was in the middle of an anxiety attachment or something, and it would just take a little time for him to feel safe. So she held the baby, standing next to him, touching Joel's chest with her forearm. His heart was pounding as if he'd been running, and she felt his breath on her neck, as he looked at the child's face.

"Isn't she beautiful, Mom?" Joel asked, his voice sounding strained. She's got blue eyes, but the doctor says all babies have blue eyes; but her hair is dark, what there is of it. She's really red, but Dr. Hossley says it's nothing to worry about. Most babies' skin is red and wrinkly like that. But look how long her fingers are! And her little feet, Mom, you should see how little her feet are! They had to get a foot print for the birth certificate, but the doctor said the ink wouldn't hurt her."

Eva handed her back. When Joel was gripping the baby again, she smoothed his hair. "Honey, you need to sit down. Okay?"

Joel nodded, and covered the baby's face again with the blanket. "We shouldn't breathe on her too much."

"Not too much," Eva agreed, glancing at Douglas, who had not moved from where he had been once he entered the room. His eyes said he was taking it all in and he was worried. Eva nodded at a chair, locking eyes with Douglas, and he nodded back, then pulled one of the chairs away from the wall and moved it behind Joel.

"Here, son," he said. "You need to sit down."

Joel did as they asked, sitting very slowly and gripping the baby tightly.

Eva pulled a pillow off the other bed in the room and laid it in Joel's lap. "Honey, lay the baby down on the pillow. You should realize that a newborn needs to stretch out, give its little lungs a chance to work freely. All right?"

Joel looked up at her smiling, beaming, really, but there was still the stricken look in his eyes. He nodded, and Eva breathed a quiet sigh, as he laid the baby onto the pillow.

"She's still got part of the umbilical cord attached," Joel said. "The doctor says it's all right, though. It's natural. It'll fall off in a few days. I never knew that," he said, looking at Douglas. "Did you, Dad? Did you know that the umbilical cord would still be attached, and then it would fall off in a few days? It's so painful looking."

*   *   *

A moment of awkward silence passed at Joel's words. Tom returned to Sharon's side and helped her slide down in the bed a little. He pulled the covers up to her shoulders and kissed her on the forehead. "Why don't you try to get some sleep?"

She nodded and closed her eyes.

Margaret and Eva moved about the room beginning to tidy it up, and Douglas watched them all, then turned to Joel. His son's almost metallic blonde hair shone in the light, his bright, new father's eyes were full of tears as he gently rocked the baby back and forth on his knees on the pillow, smiling.

Douglas went over to him, then. "Let's get a real look at what you've got bundled up in there, son," he said.

Joel looked up at him. "It's too cold in here for her, Dad."

Douglas heard the slight fear in Joel's voice. But he chuckled and moved Joel's hands off the baby's blanket. "You're not cold are you?"

"No, but Shara's so helpless, so tiny."

"But she's not cold, either, son. Her little heart rate is rapid and she's probably hot in there. Let's have a look at this little thing."

Then he knelt down beside his son and opened the blankets. The baby was asleep, its little stomach rising and falling rapidly. It was wearing a diaper that slightly covered the navel, and it had on a little knit shirt that was pulled askew. Douglas pulled one of the baby's arms up, pulling the shirt down over its little chest. Joel sucked in a surprised breath. "Don't pull so hard, Dad! You might dislocate her shoulder!"

But Douglas chuckled, again, locking eyes with his son. "Babies are a lot more resilient than you think. Sure she's little, Joel. She's red and splotchy, and helpless, but she has good genes, what with Sharon's Germanic background and either yours or Tom's own healthy blood."

For the first time, Joel seemed to relax, but he covered the baby up again. He smiled at his mother, then. "It's just she seems so very helpless, Mom." Then he began sobbing softly, his chest jerking. "I never realized…how little she'd be!"

In an instant, Eva was at Joel's side. "She'll be all right, honey. Even when you think she's seriously ill, when her little nose gets stopped up and she cries for no reason, and her waste is runny and yellow, or when she gets heat prickle, or has a tummy ache. But it's just natural."

Joel wiped his tears and picked up the baby and hugged it.

A moment later, a nurse came in on rapid steps and reached for the baby. Joel turned in the chair away from her, holding his daughter tightly. "Do you have to take her, now? You might wake her up."

But the nurse smiled, holding out her hands. "We've got to do some tests, change her, and get her ready for the nursery."

For another awkward moment, it looked as though Joel was going to refuse, but he reluctantly handed the baby to the nurse.

Douglas was grateful to the nurse for the way she gently took the baby, keeping it close to her chest as she left the room. Still he sighed with relief. Then he clapped Joel on the shoulder. "Come on, son, we need to get out of here and let Sharon rest. You can come back when she's feeding the baby. Right now, I think both you and Tom could use something to eat."

∗   ∗   ∗

Joel didn't want anything to eat, and he didn't want to leave the hospital with Shara in the care of the nursing staff. In fact, his stomach was upset, and he was on the verge of tears, again. He felt them trickling out, threatening to spill. He didn't care. He'd seen the way everyone was looking at him in Sharon's room, thinking he was suddenly nuts, or something. He'd seen the frown on his mother's face, her wanting to take the baby as soon as she walked into the room. He'd seen Tom's fretful looks earlier before anyone else had arrived, him and Sharon both looking at him with that sadness.

Well, maybe Sharon was tired. She had surely worked hard in the delivery room, her face contorted sometimes with the effort, but between bouts of pain, she smiled at them both. She was a great mother, he thought, and his own mouth turned down in sadness at the thought that he and Tom had done what they had to her, making her pregnant and full of the baby—*our baby*—yet she was really the baby's mother, no doubt at all about who the mother was. He had been surprised and frightened when the baby began to come, and it was all so bloody. He hadn't realized just how bloody giving birth could be. Then the little head appearing there, where it did. It seemed backwards and awkward, and the only thing that had helped him was to remember seeing calves birthed at the farm. The difference was, once the baby had been fully birthed and cleaned a little, it was so very weak and so helpless. Sharon was weak too after what must have been eight or so hours lying there, sometimes in so much pain, Joel thought the knuckles in his hands were about to break with the strength of her grip. So, yes…she probably was tired.

Maybe Tom's own sad looks came from realizing how important it was to protect the baby, to raise her, to watch her grow and learn to walk—and then run—to her daddies. It didn't matter to Joel who the real father was, though Shara's dark hair was at least one clue that it might be Tom's rather than his, and such a strong trait it was, he thought, to come through since both he and Sharon were as blond as you could get.

He was in the back of the Caddie with Tom and Margaret and Henry. In front were Sally and his mother and father, and they were headed to the Triangle Drive-In on the west side of town, where they could order hamburgers from the car hop, and they wouldn't have to go inside and wait for service. At least that would be better, Joel thought.

He was surprised it was already dark when they left the hospital, and the damned wind was still blowing and icy, and he surely would have to find some way to keep the baby warm when they all left the hospital in a few days. He was afraid it was going to be one of those springs that left you gasping for breath.

He didn't want to work in the fields, which made him smile to himself, since he loved working in the fields, turning the soil and leaving behind a trail of dark, rich soil turned up to the sunlight of spring. He didn't know how he could stand leaving the baby at home while he went off for hours at a time. But he would have to.

He listened to the conversation in the car, and the laughter, and tried to join in, knowing he had to show them that he wasn't suddenly freaked out. In a moment of silence, he turned to Margaret.

"We're you surprised with Sharon's choice of names?"

Margaret laughed in that beautiful high lilt of hers, which sounded more like a young girl than an old lady. "I am honored, honey. It makes me feel so close to Sharon."

"What about you, Mom," Joel said, to the back of her head, which he could not see too well in the dark, with only the dash lights causing a kind of glow around her head where the out-of-place hairs glowed with the greenish light. "Do you like the baby's name?"

He saw her nod, heard the laughter in her voice, even before she spoke. "It's a beautiful name…'Shara', Shara Margaret. Is that German, Margaret…'Shara' that is?" she asked, tilting her head back in Margaret's direction.

"I've never heard it," she said, then turned in the seat so that she was looking across Joel and Tom. "Where did Sharon come up with it?"

Tom laughed, and Joel moved his hand between them, taking Tom's hand in the dark. "It's a made-up name. Part Sharon, but to us it means to share, the way the three of us share the baby."

Joel felt an awkward silence, then, at Tom's explanation, but it was the truth. It was how the three of them felt about the baby. He hoped that people would call her Shara and not Margaret or, worse, Marge, though he didn't mind the "Margaret" as the middle name because, in the way Sharon looked at it, Margaret was like a mother to her, now, and wanted to name the baby after her. Once again, tears filled his eyes.

"I like her name," Henry spoke up. "I wish it had been a boy, though, cause I don't have anybody to play with."

"You got me, Henry!" Sally said, from the front seat. "What am I, chopped liver?!"

Everyone laughed at that. "Besides," Sally continued, "all I've ever had was smelly old boys to play with, so there!"

It seemed to Joel that his father was driving too slowly, or that they were moving through molasses, but they finally arrived at the drive-in, pulling up next to a carload of teenagers, kids Joel didn't recognize as he looked out the window. He smiled at their noisy activity and the music pounding out of the radio. The car hop was delivering their food, chewing gum and flirting with the boy behind the wheel. She collected the money, and laughed at something the boy said. Then she did a little dance, laughing. Then she leaned in the boy's window and said something, laughed.

Geez, hurry up! Joel thought. All he wanted to do was get their orders out of the way and get back to the hospital. "What does everybody want?" Joel said. "Maybe we should decide, so we don't have to waste too much time, you know. Maybe"—

Tom slapped him on the thigh, and he got the message, but geez it was taking a long time for the car hop to finish flirting.

In what seemed like half an hour, the car hop finally came to their window and took their orders. Margaret was trying to read the menu printed in block letters inside the window of the café, where the cooks were slapping meat onto the grill. Joel read off the items to her, trying to keep the anxiety out of his voice, as she kept shaking her head. He took a deep breath and bit his lip. What if the baby had already been brought back to the room so Sharon could feed her, and what if Shara was then taken back to the nursery, and what if visiting hours were almost up, and he wouldn't have a chance to hold the baby, again, until tomorrow? He felt like screaming.

*   *   *

Tom could tell that Joel was about to jump out of his skin, as the hamburgers were passed around and everyone finally settled into eating them, talking little, since the noise from the cars around them drowned them out. He wasn't hungry, and it was odd, because he hadn't eaten since breakfast that morning. But his stomach was in knots, first because he was worried about Joel's sudden possessiveness, or his fear for the baby, or whatever it was. It worried him, because it was so unlike Joel to be so nervous. He had felt sorry for Eva, when she had asked to hold the baby and Joel had practically told her no, even though he did relinquish her for a minute or two. He was grateful for the forceful way Douglas had taken control there at the end, making Joel open up the blanket so everyone could get a real look at Shara.

His stomach was also in knots, because he was feeling guilty, again, as he had the night he and Joel had slept with Sharon. All through her pregnancy, it was still theoretical that she would give up her child to them, but even in the midst of birthing her daughter, Sharon seemed concerned for him and Joel and, then, in the delivery room when the baby was finally laid on her chest and she could touch and hold it, Sharon smiled first at Joel and then at Tom, "I hope a daughter is all right?" her weak voice going up in a question, as if she were afraid they would be disappointed. Then Tom had almost cried aloud when Sharon took the baby from her breast and handed her to Joel, "Here is your child, Joel. I hope you and Tom will take good care of her."

Still, Tom was sad, not only for the way Sharon seemed intent to keep her part of the bargain, but for another reason he could almost palpably taste as he bit into his hamburger, which leached all the flavor from the food. He missed his own mother terribly, having seen how happy Eva, Douglas, and Margaret were, all of them feeling in some part like grandparents. He felt he shared such a loss with Sharon, since her parents were likely never to see their granddaughter, either.

He tried to tell himself that his own mother would probably reject the baby, anyway, and surely come up with one of his father's biblical injunctions against a "bastard" child as a sign of sin. He shook off that thought—sadly, though—because he would have liked to introduce Shara Margaret to his mother, knowing that she would never be a grandmother, except through him. He sighed quietly to himself in the backseat and tried to cheer up, thinking of the baby. A moment later, however, he felt tears welling up in his eyes. He *had* given his mother and father a grandchild, but they would never know it. That seemed wrong, even if they had disowned him, their only child.

As they headed back to the hospital in the Caddie, Tom squeezed Joel's hand in the dark, and Joel squeezed back. At least, Tom thought, Joel was not so possessed of anxiety that he didn't forget him. He hoped that the changes they were all about to go through as the result of having a child in their house would not change them too much. All Tom wanted was for the core of their marriage to never fade. He did not know if he could ever be happy, again, if it did fade. He gripped Joel's hand, again, and squeezed hard. When Joel squeezed back, Tom held onto it, hoping everything would be all right. It had to, because they were now the kind of family Joel had always wanted.

Chapter 17

Homecoming

Margaret made a habit of going into the hospital just after the noon rush ended at the café, leaving Julie Ann in charge of the afternoon stragglers. It was a good time to go in, because the babies were brought to the mothers' rooms for their afternoon feeding, and Margaret enjoyed watching little Miss Margaret nursing and Sharon's far away looks as she patted the baby on the rump and stroked her little back.

They talked more now about serious things, it seemed, than they had during the nine months Sharon had lived with her. Then, it was about practical things like getting her into school so that she could get her diploma, getting her birth certificate so that she could apply for her social security card, and fine-tuning her "past," which they made simple, so that they would not slip up, if someone asked about it. Margaret had even brought her a few books to read about Montana, so that Sharon could describe its terrain and its features to people as though recalling them from memory.

But during her hospital visits, while the baby was nursing or sleeping on Sharon's chest, or when Margaret was holding the little thing in her lap and stroking its face, Margaret nudged her into talking about her feelings.

"Honey, do you seriously think that come time for you to go away to college, you're going to be able to leave Miss Margaret behind?"

Sharon smiled sadly. "I shall, Margaret. I shall give her to Tom and Joel, and they will be her fathers."

"You don't sound too convincing, honey."

Sharon looked at her and tears brightened her eyes. "I will not forget my daughter, and I will not allow her to grow up without me being in her life, this is true. But for then, when I do go to school, I will be thinking...I will tell myself that for now it is for the best, because I have this great need to become an American, to know this country I have come to, and to become a great woman such as yourself and Eva. I will earn my living and, one day, if I should return to Casas Grandes and if I should visit the community and my own family, I will prove to them that I have made something of myself."

Margaret cried for Sharon, but not in front of her. But she knew Sharon well enough when she said those things that it was precisely what Sharon would do. She was intelligent and, in many ways, reminded her of herself as a young woman, determined to live her life the way she wanted, rather than to give in to her father.

"And you, Margaret," Sharon said one day as they were walking up and down the halls at the hospital, getting her strength back, and standing outside the nursery looking in at the few babies there, watching Shara beat the air with her fists and cry or sleep. "Will you remember me? Will you visit me, perhaps, in California if it is there where I attend university? Will you make the trip to see me?"

Margaret hugged her, then. "I shall indeed, child. You have become like a daughter to me, the daughter Rose and I never had. I will not forget you, though I hope you will come home to Common when you have taken your degree. Then, maybe you and Miss Margaret and I will travel to Montana, and I will show you where I grew up, show you the first house Rose and I lived in, show you where my life began."

"You see?" Sharon said, once they were back in her room, and Sharon slipped back into bed. "We talk of a wonderful time, and whether I must leave my daughter behind for just a little while, she will know I am her mother, and she will love me, and I will not shun her."

$$*\qquad\qquad *\qquad\qquad *$$

Joel and Tom made a habit in the next few days of working in the fields, sometimes without stopping for lunch, then rushing home to bathe and change, so that they could get into the hospital to visit with Sharon and to be there when Shara was brought to the room for her evening feeding. Sharon's face always lit up when she saw them poke their heads in at the door to see if she was asleep or awake. They brought her flowers, had filled her room with flowers and cards. There were also cards and flowers from Bill and JoAnna Hoffins and from the Lawtons, who owned the major bank in town, wishing her well, and cards from Detrick and Patrick, and even one from Terrance Lawton, because Eva had had the presence of mind the night they returned from the hospital on the fifteenth of March to call everyone she could think of.

Joel would sit on one side of the bed and hold her hand, and Tom would sit on the other, and they would smile across the bed at each other. Then Joel would get up and go down to the nursery and try to catch a nurse and ask when the baby was going to be brought to Sharon's room.

He had, in fact, annoyed all the nurses so much that, when he and Tom showed up at the hospital, the nurses would duck around the corner when they saw them coming, trying to get their work done. In the end, Joel found them, and insisted with the best smile he could muster that it was time for his daughter to be fed, wasn't it?

While Joel was annoying the staff, Tom would get up and toss the old flowers and rearrange the cards and read them to Sharon, and add water to the flowers that were still fresh.

Then when the baby was in the room, the three young people would visit and talk about the future, and take turns holding their daughter.

Joel still had a difficult time leaving the baby, once Sharon had fed it and he had gotten to hold it. But a nurse would come in and take it, and when he and Tom left to go home, Joel felt empty and restless.

Fortunately, Sharon was only in the hospital for four days, including the day she had given birth, so on the day that she was to be released, Tom and Joel were at the hospital before they opened the public doors and had to go in through the emergency room entrance.

Eva had helped them pack for the baby the night before. "You'll have to change Shara into her own clothes, Joel. So take these," she said, handing him a few diapers and a couple of little knit shirts. Do not forget to dress her in this little jumper just before you're ready to get in the car. Make sure she's been changed if she's wet or messy, and make sure you've burped her just before you put her in her clothes, because sure as the world, you'll have to change her before you get home, if you don't."

By the time they had the car loaded, Joel was laughing at all the things they were taking just for the baby, including a diaper bag, a little suitcase with several changes of clothes, and blankets to keep her warm when they went from the hospital to the car.

It was clear but cold when they went into the hospital, but after waiting for Sharon to be released and visiting with Dr. Hossley, getting last-minute instructions from him on how to care for the baby's navel, the sun was well up and so was the wind. Sharon was seated in a wheelchair for her ride to the car, and she was holding the baby against her chest, then the blankets were piled on top and she wrapped them around the baby and they made their way out to the front entrance, where Tom had gone to drive the car around.

Joel was pushing the wheelchair and he was smiling as they passed the nurse's station, nodding to them.

One of the old nurses whom Joel had annoyed the most came out and walked with them to the front entrance.

"You'll let me know how your daughter's doing, won't you, Joel?"

He turned to look at her. He knew her first name was Gladys, because he'd seen her nametag often enough. But he addressed her by her last name. "Well, I sure will Mrs. Blake. Thank everybody for me for taking such good care of our baby!"

He was about to go on ahead, when Gladys stopped him. "May I tell you something, Joel?" she asked, for once losing her professional and competent frown. Now she looked rather afraid, and so Joel smiled at her.

"Well, sure."

The nurse looked around in the lobby and back down the hallway, then seemed satisfied. "There've been people in the maternity ward, looking in and talking about your baby. You must know that you can't"—

"I know…keep anything secret in a town like this," Joel said. "We're used to it."

She shook her head. "No, honey. Oh, we all knew about Sharon," she nodded at Sharon, who was looking up, clutching Shara a little closer. "But these people were from that church that came in about a year ago. Maybe you've heard about it. The Calvary, something or other?"

"No, I guess I haven't."

"Well, their preacher was in here, trying to get us to tell him where the mother lives, and if she's going to keep the baby, though we've heard through the grapevine that she's giving up the baby to you."

Joel suddenly felt a cold prickle go down his back. "Nobody talked to these people, did they?"

"Not that I know of, but I can't be here twenty-four hours a day, and that preacher and those he's brought with them…well, they're pretty persistent, and all. We've all grown to like you and your…friend. And we surely like Sharon." She smiled at Sharon, then looked around. "Of course, we know you're listed on the birth certificate, so it's not a matter of anyone being able to challenge your right to raise your child."

"Then what is it a matter of?" Joel asked. All he wanted, now, was to get out, get his baby home, and then see if anyone could take Shara away from him.

Gladys frowned. "I wouldn't know. I'm sorry. There are those, however, who might challenge your fitness, or Sharon's. So, please, just keep your eyes open. We like you."

Joel's hands were shaking on the back of the wheelchair, and he gripped the handles hard. But he managed to smile. "Thank you, Mrs. Blake. I'll be sure to keep you posted on Shara's progress. But I think we better get home."

       *   *   *

The wind was howling when Joel pushed Sharon through the doors, and dust and grit blew through the breezeway. Luckily Tom was right there to help Sharon up, by taking the baby and, as soon as Sharon had stepped into the car, he handed Shara in after her.

Joel shut her door and hurried around to the other side and got in the back seat with her. Then Tom slid into the driver's seat, shut his door and put the car into gear.

As they drove away, he told Tom what the nurse had told him, and then as they maneuvered onto the street and began moving through the few blocks that would take them out of town, Joel began to look around, watching every car that pulled up behind them. He was frightened, more than he'd been when they realized Barela had been stalking them. He remembered how persistent Paul Romaine from Tom's old church had been, how Kenneth had chased them through town one night wielding his shotgun, just for who they were. Now, it was some crazy religious offshoot, some sneaking fucking preacher, nosing around at the hospital trying to find out where they were going to take the baby.

As soon as he got the chance, he would find out just how he and Tom could protect themselves from some sort of challenge to their fitness as parents. No damned doubt, he thought, with a jolt of anger that made him frown and caused Sharon to look alarmed, if something like this went to court, there would be people who wouldn't like their being gay at all, especially now that a child was involved.

Let them try something, he thought, again. Just let them try.

       *   *   *

Out in the open country where the fields had been turned, the dust was a blizzard and the wind even rocked the heavy Cadillac, filling the car with a musty smell and causing the baby to sneeze. Its little sneeze was cute in a way that made Joel smile, and he and Sharon exchanged smiles, but he was also concerned that the baby might get choked up, and so he asked Tom to drive faster.

When they pulled up at the Reece home, Tom kept the car running and honked until Eva and Sally and Henry came out. He let the driver's side window down just enough to speak to Eva. "Are you going up with us? Get the baby and Sharon settled?"

She shook her head, holding down her hair and smiling. "I'll come up a little later, but can Sally go with you? She's been driving me nuts asking when you'd be getting home!" Eva was shouting against the howl of the wind.

Tom nodded and waited for Eva to open the passenger side front door, helping Sally in, then she stepped back and waved and hurried back into the house.

When Sally was in, she turned around with her knees in the seat beside Tom and hung over the back. "Hi, Sharon. How's my little sister?"

Joel was still nervous, but he laughed at her. "She's your niece, sweetie. You didn't know that, huh? You're an aunt!"

Sally wrinkled her nose, and the spray of freckles on her cheeks rose to match her smile. "Is Henry an aunt, too?"

Sharon laughed at that, and from under the blanket, the baby let out a whimper, or a cry, then sneezed. "I guess Henry's an uncle," Sharon said, "as are your brothers Patrick and Detrick. Don't you think?"

"I guess," Sally said, turning around in the seat waiting for Tom to pull to a stop at the bottom of the hill. "Can I carry the baby?"

Joel shook his head, trying not to feel annoyed with her. Then he smiled, "You can help carry the baby's things, and Tom can help Sharon. I think I need to carry your little niece, okay?"

*   *   *

Their small house filled up with guests that evening, once the baby and Sharon were settled into the nursery. Eva, Douglas, and Henry came up after the sun went down, bringing food in covered dishes and setting them out on the kitchen table. Then JoAnna and Bill Hoffins came, as well, bringing gifts for the baby and for Sharon. Then Leo and Frank just happened to call, but when Joel told them they had brought the baby home, Leo asked if they could come see her. "I'm living in Deming, now, he said, but we'd love to come see this miracle child."

Although he did not want them to, Joel agreed. He did want to see Frank, and figured that once everyone got a look at the baby, maybe they'd be left in peace the rest of the week. Then Tom called Margaret and invited her out. "I guess we're having a homecoming for the baby and Sharon," he said.

So within a couple of hours after sundown, a dozen people filled their house, all looking in on the baby and trying to wait on Sharon. But at least she did not seem to be overwhelmed, so much as happy to see everyone. For that, Joel was relieved. But when he had a chance, he slipped off to check on Shara, and to make sure that she was asleep in her bassinet, or dry, or not crying.

At one point in the evening, Joel took JoAnna and Bill in to see the baby and held his breath while his old coach lifted the baby out of the bassinet and sat down in the bentwood rocker, and held his breath again, when JoAnna changed places with her husband, both of them adept at handling a newborn, and then Joel remembered their own son, and relaxed, knowing that their hearts must ache at the thought of having a child of their own, but having to keep him at the children's hospice.

Then later, he took them aside and related what the nurse had told him. "Have you heard of that church?"

Bill shook his head, but JoAnna said she had. "In fact, Joel, I was there at the hospital one day visiting Linton, and when I was checking on your own baby, there was a woman there who was asking which one was that—sorry for putting it like this, but asking which one was that homosexual's baby."

"Did they tell her?" Joel asked, feeling the prickling down his back again. "Any of the staff I mean?"

"They did not, and one old nurse threatened to have the police come and take her away."

Joel was relieved. "I guess that was Mrs. Blake, bless her heart. So you do know about the church. Where's it located? How many people do you think attend? Is it one of those new cult churches we've been hearing about? Or is it just another splinter off some church here in Common?"

"I don't know all that," JoAnna said, "but I can sure find out who the preacher is and how many people attend. Maybe even find out who some of the members are. But more to the point, I'll find out what kind of legal issues are involved."

"People in this town don't give a shit about abused children," Bill said, "or there wouldn't be as many kids at the hospice as there are, and you see poor kids in the schools every day with rags and sorry-assed lunches. So, I'm thinking the only thing you have to really worry about is that church stirring up some kind of trouble that won't mount to a hill of beans if you just ignore it."

"Thanks," Joel said, feeling not the least bit relieved, though he tried to put on a brave face with his friends. "I'm not in the mood to go through any of that religion bullshit again. Tom and I put that to rest five years ago."

Later on, when Bill and JoAnna and Douglas were visiting with Margaret, and Eva and Tom were doing the dishes, Joel sat down on the couch and visited with Leo and Frank. Tom was right, Leo was finally beginning to treat Frank with the kindness he deserved. In fact, Leo was beginning to fill out a little and to look less wispy and act less campy, and he was downright the model of social grace among the rest in their small house. When Frank was about to light a cigarette, Leo stopped him. "I don't think we better stink up their house with our smoke. We can go out on the porch if you want."

"I'll join you," Joel said and grabbed a Levi jacket off the coat rack next to the front door. A moment later it was just the three of them standing in the nippy air of the porch and looking out over the darkened silhouettes of the Florida mountains toward the east.

"Have you heard the latest on Barela?" Frank asked, once he'd lit a cigarette.

Joel said that he had not, having not thought about that for several weeks. "Has his trial date been set?"

"We go to court the beginning of April," Leo said. "I'm pressing charges, finally, for the beating that bitch gave me, and Frank is pressing charges for kidnapping and torture."

"We've also thrown in charges of rape," Frank said, snorting smoke through his nose, "but our lawyer says that would be less likely to carry any prison time; says a jury of the cop's peers just wouldn't think too much of it, and probably won't even know how a man can be raped."

Leo laughed one of his characteristic shrieks, then took a deep drag on his cigarette. "I could tell them how it's done, but who would take somebody like me that serious?"

Joel couldn't laugh. It was so true that Leo was rarely taken seriously, and he felt sorry for him, as he always had in school. He saw the old Leo under his new, more substantial appearance, the skinny kid with a lousy self-confidence. "Well when you go into court and testify, Leo, just give the jury a list of your injuries, and tell them how long it took for you to recover. They'll take that serious enough."

The front door opened just then and Henry stuck his head out. "Hey, Joel," he said, "Margaret's asking for ya."

"Tell her I'll be there in a minute, Henry. Is anything wrong?"

Henry shook his head and shut the door.

And so it went for the rest of the evening. Joel felt pulled in every direction, but he realized he was feeling less and less anxious with what the nurse had told him at the hospital. When everyone had finally left and it was just him and Tom, the baby, and Sharon, he let out a long breath, as if he'd been holding it the entire evening.

CHAPTER 18

A PHONE CALL AND A DEATH

Eva settled into the easy chair in the living room with a cup of coffee. Douglas and Henry were still outdoors. This late in March, the sun was up a little longer, and it was easier to believe that spring had finally arrived. She had a roast in the oven staying warm. The cooking dishes were done. Sally was up at Tom and Joel's, no doubt pestering them both about the baby, an image Eva laughed at as she took a sip of coffee. Slanting sunlight coming in through the west windows cast a golden, warm light in the otherwise darkened space where, Eva had to admit, she and Douglas spent entirely too much time now that the twins were off at college. But now that there was a newborn in the family, she figured she'd soon be sitting for the baby when Joel and Tom were working and Sharon returned to work at the café.

Eva took another sip of coffee, and thought about the twins. It seemed like they'd had them such a short time before they were finished with high school and out of sight, except for the holidays. It was odd, but she worried so much more about Detrick, down in West Texas than she did about Patrick, who had chosen the west coast for his schooling. Why exactly, she could not say, and of course she worried about them both. But Detrick just seemed more vulnerable. Maybe because he had taken so much longer than Patrick to fit in well, here, when they were adopted.

Even the way Henry and Sally were growing up alarmed Eva, and then it would be little Shara, first learning to walk, then walking out the door on her first day of school. But for this evening, for just a little while as she watched the gathering gloom of late afternoon settle inside the house, she was as content as a mother could be.

Then the telephone rang, right beside her, nearly causing her to spill her coffee. She grasped the front of her blouse, laughing at herself. "My goodness, I've become jumpy," she said aloud. On the second ring, she leaned over slightly to retrieve the receiver from the base and brought it to her left ear.

"Eva Reece," she said, as had become her habit in the last few years. She didn't know why she had become more formal, but it got a lot of nonsense out of the way. "Hello?"

There was breathing on the other end, then, "Mrs. Reece? This is Livia Allen. I don't know if you'll remember me. I'm Mrs. Allen…Thomas' mother."

Eva jumped again, though inwardly, but her breath caught in her throat, so unexpected was the call. "Tom's mother? My Tom?"

"Uh, yes, if that's the way you see it."

Eva felt like slamming the phone down as she had done many years before in her last conversation with the woman. She took a deep breath as she held the receiver away from her mouth. "It is the way I see it, Mrs. Allen, after all"—

"I'm sorry, Mrs. Reece. I do not mean to offend. I hope Thomas is still with you. He is, isn't he?"

"Well, yes. He and my son, Joel, are still together in their own home." In a way, Eva hoped that her own words offended, just a little.

"I'm relieved to hear that, Mrs. Reece."

A moment of silence ensued, leaving Eva with no real response. She wondered why Mrs. Allen would be calling in the first place. She waited. Then, very faintly on the other end, she heard what must be crying, though it was almost imperceptible.

"Mrs. Allen? What is the matter? You have left me a little confused."

A moment passed. "I'm sorry. This is difficult for me, considering how we left things, before. I do not mean to intrude on your lives. It's just that my husband has recently died, and I thought Thomas should know."

Eva collected her thoughts, now that the conversation was more focused. She felt a welling up of anger since, as Livia Allen had just alluded to, things had been left extremely bad for Tom the last time they talked. Something like "until Tom can change his ways, I consider my son dead." But under the circumstances, she could not remind the woman of that. "What would you have me do, Mrs. Allen? Would you like for Tom to call you? Do you want me to pass on this information?"

"No. I"—A moment more of silence and the barely audible crying. "I am here in Common. I would like to see him."

"Oh! My!" Eva said, involuntarily. "Then you have already buried your husband?"

"His body has been shipped back to Waco, to be placed in the family mausoleum. Our church held a memorial for him, but it was not quite the same. I do not want to move back to Texas. I am not certain what I would like to do...other than make amends to Thomas."

"That will have to be Tom's decision, then," Eva said, trying and failing to hold back any sympathy she felt fighting its way past the anger she had harbored against this woman. "Do you have a number?"

Mrs. Allen gave Eva the telephone number of the motel where she was staying, then "I...you must realize, Mrs. Reece, that my husband was a powerful individual, would brook no...ah...disobedience, either from Thomas or myself. So now that he has left me, as it happens, I find that my finances are not nearly as set as I had believed."

Again, came a wave of sympathy from Eva. "But surely he had life insurance? A savings?"

"Some. Yes. But a preacher's salary in these small congregations. Well, they never paid much. So, as well, I find I must stay in this climate. My asthma...I must take that into consideration. I was hoping to find some sort of employment here or nearby, because despite how we might have left things a few years ago, I want to be near my son. I really have no other family that I care to"—

"I see," Eva said, interrupting Mrs. Allen. "Excuse me a moment." She took a sip of coffee. It had grown cold in the cup, and the darkness of dusk was beginning to settle into the living room. Just a faint glow of sunlight still shone in the sky through the small west windows. For reasons beyond her own immediate understanding, Eva was upset at the prospect of having Mrs. Allen back in Tom's life. Perhaps, she thought, taking another sip of coffee and regretting its bitter taste, he had become like a son to her as well, and she felt threatened. The call had come so suddenly, so unexpectedly. She closed her eyes, took a breath, and spoke into the phone: "I cannot promise you, Mrs. Allen, that Tom will even want to see you, after all these years. You and your husband left a quite broken-hearted young man, and you never so much as once tried to make amends when it would have mattered most."

"I realize that, I thought I had explained"—

"No, Mrs. Allen. You have not explained it—at least not to my satisfaction—but that is not for me to judge. You must explain it to your...son's satisfaction. So I will tell him you called and give him the number. If he is amenable to seeing you, I will go along with his wishes and, if you are in as difficult a position as you say, concerning your finances, I will see what I can do to help you find employment of some sort. But let's let Tom speak with you first."

"Thank you, Mrs. Reece," Livia Allen said. "I won't leave my room until I hear from him. It will be this evening, do you think?"

*   *   *

Eva made the short trek up to Tom and Joel's house, instead of calling to send Sally home for supper. It was a lovely time of the day, now that the interminable wind had calmed down. She passed through her garden, quickly, trying not to think of the work ahead of her with the planting and such, but set her feet quickly one after the other, feeling dread at what the arrival of Mrs. Allen (she could not think of her as Tom's mother) meant, what it would mean—if anything.

Yet she also felt a kind of gladness that Tom might be able to retrieve something he had lost, if he chose to have his mother back in his life. She wondered what the woman would think of being a grandmother. With that thought, she felt a wave of sympathy for her, knowing as she had that her gay son was unlikely to ever give her grandchildren, although now he had. She hoped the woman had enough sense to appreciate it, and not find something sinful in the fact that her grandchild was born out of wedlock.

Outside the garden, on the north side, she entered Douglas' domain. She passed the work shop, where he and his sons maintained the farm equipment. It was lined up in rows: harrows, deep-cut plows, cultivators, cotton pickers, tractors, planters. She passed the new barn, which Douglas had built a few years before when he decided that, with all his new children, he could afford to expand his operation. Then she was walking along the road that led into the east fields, crossing over the irrigation canal that carried water from the irrigation pond to the fields, and finally came to the driveway that led to her son's house.

Sally was playing on the porch, barely visible under the porch light.

"Sally!" Eva called, as she walked through the gate at the bottom of the hill. "Why don't you run on to the house and set the table? Dad and Henry should be in soon."

Sally ran past, "Okay!" and Eva reached out affectionately to swat her bottom, which she missed as cleanly as she always did. Eva felt less cheerful than she let on, but walked up the flagstones and entered the house.

They all greeted each other. Eva said hello to Sharon and cooed at the baby, which Sharon was feeding on the couch, and then Eva went straight for the heart of the matter.

"Tom, your mother just called. She's here in Common at the Lamplight Inn." She pulled a slip of paper from her apron pocket, handing it to him, catching a glimpse of his face in the yellow light. It was blank, though his eyes narrowed a little.

"She called? Just now?" Tom asked. His voice was shaking, and Eva knew right then that he had never been able to get over the hurt his parents had caused him. She almost regretted having given him the news.

"Your father has passed away and she needs to talk to you, Tom. I would tell you more, but I believe you need to hear it from her."

She noted and approved that Joel automatically put his arm around Tom's shoulders. They were sitting side-by-side on the other couch, and she was glad that her part in this was now over, glad that Joel was there for him. She nodded and turned. "I've got dinner on, if you would like to join us." She included Sharon in the nod.

"Sharon's going to show us one of her soup recipes," Joel said, "once Shara's been put to bed. But thanks, anyway."

*   *   *

Joel walked down the hill with Tom and kissed him. "Will you be all right, honey?" he asked, giving Tom a long hug.

Tom hugged him back. "I guess so," he said, and got into the pickup.

Joel watched as Tom drove off. The news of Tom's mother, back in town after what, three years, reminded him of that difficult time for Tom, the way the preacher Allen had kept them apart, then when Tom had stood up to his father, the way the preacher and his wife had disowned him. Nothing, however, could cause Tom to totally give them up, and news that his mother was in town and wanted to see him was all Tom had needed. All the years of trying to get over them and his brave protests to the contrary, he was anxious to see his mother again. Even though Joel didn't know what his own mother thought of it, he was plagued by the same sense of dread as she; and like his mother, he knew it would have to be Tom's decision to let Mrs. Allen back into his life.

Joel returned to the house, and it felt very odd, suddenly, for him to be at home, without Tom and, instead, coming in to Sharon and the baby. In a weird twist, he could imagine what it would have been like had he been straight and was living with his wife and child. But the thought left him feeling uncomfortable. He sat down a moment later on the couch opposite Sharon. She had finished nursing Shara and had put her to bed. After a moment of silence, he smiled. "Well, I guess you understood that Tom's mother is down at the Lamplight Inn. This is the first time he has seen her, Sharon, in at least three years."

Sharon's face lost its smile, and she nodded gravely. "I hope that this meeting goes well, Joel. It is a hurtful thing to have one's mother turn her back."

"Do you think Tom should welcome her just like that?" Joel asked. His own resentment was too great to know what the right thing was.

His question brought a frown to Sharon's face. "You know, Joel, I would wish my own parents would know this…ah…how do you mean make a real…real?"

"Realize?" Joel asked. "You wish your own parents would realize…?"

"Yes!" Sharon said. "I wish my own parents would realize that it hurts to lose them. They have put their religion in front of their love for me."

"Yeah," Joel said, smiling wistfully at Sharon. "That's exactly what Tom's parents did, too. They disowned him. Or shunned him as your parents did you. He was so hurt. His mother said she considered him dead, as long as he wouldn't give me up, and give up his notion that he was gay."

"This is horrible!" Sharon said. In the lamp light of the living room her blonde hair and her face shone. Her hair was what his mother might have called a honey blonde, and he noticed it had highlights of almost white hair. Her lips were pursed, but looking at her, Joel thought how pretty she was, and he remembered kissing those lips, finding for the first time in his life that kissing a woman was pleasurable. Of course, he reminded himself that, by the time he had kissed Sharon, he was already aroused by the tequila and by the fact that Tom had gone first with her in an attempt to make a baby. Still, for a moment, he remembered.

There were tears in Sharon's eyes, but she was smiling at him. "This is why it is so much of importance for Tom to be with his mother," she said. "She has, after all this time, made a try to realize, maybe the hurt she has caused, and wished she had not."

"Yeah. The wish," he said. He remembered times when he and Tom would be in the grocery store and might run into Tom's parents. Tom would either pull Joel back into another aisle in an attempt to hide from them, or on nights when he was feeling defiant, he would push their cart, with Joel following quickly behind him, right behind his parents and tell them hello. Not one time that Joel recalled, did either his father or his mother ever acknowledge Tom's existence, even when he spoke their names. And for this, Tom always got hurt, though many times he tried to pretend he wasn't. Even when he laughed about the incident later, there was the same sort of hurt defiance in his voice as had been in Margaret's when she talked of her father.

"But you can understand, can't you, Sharon, that Tom might have his hopes crushed again? What if she has come to lay blame on him for his father's death?"

She nodded. "That is a chance he has to take, I suppose, Joel. But if that's the case, then a break with her this time will probably be more final for him."

True, Joel thought, but his stomach was in knots for Tom, anyway. He looked at the clock on the wall behind Tom's desk. Through the front door he saw it was completely dark and, in his mind's eye, Tom and his mother were having at it in an even more dimly lit motel room.

✳   ✳   ✳

For an instant, Tom did not recognize the woman that stood before him at the doorway to the motel room, and he thought he'd knocked on the wrong door. She was not only thin, the way his mother always had been, but gaunt, almost skeletal. But he recognized the powder blue dress almost immediately, one that his mother wore for church services and for special dinners, when his father had invited over this or that elder or deacon and their wives. Tom even had a photograph tucked away somewhere at home of his mother in that dress, and yet it hung on her frame, now, as though it were a hand-me down.

It brought tears to Tom's eyes at the change he saw in her.

"Mother?"

She smiled, but it was wan. She stepped back, rather than toward him. "Come in, Thomas. I am glad that you decided to come see me."

Her voice was the same soft-spoken, hesitant voice that she had always used, especially when she was nervous, and he could not think of a single time, at the moment, that he had ever heard his mother laugh out loud as Eva Reece did.

But he hesitated. He wanted to run. He took a deep breath and stepped into the room with her, shutting the door behind him. Then forcing himself to risk rejection, he pulled her to him and hugged her, feeling how thin she was beneath her clothing. For a moment, she allowed herself to be hugged, and Tom was afraid that she was going to pull away. If she did, he would release her, turn on his heel, and walk out. He did not think he could stand it, if she could not return his hug, even though she had always been withdrawn and still.

Then she did hug him, so hard, he felt his breath squeezed in his chest. She clung to his neck. "You've changed so much, Thomas! You are positively a grown man. So strong," she said, finally releasing him.

They looked at each other as they never had before. It hasn't been that long since you and father were here in Common, Mother. I couldn't have changed that much."

She moved away then and sat in one of the chairs next to the bed, looking up at him. "It has been three years, Thomas. And I didn't see you very much when I was here, after…" She trailed off. "Please, sit." She indicated the bed.

Her suitcase still lay on the foot of the bed, apparently unopened, and he wondered if she had been afraid to unpack, if he had not agreed to see her.

Tom felt sweat trickle under his jacket from his armpits. His back had broken out in a cold sweat as well. But he no longer wanted to run. There was so much to say to his mother, and he was afraid that much of it would be said in anger.

"Was it a heart attack or something?" he asked, almost desperate to keep their conversation moving.

She shook her head. "A stroke. An aneurysm. It was sudden, and the doctors said he did not suffer any pain. You know how red he would get when he was angry, how his veins would pop out on his forehead, how controlled he was?"

And controlling, Tom wanted to add. But that could wait, even though he knew now that he would tell her that. "Didn't you think I might want to go to his funeral, Mother? Couldn't you have at least relented in that? I loved Father, even if he did disown me."

She raised both hands, as if to ward off his anger. "Please, Thomas. I know it was wrong of me not to have a funeral for him. But I didn't wait for that. As soon as he was dead, I instructed the hospital to ship his body back to Texas. I'm letting his family take care of him, now."

Tom was surprised at this, but did not ask her why she didn't have a funeral. That too would come later, he supposed. "I don't understand," he said, in reference to what she had just said. "You obviously had your reasons, if even you didn't want a funeral. But I guess that's somehow not really important right now, is it?"

"No, it is not." Her voice was surprisingly strong in response. "What is important to me, and I hope to you, Thomas, is that we can have some time together. I know you are hurt and angry with me. But I am hurt, as well. I have dreamed of this moment for many years…I…"

She got up and opened the suitcase. Her mouth was set, but there were tears in her eyes as she moved aside some things in the suitcase and pulled out a much creased white envelope. She unfolded it and pulled out a scrap of paper that looked as if it had been torn from a spiral notebook. She looked at it a moment, as if she intended to read it, but she handed it to him. "I have kept this with me, Thomas. I have thought about this letter from you for so long, and have hoped"—her voice caught on a sob.

As soon as Tom took the sheet of paper and looked at the words on it, he recognized his own boyish hand, remembering the details of that afternoon when he had hurriedly written the letter to his mother. From deep down within, a sob began, coming up from his stomach, as though he were retching, then it rushed into his chest, causing him to shudder. Tears sprang from his eyes. "You've kept this? You read it that day and you kept it? But I thought you hated me for what I'd done, defying Father." He could hardly speak, his throat filling with the sob, choking him.

She sat beside him on the bed and smoothed his hair. "I have never stopped loving you, Thomas. Never. Even when I had to say things, as I did to Mrs. Reece. Your father was there when I talked to her. Your father"—

Tears welled up in Tom's eyes as he listened to her try to explain. But he was not crying for the hurt that she had caused him, but the hurt that she herself had to endure from her husband, the preacher. He could not blame her for her silence of the last five years. Not at all, because it had taken a great effort for him to defy his father. If it hadn't been for Joel and the love he promised, Tom knew he would not have been able to break away from his father, either. How much harder it must have been for her. The evidence was sitting before him, gaunt and frail.

Oh, yes, there was so much to talk about, so much to learn, so much to say, and no doubt many tears to go.

*　　　　　*　　　　　*

It was near midnight, as it turned out, before Tom got home. Joel had been worried in a way, but as the hours passed and Tom had not called, he became more and more certain that this first meeting with his mother was going well. Otherwise, he figured, it would have been a short, devastating meeting, and Tom would have left in anger or hurt or both.

Sharon had sat up with Joel until almost eleven o'clock, but had finally begun to feel tired, and Joel gently told her she needed to rest.

"Would you not like the company?" Sharon asked.

But Joel shook his head and kissed her lightly on the forehead. "Goodnight."

Then he was alone in the living room and his thoughts returned to Tom. Finally, when he heard the pickup drive up, he didn't know if he should go outdoors and meet him or wait in the house. But even as he was debating, Tom came through the door.

At first, when he saw Tom, Joel's heart lurched. His eyes were red from crying, and he looked very tired, as though he had been in a sustained argument. But when he smiled and hugged him, Joel knew that his meeting must have gone well.

Of course there would be tears, he thought. How could there not be? Still, when Tom sat beside him on the sofa, Joel said, "I take it you and your mother had a good meeting?"

Tom sat forward, as Joel had seen him do so many times, with his forearms resting on his thighs then looking at him intently. He smiled, however. "It was so much better than I could have hoped. All these years I thought that Mother had taken my father's side, Joel. But she hadn't." Then he looked sad. "She looks terrible. She is so skinny, babe, I almost didn't recognize her. She's been eating herself up from the inside."

"And what does she think of you and me?" he asked.

"She was actually great about it, tonight, babe. She said she'd had many years to think about it. She said that if I was willing to be disowned by my family all for the love of someone, she could not condemn it, herself, and it was up to God in his grace and mercy to judge me." Tom smiled as he was saying this. But Joel could imagine how it would be with his mother—both she and Tom having come from such a strict religious background.

Tom, of course, had been able in the last few years to see through much of the doctrine of such a fundamentalist teaching. Through his and Joel's continual contact with the Unitarians in Common, and with their ever growing friendship with the Rev. Suskine and Bill and JoAnna Hoffins, Tom had come round to a much more enlightened way of viewing Christianity, per se, and religion in general. Joel had to admit, even though he was no closer to believing in any of it, that the religious urge and how it helped many people through life was something that should not be condemned nor scoffed at. *For those who need it,* Joel reminded himself.

"Did you tell her she's a grandmother?"

At that, Tom grinned. "I waited until we'd mulled over all the hurt of our past, and after she'd told me why she did not want to move back to Texas with Father's family. I'll let her tell you about that one of these days, Joel. But to your question, I finally told her what you and I had been doing these past few years, building up to the big news, you know?"

Joel nodded, smiling.

"I told her how much you had always wanted children, to see what she would think of the idea. And she did object, saying she didn't know if that would be good for the child."

"That's really understandable," Joel said. "I can't blame her for fearing that, even though I know we're going to be great fathers. So…?"

"So I asked her how she would feel if I told her she was a grandmother." Tom looked sad for a moment. "Just the question made her cry, honey, and she said she knew it was never going to happen since I was the only child, so then I just blurted it out. I said, 'well, guess what, mother? You *are* a grandmother.'"

"And how did she feel about that?"

"Well, she cried even harder, but this time I don't think it was from sadness, though I'm sure, at first, she was afraid to believe it, or she just couldn't grasp that it was true!" Tom laughed for the first time like the young boyish lover he had been when they had first gotten together. So, I invited her out. If you think it's all right."

Joel did not hesitate to answer. "Of course it is, honey. I can't believe that Shara is gaining grandmothers by the day!"

CHAPTER 19

THE VISIT

It was the first Sunday since Sharon had been released from the hospital, and the first day she had returned to work at the Red Rooster. Margaret had not wanted to push her but Sharon had insisted, saying that things had to get back to normal. Now that the baby was home, she told Margaret, she needed to get her strength back.

Tom was helping his mother get settled into a house he had helped her find and, when they were done, he was bringing her out to the house to meet her granddaughter. So, Joel was at home alone with Shara. It was the first time he had had the baby all to himself, and now he had her on his and Tom's bed in the back part of the house. He had bathed her and fed her a bottle of Sharon's milk, which she had put aside, for times when she was not there to nurse the baby. He was lying on his side, just studying Shara as she slept in her little pink jumper with the feet in them, like a kid's pajamas. It was warm in the room and so he had taken off the blanket so he could see her better. She was gripping his finger with her little hand, which was no bigger than the end of his thumb. It was amazing, Joel thought, how perfect her little fingers were, including the minute fingernails, the little knuckles, and the back of her hand. It was no more than three inches from her wrist to her little elbow, and just another few inches to her little shoulder.

There were tears in his eyes as he studied her hands, her face, and watched her stomach rise and fall in such rapid breaths, he thought he'd hyperventilate if he breathed that fast. He had tried to synchronize his breathing with hers, just to see what it would feel like, and he couldn't keep up.

He laid his head on her chest, careful not to put any pressure on her, and listened to her heart beating, as rapidly as she was breathing, and again he was amazed. He cupped the entire top of her head in his palm, feeling the utter softness of her brown, almost black, hair.

"Oh, honey, you are so precious," he whispered, unconscious of his own beautiful face, and the look of utter love in his eyes for his little daughter. Shara Margaret Minninger Allen-Reece. That's who she was, although her birth certificate said her last name was Minninger and that he, Joel Hale Reece, was the father.

We did things backwards, Joel thought. They should have first had their last names changed legally to Allen-Reece, so that the birth certificate would have also included Tom's last name. Although Tom said he didn't mind, Joel minded a little. *We should have done that first*, he thought, *then* had a child. He would never have married a woman just so his child would bear his last name. But now, he did want to find some symbolic way to show that Sharon was part of their lives, as he and Tom had done by wearing their wedding rings. But of course he did not want the wedding band to be that symbol. That was reserved for him and Tom. He agreed with Tom that *official* pieces of paper like birth certificates and marriage licenses were not the true measure of real life. He and Tom were not legally bound to each other, except in their wills. They were not legally married and would likely never be. But in the end, it simply didn't matter. They were married in every other sense.

He had what he wanted, now. A family. Him and Tom and Shara. A troubled looked passed over his face as he watched his daughter sleeping. Their little family did include Sharon in a way, but he didn't know quite where to place her. At the hospital, when she had handed Shara up to him, she said, "Here is your baby, Joel." Just as Tom did, he took that to mean that she was holding up her end of the bargain. She had offered to have a child for them and had agreed to their terms.

But the reality was, Joel didn't want Sharon to relinquish her daughter. Shara needed a mother, too.

Oh, he had planned on finding someone who would carry their child and then disappear, but it wouldn't be right, no matter how you sliced it. He hoped Sharon would not disappear from her daughter's life—or theirs. She was too special, too downright beautifully wonderful for that.

He was glad that Tom agreed, and they were glad that Sharon seemed to feel the same way about them. She would go to college and be free of the responsibility of a child for as long as it took. But she was also free to return here any time she was ready.

He picked up the baby, trying not to wake her, and scooted up to the head of the bed, lying on his back, placing Shara on his chest, and covering her with the blanket. He shut his eyes and breathed in the fragrance of her little body, the powder and lotion and her skin. He felt her thumping heart in his chest and her breath on his neck, as he fell asleep.

*   *   *

When Tom brought his mother home, he had decided that she should see the way he and Joel interacted. They would not change the way they greeted each other or where they sat, or even if they kissed each other. So, when he walked his mother to the house, up the flagstones, and opened the front door, he called out: "Babe? We're here!" Then he let her walk into their house ahead of him, expecting to see Joel standing in the living room or coming out of the kitchen.

But she stood in the middle of the living room, catching his eye and smiling nervously. Joel did not appear.

"Maybe he's in the nursery," he said, and opened the door. Neither Joel nor the baby were there. "Sorry, Mother," he said, "I guess Joel has gone off somewhere. Would you like a cup of tea? Coffee?"

She agreed and he led her into the kitchen. Then he saw down the short hall that led to their bathroom and bedroom that their bedroom door was open, and he could just make out Joel's bare feet on the end of the bed. Fear clutched him, suddenly, because if Joel was taking a nap, where was the baby?

He left his mother standing in the kitchen and quickly walked into the bedroom, then he smiled and motioned for her. "You've got to see this!" he said, standing aside.

Joel and the baby were asleep. All that was visible of Shara was her little head, nestled into Joel's neck. The rest of her was covered with the small blanket and Joel's hand. His mother smiled, and Tom was surprised that she tiptoed to the edge of the bed, at first just standing there, looking down on her grandchild, her hands clasped in front of her. Then she reached down and tried to take Shara from Joel's chest.

Joel came awake slowly, his hand tightening on the baby, until he opened his eyes, blinking, and then, "Oh!" he said, surprised. "Oh! Mrs. Allen."

A moment later, he sat up still holding Shara, then handed her to Tom's mother. "Meet Shara Margaret."

*   *   *

Later, when the baby had been changed, again, after waking up and being fed a little more, Tom, Livia, and Joel sat in the living room. Reminding himself of his earlier decision that they should not change the way they interacted, Tom had sat down by Joel on the couch and offered his mother the other couch. Joel had raised his eyebrows at this, but Tom just winked.

His mother did not give any indication, one way or another, that this bothered her and, in fact, they were now having what seemed to be a long-needed conversation. Livia had been talking to both of them, but more importantly, Tom thought, she was telling Joel about her life with her husband. Tom realized that he'd been right when he had lived at home to think that his mother was just as much a prisoner of his father's iron-fisted control as he was.

"It was not so much that I didn't have a choice, Joel. I could have left him many times, and perhaps I should have. But I also had Thomas to think about. There were times I just wanted to take him and leave, but then I would think, what am I going to do with a ten-year old son and try to work. I don't have a supportive family in my own parents and never did. Not like it appears that you have. Nor was my husband's family any more inclined to offer a way out. So I felt I was stuck. When Thomas left to be with you, I guess I had just gotten used to Milton's abuse."

"Did he abuse you, Mother?" Tom asked, his gut wrenching.

She looked at him and smiled sadly. "Not physically, dear, not like that at all. But think of your own experiences. That is how I felt."

After a while, their conversation drifted back to the baby, and Livia said, "Thank you. Both of you for allowing me the pleasure of seeing your child." Her eyes crinkled with pleasure in a way that Joel had never seen in the few times he had spent at her house. "I know it is a mystery who the father really is, and that must have been the way you intended it." She clutched her blouse and gave off a small laugh, a kind of surprise, Tom thought, at herself "Listen to me, will you? My husband would have popped a vein at this situation, but I think it is rather amusing." Then her eyes crinkled even more. "But it is my opinion, having got a good look at Shara, that she has Tom's hair and his mouth!"

Tom glanced worriedly at Joel, wondering if he would like the notion that it might not be his baby. But Joel was nodding. "I think she does, too, Mrs. Allen. But if she's short, like me, or maybe if she has my eye color, once they change, then we'll just have to wonder all over again."

Tom studied Joel for a moment, noting that he had bathed and shaved for his mother's visit. He was wearing a clean pair of Levi's and a favorite, casual Hawaiian shirt. His tanned skin, the smooth shaven glow of his jaw, and his slicked down blond hair radiated his youth and vitality, which never failed to take Tom's breath away.

Livia smiled at Joel's rejoinder about who Shara favored. "You were always one of my favorites, Joel, of Thomas' friends. But do you know why?"

"No, ma'am," Joel said, seeming embarrassed by Livia's sudden change of subject.

"Well, I will tell you. It is precisely because you had a way of teaching Thomas that he did not have to completely subdue himself to his father."

"But I didn't try to do that!" Joel said. Again, he seemed embarrassed.

She held up a hand, nodding. "Oh, I know you did not, intentionally, but as your friendship with Thomas blossomed, he was sometimes distracted from his religious duties, just so he could be with you. So, I knew you were having a positive effect on him. You see, when we moved out here to this part of the country, even my husband was worried that Thomas was too delicate…that is, he seemed to have no real ambition. Of course, I thought of it as a lack of self-identity, and he always gave in to my husband's least demands. He was not in any way a rebellious teenager."

She turned to Tom with a determined look in her eye. "And that worried me, dear. You didn't know that, did you? That I would worry that you were not having a normal teenage life?"

Tom was surprised. "But you always told me to do as my father said. You said he knew what was best."

His mother nodded again. "Yes, I did, after awhile. But you do not know how I tried to raise you. Perhaps by the time we had moved here, I had given up."

She looked at Joel. "Until you came along, Joel. That's when I saw Thomas becoming his own person, and I was secretly happy about that."

Tom sat back against Joel's arm, which was on the back of the couch, and Joel dropped his arm down on Tom's shoulder. For just a second, Tom felt uncomfortable, but it was a natural movement for Joel, and so Tom settled into his shoulder. He still could not believe that he could be this way in front of his mother in their living room. That she was in his home, at all, after five years of being estranged, was also miraculous, Tom thought. Yes, there was going to be plenty of time for him and his mother to get reacquainted, and for her to get to know her granddaughter and Joel. But Tom still had questions about how much she was able to accept him. It was difficult to believe she was not still the estranged mother she had been for the last five years. He hoped she was not hiding her real feelings about them, afraid to criticize him for fear he would now shun her.

But wouldn't that be trading one kind of subservience to her husband for a kind of subservience to him? Tom shook off this thought as soon as it came to him. He would just have to trust her, hoping she was as happy to see him as she seemed.

"Would you like some more tea, Mrs. Allen?" Joel asked.

She nodded. "Yes, thank you. But may I ask, if you don't mind, Joel, to call me Livia? I think we should be less formal. Formality, even at home was something my husband insisted on, but I never felt comfortable being so formal around people, unless it was among the elders of the church, or it was a formal dinner."

Joel sighed and smiled. "That's fine with me, Mrs.—Livia. My parents are about as far from formal as you can get."

They spent a pleasant hour or so getting reacquainted but, as the sun began to fall toward the west, Sally and Eva came into the house to invite everyone to dinner. The baby woke up, and Eva took Livia into the nursery. "You might as well start pitching in with your grandchild," Eva said, with laughter in her voice. "I tried to warn the boys about a newborn's cycle of sleeping, eating, messing, and then doing it all over again."

Livia laughed with Eva as she followed her. Sally sat on the couch with Tom and Joel for a minute or two, but she could not stand it, and soon went into the baby's room as well.

Left alone for a moment, Tom kissed Joel. "I think our visit with Mother went well, don't you think?"

Joel kissed him back. "I'm glad she came back to Common, honey. I'm sorry your father died without knowing his grandchild."

Tom was about to say, "I'm not," but then thought better of it, because a part of him was still saddened by his death, still haunted by the thought of what could have been. But he brightened. "At least Mother is here, and that's worth so much to me, and to her, too, I hope."

＊   ＊   ＊

Later, Eva and Sally took Shara up to the main house, and Tom and Joel took Livia on a short tour of the home farm. They drove her around the fields and showed her the equipment, Eva's garden, the barn and livestock, and told her about the other farms that were part of Reece Farms, Inc.

"And are you a part of this…this enterprise?" Livia asked Tom. They were driving to a stop at the bottom of the hill. Her eyes shone with surprise and pride.

Tom laughed. "Yes, Mother, I am. Mom and Dad Reece consider me part of the family, and they consider me Joel's mate, as surely as they consider their daughters' husbands part of the family. They've all treated me very well over these last few years."

"You were lucky and blessed, then," his mother said. "I think it is shameful that my husband and his family all agreed to disown you and write you out of their wills."

"Is that why you are not returning to Texas?" Tom asked. Joel heard a sob in his voice and hoped he wasn't about to cry.

Livia patted his leg, then withdrew it to the middle of her lap where she kept her hands folded. "That is certainly a great part of it, dear." She leaned forward, speaking directly to Joel. "I want you to know, Joel, that I went along with my husband. That was my duty as his wife. But in my heart, I never gave up on Thomas. Milton is the one who lost out."

Joel sighed again and felt tears sting his own eyes. He looked at Livia and smiled, then rolled to a stop and shut off the engine. "I'm glad you didn't give up on Tom…ah…Livia. He's a great man."

Her eyes crinkled, again, with the smile that became more frequent as the afternoon came to a close. "Thank you for sticking with my son. I had always heard that…such as you…were flighty and undependable, which is one of the reasons my church…" she trailed off.

"There's good and bad in all people," was all Joel could think to say, and he too grew quiet as they made their way into the yard.

"Finally," Joel said to Livia, "I hope you've noticed our little yard, here. When Tom and I first moved in, while I was out working in the fields, he spent the first few months doing all the yard work by himself. He laid most of the flagstones and did most of the terracing of the yard."

Tom nodded, appreciating the fact that Joel was being so generous in his description of how their yard had come to its present condition. "Joel's not being entirely truthful, Mother," he said. "Everyone worked on it. Douglas used one of his tractors to dig up all the mesquites. The twins helped me a lot in carrying in the flagstones. Joel and I built the fence around it."

"But you did dig most of the post holes," Joel said. "Don't be so modest, babe. Your mother needs to know that you're not lazy."

"Oh! I never thought that," Livia said, taking Joel's teasing too seriously. "I remember that summer when Thomas was out here helping you take care of the place while your parents were on vacation. Milton came back beaming."

It was the summer when all hell broke loose, Tom recalled. He wondered at his mother's reasons for mentioning that particular summer, but he decided not to interrupt.

"Of course, it was shortly after that, when that horrible boy took those pictures of you and Joel," Livia said. "What was his name, Thomas?"

Tom felt his stomach clench at the direction his mother was taking the conversation. "That was Paul. Leon Romaine's son."

She nodded vigorously. "Yes, that's him. He was a trouble maker, and he just could not let things proceed at their own pace. I really hated the way it all came down around our ears, Thomas. Your father was so embarrassed and therefore angered by it."

Again, Tom was wary of the direction his mother was moving.

"Father would have been angry no matter when he found out about me, Mother. I blame Paul only for being a spiteful sneak, but not in what happened once Father found out about me and Joel."

His mother frowned. "You are right, Thomas. Your father was unbendable, regardless of the entreaties I made on your behalf. Joel, I don't want you to think I supported my husband in this."

So that was it, Tom thought, and he wanted to wrap his arms around his mother's thin shoulders. She had continued to feel guilty about the way his father and she had treated him after they found out, and she was trying to show that she had had no choice.

Tom did not want her to try to justify herself. "Mother, please. You don't have to feel guilty about all those years. They were lost years as far as Father is concerned, because he's no longer alive. You and I have the rest of our lives to set things right with each other. Let's just be thankful for that and forget the past."

"And you think we can do that, Thomas?"

*　　　　*　　　　*

Joel wished that he was anywhere else, at the moment. He felt as if he were intruding on a very private conversation between Tom and Livia.

*　　　　*　　　　*

Tom was glad Joel was there to hear this. He looked over at him, smiling, as they entered the front porch, but he saw that Joel was uncomfortable. When he was uneasy in a situation, Joel's cheeks turned splotchy red, despite his deep tan.

"Who knows," Tom said, "Maybe one of these days even my aunts and uncles and all my cousins will come around."

His mother smiled sadly. "Maybe they will, Thomas. We can only pray that they do." Something in her voice, however, told Tom that they would not.

CHAPTER 20

BETRAYAL

Livia Allen was pushing fifty when she returned to Common, New Mexico, as a widow and a new grandmother. But after having met with Tom and visiting with Joel and his family, which had made loving room for her granddaughter Shara Margaret, she felt young again. It was all just a matter of perspective she thought as she went through her husband's clothes. Pulling them out of boxes the men had packed for the moving van.

Tom had found her a lovely house, she thought, in the neighborhood near the church where her husband had been a preacher for a couple of years. It was attached by a breezeway to the old Victorian where her new landlord, a widow by the name of Mrs. Cox, lived. But Mrs. Cox called it an apartment when she showed it to her, hovering over her and Tom as they looked through it. "I do hope you like it, Mrs. Allen," the old lady said. "I'm delighted to have such as yourself renting it. It's so difficult to find responsible adults, you know. I tried renting to the seasonal farm laborers a few years ago, but they lived like animals if you want to know my opinion. Being so far from the university, it was not practical to rent to students, either, though I can't say as I would have, anyway; they're irresponsible, if you ask my opinion."

She had led them through the large living room, which had a fireplace, but which had been converted to gas, into a large kitchen with what looked like nearly new appliances. When Livia had remarked on them, the old lady said how she had swapped them out of a house she had sold recently. "An awful part of town, but my husband was always thinking about my later years," she said.

"He was a lovely man, but stricken with emphysema, you know. Terrible disease, and so debilitating."

Off the kitchen was a dining room on the south side of the house that could have been bright, had it not been for the breezeway that shadowed its French windows. Livia had directed the moving men to set up her own dining room set, there, but she had not yet oiled the surface of the table. It was still covered with open, half-emptied boxes.

"I can remove the furniture when your own arrives, dear," Mrs. Cox had said, standing between Tom and his mother when they were looking at the main bedroom. "But for now will you need a bed…or two?" she asked, looking oddly at Tom.

"Just one," Livia had told her.

"But you have two bedrooms." she insisted, again looking at Tom.

"The other will be my office."

"Then I am relieved," Mrs. Cox said, her voice going up to match her eyebrows. "I take it you're not moving in here with your mother, are you?" she asked frowning at Tom. "I don't hold with young men such as yourself coming home to roost, if you know what I mean."

Tom had tickled the old lady with his response. "No, ma'am. I have my own place. And to tell you the truth, I wouldn't want my mother living with me, either, so you needn't worry."

In the second bedroom, which was a bit smaller than the first, Livia had set up her husband's office furniture, though she intended to go through all of his papers and the tracts he had written over the years and donate them to the divinity school where he had received his doctorate. She would, in fact, rid herself of as much of his presence as she could, she thought, as the pile of his clothing grew as she emptied several boxes.

She was sitting on the sofa in the living room with the bright overhead light burning. Even though it was midday, the large trees in the small yard outside the living room window blocked much of the light. She would be glad, she thought, as she tossed his clothes onto the carpet, sorting through them, to finally be settled, but going through twenty-five years of his belongings and hers was going to take time.

Later, she would put them back in the boxes, labeling them for the church she had discovered so that they could donate them to needy families. At least that is what the Reverend Billy Conger had said would be done with the clothes a few days before, when he had called her. At first, she wondered how he had gotten her telephone number, but from the initial conversation, she could tell that the man had been dialing numbers at random, since hers was not yet listed in the telephone directory.

"May I speak to the gentleman of the house?" the voice on the other end
had said with a southern drawl, and when she had replied that there was no
gentleman of the house, that she was a recent widow, the caller identified himself. "Sorry to bother you, ma'am," he said. Soft southern laughter washed into
her ear, and she thought he was a real charmer and was about to hang up when
he said he was looking for donations for his congregation.

"You may have seen our flyer?" he asked. "We've been putting them up all
over town, now that the blessed Christmas season is over, our small congregation is hoping to extend that most blessed season of our Lord to those less fortunate. Would you not have some old clothing or something you might
donate?"

She had as a matter of fact seen the flyer he had referred to, but had put it
out of her mind until he reminded her of it; she had discovered it stuck under
the windshield of her Ford Galaxy one morning. "I do, indeed, have clothing
that I will never use, and I must tell you it is good, some of it practically brand
new. As I said, I am a widow, but my husband"—

Again the laughter. "The Lord works in mysterious ways, Mrs. ah…? What
did you say you name was?"

"Livia Allen," she told him. "My husband was a preacher here a few years
ago."

"The Reverend *Milton* Allen?" he had asked, surprising her.

"Why, yes," she said.

"Then once again, this just shows the Lord at work," the Rev. Billy Conger
said, his southern drawl seeming to get more thick. "I worked with your husband, as it were, a few times. He was a great champion of the poor. Was he
not?"

Livia felt herself warming up to the man. "He was," she agreed. Then she
told him again she would be delighted to donate his clothing.

"Just follow the directions on the flyer," he said. "Call us before you come
over so that I will be sure to greet you, as I am out quite often ministering to
the less fortunate, myself."

Not only by his choice of words on the phone that day, but from the scrip-
ture quoted on the flyer, she knew this church was of the same vein as the ones
her husband had preached in, though not Baptist, really, even though the flyer
announced itself as the John the Baptist Calvary Mission. But she could not
think of a better way to rid herself of her husband's things than to return them
to the kind of ministry he had always engaged in. "*Suffer the poor and the needy
and the Common Man,*" he had preached all his life, "*and you shall enter glory.*"
It was not a quote from the Bible, of course, but Livia did respect it from her

husband. His ministry to the needy and the less fortunate was, she thought, the most likely thing that would get him into heaven, if anything would.

She was not resentful of the years she had spent with him but, as she went through his stuff, she felt her spirits continue to rise. It was almost as if by casting off his presence in her new house, she was freeing herself from his grasp. She *had* resented his iron-fisted grasp on her, so as she carried the boxes out to the car, she almost felt like singing. "There you go, Milton. I'm sure your clothing will outfit some of the poor of the Calvary Mission in finer clothing than they've ever worn."

Then she spent the remainder of the afternoon putting up dishes and pots and pans and creating a space she could live in without feeling too flustered with the boxes that yet remained unpacked. As she worked her way through the house, she was smiling unconsciously, wondering if she should make a little area for the baby, for surely, with Sharon working so close by and her son and Joel having so much farming to do, there would be times when they might want her to baby sit.

Telling people she was a grandmother made it more real when she met those she knew in the grocery store or other places she had gone to in town as she got settled. She could not yet talk so freely about it as she would have liked, however, since relating such news inevitably brought a question to her listener's face. "And how is your son, Mrs. Allen. I thought…well, you know how news travels in this town."

She recalled one conversation she had had just the day after she had rented the house. She was buying an inhaler at the Rexall Drug Store, because the dust she had raised cleaning had caused her asthma to kick up, when someone called her name.

Looking around to see who it was, she met Ruth Todd, one of the elder's wives from the church where her husband had preached.

Mrs. Todd smiled, though she looked a little confused. "I thought you and Milton had moved to Arizona. I haven't seen you in several years."

She told him what had happened and suffered through Mrs. Todd's condolences. "So, I've decided to return here. I always liked Common, you know? Nice dry air. Warm winters."

"Are you going to be attending the old church?" Mrs. Todd had asked.

Her question was odd, Livia thought. "The way you say that, Ruth, it sounds as though you no longer attend. Is that right?"

Ruth smiled and her eyes lit up. "It is, dear. How perceptive of you. My husband and I have begun attending a new church, since it's not as liberal as the old one."

"But wasn't that quite a sacrifice for your husband, since he was an elder?"

Mrs. Todd smiled somewhat condescendingly, Livia thought. "We do not consider it a sacrifice, at all, since my husband has already advanced to head elder at our new church. You may not be aware," Mrs. Todd said, lowering her voice a little, as if confiding a secret, "the preacher who came after your husband was a *northerner* and simply too liberal for some of our tastes. To me, it was as much of a scandal as it was for you after your own son…well…when all that happened."

Livia did not know how to respond and sought to move off, but Mrs. Todd put a hand on her forearm. "Now that we've spoken, our little congregation would love to have you, if you've a mind. I think you would find our preacher's good old southern fundamentalism a refreshing change."

That was the last thing Livia wanted, but she deferred her answer, because she had not yet decided if she wanted to get wrapped up in any church so quickly. "I will have to think about that, dear. As I said, I've just recently returned here. My house is a mess at the moment. There's so much work to do."

"Do you have a phone yet? I would love to give you a call sometime, to see how you're doing."

Livia had fumbled in her purse for the number, since she had not yet memorized it, then gave it to her, along with her new address.

Now, she looked around the house, satisfied that she had made enough progress for one day.

Then she bathed and fixed her hair and changed into a new dress she had bought—one that she had picked out herself, rather than one that Milton had insisted she buy. She called the number on the flyer and spoke to Billy Conger's wife, Mary, saying that she was bringing over some stuff to donate. "I will tell my husband that you called, Mrs. Allen."

Livia locked up the house and, with purse and keys in hand, she set off for the north part of Common, crossing the railroad tracks that ran east and west, and found her way to the new Calvary Mission church, which had set itself up amid the squalor of adobe buildings and trailer houses in what looked like a very poor, very rough part of town.

The Calvary Mission was a rather small, blank, stuccoed structure, whose name and apparent ambition was bigger than the church building.

"Bless you, sister, for your generosity," the Reverend Billy Conger shouted, when he saw all the things she had in the car and helped her to carry them into the church building. He was a big man, dressed in a much worn suit with a shirt that had seen much better days, and a tie, she thought that must have come off some Salvation Army store rack, of at least a 1940s vintage, though the mustard stain, or what ever it was, looked recent. He was by no means a handsome man, she noted, but his face was pleasant enough. But like his suit, what must have once been a charming southern appearance had also gone to seed.

"You should try on some of my husband's suits, yourself," she offered, noting how large he was, as he invited her into his office, which was a small travel trailer behind the church building. She looked around, ready to leave in an instant. Though the place was tidy, and she gave him that, from many years of experience, she knew that the Rev. Conger was a fundamentalist even farther on one side of the protestant faith than her husband, though she doubted that he was of the snake-handling brand she had encountered in Louisiana, when her husband was assigned to that horrible church in Baton Rouge. The walls of the trailer were lined with bookshelves, and she was able to read a few of the titles. Some were familiar to her, though others whose spines were almost homemade looking were not familiar. On one wall was a poster board, where amid many sheets of paper, his divinity school credentials were proudly displayed, though she had never heard of the school.

The preacher seated himself behind his desk, and offered her a rather overstuffed and somewhat stained chair on the other side of the desk.

"I don't really have much time to stay"—

"You must meet my wife," he said. "At least."

Before she could object, a woman who looked as run-down as the preacher looked energetic creaked into the trailer carrying a tray upon which two mugs and an aluminum pot had been placed.

"I'm Mary Conger," the woman offered setting down the tray and pouring steaming coffee into the rather large, heavy looking mugs. "I spoke with you just a little while ago." Her hair was gray and in terrible need of hot-oil treatments, Livia thought. Her dress, a vintage shift from the same era as her husband's suit, and faded to pastel green, reminded Livia that she should also go through her own clothing.

"Livia Allen," Livia offered, shaking the woman's hand and sitting down in the chair to avoid hovering.

The preacher suddenly nodded to his wife, who had been left standing. "You may go. I'd like to visit with Mrs. Allen for a few minutes, alone."

Although Livia was reminded of being treated the same way by her own husband, it was not until the man had dismissed Mary, or rather given her permission to leave, that Livia saw how distasteful such a presumption was for a man to treat his wife so subserviently. But she tried to smile, now that she was seated. She would give him a few more minutes of her time and then leave.

"As I said, th'otha day," The Rev. Conger said, in his southern drawl, leaning back in his chair, "I worked with your husband. You and he left town… what…two…no, three years ago?"

"Yes, that's right," Livia said, though she couldn't see of what interest that might be to the man. "We got an offer from a church in Arizona, and my asthma was kicking up a little worse."

"Too bad," Mr. Conger said, taking a loud sip of his coffee. "Too bad, indeed. As I said, I knew your husband, ma'am. He was a good man."

Livia did not doubt that someone like the Rev. Billy Conger would know her husband. "So how long have you been here, Mr. Conger?"

"Oh, not long. Not long, this time, that is. As you might have guessed, I was born in the South, my accent and all."

"Yes, so I did."

"I was called to bring the gospel to these people," he said, looking around him, as if they were standing outdoors, and Livia imagined that he was talking about the neighborhood.

"Here in Common?" she asked.

"Yes, but especially here on the wrong side of the tracks. These are God's forgotten. But He called me here, to bring the light, the true Way. And do you know why?" He asked, sitting forward, almost leering at her, she thought. She began to feel uneasy.

"No, Mr. Conger. Why? My own husband felt a similar calling," and she quoted his favorite line about the poor and needy.

"That is certainly part of it. But I was called to minister to these people, of all the people in this town, because their lives are torn from drink and child-birth out of wedlock and a whole host of sinful ways. Do you know, Mrs. Allen, that it is from such sin as this that arises other more foul and wicked ways? Deeply foul and a scourge on the face of Jesus!"

"I have seen poverty at its worse," she replied, though she really knew she had to be leaving soon.

"Are you ch'uched?" he asked, suddenly standing. "Are you saved, Mrs. Allen? Was not your own son among the lost a few years ago?"

She stood as well, and began backing toward the door. "My son? I don't think that's any of your business, really."

He came around the desk quickly, and it was all she could do to keep from running. "Everyone in Common knows your sodomite son and the dark evil he has brought on this town!" he said, his eyes burning. "We noted his movements shortly after he and his devil's mate had spawned their unholy child!"

"Really! Mr. Conger, I think I've heard quite enough. It's"—

He grabbed her wrist and sank to his knees. "Pray with me! Call on the Lord to give you the strength. Work with us. The child can be saved, Sistah Allen! As can the mother. We know where she works, you know."

She attempted to pull her hand free, but he grabbed her wrist with both hands, tightening his grip, hurting her arm.

"Please!" she said. "Let me go! You are stepping way beyond your bounds, here."

But he began to pray and then to jerk, and he began what she knew was speaking in tongues.

She pushed him with her free hand and then grabbed onto the desk for support. She felt herself losing balance, as he continued to pull her down—

She grabbed the mug of coffee, bringing it down on top of his head, aiming for a bald spot, where a mole sprouted—

Hot coffee sloshed onto his hair and the back of his suit jacket, and he cried out, falling sideways, one of his hands releasing her wrist, though the other hung on. She brought the mug down, again, this time on his hand that clutched her own.

He lost his grip and Livia turned, stumbling out the door, digging for her keys as she ran for the car, tripping once on a pipe that stuck out of the ground, rounding the corner of the church, and practically knocking Mary Conger over.

"It was no accident!" Mary called. "No coincidence!"

Livia heard but did not stop to respond as she ran for her car, flung the door open, and jammed the key into the ignition. A moment later, she threw the car in reverse, with the door flopping wildly. Then she threw it into drive and stomped the accelerator, causing the door to slam shut. She gunned the engine and careened onto the street, catching the frightened look on Mary Conger's face in the rear-view mirror.

Her hands shook on the wheel as she slowed down for the railroad tracks, re-entering downtown Common. She turned right onto Main, and parked around the corner from the Red Rooster; then, trying to compose herself, she walked unsteadily to the café.

Tears welled up in her eyes, and her breath was shallow. She hoped Sharon was there, as well as Margaret Jost. She could not tell such a thing to Tom—at least, not yet. She feared he might blame her.

*   *   *

"But what did she mean, 'no accident, no coincidence?'" Margaret asked.

She and Sharon were sitting on the couch in Margaret's living room. Livia was sitting on the chair, gripping a mug of hot chocolate and crying. After all the years in which Margaret had thought so very little of Tom's parents, but perhaps especially least well of Livia Allen for the way in which she had apparently rejected her own child, she now felt great sympathy and a kind of surprised awe. When she had walked into the café a half-hour ago, looking as though she might faint, Margaret had first attempted to find out what had happened. The café was beginning to fill up for the dinner hour, and would soon be hopping, straining the entire staff.

But she soon saw it was not going to work, there in the café, with so much going on. As soon as she was able, she turned the operation over to Julie Ann, who had looked stricken but, good girl that she was, had bravely agreed she could hold things together for awhile.

"I really have no idea what Mrs. Conger meant," Livia finally said. "I was so shocked at her husband's attack, I couldn't think straight."

"But surely, dear," Margaret said, "this Mary Conger was trying to tell you something."

"I fear I know," Sharon said. She placed a hand on Margaret's shoulder. "When we were leaving the hospital with the baby, one of the nurses told Joel about this new church, and how a man had been lurking about, asking which one was mine. She warned Joel about it. Joel was frightened for the baby. I was frightened at this woman's words, but did not know what it meant."

Margaret nodded at Sharon's words, but they didn't make sense, other than that this church, this Calvary Mission and its preacher, did not like the birth of the child. It was also no surprise that people would have known about it.

"Tell me, again, Livia, how you came to take your husband's clothing to that church—which turns out coincidentally to be the same church that took such a great interest in our granddaughter."

She told them how she had found the flyer under her windshield and then a few days later got a random phone call from the preacher.

Margaret was greatly troubled by that. The afternoon was quickly turning to evening, and she was also troubled about having left Julie Ann there with only two waitresses on duty. But she shook off this thought, looking first at Sharon, then at Livia. "It doesn't sound like the telephone call was so random, dear."

Livia shook her head. "It had to be. When he came on the phone, he asked for the man of the house, and I told him that I was a widow and, of course, identified myself. That's when he said he knew Milton." She nodded at Sharon. "My husband. Besides, my phone is not listed yet, and nobody except Tom and Joel, Eva, and you and Sharon know it."

"Are you quite certain?" Margaret asked. "It was simply too coincidental, don't you think that the flyer was under your windshield, at your house, and then"—

"Wait!" Livia said. She took a sip of hot chocolate then set the mug down on the end table. "I did give my number to a woman who used to go to my church, back in 1965. Mrs. Todd. Her husband was an elder, and she did tell me that she and her husband had switched churches, saying how they didn't like the new preacher at the other church. But surely"—

"My dear, is she the only other person you can recall giving your number to?"

Livia put a hand to her mouth, as fear rose in her eyes. "I also gave her my address. My Jesus! That's how they knew to put the flyer in my windshield. And when I didn't take the bait, they gave me a call." Her face lost its fear and a kind of determination came over her. Margaret was reminded of Tom. She had seen the same look in his eyes when he had finally agreed to get the wedding rings that Joel wanted, even though he had tried to argue him out of it, saying that people would not like it. Once he had decided to do it, however, that determined look came over his face.

"Now," Sharon said, sitting forward. "We just need to decide if they will try anything else. I am thinking they wanted you to join them. To perhaps take your grandchild and bring it into their religion. Did you not say that this...um...minister said the child could be saved?"

"If that's what they really want," Livia said, finally settling back in her chair, as though relieved. The color had returned to her cheeks, though her slight bit of makeup was ruined from crying, earlier. "Believe me, I know how these splinter groups think. I don't think they will give up so easily."

But Margaret was not relieved at all, though she thought better of voicing her further concern. The dinner hour would be well under way by now, and she did have to get back. She smiled at Livia. "The preacher is going to have more than a sore head, after the knot you probably gave him." She still reveled in Livia's quick thinking on that score, and her smile increased. "I think we should tell Tom what happened, though. He and Joel need to be aware that this preacher and certain members of his church lured you over there." She nodded at Sharon. "The old nurse at the hospital was right to have warned you."

*   *   *

As she drove home, Livia did not think she should tell Tom what had happened. They were just beginning to trust each other after the last few years, and she felt that their relationship was still too tenuous to jeopardize it.

They know where I live, she thought as she drove into the small driveway provided by the landlady. It was already dark outdoors and, this late in March, still grew cold as the sun went down. She had left no lights on in the house having left what seemed hours ago when it was still daylight, but it was really only a little over two hours at most. As she stepped out onto the concrete slab and shut the door to the car, she locked it, had never been in the habit of doing so, but decided it was a good habit to be in.

Although she was no longer shaking, a dread had settled into the pit of her stomach. She had never been in a situation like that in her life as when Billy Conger, a man as large as her husband, had grabbed her and would not let her go. Nor had she ever struck another human being as she had him. No doubt the heavy mug and the steaming coffee had given him a sore, if not a bloody, head. She did not remember seeing any blood, at least, but the image of her actions and the situation she had gotten herself into was ugly.

She unlocked the front door and turned on the lights. The living room was still a shambles, but she could tell she had made progress. The silk brocade couch and the coffee table in front of it were cleared of all Milton's boxes, but there were still boxes piled up on the two matching chairs, flanking either side of the couch. She had set out a few knick knacks on the fireplace mantle, but boxes were stacked on either side of that and, against another wall, the console radio, with the record player was also piled with assorted boxes marked "living room."

She was too tired and rattled to think about doing any more unpacking. She went into the kitchen and put on a pot of water for hot tea. Milton had liked hot tea in the evenings as he worked at his desk; she preferred coffee, but did not want to jangle her nerves any more than they were. She ran a sink of water and was washing up her breakfast dishes when the telephone rang, causing her to jump.

She found a towel in one of the open boxes on the counter and dried her hands as she made her way back into the living room.

"Hello?" she said, half fearing that it might be Billy Conger or his wife, or maybe even Ruth Todd. She would give Mrs. Todd a piece of her mind, if it was her.

"Mother?"

She sighed with relief, as she sank to the couch, listening to Tom's voice on the other end. *How dare that preacher to imply that my son is some sort of evil influence on the whole town.* Now she understood perhaps even a little more how Tom must have felt and she stopped herself from crying, yet again. Crying could get to be a habit, she thought, if she let other people's bad intentions and dislikes upset her. From what Tom was saying, he was in a happy frame of mind and, again, she did not want to let him know about the ugliness at the Calvary Mission.

"Can you come for dinner? Or have you already eaten?" he wanted to know, once he had filled her in on the baby's day and her bout with what must have been an upset stomach.

She glanced around the room and caught her reflection in the bare windows, where she had not yet hung curtains. It depressed her to think of spending the evening alone. This house was too quiet.

"I would love to come, dear. Give me a half-hour?"

She was smiling when she dropped the receiver into the cradle, anxious now to see her granddaughter. All she needed to do was clean up her face and put on a little more makeup. It shouldn't take long, at all.

As she turned to make her way to the bathroom, the phone rang again.

Thinking maybe Tom had forgotten something, she picked it up without hesitation. "Yes, dear?"

"Now, ain't that a friendly way to greet people," the drawling voice of Billy Conger said on the other end. "You've injured me, bad, Sistah Allen. Did you know that?"

Livia almost dropped the phone. Her heart began to race, and her knees felt as if they were about to buckle. "Mr. Conger, I suggest strongly that you not call, here, again. I've no cause to feel sorry for breaking away from you. I have never been put into such a"—

"Now, Mrs. Allen," the preacher drawled, his southern accent soft and low. "I just want to apologize for my behavior this afternoon."

"Fine. Thank you," she said and hung up, and then she began to shake, his voice having brought all of it back. She did not like the idea that he had her number. Well, that could be changed, she thought, and tried to pull herself together.

It was quite another matter of changing one's address, however. Although she really liked the small house she had moved into, the pleasure in it had been tarnished, since people she wished to never see again knew where she lived.

CHAPTER 21

A MISUNDERSTANDING

There was something wrong with his mother that Tom could not put a finger on. As soon as she had entered their house and had greeted them by kissing them both on the cheek, Tom thought he felt her trembling. Then, when they let her into the nursery, where Shara had finally gone to sleep after spitting up and crying all afternoon, she only stayed a short while, bending over the bassinet, toying with the blanket, feeling to see if her granddaughter was wet, then turning and flipping out the light and following Tom back into the living room.

He had expected his mother to sit in the rocker and watch the baby sleeping at least for a little while, as he and Joel both did. The newness of the baby— *their baby*—just never seemed to wear off. Even Eva came over to the house every day and spent at least an hour, sometimes two, checking the baby, giving it a bath, even against both their objections that she'd had one not more than an hour before.

But Tom's mother had spent less than five minutes in the room with her granddaughter, nor did she express much interest in joining him and Joel in the kitchen as they put the final touches on the dinner. Tom thought that they could at least catch up on news from Sharon. So Tom came and went from the kitchen to the living room for the next half-hour, checking on her. She was much too still on the couch and had not touched a single magazine they had laid out on the coffee table. Rather, she just sat where she was looking dazed.

"Mother?"

She looked up. "Yes, dear?"

"Would you like something to drink before dinner?"

"No, dear, I'm fine." Her smile beneath the table lamp was thin.

Tom went back into the kitchen, beginning to feel a knot in the pit of his stomach. Something was just not right, and he said so to Joel.

Joel was at the sink washing the cooking dishes. "Are you sure, babe?" he asked. "She seems fine to me. Maybe she's just tired."

"Maybe," Tom said, standing next to him.

Then he went back into the living room and sat on the couch opposite his mother, leaning forward with his forearms on his thighs. "Have you made much progress unpacking? Are you overdoing it?"

She looked at him. Her face was still gaunt as it was on the first day he had seen her. She shook her head. "No, I'm not tired. As for my progress, things are coming along."

He studied her for a moment, trying to lock eyes with hers, but she looked away, then looked back and smiled thinly.

"Are you sure, Mother? You seem…subdued this evening."

"Well…perhaps I am a little tired, dear. I went through a lot of boxes, took Milton's clothes to…ah…got rid of them."

"Did that bother you?" he asked. "You know, going through his things?"

"I was glad to get them out of my hair to tell you the truth. I'm sure they will be appreciated."

"So did you find the Goodwill station?"

She shook her head.

Joel popped his head into the room. "Dinner's ready, Livia. Tom."

Tom extended his hand to his mother. Her hand was icy as he helped her to her feet. She withdrew it quickly and followed Joel into the kitchen.

The dinner was awkward, Tom thought. His mother did not volunteer anything, except to answer questions put to her and, once she had tasted her food, making what sounded like obligatory complements, hardly touched her meal.

She brightened a little when they were telling her about Shara.

"Did you see Sharon, today?" Tom asked.

"Yes, I did, but just for a little while late this afternoon."

"How is she?"

"Fine, dear."

"And Margaret?"

"They're both fine," his mother said. She set her fork down and folded her hands in her lap, a gesture that almost broke Tom's heart, recalling that she had done that at almost every meal with his father, because he would not permit anyone to leave the table until he was finished.

When the telephone rang and his mother jumped, grasping the front of her blouse, Joel got up to answer it, and Tom was left staring at his mother, as the tears began to shine in her eyes. He heard Joel in the other room, laughing, telling someone about the baby, then listening. He tuned the conversation out, since it didn't sound important. He turned his attention back to his mother.

"Mother. Something is wrong. I can tell. Are you having second thoughts about our baby? Or about me and Joel, because if you are, I hope you know that we're good for each other. I know it's maybe really difficult for you to accept us. Maybe you can't. I just don't know. I thought we were getting off to a good start."

When her tears began to run her makeup, she got up from the table and went into the living room, where she rummaged in her purse. Then she returned to the table and sat down, wiping her eyes. She reached out and touched his hand, squeezed it. "It is none of those things, Thomas. Please understand that I am happy for you and Joel. It is not something I would have chosen for you, but you two have been together for almost six years. That is remarkable and, as far as I'm concerned something that you and Joel will have to work out with God. It is not for me to say."

"Then, what about Shara?"

She smiled and blew her nose. "I have even fewer reservations about her, Thomas. I am truly happy to be a grandmother. Something I gave up on six years ago."

"Then what is it? You've got me worried."

Just then, Joel came back into the kitchen and sat down, looking from Tom to Livia, appearing to be confused, seeing that Livia had been crying. But he didn't say anything; rather, he finished his meal, glancing at Tom with questions in his eyes.

Livia finally composed herself. "Oh, Thomas! I feel I was betrayed."

That made Tom's heart pound. "Betrayed? Who...what do you mean, Mother?"

It all began to spill out, then, her meeting with Ruth Todd. "You remember her, don't you? Or at least her son, Kevin. I know you spent time with him at those monthly dinners."

"The elder's son," Tom said. "Yes, of course. But you said 'Ruth.' Did she do something to you?"

She nodded. "I gave her my phone number one day when I met her in the drug store. I also gave her my address. Then I got this flyer stuck under my windshield one day. I didn't think anything of it. It was just some mission, I thought, asking for old clothes, dishes, anything they could give away to the needy." Then she told them about the telephone call from the Rev. Billy Conger.

At the mention of his name, they both shook their heads.

"He runs the John the Baptist Calvary Mission, across the tracks. He called me up"—

"Wait, Livia," Joel said, frowning. "Did you say the *Calvary* Mission? I heard of that. This old nurse at the hospital was telling me about this guy."

Livia nodded, and then filled in the details, and then told them about taking her clothes out to the mission, and finally his insult. "Thomas, he called you and Joel devils, or accused you of doing the devil's work. Some nonsense like that." Then she told them how he had grabbed her and demanded that she pray with him and how she had struggled to get away.

As her tale unfolded, ending with her flight from the premises and, still later, Billy Conger's telephone call, Tom became so angry he got up and paced the floor, while Joel tried to calm Livia down.

"See there?!" Joel said. "Babe, I told you. Looks like the religious nuts are after us again."

Then they told her about their experiences, beginning with the first time they had kissed and were caught at the country/western dance by Joel's friends, ending with Tom's leaving the church.

*   *   *

More than anything she had done to try to rectify her feelings about the relationship between her son and Joel Reece, hearing their side of the story after all these years helped melt away some of her dread and misgivings about them. She had not told them how much she had prayed for guidance as she re-entered their lives, how much she still disliked their homosexuality, how she still feared for their souls. But there was something liberating, finally, in hearing how they had suffered at the beginning of their relationship, how Tom had fought it, just as his letter said, and how they had, in the last six years, grown so confident about the rightness of their love for each other that they had no misgivings about their right to have a child.

Livia was glad they allowed her into their lives, where Eva Reece had been since the beginning. So, as the evening wore on, and the three of them sat in the living room talking about their past, with all the misunderstandings that had arisen, Livia began to feel less fearful, even though she knew she was going to have to face the religious bigots of the town, a group of people she had once been part of in a way—not by her own actions, she thought, but by her lack of action.

Years ago, she realized, she should have told her husband that she did not intend to disown her son, that he was too much a part of her to just cast him off.

By the time Margaret brought Sharon home for the night, near ten o'clock, she felt better than she had all evening. She visited with Sharon for a just a few minutes, then decided it was time for her to go.

She hugged Sharon, her son, and Joel, kissing their cheeks, and having one more look at her granddaughter. Then she asked a question that she had been afraid to ask, as she was standing by the front door, slipping on her jacket.

"Would the two of you think about bringing Shara by the house and letting me have her for the day, sometime? I could watch her while Sharon is at work, and then when she got off work, I could bring her and the baby out here."

Both Tom and Joel were beaming at her. "Of course you can, Livia!" Joel said. "There'll be times, I'm sure, when we're going to be so busy, we won't be able to watch her. Maybe when she's a little older and we've switched her to solid foods, she could spend the night with you. Would you like that?"

Livia's eyes stung with tears. "I would, Joel. You don't know how much."

*   *   *

As soon as Livia got home and was coming through the door, the phone began to ring. Her heart thudded, hard, but to test her new resolve to stand up to the religious bigots and the likes of the Rev. Conger, she tossed her purse onto the sofa and snatched up the receiver.

"Mrs. Allen?"

"Yes…is this Mrs. Conger?"

"It is. I want to a"—

"Listen to me, Mrs. Conger. As I told your husband earlier in the evening, I will not tolerate any further calls from you or members of your congregation. And if you do not stop calling, I will notify the telephone company that I am receiving harassment calls. They will"—

"Please!" came Mary Conger's voice. "Please! You misunderstand. Just a moment of your time."

Livia was in no mood to listen, but she sat on the couch. "You have one minute."

"Thank you. When you were leaving this afternoon, I tried to tell you it was no coincidence. You were manipulated into visiting my husband."

"Tell me one thing, before I hang up on you, Mrs. Conger," Livia said, her anger still rising. "How is it you are brave enough to be calling me, at this hour, or at all, when I saw clearly how your husband treats you? How can you possess the courage to call me to explain anything?"

There was a moment of silence, in which Livia was about to slam the receiver down. Then, "You don't know how hard this is for me. I can only say that my husband is spending the night in the hospital, so I know that he will not find out I have called you."

"Oh? He called me himself, not more than four hours ago."

"Yes, I know, Mrs. Allen. But right afta' he went into convulsions. I think that knock on the head you gave him caused a concussion or something."

With that, Livia sagged, suddenly feeling guilty. "Then I owe you an apology, Mrs. Conger. I never intended to hurt him that badly."

"The doctor says he will be fine. I didn't call to scare you. I called to tell you I'm sorry and that my husband...that some members of the ch'uch are talkin' 'bout your son, and the woman who had this baby. I am not a part of it, and...well, I guess that is all I want to say."

"Then I thank you for that," Livia said, her feelings confused. "I'm not used to this sort of thing. I have never struck anyone before, neither out of anger, nor with a weapon. I was only trying to get away."

"I understand, Mrs. Allen. Thank you for listening to me."

"That's—

The telephone went dead and Livia stared at it for a moment before dropping it into the cradle, not knowing what to think—other than she intended to meet with Mary Conger. This woman needed her help and, in a way, reminded her of herself.

CHAPTER 22

TOM'S ANGER

Tom waited until after Sharon had bathed and nursed the baby and both were asleep in the nursery before he talked with Joel about what the preacher Conger had done. He and Joel were in the back part of the house in their bedroom. Joel had also bathed, since he had spent a long day in the field, finishing up the plowing. He was naked and lying back on their bed. Tom was sitting on the edge of it still dressed, absently caressing Joel's chest, but still too angry to make love or go to sleep.

"It really scares me that Conger's got the members of his church out finding out about us," Tom said, "like going to the hospital and trying to get information from the nurses, or like Elder Todd and his wife getting Mother's address and telephone number, so he can call her up and pretend it was just a coincidence."

"Maybe Mrs. Todd didn't realize she was doing anything wrong," Joel said, "if she's the one who gave that preacher your mother's phone number."

Tom felt angry at Joel, then immediately felt sorry, knowing that Joel usually trusted people and was often surprised when he found out later that their motives were sneaky or underhanded. So he smiled, trying to keep his own emotions in check.

"I'm sorry, honey, but I do think Ruth Todd knew exactly what the preacher had planned. After all, *someone* had to know where Mother lived to put that flyer under her windshield, and I'm afraid it was more than coincidence that Mother got one to begin with. I think it was Conger's way to entice her out to

192

his church. Then, when she didn't respond, he called her up—and Ruth *had* to be the one who gave him the telephone number."

Joel just nodded, and Tom wondered what was going through his mind. It reminded him of the times he had spent the night at Joel's when they were both teenagers—especially after everyone knew they were gay, and they wondered where the next problem would come from.

It was much the same kind of fear that gripped Tom, now, as he thought of what Conger had done to his Mother at the Calvary Mission and what he might do next.

"What do you think, honey?" Tom asked. "You're not saying much."

Joel smiled at him, but his smile was thin. In the light from the lamp next to their bed, his face was soft, his skin a beautiful golden color. "We need to find out what JoAnna has discovered, don't you think? She said she was going to find out who the members of the church are. Maybe if we know more about them, we'll know what to expect."

"But what about Mother, Joel? I think she's in danger, now, don't you? I mean, especially since she banged Conger over the head. If he's a crazy kind of preacher like my father was, he's not going to let that go lightly. You heard Mother, saying how he'd called her just before she came out here. That scared me."

"I *was* thinking about your mother, honey," Joel said. "It was Conger's idea, I bet, to work against us through her. So we need to see if JoAnna has any ideas. She needs to meet your mother, and stay in touch with Margaret, too. We've also got to find a way to shield Sharon from them, as well."

Tom realized that their roles had been reversed. Joel was the one urging caution and to wait to find out more, while he was the one looking for something immediate to do. He sighed in frustration and began undressing, realizing that there was nothing to be done, at least not tonight. "Then first thing in the morning, Joel, I'm going to call JoAnna and see what she's found out."

Joel got up then and helped Tom undress, but he did not kiss him, once they were both naked. Instead, he put his arms around Tom's shoulders and hugged him close. "It'll be all right, honey. I know you're anxious about Livia. It's just too bad she had to get into the middle of it, especially with all she's had to deal with, with your father dying and then coming here, hoping to get back with you."

They laid down and Tom switched off the light, then snuggled against Joel. It was so much like the problems they had faced almost six years before. He took comfort in the thought that they had made it through those times together, and they would make it through this.

When Joel had drifted off, no doubt tired, Tom cradled Joel's head on his chest. His anger had not dissipated, but he tried to block it out of his mind, caressing Joel's neck, running his hands down his husband's back.

*   *   *

As with most things, problems looked different in the light of day, less threatening, at least, Tom thought. He was standing on the porch with a cup of coffee, watching the faintest daylight begin to glow in the eastern sky. He breathed in the crisp air. It cleared his head, and he found he could think clearly about his fear and anger of the night before. He and Joel had already eaten their breakfast, and Joel had left for the equipment yard, where he and Douglas were getting the cultivators ready. He had told Joel that, after he dropped Sharon off at the café, he was going to visit with his mother; but by the time he was in the kitchen cooking breakfast for Sharon, he had changed his mind.

Sharon came into the kitchen a few minutes later, wearing her yellow robe. Tom complimented her on it.

"How's our little girl?" he asked.

Sharon poured herself a cup of coffee and sat down at the table. "She is fine. I believe she must be already gaining much weight."

"And you?"

Sharon laughed. "I believe I am a little tired. It is almost sunup, and I could still sleep more."

"Did Shara keep you up?" Tom asked. He turned the burner off beneath the frying pan.

"Some," Sharon said. "But I was worried about Margaret. I could not sleep much of the night. I do not like leaving her this way. She has been so very well to me, Tom."

Tom smiled at Sharon's grammar, although her accent and strange way of putting most things had improved in the last nine months.

"How much longer do you think we should breast feed, then? We could try the formula, see if you can stay with Margaret, if that would be better."

She took a sip of coffee, staring thoughtfully into space. "I do not know. This is all so strange to me, this idea that all babies are not nursed. In my community, if it is sometimes the case that the mother is not able…um…if her milk is not good, there is always someone else who will share and nurse the baby. We have none of this, this…formula."

"You know you can decide to do whatever you want," Tom said, sliding the eggs onto a plate and placing strips of bacon and a slice of oven-toasted bread beside the eggs.

Sharon smiled, looking at him. "This is so strange to me, as well. I am thinking how much friends you and me and Joel are, how you will keep Shara, and I will live where I want."

"Do you regret your decision?"

She salted her eggs and began cutting them up. She shook her head. "Not so much. I tell Margaret the same thing. I wish to make myself a success. I wish to be a great woman as is your Eva and as is Margaret. I see Shara and wish that she will be happy with her two fathers, and when I come back from university, she will know me."

Tom smiled at that. He had thought how difficult it would be for Sharon, as had Joel. But the three of them would remain friends, all sharing their child. "Never be afraid that we will not teach Shara about you when you are away at school and she asks about you."

A few moments passed in silence, then Sharon frowned, looking at Tom. "I felt sorry for your own mother. She was so upsetting...upset."

This brought Tom back to the problem at hand. He waited for Sharon to finish eating then gathered up the dishes and ran water in the sink. He poured himself another cup of coffee and sat down opposite Sharon.

"True. Mother didn't need this kind of problem. But Joel and I talked about it. You know JoAnna Hoffins?"

Sharon smiled brightly. "Oh yes, Tom. She has helped me in so many ways. Because of her I am getting into night school. I will have my diploma in a few months."

Tom nodded then told her how JoAnna and Bill had helped him and Joel. "They're the ones who introduced us to the Rev. Suskine. You met him at Joel's birthday party." He told her about the Hoffins' son in the children's hospice. "They've been so much help to so many people," he continued, not knowing where he was headed with the conversation. Then he told her of JoAnna's plan to find out more about the preacher at the Calvary Mission, and to find out who the members were.

Sharon looked thoughtful. "You know, Tom, I have met many many people of Common, as well, there in the café. It would not be difficult to find where they go to church."

Tom didn't like the idea and said so. But Sharon laughed. "It is not so difficult, nor dangerous as you say, because people in America do not hide their true opinions. I already know those who do not like that I should be the mother of a child, and her fathers are"—she screwed up her face—"'them there two faggots 'at brought disgrace on this town!'"

Tom burst out laughing at the perfect good-ole boy accent she had mimicked. "Where did you hear that?"

She smiled back, then frowned. "In the café, Tom. I have heard many bad things said of you and Joel—and maybe even when people thought I did not hear, they said bad things of me. Though I think they knew I could hear perfectly. So it is not dangerous for me to discover their religion. I feel certain that such people will be glad to name their religion. They are like the elders in my community of Brethren, who tell others how they should be and tell them who to shun."

*   *   *

The wind was already kicking up when Sharon and Tom left the house. Shara was bundled up and dressed for the short trip to her grandmother Eva's, and Sharon was carrying the various bags. Tom was holding the baby against his neck, trying to keep the wind from whipping the blanket off her face. They hurried to the pickup and drove past the equipment yard. Tom honked as he drove by but did not stop.

After they had dropped the baby off at Eva's house, Tom took Sharon directly to the café. He didn't get out. "Tell Margaret I said hello," he said, as Sharon got out of the pickup and shut the door. She waived and made her way into the café. He watched her, frowning to himself.

Why people took such interest in them—him and Joel, and now Sharon and their baby—and why they could not leave them alone, Tom did not know. He frowned, too, thinking of his mother's tears of the night before, so soon after coming back to town. She should not have had to deal with a man like the preacher Conger nor be afraid of her own son's reaction.

But he would take care of things, show her that she had nothing to fear from him, that she could trust him—especially that he *had* learned to think for himself, which had been her wish for him—that he was strong like Joel, when it came to standing up for himself and those he loved.

As he headed north, across the railroad tracks, looking for the Calvary Mission, he thought Joel would be proud of him, if he knew that he was, for once, taking action against those who threatened them, rather than leaving it for Joel to handle.

The wind and dust were worse, if anything, north of the railroad tracks. Even though there were old neighborhoods, here, they were rundown, and the yards were barren of grass. Everywhere were junked cars and trash and mean looking dogs that barked as he drove slowly by.

When he spotted the Calvary Mission, it was almost exactly what he had imagined it would be, based not only on his mother's description of it, but on what seemed to be an architectural model for such a church, with a poor congregation and a fundamentalist preacher that speaks in tongues. The woodframe mission with a tin roof was, if anything, a blight on the neighborhood of poor and desperate people with their barren yards and their grinding poverty.

No doubt the good preacher called on them to give when the tithing plate was passed around, promising salvation for their dollar bills. A buck a miracle, Tom thought, not realizing that he was scowling as he drove up to the church building.

Then he saw his mother's car next to a travel trailer at the back of the church.

He slammed the pickup door and raced across the barren ground past the church, fear driving him toward the trailer. As he drew near, he saw that its door stood open. If Conger was inside, Tom knew he would fly into him with his fists and ask questions, later.

He skidded to a halt at the three steps leading into the trailer and, in one leap, entered the doorway, looking into his mother's and another woman's startled faces, both of them caught in mid-sentence.

A moment passed as each assessed the other.

"My Jesus! You scared me, Thomas!" his mother said, taking a breath, then smiling with relief. "I was just telling Mrs. Conger about you. Thomas, this is Mary Conger, the preacher's wife." She nodded at the other woman, who was sitting on the other side of a desk piled with papers, fear still lingering in her eyes.

Tom was still confused, and he could hear the blood beating in his ears. "Where's Conger?" he asked, when he saw that his mother was not in danger. "And why are you here, Mother?"

Mary Conger cleared her throat. "My husband is in the hospital. Livia gave him a concussion."

"And I'm here to find out a few things," his mother said. "We don't have much time, Thomas, since Mr. Conger will be expecting Mary in about an hour."

At the news that the blow his mother had given the preacher had hospitalized him, Tom was even more alarmed but he pushed that out of his mind. "What kind of things?" he asked, for the first time letting his eyes rove over the contents of the trailer, scanning the titles of the religious tracts. Then he saw that the desk was piled with religious tracts as well. These were, Tom knew, more important to the fundamentalist churches like this one than the Bible, itself. Just like his mother, he could almost determine from the titles of the tracts alone that the members of this church engaged in glossolalia—speaking in tongues. And a cousin of this church, or even some of this church's adherents were probably into snake handling.

It all made Tom's head spin and, again, he asked, "what kinds of things is Mrs. Conger showing you?"

His mother looked at him and her look said she realized he was suspicious. "Please don't think I'm here to be converted or to embrace this..." she waved a hand over the desk, as if to indicate the material.

Tom was immediately sorry that he had let his fears show through. He shook his head. "I didn't think that, Mother. But what are you doing?"

Mary Conger cleared her throat again, and Tom realized she was not only nervous, but frightened, so that she could hardly speak. "I just wanted to show your mother what my husband is preaching, here." Her voice was soft and her words tentative. "You can see from these, she said, nodding at the desk and then at his mother, "that my husband is teaching Levitical law."

"He's preaching Old Testament justice," his mother said. "You know what this means?" she asked.

Tom's stomach felt leaden and his legs began to tremble. It was as close to this sort of church as he ever wanted to get, because he knew the importance of what both Mary Conger had said, and what his mother was discovering, here, in the poorest, most vulnerable part of Common. The Reverend Billy Conger was preaching the most virulent form of fundamentalism, one that wanted to return the country to something akin to the witch hunts of early America, one that taught stoning as a form of punishment of the wicked.

He studied Mary Conger's face as she glanced nervously from him to his mother and back. He saw the faint trace of bruises on her cheeks, the fear in her eyes, and he knew it took a great amount of courage for her to reveal her husband's teaching to his mother.

"We've got to get you out of here, you know," Tom said to Mrs. Conger. "If your husband finds out you've showed us these..."

"He'll find me," she said. "He always does. Where am I going to go?"

"That's something I'm going to work on, Mary," his mother said, standing up. "Call me when you get a chance, and please make sure that you get these back in the shelves before you bring your husband home."

Mrs. Conger also stood up, attempting a smile, even as tears shone in her eyes. "He'll see these books have been moved. I'm not worried about that. He expects me to clean his office. Just please don't tell anyone you've been here."

*   *   *

Tom followed his mother home in the pickup and parked behind her car at the house. Once inside, they visited for a little while, both of them shaken by what they had seen, both knowing first hand what the preacher Billy Conger was capable of. Both agreed that Mary Conger needed help, to be taken away from what was apparently a lifetime of abuse. And they both knew something else. Billy Conger simply could not entrench himself in the town with his brand of religion. It was too dangerous, too reminiscent of the backwoods churches of Louisiana, Mississippi, Alabama—places where snake handling churches and the Ku Klux Klan were inbred, where hatred and not Christian love was the true religion.

His mother prepared a pot of tea and, as they sat on the couch together trying to calm themselves down, Tom smiled at her. "You scared me, Mother. I thought you were in real trouble over there. I didn't know Conger was in the hospital."

She took a sip of tea, holding the saucer in one hand, the cup in the other. She returned his smile, but it was wan. "Yes, I know you didn't. I didn't find out he was in the hospital, either, until I got home last night. Mary called to apologize for her husband's behavior. I didn't know I'd given him a concussion."

Tom played with his cup, running his finger around the rim. "She was taking a chance. She reminds me of Edna Stroud. You remember her?"

His mother looked sad when she nodded. "Of course I do. You're right. Poor woman. I was glad when Eva and Douglas adopted her children, though your father, of course, was against it."

"I figured he might be," Tom said. "I'm surprised that he resided over the funeral for the Strouds, the way he felt."

His mother nodded, again. "Leon Romaine talked him into the wisdom of it. If there was anyone in that church who could talk your father into sense, it was Leon. He always asked us about you, Thomas, did you know that? While we were still here?"

It was Tom's turn to look sad. But he smiled through it. "I bet that made Father angry, didn't it, for Leon to mention my name?"

She smiled, and there was a hint of a twinkle in her eye. "It did. But your father couldn't very well demand that Leon not talk about you with us."

Tom set his cup and saucer on the coffee table and looked around the room. "This is a pleasant house, don't you think?"

She followed his gaze. "It is. I cannot describe how it feels to be on my own. I will be needing to get a job, soon. But I'm not quite ready. It's like I'm getting to know myself, after so many years with your father."

Tom nodded, noting the way his mother straightened her back as she spoke. Then he laughed softly. "It has taken me all these years with Joel, too, Mother, to get to know myself and to realize what I am capable of."

"Like standing up for yourself?"

"Exactly. That's what you're discovering too, isn't it?"

She smiled in return. "It is, and in meeting Mary Conger, and seeing how she is, I've realized that one thing I *am* capable of doing—or at least strongly considering"—she stopped.

"What, Mother?"

She smiled again, this time with a look that he did not remember ever crossing his mother's face, a mixture of happiness and something else. He waited.

"I'm thinking about finding a way for Mrs. Conger to break away from her husband."

"And?"

"I will have to do some research. Talk to a doctor, or a psychologist, maybe, about…what is it they're calling abused women these days? 'Battered?'"

Tom nodded, though he had no idea. "Whatever they call it, I just thought Edna Stroud was badly beaten. You know it's going to be difficult, if not impossible, to get Mrs. Conger to leave him—even if she is abused. Edna never did."

She looked sad for a moment. "That is true, Thomas. But she had all those children to think about. Mary said she and her husband don't have any children of their own. There's not much to keep her there, if you ask me."

"Except fear," Tom said.

CHAPTER 23

A NEST OF SNAKES

JoAnna Hoffins could not concentrate on the mountain of paperwork on her desk. Her office looked out over the sweeping driveway in front of the high school where visitors to the school came, or parents dropped their children off, or in the mornings, where students who lived in town gathered before the first bell, congregating on the well-kept lawn that ran the length of the high school. It was here too where students let out in mass during fire drills. But this morning the wind and dust flew past the window, gearing up for what looked like a real howling afternoon of stinging sand. She could barely see the flags flapping on the twin poles at the end of the sidewalk; but she heard the constant metal ringing as the tortured ropes hit the poles.

She counted the days until the end of March and then April, hoping that the spring winds would be calm by then. They usually were, but some years, the wind and the blowing dust didn't stop until May. She hoped it would not be one of those springs. It seemed to put everyone on edge. Students got into more fights, teachers and administrators had tiffs, and the number of students needing counseling increased so that her office was bursting at the seams.

Today, however, it was not the wind, or the number of windy days left in the season, or the number of students who needed counseling, nor was it her very difficult boss' attitude that had sometimes made her feel like quitting. Margaret Jost had called her just a few minutes ago with disturbing news. Tom Allen's mother, Livia, just back in town after three years, had apparently been involved in an ugly scene with the preacher of that fundamentalist church, the

Calvary Mission, the very same church and the very same preacher that had been trying to cause trouble about Tom and Joel's baby.

Exactly what the scene was, or how Livia had gotten involved, or whether she had been hurt was not clear. Ever since the day she and Bill had gone to the Reece farm to welcome home the new baby, Shara, she had been trying to find out exactly what sort of threat the preacher and the members of his church posed. Their objection, of course, was that the baby was born into what they characterized as an abusive, unhealthy, unholy, and totally unacceptable home, further scandalized that the baby's mother (according to them) was a harlot.

She toyed with her hair, she re-stacked the folders of student cases on her desk, pulled one to the top and opened it, tried to read her notes, then looked out the window, again.

Over the years, she had become as fond of Joel and Tom as her husband was. The two young men had continued to be a presence in their lives, since they all attended the small Unitarian church, and JoAnna had watched as they matured. Although she had been as surprised as Bill (and a little appalled) when they found out that Joel and Tom had gotten a young woman pregnant, her misgivings about that faded, once she learned the entire and more truthful version of it from Margaret Jost.

She and Bill knew Margaret was homosexual, and they saw the twinkle in her eyes when, one day, she introduced them to the very pregnant Sharon Minninger. Just as everyone else in the small town had, they had heard the rumors of the "queers' baby," and had heard the rumors that the old dyke who ran the Red Rooster was keeping the girl in her hire so that, when the baby came, she would force the girl to give it to the two men. Margaret's homosexuality, however, had not been an issue with JoAnna or Bill, nor with the members of the Unitarian church. But it had troubled them both that such ugly rumors were once again flying around town.

JoAnna had even heard the talk as it spilled into the high school among the students, staff, and faculty. So as soon as she had a chance she decided to find out the real truth of the matter. Once she had met Sharon and had talked with the girl, she continued to listen to the rumors, as well, to see what further ugly twists and turns the story took.

When she learned that there were people hanging out at the hospital to find out about the baby and where it was going to live, she increased her vigilance. She had quite easily discovered who the preacher of the Calvary Mission was and knew quite a few of the members, through her contact with the high school students who came to her counseling office.

It seemed almost predictable that the parents of the most troubled youth—those with real emotional problems—were members of the Calvary Mission church. Further, with each new discovery, she exchanged information with Margaret, which is how she learned of the preacher Conger's attack on poor Livia and how Livia had been manipulated into visiting the church; apparently it was the preacher's desire to save the baby from eternal damnation. The only thing wrong with that, JoAnna thought, was the disturbing frequency of what she considered real child abuse there in the Calvary Mission church. She had counseled depressed students who felt estranged from their parents, discovering that shortly after joining the church, their parents began to think the end of the world was at hand, or they had smashed their television sets, and could talk of nothing else but Satan being loose in the town of Common. Though JoAnna could not discuss religion with those students she counseled, she could discuss religion with the parents in certain contexts and gained from them a better understanding of just how controlling—and effective—the preacher Conger was.

Such fear mongering and the perverted use of religion was an assault on JoAnna's own religious sensibilities. So, shortly after the baby's homecoming, JoAnna was ready to act on the information she had gathered. What form such action would take, she did not know. She had discussed the problem with David Suskine, their minister, as well. He cautioned her against attempting to change any of the minds at the fundamentalist church and tried to assure her that, as far as he knew, there wasn't much that such a nutty congregation could really do to threaten the safety and well-being of the child in question, unless it was something illegal; and then, well, it could be dealt with. Nor did he think there was much that group could do to take the baby away from the biological mother, or even the biological father.

"I'm not saying that a court wouldn't have difficulty with the Allen or Reece boy's homosexuality," he said. "As far as I am aware, only we Unitarian Universalists have taken a positive position as regards that issue. But the court system is equally unprepared to take children away from their parents, unless it's a case of gross neglect or physical abuse."

Bill had said the same thing, so when JoAnna had told him that she intended to visit the church, to see if she could discover any overt activity the members might be planning, he had put his foot down. "In this, Jo, I simply can not go along with you."

"What! You can take the kind of chance you did with Joel, when he came to you that first time, asking about his feelings for Tom, remember? But I can't attend the church? I told them I would try to help."

Bill had prevailed, however, saying that too many of the students and some of the parents in the church would recognize her. "They know what church we go to, Jo, and you'll do nothing but arouse their suspicions and raise their ire."

She hated to admit that he was right and was trying to think of another way she might discover the Calvary Mission's activities but, until today, she had come up with few ideas.

When the morning was finally over, she and Bill fought the wind and the dust to get home for their lunch break, and were sitting down to leftovers, when Tom Allen called.

He sounded faint, as if the wind had invaded the phone lines, and worried, as if something worse might have happened since Margaret's call, earlier.

"Is your mother all right, Tom?" she asked, as Bill sat at the kitchen table listening to her end of the conversation. At her question, his eyebrows went up, and she just nodded at him, listening to Tom on the other end.

When she got off the phone, she sat down and continued eating. She filled Bill in on the news of the morning and then, "I guess you gathered that was Tom Allen. Livia is fine, but Tom said he got a scare when he found her at that Calvary Mission church."

Bill looked surprised, but nodded. "I guess Tom's mother must have had the same idea you did. So…?"

"It's too long to go into," JoAnna said. "But Tom did ask me to drop by Livia's house this afternoon, after I leave school. You're welcome to come."

He shook his head. "I would, ordinarily, Jo, but baseball practice is shifting into high gear."

She understood and, so, when she returned to work, she spent the afternoon trying to clear up as much of the paperwork as she could. Although the afternoon was almost as interminable as the morning, it finally came to a close. She stopped at the baseball field where the sand was scouring her husband's face raw and promised to return to pick him up by six.

Within five minutes of leaving the school, she pulled up into the driveway, where she recognized Tom and Joel's old pickup. There were two other cars at the house as well, one a relatively new Ford and the other of such an age and ill condition, she couldn't imagine what kind it was.

Her knock was answered instantly. It was Tom. He led her into the living room and introduced her to his mother. Then in a rather startling introduction, she met Mary Conger, the preacher's wife. After a quick exchange of greetings, Tom said, "We've managed to find out quite a bit from Mary. Only problem is she doesn't have too much time. Her husband is asleep, but she doesn't think she can be gone too long."

"She's supposed to be grocery shopping," Livia Allen said.

Mary and Livia were sitting on the sofa. Tom was sitting in a matching chair closest to the door, and JoAnna was seated in another matching chair next to the fireplace. The three of them looked liked conspirators and JoAnna wondered what the real urgency was; she could even hear it in Tom's voice. The light in the living room was dim, but even from the lamp that burned between the sofa and the chair she was sitting in, JoAnna could see that Mary Conger was not a healthy woman. Her hair, while apparently clean, was like straw, her forehead had wrinkle lines and the rest of her face was lined, as well, due less to age, which JoAnna guessed was mid-forties, and due more to what she thought might be a protein or vitamin deficiency of some sort.

Mary would not look directly at her and was sitting on the sofa with her purse clutched in her lap, as if she were about to leave at any moment.

Livia Allen was in every way the opposite in appearance, from her head of lustrous dark hair, to a rather youngish, if thin, face, though she knew her to be at least fifty, considering Tom's age. But there was a connection between the two women that intrigued JoAnna.

"Mary has been a big help in the last couple of days," Livia said. "Now we'd like to help her."

Still Mary did not answer, but kept her face focused on Livia, only turning to JoAnna and nodding.

JoAnna waited, as apparently Livia and Tom seemed to have important news. Tom sat forward in his chair. "Mary told us what her husband has been up to regarding the members of the church and their interest in my daughter. Mother was tricked into going over there yesterday, as you've probably heard by now. Conger was rough with her, and Mother ended up knocking him over the head with a mug of coffee."

At this, JoAnna wanted to laugh, as unlikely as it seemed for Livia to be the sort of woman who would first of all get herself involved in a situation like that, and second that she would fight back as she did. But she didn't say anything, because she saw that something else was coming.

"We thought you'd be able to counsel Mary," Livia said. "She's been physically abused by her husband, and we're trying to convince her to leave him, sooner than later."

JoAnna was surprised. She was also dismayed to see that the Conger woman was so far abused that she no longer felt she could speak for herself. It was a classic sign of chronic abuse and, from what she knew of such cases, it would be next to impossible to get her to take the real steps necessary to leave the abusive relationship. But she didn't say that. "Of course, Livia, I'll be glad to help in any way I can."

It was then that Mary finally spoke up, looking directly at JoAnna for the first time. "I don't know about leaving my husband, Mrs. Hoffins. I've tried in the past, and he's always found me and brought me back."

The classic feeling of lack of power, JoAnna thought. She nodded. "I am sure it is difficult, it"—

"I am more concerned," Mary said, cutting her off, "that folks in this town learn that my husband's chu'ch harbors a nest of snakes."

"You don't mean actual—?"

"No, ma'am. Though we do keep a few rattlers for special services 'an all."

JoAnna could hardly take a breath at the thought; she nodded, feeling completely unable to offer any intelligent response.

"Then what exactly do you mean, dear?" Livia asked.

Mary turned to her. "Snakes who want your grandchild, Livia. Snakes who use the innocent babies what are already in the chu'ch," she said, turning back to JoAnna.

JoAnna leaned forward, feeling apprehensive, though still not comprehending what Mary was really trying to say. In truth, the woman sounded like a nut case. In leaning forward, she saw old bruises that had gone to yellow spots around her eyes, but which were barely visible.

"What do they do with the babies, Mary? Who does these things?" Again, it was Livia who spoke, who still had her wits enough to follow Mary's words.

"The babies are punished for the sins of the fathers," Mary said. Her voice had become low, again, and she looked down, rather than maintaining eye contact. "Punished by the fathers."

"How old are the babies?" JoAnna asked. She touched Mary on the leg, resting her hand there for a moment, feeling her trembling. She realized that Mary was just barely able to maintain control of herself. It was taking tremendous courage for her to speak at all.

"Younguns, mostly," she said, looking up again and looking JoAnna in the eyes. "Girls, mostly, too."

"Is your husband one of these men?" Livia asked.

Mary shook her head. "No."

"No?" JoAnna asked, wondering if Mary could admit it, even if it were true. "You can tell us, Mary. Your husband will not find out you've talked to us."

Mary shook her head. "He does not punish the children," she said. "He believes that each father must punish his own child. His is the voice of God. The fathers are like Abraham. Those who would do as God says are the true believers—even if it is to sacrifice their own children."

Outside the wind had begun to die down as the sun moved toward the horizon, and by sunset, it would be calm. JoAnna looked at her watch and saw that it was already half-past five.

"Mary," she said. "I am a guidance counselor at the high school, here in town. Which is probably why Tom and Livia wanted me to come over this afternoon. I'm not clear on exactly what you say, but it does not matter. Right now I am more concerned for you. I know it took a lot of courage for you to tell us about your husband and the activities of the men in the church. These things ought to be investigated. If innocent children are being harmed in some way, and if it is with the...ah...direction of your husband, the State should look into it. But do you wish to leave your husband?"

Mary nodded, and JoAnna maintained eye contact with her, watching for signs that she was shutting her out or had ceased to listen. She could read such signs in the students she counseled, but so far, Mary was listening. So she continued.

"All right. Good. Would you like to do that this afternoon?"

Mary's eyes flickered, began to look away.

"Please, Mary. Listen to me! Just for a moment more."

Mary looked at her, again, beginning to visibly shake. "We're a small community, here, in Common," JoAnna said, "and though there are those who do not help each other, and others who are responsible for a lot of the hurt that takes place, you are among those right now who can keep you safe from your husband."

"But he'll find me. He always does." Her voice was almost inaudible.

JoAnna nodded. "This time, Mary, he'll know exactly where you are, but he won't be able to hurt you, or talk to you, if you don't want him to."

Mary looked doubtful, but she did not look away. "Then how? I'll do it. But if it's just the three of you, I'm sorry to say, you're wrong. He'll get me right back."

Livia had been quiet for a few minutes, but now she moved a little closer to Mary on the sofa and touched her on the shoulder. "It's not just the three of us, dear." Then she looked at JoAnna. "Is it?"

JoAnna sensed Livia's doubt as well. But she said, "No, it's not just the three of us." Now she had to come up with something that would protect Mary as she had just promised. If she backed away because she herself was afraid of the consequences, Mary would lose trust in her, and she would never leave her husband.

"May I use your phone?" JoAnna asked.

"Use the one in the kitchen, dear," Livia said, "by the refrigerator."

A few moments had passed, and JoAnna tried to look confident as she dug through her purse, as though looking for something. It was a tactic she had learned with the students she had counseled, the particularly vulnerable and frightened ones, those who were afraid to go home because they were pregnant, or as in the case of Leo Johnson, the homosexual friend of Tom and Joel, afraid even to leave her office. She pulled out a fat notebook that she carried with a list of telephone numbers of contacts in other schools, hospitals, juvenile detention facilities—her own kind of bible. It's very bulk and worn edges gave students the sense that this was an important kind of notebook; even if it was not one that held all the answers, it was the way in which JoAnna used it that set their minds at ease.

The tactic worked on JoAnna as well, because as soon as she flipped through the notebook, an idea came to her, and she got up then, feeling as confident as she had tried to look for Mary's benefit. She knew exactly who she was going to call, and she knew that he would help her.

CHAPTER 24

THE GAME,
AS THEY SAY, IS UP

When the telephone call came in from JoAnna Hoffins, Doctor Albert Hossley was at the children's hospice. It took only a few minutes of conversation for him to agree.

"You bet, Jo. We'll put Mrs. Conger up at my private clinic, and we'll hold her there for medical reasons, if she's as run down as you say.

"What? Restricted access? Of course I can, especially in the case of abuse.

"No, that shouldn't be a problem, either."

He began scribbling notes, which he would pass off to one of his assistants.

"I will check my records. You say for the child abuse cases?

"Right. I have noticed that trend, as a matter of fact."

He hung up the phone and from a hook by the door, he pulled on his white lab coat.

Albert Hossley was a general practitioner, but specialized in pediatrics. He was nearing retirement age, and would be relieved to settle down at home with his wife of 40 years, who had not only been his devoted companion, mother to his six children, but also his nurse in his private clinic. Together, they had built up a lucrative practice, as well as having been instrumental in gathering funding for the children's wing on the county hospital. It had become known as the children's hospice, since many of the children who were admitted into that wing ended up living there until they died, or until they were institution-alized elsewhere.

He was a practical man and a good doctor, but he saw the writing on the wall as concerned the eventual demise of the children's ward if they could not attract more doctors to the small town, young ones who would have the stam-ina, both physically and emotionally, to deal with the horrors he had seen of the children who entered the hospice. He had, therefore, spent much of his later years traveling the country, speaking at medical conferences and practi-cally begging the newest medical school graduates to think about starting their practice in the rural counties of the country—but most importantly *his* rural county. Within the last year, he had snagged two bright doctors, one of whom had arrived roughly about the same time that Sharon Minninger had given birth to her daughter, the other doctor, a woman, had arrived not more than a week ago, and as he left the office, he asked her to accompany him on his rounds at the hospice.

Her name was Clara Tyler. She was only in residency at the hospital, but Albert hoped to convince her to stay, once she had put in her two years. She was energetic, pretty, and had studied general medicine, but had agreed to come to Common to further specialize in pediatrics. Although her duties saw her make rounds and take cases from the main part of the hospital, she devoted three days a week to the children's ward.

They entered the children's wing, and Albert led her through the rooms where the long-term patients lived.

"Do you know anything at all about autism?" he asked. He handed her the file on Linton Dean Hoffins. "Note my entries. We've made absolutely no progress whatsoever. This child is eight years old and still does not speak, engages in bloody, self-destructive behavior, and if he's not restrained, he's medicated." He hoped, by his descriptions of the horrors and hopelessness of some of the cases, to charm her into staying. Following the call from JoAnna, he had an even more immediate need.

Doctor Tyler was a brunette with short-cropped hair and wore John Lennon glasses, crisp white blouse and skirt and what he could only think of as hippie beads around her neck. She was petite and thin-hipped, munched on apples and other fruit when she was not busy or reading reports, and made friends with the nurses, both male and female, and had them eating out of the palm of her hand.

"The current theory holds that autism has an emotional, rather than a physiological cause," she said in answer to his question. "Therapy involves operant conditioning."

"Which means?"

They had seated themselves at the patient's bedside. At the moment he was calm and sitting up in bed with a beatific glow on his face. There were bruises on his forehead, where he had beaten himself with a spoon someone had forgotten to remove after his meal. Doctor Tyler took his pulse, shined a penlight into his eyes to check for pupil dilation, and handed the file back to Albert. "It means that, as far as autism is concerned, we're nothing more than witchdoctors. There has to be something wrong with their brains, Albert."

He nodded, taking note of her passion, finding himself attracted to her rather luscious mouth, the curve of her neck. "Why do you say that?" he asked, as they left the Hoffins boy and went into a room where two children were sitting up in bed reading. Cancer patients. They did not stay to disturb them. Clara tucked their files under one arm, as they entered the next room, where a little girl, not more than four years old, lay unconscious, with bruises and contusions around her eyes. One arm was enclosed in a plaster cast from her hand to her shoulder; the other displayed burn marks.

"Her father used her for a god-damned ashtray," Albert whispered. He looked at his notes from the phone call and checked the surname on the folder. Sure enough this was one of the children whose parents listed their religious affiliation as the Calvary Mission.

Clara checked the child's vital signs, opened one of her eyes and shined the penlight. She spun around. "Why do I say autism has to be physiological, rather than psycho-emotional?" She asked, visibly shaken by the girl's condition.

Albert grimaced, looking at the little girl and shaking his head. "Why?"

"Because perfectly healthy, well-cared for and much loved children get autism. Then you have something as grotesque as this." She indicated the little girl, studying the chart at the foot of the bed. "Children like this are physically and psychologically tortured and, yet, they speak and interact with other children, go to school, and in many cases hide their hellish lives from the teachers, until one day, their frigging parents beat them to a pulp. But no autism. The quack psychotherapists who practice Skinnerian Voodoo tell you that, by rewarding appropriate behavior when the autistic child even remotely approximates it, you can instill a conditioned response to, say, getting the child to look you in the eyes when you're talking to him. You also withhold your reward when the child does not perform."

Albert nodded. "So you're saying it doesn't work?"

"It makes the therapists feel good, I suppose," Clara said.

Albert laughed. "Well, see what you can make of the Hoffins boy. His parents are about ready to call in a witchdoctor, anyway. They've tried everything else."

They made their way through the rest of the ward. Some of the children were only in for short hospital stays, and then they would be sent right back to the environment that would more than likely send them back in six months.

"Then we have this child," Albert said, standing outside a room and handing Clara a file. She opened it to a single sheet of paper. "Bruised labia, tearing, vaginal blood," Albert said. "She's a new admit. Came in last night."

Clara scanned the sheet on the girl. They looked into the room, but the lights were dimmed and she was asleep. "Do they know who did this to her?"

Albert nodded, as they walked into the doctors lounge, where he poured himself a cup of coffee, and Clara found a teabag and poured hot water into a cup. They sat at a table next to south-facing windows that looked out onto a playground, which was invisible in the dark, since the windows were reflecting the lounge in its panes. He took a sip of coffee, then folded his hands under his chin. "There's this church that operates in the north part of town." He indicated the folder that Clara had set aside. "Angela is the youngest of eight children in the...Franklin family. Three boys and five girls. Every girl child in that family, as well as several other girls whose families attend that church have been in here in the last year. The god-damned church has only been here a year, but the preacher...Billy Bob something or other has been packing 'em in, or so I hear. And every sharecropping, pig-slopping, beer-sucking redneck in the county and their enormous child population have suddenly got religion."

"You sound angry," Clara said, smiling, dipping her tea bag up and down in the steaming water, looking up at him, then back down as she took a spoon and squeezed the strong vestiges of tea out of the bag. "Is it because he's attracting all the poor people to his church? Or because they're rednecks?"

Albert laughed and grimaced. "A little of both, maybe. But I'm angry because until that church came, we saw occasional abuse; now we see it regularly. But if I hadn't dug a little, trying to find out what the common denominator was between apparent disparate cases, I never would have discovered that *all* the children go to the same church. I'm an old man, Clara, and I would retire five minutes from now, if I could, but we've got some kind of stinking plague on our hands." Then he told her about his call from JoAnna Hoffins. "I'm going to be admitting the preacher's wife to my clinic this evening. She's in for observation, but Mrs. Hoffins, the mother of the autistic child you just met, says that Mrs. Conger, the preacher's wife, has been sharing some interesting information about her husband and some of the other men from the church. Which brings us back to our child-abuse cases. If that cracker's not at the head of the line, he's somehow behind it."

"Meaning the preacher?" Clara asked.

"You tell me," Albert Hossley said. "There's something more, too."

Then he told Clara about his recent new mother, Sharon Minninger. He told her about her child's two fathers, naming them, telling her he had objected to it, the way the two young men had gone about fathering the child.

She was smiling oddly. "Why are you telling me this, Albert? Aren't you just gossiping?"

Her eyes were lit up with something Albert could not put his finger on. "Of course I'm gossiping, my dear. But I'm telling you about Joel Reece and his homosexual partner, Tom Allen, because I'd rather you hear a simple, sane version of it than the wildly provocative rumors that occasionally fly through the town—most of them now coming out of that same church I've been telling you about. I have been the family doctor to the Reeces for twenty-five years, and I've treated their son, Joel, for everything from a dislocated shoulder when he fell out of a tree, to broken ribs when he got beat up by his pals on the boxing team a few years ago. He and Tom assisted with their daughter's birth. That child is going to grow up happy and healthy and as well treated as I treated my own children—maybe better. But I've heard from the staff in the maternity ward that our good friend, Billy Bob, is whipping up his redneck congregation about our gay boys, warning of child abuse, of course with Satan thrown in. Yet…look where the perversion is coming from."

Clara smiled then, and the look in her eyes meant that he'd fired her up. He hoped he'd shown her enough in one day to challenge her Hippocratic enthusiasm for the next ten years.

"You really know how to perform PR on a new, enthusiastic recruit, don't you, Doctor?"

He grinned. "I'm too old to keep this up, young lady. In this ward, you need to not only be a doctor, but a god-damned detective and a frigging cop."

"Meaning that in this ward, you go well beyond the call of duty? What if the child's parents get upset? What do you do, make house calls?"

"Something like that," Albert said. "Or you just keep your ear to the ground and listen to the gossip you hear. Now you want to hear just how small this town is?"

Clara shrugged, smiling.

"I treated the preacher just yesterday for a concussion and released him this morning."

"Somebody in his congregation beat him up? What?"

"No, Tom Allen's mother attacked him, according to the preacher. He was ready to file assault charges against her."

This time Clara grinned, and the odd look in her eyes was back. "You're talking about one of the gay boy's mothers?"

"Indeed. Had I strictly taken the preacher's word for it, I would have thought Mrs. Allen was just a fringe lunatic and dismissed her. But it didn't take long to find out she was considered one of the upstanding citizens of our fair community a few years ago, when her own husband was the preacher at a church here in town. She's now the proud grandmother—or possibly the grandmother—of Sharon Minninger's child."

"And we come back full circle, I take it. So what did you find out to be the real truth in this assault?"

"I haven't looked into that. But I suspect that my new admit, Mrs. Conger, will fill me in on the details."

"And you want something from me, right?"

Dr. Hossley grinned. "You're a doctor aren't you? In this little town we still make house calls. But back to our problems with the increase in child abuse, might I suggest that you at least meet the mother of the baby that church is so excited about? Her name is Sharon Minninger. She works at the Red Rooster Café, run by a handsome old lady by the name of Margaret Jost; probably Germanic. I think you'll like her. She's the one who brought Sharon to me when the girl turned up pregnant. She's taken Sharon under her wing. Sharon even lives with her, I believe. And even though some say Margaret is a female homosexual, I doubt that she's helping the girl out of some selfish interest like that."

Clara's face went through so many contortions, he just waited for her to compose herself, sipping his coffee and grinning at her.

"You mean the mother doesn't live with this Tom and Joel?" Clara finally asked. "I would've thought"—

Albert laughed, smiling at her and winking. "The baby does. But not the mother, as far as I know. I think that was the deal they made with her."

This time, Clara frowned. "That's horrible! She gave up her own child?"

"It's a lot more complex than that, Doctor Tyler. Now, about those house calls..."

*   *   *

That evening, as soon as Clara looked in on her last patient and read over the nurse's reports, signing paperwork and otherwise completing her duties at the hospital, she drove home and changed into casual clothes. Then she made a few phone calls, took a few notes, which she kept in a steno pad, and headed out the door, her heart and mind ready for her duty as a "detective." *That sly old fox,* she thought, smiling to herself at Doctor Hossley's home-spun wisdom. She also smiled with satisfaction at how damned easy it was to find out just about anything about anybody in this small town. Having come from Chicago, where it was easy to lose oneself in the crowds, she was actually amazed that meeting one person would soon put you in touch with almost anyone else.

She doubted that the good doctor realized she herself was a lesbian; and she was glad she would meet another woman of the same "religion" here in Common. She had fully intended to put her personal life on hold, until she completed her residency, then head right back to Chicago or some other civilized place to practice medicine. She had not been prepared, either for the interesting and heart-rending challenges of practicing medicine in a rural community, or the refreshing friendliness of the small town.

She parked her VW bug around the corner from the Red Rooster Café and tucked the steno pad into her canvas bag. At twenty-eight years old, dressed as she was in a long skirt, sandals, and a rather tight-fitting tie-dyed T-shirt, over which she wore a light denim jacket, she looked no more than eighteen or twenty-one. She hoped her rather innocent looks would disarm anyone into talking to her.

But on this interview with Margaret Jost and her waitress, Sharon Minninger, the mother of the controversial baby, she doubted she'd have much trouble getting them to tell her what she needed to know.

The air was chilly on her back as she walked east on the sidewalk, but a moment later, she entered the cozy atmosphere of the café. She liked the feel of it immediately. She recognized Margaret Jost as soon as she laid eyes on the rather striking woman behind the cash register. The way Doctor Hossley had described her fit perfectly. She was handsome, indeed.

"You can sit anywhere you'd like, dear," Margaret said to her, as Clara stood next to the counter looking about the room. "We won't be busy for another hour."

Clara smiled at her, then introduced herself. "I've actually come to see you Miss Jost and the new mother, Sharon Minninger. I work with Doctor Hossley at the children's hospice. He was telling me about Miss Minninger. She was his patient during her pregnancy. The baby's what...two weeks old, now?"

Margaret's face went from a friendly smile to a large grin. "Oh, yes, child! Sharon's baby is growing fast, gaining weight right on schedule." Then she lost her smile. "But *why* did you say you have come? Sharon takes the baby in for regular check ups."

Clara touched the old lady's hand. "I'd prefer to sit down for a few minutes, if you don't mind. He's sent me on a rather non-medical mission, and I do think you'll be interested in hearing what I have to say."

"I'm afraid that Sharon is with the baby, right now," Margaret said. "But if I can be of help, I believe I can take off a few minutes. I do have an office where we can talk in private."

A few moments later, Margaret showed Clara into what turned out to be a store room as much as it was an office, and she looked around at the stacks of paraphernalia that had more to do with displays she imagined than the nuts and bolts of operating a restaurant.

Margaret indicated a couch on one side of the room, which Clara had to share with a brood of plaster chickens, while Margaret seated herself in a rocking chair, rather than behind her desk, which was piled up with bundles of restaurant checks, rolls of register tape and an assortment of napkin dispensers, salt and pepper shakers, and a lone photograph in a standing frame. It was turned toward the couch and Clara studied the picture of the woman in the photo. She was standing beside a car that Clara could only think of as gangster era.

Clara leaned over and picked up the photo. "Is this you, Margaret...ah... you don't mind if I call you that, do you?"

Margaret watched her study the picture, then smiled. "No I don't mind. In fact I prefer it—or Marge. No, dear. That's not me. Her name is Rose."

"She's beautiful!" Clara said. Her heart skipped a beat, but she decided she was going to come out on the spot. "I could settle down with someone like that, if you know what I mean." She watched Margaret's reaction, and regretted her boldness. Margaret blushed and fought to keep a smile on her face.

"Clara? Is that what you said your name was?"

Clara nodded.

"If someone has put you up to this"—

"No! Please, Margaret! No one has! I really mean I *could* choose a mate like Rose. I am not trying to be cruel or play some trick on you."

Still, Margaret did not quite relax, though now she smiled a little, her embarrassment appearing to make room for curiosity. "I don't think I'll even ask you from whom you might have learned my little secret—or maybe I just look like a dyke."

Clara still felt badly for her boldness. She shook her head. "You do not look like a dyke. I just hate that word. It puts us in such a limited and convenient box. Not that there's anything wrong with being butch..." she trailed off but was glad to see that Margaret was now smiling, again, even if it was tentatively.

"My! I haven't heard those terms in years! I can't think of the last time I've used them, myself. But I don't think you are here, are you, to...what is the term? Come out to me? You mentioned your mission? Something to do with Sharon?"

"I have to confess that I didn't intend to discuss our mutual kinship. I just couldn't help it." She realized she was still holding the photograph and gently replaced it on the desk. "So, let me be brief, then."

She told Margaret of Doctor Hossley's suspicions that the Calvary Mission church and its pastor was either encouraging or instigating child abuse and some of it sexual in nature. "There've been too many cases in the last year—all of them from that church—for it to be mere coincidence." Clara told her.

Margaret then told her about the people from that same church coming to the maternity ward when Sharon's baby was born, the warning from one of the nurses, and the assault on Tom Allen-Reece's mother. "She was so distraught when she came to me for help," Margaret said. "And so fearful, not only for the safety of the baby, but that her son would somehow think she was to blame for the church's interest in the baby—which of course was unfounded. Still, it caused her some grief and fright."

"The preacher told Dr. Hossley that Mrs. Allen attacked *him*," Clara said. "What did Mrs. Allen say?"

Margaret related Livia's story; then after a moment of silence she said, "I'm afraid, however, that I can be of little help about this other, this sexual abuse, though I wouldn't put anything past those religious zealots." She also told Clara about the ugly incidents in the café and elsewhere from some of the other people of the town toward Tom, Joel, and even Sharon. "There's a cop in jail, right now, who was stalking the Reece family, but especially Tom and Joel. Joel confronted him one night, which…well, it's hardly relevant to your project, do you think?"

Clara had been jotting down the names of some of the people Margaret had mentioned. She did it openly, so that Margaret could read her notes as she wrote them. This newest revelation about yet another set of incidents interested Clara, but she nodded. "I agree, it's probably not relevant to the case of the Calvary Mission. But I would be interested sometime in learning more about it."

They visited, then, and Clara was gratified to hear of Margaret's long relationship with Rose. Then she got up and, when Margaret also stood up, she hugged her. "Thank you, Marge, for your help. Do you think it would be too forward of me to call on these two young men? Of course, I'm mainly interested in what they may have found out about the church, but I'd like to hear how they feel about being gay in such a small town. I thought I was going to have to just bury myself in my work and forget about my personal life. But it's difficult to be so isolated."

Margaret's eyes were bright with tears, but she smiled through them. "I dare say it has been that way for me, which is why I go to the Unitarian church, if you want to know the truth of the matter. I am *out* to certain members, there, though I suspect that, despite your saying I don't look butch, my appearance gives me away to the more alert customers."

At this they both laughed and hugged, again. Then, as Clara was leaving, Margaret invited her to come that evening for coffee. "You'll at least think about it?"

Clara smiled as they were once more standing at the cash register. "I will definitely be there. What time?"

"I'm usually home by nine." She wrote her address and telephone number on Clara's steno pad. "I think I can persuade the boys to stop by as well. It will make for an interesting evening."

That it would, Clara thought. In her mind she checked off people she had intended to see. After tonight, she would find a way to investigate the church and its members. Though what tactic she might use to discover what, if anything, was being done in the church to cause the rash of child abuse, she had no idea.

*   *   *

When Albert left the hospital, he went straight to his clinic and, as good as her word, JoAnna Hoffins led the woman, Mary Conger, into his office.

"I really hate to run, Albert," JoAnna said, "but I've left my husband at the high school, and he's probably not real happy with me for that."

Albert nodded and barely glanced toward the door as JoAnna left. He introduced his wife to Mrs. Conger, and told her he wanted to keep her there for the night, and give her something to help her sleep. He seated Mary on the edge of a bed in a small room off the office.

"But what about my husband, doctor? You know he's had that concussion, and I left him home this afternoon."

Albert took a breath. "Your husband will be just fine, Mrs. Conger. He's an emotional man, and I daresay that most of what brought on those convulsions was just a little bit concussion, a touch of temper, and some pretty good acting."

Mary looked at him and a very thin smile crept onto her face. "Then you think he's going to be all right?"

Albert smiled, as well. "It is your intent, isn't it, to leave him? That was my impression from Mrs. Hoffins."

"I cain't say as I'd particularly like to go home. You don't think that's a bad thing?"

"I'd say, Mrs. Conger, if you're feeling poorly, now, it's a good thing if you would permit me to keep you here, safe, for a few days. I'll be sure to let your husband know you're under a doctor's care."

At this, Mary Conger's eyes widened in fear. "He ain't gonna like that."

Albert grimaced. "I can't say as he's got much choice in the matter, unless you object. Do you?"

Mary appeared to relax. "I don't object. I just knew his evil ways were going to need light shined on them. I just wisht, now, it hadn't taken me so long to do it."

"At least you've finally done it, Mrs. Conger. So the game, as they say, is up for your husband. I suspect that in a few days that church is going to change preachers."

PART THREE

CONSEQUENCES

CHAPTER 25

A PASSING WIND,
A CHANGE OF SEASONS

It seemed to Joel that a kind of blind season had passed through their lives in the last year. He was reminded of that old saying that when rattlesnakes are shedding their skins, they're blind and feel vulnerable and strike out of fear at anything that moves. It had been that kind of year, he thought, where the people he knew and even those whom he loved had struck out at one another, sometimes blindly, sometimes feeling vulnerable or fearful of one thing or another. He also knew that he had brought about much of the trouble by finally getting his way, finally getting a child of his own, a child he could be a father to. And then, of course, because of the scandal it had caused among the townspeople, others in his family had been affected, or threatened. Whether it was the police officer Barela, who sneered at him and Tom for the marriage they had, or his old friends. Just as they had turned against him six years before when they found out he was gay, they struck out at him and his family, again, when they found out that he and Tom had gotten Sharon pregnant. Then it was the religious nuts of Common, once more threatening their lives by threatening their baby.

He thought of all this because, this morning, as he read Common's only newspaper, *The Common Voice*, there were two articles in that week's edition that had caught his eye, reminding him of the bad times just past. First, in a final segment of a story the paper had carried for weeks, he read that Eugene

Barela had been not only convicted of kidnapping, but the district attorney had also managed to tack on and receive a conviction for attempted murder— both charges came back from the jury with a "guilty" verdict. The second article, which Joel read with even more attention and relief was the one about Billy Conger, now convicted felon and former pastor of the John the Baptist Calvary Mission. Both the accusations and charges against him were more vague in Joel's mind, and the writer of the article only referred to statutes and child welfare; but for weeks, that particular trial had caused the greatest stir in the town since he could remember.

Even though Conger was not charged with child molestation, members of the congregation had been; and the testimony of Conger's wife, Mary, had implicated the good preacher in the middle of it. "Inciting already disturbed individuals to act inappropriately and even harmfully," the paper said. Women and men, husbands and wives, *heterosexual* people, Joel thought. *And they thought we would do bad things to our daughter?* The article disturbed him, deep down, the same way he had been bothered the year he and Tom volunteered in the children's hospice and had witnessed, first hand, the horrors that parents could do to their children. As he read, he wondered how anyone could do such things to innocent and helpless babies.

It helped Joel to know that people talked about a renewal of morality in the small town of Common. With the ouster of the preacher Billy Conger, and his subsequent conviction and jail time, Joel felt his relief rising, again thinking of the bad time that had passed through the town. But the storm, like the howling spring winds, seemed to have subsided.

Margaret had said that people had even lost interest in them, their baby, and Sharon Minninger. So, it looked as though he and Tom could finally begin enjoying their new lives as parents.

He put the paper aside. He was sitting at the kitchen table holding the baby, Shara. A couple of weeks before, they had successfully switched her to formula, rather than Sharon's breast milk and, though she didn't like it at first, now she hungrily nursed the bottle Joel held. He looked down at her, smiling at the way she gripped the bottle with both her little hands. She was growing like the weeds in the field, he thought.

She was looking at him, seeming to study his face. Her eyes had finally begun to show their true colors and he was secretly thrilled, as he looked back at her. They were gray like his own, and if those little blue striations stayed in her irises, like his, there was just as much chance that she was his baby as there was that she was Tom's. He and Tom had bantered good naturedly back and forth about her different traits.

"She has my hair color."

"She has my hands."

"Yeah, well, she's got my mouth."

This morning, he whispered to her, so Tom couldn't hear. "You've got my eyes, don't you, Shara?"

"I heard that, babe," Tom said, coming to the table with two cups of coffee. He set one down in front of Joel, then sat in the chair next to him. He set his own cup down and leaned over the baby.

"Sha-a-a-ra?"

The baby turned her attention to Tom at the sound of his voice, letting the nipple of the bottle slip out of her mouth.

"Let's see those eyes," he said, looking down at her, then up at Joel. "Nope. It's just the way the light hits them. Besides, Sharon's eyes are pale blue, so there you are."

They both laughed.

"She really seems to recognize our voices," Joel said, as they both looked at their daughter. Sure enough, Shara looked back at Joel when he spoke, and grinned toothlessly.

As they sat there playing with the baby, talking about little things they'd noticed about her, the sun began to rise above the Floridas to the east, making the living room, then the kitchen, glow with rosy light.

In the past month, the temperatures had risen, as well, so that it would reach into the nineties by midday.

Shara was still dressed in a little yellow sleeper that Sharon had brought her one day about a week before, surprising them both when she knocked on the door and they asked where Margaret was.

"I drove by myself!" she said. "I have been keeping it a secret from you until I could drive out here. It is not so difficult, since I could drive at the community, though only the boys were permitted to drive beyond the farms."

Then she went straight to the nursery, where Shara had been put down for a nap.

They followed her into the room and Joel watched her looking at her baby. She had been living back in town with Margaret for about a week, and Joel thought he could detect a look of sadness in her eyes, when she picked the baby up. Neither he nor Tom objected, even though Shara had been asleep for less than half an hour.

"I miss you little Shara Margaret!" Sharon whispered to the baby. She held the baby close to her chest, handing the new sleeper to Tom. "I picked this out for her the other day."

Later, just before she was leaving, Sharon told them she had gotten her driver's license. "I passed the written test. I missed three questions, and the police officer who went with me on the drive said I was a safe driver—even though Margaret's car is so huge and the steering is...loose. Is this the right term?"

It was, they told her and walked with her down the flagstones to the gate. Then they watched her drive off in Margaret's old Buick.

"Joel?"

Joel looked at Tom. "Did you say something?"

"I said I think Shara just pooped."

They both smiled down at her, and Joel got up, setting the bottle on the table. "Guess I was thinking about Sharon. She's going to need a car, don't you think?"

Tom nodded. "Funny I was thinking about that the other day when she was out. We're going to have to do some serious thinking, how we're going to swing one."

Since Joel did not handle the checking account or the savings or, for that matter, involve himself with any of the bookkeeping, he just looked blankly. "We can't afford it?"

Tom smiled. "We can, honey, but I'm trying to think if it would be better to buy the car outright, and drain our savings that amount, or put it on payments."

"I'll go along with anything you decide," Joel said. "Now about this diaper changing..."

*   *   *

When they left the house it was almost seven o'clock, but the sun was not yet too hot. The sky was a clear blue, and Tom looked around as they walked together down the flagstones. The grass was a rich green, and the leaves of the trees were filling the branches, now, casting parts of their yard in shade. Joel was dressed in Levi's, boots, and a T-shirt and had tied a bandana around his hair. Tom was dressed the same, except for the bandana. In its place he wore a cap. He was carrying the baby. They decided to walk, since Joel would be taking a cultivator into the fields, while Tom would be helping the twins tune up the Reece's Caddie and the twins' vehicles.

It would be a good idea, Tom thought, to ask them what kind of car they thought would be the best. Tom wanted Sharon to have as carefree maintenance on it as possible. He had never owned a vehicle of his own. When he had come to live with Joel, they had always used Joel's pickup, and even now, Tom couldn't imagine needing anything beyond a pickup, since they had rarely taken a road trip of any real distance.

They walked over the irrigation ditch and made their way to the equipment yard. Joel had his arm over Tom's shoulder. "Take good care of my girl, babe. Tell her I'll be home for lunch."

A few minutes later, they passed the barn. Henry saw them, but he didn't stop to visit. He was carrying alfalfa flakes into the barn, where his calf was waiting. He was raising a calf as a 4-H project, getting it ready for the fall fair and livestock show. "Hi, Shara!" he sang out, as he pushed the barn door open with his foot.

The baby wriggled in Tom's arms, as if she wanted to see who had called her name.

When they arrived at the equipment yard and Patrick and Detrick saw them, they dropped their tools and trotted up to them.

"So how's our little niece?" Patrick said. Like Joel, he was wearing a bandana around his long hair, which was much longer than Joel's.

"Yeah, is she walking yet?" Detrick asked on the other side of Tom. His hair was short, and he was wearing a wide-brim Stetson hat. He pulled the blanket away from the baby, and Tom immediately put up his hand to shield her eyes from the burst of sun.

Detrick's look lingered, then he glanced at Tom's face. "She's beginning to look kind'a like you. Did you know that?"

Tom grinned at Joel. "Told you!"

The four of them laughed, since they all shared in the bantering about whose baby Shara really was. It was no longer odd to Tom that those in this family, his own mother, and even some of the members of their church talked about the confusing fatherhood. He had felt uncomfortable about it at first, fearing that the baby might be confused if people brought it up all the time. Now, he thought that, by the time Shara was old enough to wonder where she came from, people wouldn't be talking about it, and he and Joel would have a chance to discover their own way to explain it.

"You guys glad to be back for the summer, again?" Joel asked the twins. "Of course," Patrick said. "You bet!" Detrick echoed. Then Joel took the baby and kissed her on the cheek. "You be a good baby, for your *real* daddy, okay?" He and Tom locked eyes at this and grinned at each other. Then they kissed quickly.

Again, nobody seemed to think it odd, and Tom barely registered the thought himself. Tom took the baby back and called over his shoulder as he was leaving the yard. "I'll be back in a few minutes, guys. I've got something to ask you."

Sally was the first one to greet him at the main house and, at her insistence, he gently transferred Shara to her arms, though he could not quite take his hands away.

"I won't drop her!" Sally protested, but even as she said it, Shara overfilled her arms and Sally's grip increased around the baby's middle as if she were holding onto a squirming puppy. Tom allowed this to continue for a moment, until Sally awkwardly kissed her niece on the forehead, causing the baby to look startled. She handed her back to Tom with a look of relief. "She's heavy!"

Then Eva came into the living room, dressed in jeans and a blousy shirt. She took Shara, clucking her tongue and smiling. "Where are you going to be in about an hour?" she asked Tom.

"Probably at the equipment yard. "You glad to have the twins home?"

Eva smiled down at the baby in her arms and then at Tom. "Of course. All my children are home, at least for awhile. I think we should plan a very large dinner. A real sit-down affair, this time with us, your mother, Margaret, and Sharon. What do you think?"

"It would be great, Eva," he said, noting that she had placed Sharon outside the "us" and didn't know how he felt about that.

As he made his way back to the equipment yard, the sun was beginning to heat things up. Everything was green and beginning to shimmer on this last day in May, and yet not too far distant, Sharon would be away at school. Gone out of her baby's life, and he felt a little sad at the thought.

It was difficult to think of her as the same age as the twins—even a year younger—and yet they thought of her that way. Patrick's best friend Terrance Lawton seemed to think of her in an even different way. Although Tom smiled about that, he didn't know if he really liked Terrance's interest in Sharon. As far as he knew Terrance was a good kid, but he didn't want Sharon to get hurt by someone who might not be as mature as she was.

The day after Patrick had arrived home from college, Patrick and Terrance had come to their house, not only to look at the baby, which had been Patrick's reason for calling on them, but to visit with Sharon.

Terrance's interest in Sharon was especially evident, but so was Sharon's interest in him. She and Terrance and Patrick had soon gone out to the porch to visit, leaving him and Joel alone with the baby and Sally, who was always visiting them.

When Detrick got home from West Texas, he also made the trek up to their house with Patrick in tow. Sharon had not been there that day, but Detrick seemed even more interested in his little niece than his twin. He had held her for much of the evening, playing with her and making faces and swearing that she was trying to talk back. He had even followed Tom into the nursery when she needed changing, then watched as Joel gave her a bath in the kitchen sink, in her little tub.

When Tom arrived at the equipment yard, Douglas was there. He pulled his head out from under the hood of the Caddie. "Shara with grannie?"

"Safely deposited," Tom said. He smiled at the way "Grannie" sounded coming from Douglas, who had always referred to Eva using her name and, sometimes, honey. But now it was Grannie and sometimes Grandmother Eva, when he was distinguishing between her and Tom's mother, whom he referred to as Grandmother Livia, but never Grannie.

Like Joel, as the spring winds had died down and everything began warming up, and as the trials for Barela and Conger ended, Tom had felt a rising sense of relief. But unlike Joel, there was that nagging sadness that did not go away, even as the nights were scented with roses and lilacs blooming in their yards, nor when the cool air came through the kitchen window when he and Joel were cooking dinner, and Shara was in her bassinet in the kitchen with them cooing and playing.

Sharon would be gone soon. He wondered how she felt about it, or if she tried not to think about it. She always seemed happy, always learning new things, beginning to dress even a little more stylishly than she had with the first set of clothes he and Joel had helped her pick out. Though she still did not wear makeup, the texture of her skin and the natural color of her lips were complemented by the clothes she bought for herself.

Soon it was Henry and Douglas, the twins, and Tom working in the equipment yard, moving one vehicle out of the large bay and moving another one in, their talk good-natured and joking, and Tom worked alongside them feeling a sense of belonging, as he never had anywhere else.

Still, there would come a time when the twins would be gone for good, pursuing their own lives, when Henry, and even Sally would be grown up, and even Shara would be gone. The endless summers and the years the family had spent together would be only memories.

When Tom smashed his thumb with a wrench that brought blood under his finger nail, he was snatched back to the present, and was glad of the pain.

CHAPTER 26

BECOMING AN AMERICAN

Sharon did not know to what she owed her good fortune. She often thought back to those terrible times on the farm, among the Brethren, the girl she had been, lying awake nights dreaming of a different life, though all she had ever known was right there among her people. So when she dreamed, the images of what could be were so vague, she could not open her eyes to the darkness within her bedroom and risk losing even the faint image of her dreams. Her eye would catch on the starlight coming through the curtains and touch the surface of the kerosene lamp, and she would be fully back on the farm. So she closed her eyes, stilled her breathing, catching glimpses of what might be. Perhaps the vague dreams came from the times in Casas Grandes when they were in town selling their vegetables, and a rich Americana would approach their tables and, in English, Sharon would ask her with a small voice where she was from.

Tourists told her they were from places like Houston, Pennsylvania, or San Francisco, and Sharon would say, "I am never to have been there," embarrassed because she knew her English was not correct. But then one of the Americans had shown her pictures, had even given her one, saying, "San Francisco is the most beautiful city in the world. It sits on the bay and overlooks the Pacific Ocean and, at night, during the summer, when the nights are warm, the city lights up and reflects itself on the dark waters."

And so Sharon would dream of the most beautiful city in the world, looking at the photograph she had hidden in her room, trying to imagine what it would be like to walk the streets of that city and to see so many lights, and try to see herself there. When she would sneak out of the house and go down by the lake, she would pretend she was sitting by the Pacific Ocean, and the starlight reflecting in the lake's still waters would be the lights of the city shining in the bay.

Then came the time that she was caught by the lake and brought before the elders and questioned, looking on their grim faces for a little kindness and was met with ice; and then was shunned. She recalled then, her days on the streets of Nuevo Casas Grandes, begging for food, and sometimes it would be the rich Americanas who were friendly and gave her a little money. Then came the day that the two beautiful young men introduced themselves and smiled and were so kind.

She relived their kindness many times after they had brought her to the United States, to the town of Common, where their child grew in her belly, and she was taken in by the greatest Americana she had ever met, Margaret Jost, who not only taught her better English but spoke to her in German and Spanish, and took her to the doctor for her baby, and paid what to her were enormous amounts of money with which she could continue to add to her clothing. When the baby was born and she once again had a family in Tom and Joel and Douglas and Eva and Margaret, she was happy.

Still she dreamed and lay awake at night, not knowing how she had been so fortunate, but knowing it was through her baby's fathers that so many good things had happened.

She knew she was fortunate. She now had her birth certificate that JoAnna Hoffins and Margaret had helped her get, then came her Social Security card, and then she was able to open her own bank account, and now she could open her purse and pull out her wallet and there was her driver's license.

Slowly, but steadily, she felt she was becoming that which she had pretended to be, an American, a citizen of the United States.

There were bad times, as well there should be, she thought, when the bad people with bad intentions, like that Jeannie Lynn and Bill Crawford and others pretended to befriend her, then tried to make her sad in the Angus Iron restaurant. But as the weeks and months passed, those bad memories faded and joined the bad memories of her time on the streets of Casas Grandes as a beggar.

And still yet her good fortune did not stop, for among her family were the twins, Patrick and Detrick, who took her out with them to the movies when they returned from university, and they brought with them the very handsome and nice Terrance Lawton, who made Sharon feel things; though he seemed much younger to her than Sharon felt of herself. But he and the twins talked of school, and Terrance and Patrick told her that she should come to Berkeley, once she got her high school diploma, and they would take care of her at UC.

"You're smart and beautiful," Terrance had said one night. "You'll love Berkeley." She had asked where that was, and when he said near San Francisco, her heart began to thud. "Am I truly smart enough?" she asked, though her throat was closing up with emotion, "to go there?"

Terrance had only laughed and got this look in his eyes and she knew he wanted to kiss her, and she wished that he would, but he did not and she nodded to herself. It was good that he was hesitant to do so.

Then came the day when Tom and Joel came into the Red Rooster smiling broadly and looking much as they had when they befriended her in Casas Grandes, when they put her into the hotel to get her off the streets.

It was a hot August morning, and they said they had dropped Shara off with Grandmother Livia, because they wanted to take her shopping, and Margaret had smiled, apparently knowing what they meant. "Go, dear! Now that I've got Cindy Coleman working here, I can afford to let you take off the day."

"But I do not need anything," Sharon said, eyeing all three of them and wondering what they knew that she did not. "I have many clothes. What else do I need?"

"You'll see," Joel said.

"I've heard from JoAnna," Tom said, "that as well as you're doing in night school, you'll have your diploma in no time, so if you want to attend UC by next fall, you'll need just one more thing."

Still Sharon could not guess, so she went with them in their pickup and they said they were taking her to Deming. So they drove the five miles across the desert to the much larger town, but did not enter it. Instead they came off the interstate and came to a stop at a place that said Brem Chevrolet. From the middle of the pickup where she was sitting, Sharon saw what must be a field of bright, new cars.

She began to cry, for it was then that she had guessed what they were about to do. "I can not allow this!" she protested as both of them got out and waited for her to follow them. "If I need a car to get around, I will use Margaret's."

But Joel laughed, smiling brightly. "Margaret's old clunker wouldn't make it to California, Sharon."

"And she wouldn't let you take it, anyway," Tom teased, both of them looking at her.

But she continued to cry, because she thought about one of the promises she had made to herself when she had left her people and was begging for food in Casas Grandes—one day, she would return there and she would be driving a bright new car and would give dimes to the children and buy Tarahumara pottery and hold her head high.

"I can not!" she insisted, trying to keep herself from grinning. "It is too soon! I am not yet a great woman as is Margaret or Eva!"

She saw the confusion on Tom and Joel's faces, but they could not keep from grinning, either, and led her to the field of cars.

"But you *are* a great woman," Joel said and kissed her on the cheek.

"You're a great mother, too," Tom said, and kissed her on the other cheek.

So they walked among the cars and, used to the American dollars by then, and the many months' worth of income it would take to pay for a car, she felt nervous. They quickly got rid of a loud-mouthed salesman who kept calling her little lady and squinting at Tom and Joel.

Joel took the guy aside after a few minutes as Sharon and Tom walked around looking at the Impalas and Biscaynes and Chevy IIs and, from the corner of her eye, she saw Joel shake the guy's hand and slap him on the back. When the salesman left, Joel came up to them. "What d'you think Sharon? Any of these suit you?"

Sharon had been eyeing a pale blue Monte Carlo, but when she saw the sticker price, she had moved quickly away. "They are all so expensive," she said, beginning to feel sick to her stomach. "Let us go back and I shall come with Margaret and she will tell me."

But Tom and Joel were both grinning at her. "Margaret would put you in something from the 1950s," Tom said. "Something made of cast-iron."

"You like the Monte Carlo?" Joel asked.

Sharon tried to hide her grin. "It is much too expensive," she protested, glancing back at it, where it sat among the other cars, feeling both sick and something sweet in the pit of her stomach.

"I'll tell you what, Sharon," Joel said, "you take it for a spin, and if you don't want it when you get back, we'll look at something else." His eyebrows went up and his smile also made Sharon's stomach feel sweet.

A few minutes later, the same salesman was back, handing her the keys with a paper tag hanging from the key ring.

A few minutes after that, Sharon was sitting in the driver's seat with the engine running, listening for the sound, though she could hardly hear it, then she put the car into Drive and maneuvered out of the lot, choosing her route carefully. She was by herself and glanced in the rear-view mirror at Tom and Joel standing side-by-side looking in her direction.

Still later, she was sailing down the interstate, listening to the smooth running engine, even when the air-conditioner was turned on, nudging the car up to fifty, then sixty. It was so responsive to her foot on the gas pedal that she felt

free, feeling as if she could drive forever, and not tire out. She cried and
laughed, alone in the car, and sang, and grinned at herself in the rear-view mirror and waved to cars that passed her; then, at the exit that came up within a
few miles, she followed the directions to get onto Interstate 10 West, and
headed back toward the Brem Chevrolet.

As she maneuvered the car back into the lot, Joel waived to her. He was
standing next to the building with the large glass front. Inside were other cars.
She rolled to a stop, turned the key in the ignition and, when the engine died,
she stepped out.

"Well?" Joel asked, still grinning.

"It is so...smooth," was all she could think to say. Then she laughed. "Poor
Margaret! Her car is like a tractor! I never realized."

Tom came out of the building with the salesman on his heels. "You like it?"
Tom asked, standing next to Joel.

She looked from one to the other, and recalled fondly that she had thought of
them as her saviors, and now they were her friends, and her heart was bursting
with the love she felt. "It is beautiful! But it is too expensive!"

"But it's already yours," Tom said.

*   *   *

There were papers to sign, and Sharon proudly took out her driver's
license and signed her name, watching it unfold under the tip of the pen. Her
heart was racing, but Tom and Joel were there, joking with her and gathering
up the papers, and the salesman was trying to conduct his usual business,
giving last minute instructions. "Bring 'er back if you have any trouble, little
lady, and we'll check 'er out. Your maintenance schedule is here in your
owner's manual."

Her head swam and she felt frightened and said so, once she and Tom and
Joel were outside by themselves.

"We'll help you, Sharon," Tom said. "There's nothing to it. Besides, we don't
need to bring your car back here, unless something goes wrong with it that
shouldn't. We do most of the minor work on all the vehicles at the farm."

Then it was time to leave and Sharon was once more behind the wheel of
her new car. Joel got into the passenger side with her, and Tom got into their
pickup. "He'll follow us home," Joel said, sitting back and running his hand
along the dashboard. "You do like it, don't you?"

Sharon could not speak as she started the engine and put the car into Drive.
How could she tell Joel that she was dreaming? How could she begin to explain

what it meant to have become an American. She opened her mouth: "I…" then shut it again.

Joel laid his left hand on her shoulder. "You know, when we get back to town, you're going to have to give everybody a ride."

"You mean Margaret?" Sharon asked.

"And Mom and Dad, and that new friend of Margaret's…Clara? And Livia and of course Henry and Sally. Everybody."

She drove out of the lot and back onto the interstate, heading east, feeling the engine respond to her foot. "Why is this, Joel?" she asked. "Why do I need to give everyone a ride?"

Joel began laughing. "Oh, Sharon, you're so cute! It's just what you do when you get a new car."

Again Sharon could not speak, but she did laugh. It was too much, she thought. Every day she had been in America, among her new family and friends, she would think she knew things; but every day, there was something else to learn.

Sure enough, when they got to Common, and Sharon parked on the street at the café, Margaret came out and looked at the car, beaming at her. "You'll have to give me a ride, child! How about driving me over to Livia's, and you can give her a ride."

When they got there, Margaret reached over and punched the horn. A few moments later, Livia came out holding Shara, and Mary Conger was there, and both women got into the back seat, with Livia holding the baby.

Sharon turned in the seat, and her daughter squealed when she saw her. "See your mother's car, little Margaret?" Sharon asked, and Shara squealed again, making the women laugh.

Sharon drove them through the streets as they oohed and ahhhed. She drove them to the Triangle Drive-In, and bought drinks. As the sun finally began to fall toward the western horizon, turning the light a gold, Sharon began to get used to the idea that she now owned a car, and then she felt suddenly alarmed, realizing that her time among all her friends here in Common was coming to a close.

When she dropped Livia and Mary Conger off, Sharon asked if she could take the baby for a while, trying to keep a smile on her face, and to hold back the tears that began to gather beneath her lids. Then she took Margaret back to the café and dropped her off, promising to be home within a couple of hours.

Finally, it was just her and Shara in the car. She bundled her baby up in the back seat, and drove back out on the highway, realizing there was no place of her own where she could go to be alone with her baby. She settled for a rest area a few miles out of town. When she had parked near a picnic table away from the other cars, she brought Shara up to the front seat with her. She was crying, and Shara looked intently at her with her gray eyes with their strident slashes of blue, reaching out for her mother's face.

"Oh, my sweet child!" Sharon said to the baby, looking into her eyes. "You will remember me? You know that I am not shunning you?"

Shara listened and cooed, and Sharon held her, feeling her warmth, hugging her and rocking back and forth, crying softly.

CHAPTER 27

FREE WOMEN

Livia Allen sat in the classroom at the high school, looking out the window, then down at her watch. This late in December, just before the Christmas holiday, it was dark early. Still, with the street lights that ran along the outside of the building, she could see the cars lined up along the sidewalk. It was coming up on seven o'clock, and she was getting anxious. This was a small ceremony, unlike those held for the regular graduating seniors, which filled the football stadium to accommodate friends and relatives of the graduates. Tonight, she had come to see the graduation of only one person, and Sharon Minninger had passed before the podium several minutes before wearing a cap and gown of blue, her blonde hair flowing behind her as she stopped, shook hands with the principal, and took her diploma. Like the rest of the students who were graduating this evening, Sharon was older than the normal seniors, but not by much. She was quite young, Livia thought, and exactly the kind of girl she would have chosen for her son.

Livia was sitting next to Tom and Joel. Joel was holding Shara, who was awake and busy playing with a set of plastic keys, with an intense concentration that made Livia smile. Next were Douglas and Eva Reece, Bill and JoAnna Hoffins, and Margaret Jost and Clara Tyler. They took up a whole row of seats, as a matter of fact, and were there to see Sharon graduate. In the few rows ahead of them were children and other adults. The Reece children, Henry and Sally, were sitting with some of their friends from school, and Livia imagined that some of the much older graduates getting their diplomas this evening were their parents. In all, there were about forty people in the class room, not counting the graduates.

Once Sharon had taken her diploma and rejoined her fellow graduates on the front row of seats, Livia's mind wandered. It was not so much that she was bored. Far from it. She even intended to go over to Margaret's house after the ceremonies, where Sharon would be the guest of honor and would open presents. Everyone had gotten together and decided she should receive gifts she could use when she went to college next fall, including a briefcase, a typewriter, and a set of luggage. There was one very special gift, however, that Sharon needed most. JoAnna, working through the arcane system of applying to colleges through the high school counselor's office, had gained Sharon acceptance at the University of California at Berkeley for fall 1972. JoAnna was going to give her the letter of acceptance tonight at the party.

Livia was glad for the girl, and over the several months that she had come to know her, she admired Sharon's tenacity and intelligence; like Eva, Livia thought that the last thing Sharon needed was to be tied down to her child. But like her son Tom, and even Joel, she also hoped that once Sharon had been out in the world for awhile she would come back to the small town to live and settle down.

Livia smiled, too, thinking about how different it was for herself this time back in Common, and she was happier than she had been in many years, if not happier than she had ever been. She was nervous, however, this evening, and anxious, glancing once more out the windows and again at her watch.

The preacher Billy Conger had suddenly been let out of jail on probation. Mary Conger had called with the news and, then, had said she intended to see him.

She had assured Livia that this visit with her husband was going to be her last. Livia regretted—and even feared—Mary's decision. Until now, she had been doing so well. She had moved into a small efficiency apartment on the same street where Livia lived, renting the apartment from the landlady, Mrs. Cox, who appeared to be a property holder of quite significant means in the small town. She had been less amenable to renting to Mary than she had been to Livia, but had taken into account Livia's recommendations; thus far, Mary had paid her rent on time and had otherwise impressed the old lady.

But like many women who had been controlled by their husbands—especially the abusive ones—Mary was a little more unstable when it came to working. Livia had seen to it that Mary stayed focused on her new goals: to become a self-sufficient woman, free of her husband. When he called, however, it was all Livia could do to convince Mary that she should at least wait until she got off work that evening. Now, Livia was afraid that had been a mistake. It was dark out, and someone like Billy Conger preferred working in the dark.

Livia knew the kinds of fear and reticence Mary had about holding a job, paying rent, and living on her own. She had the same problems in her own life, once her husband had died. Livia had landed a job in April at the Common Public Schools administrative offices through the help of Eva Reece and JoAnna Hoffins. Eva had apparently stiff-armed one of the personnel managers into at least giving her an interview, and JoAnna had helped her prepare a resume and brush up on her typing skills. The pay wasn't much, but Livia's expenses were low enough that she could even put away a few dollars each week. Still, in the ensuing months, until now, just as the Christmas holiday loomed, Livia had moments of anxiety, when she was hit with an especially tedious or rushed job. But as the months passed, she had gained steadily in confidence.

It was that self-confidence she had fought so hard to help her new friend Mary Conger realize. Mary was, if anything, in a worse situation with far fewer skills than Livia, and she had threatened to quit her job as a desk clerk at the Lamplight Inn many times in the two months she had been working there.

Livia would not hear of it. "Listen to me, dear," she had said, with Mary in tears on her sofa in the living room. "Guests are going to be upset occasionally, and they're going to take it out on the first person they see, or the last. But if you're going to survive without your husband, you've got to maintain your perspectives."

But today, Mary's call had been a blow.

Livia's heart had almost stopped at the news, and she heard the tension in Mary's voice over the phone. "I would advise you not to do it, Mary," she had said. She didn't think the man was capable of changing. The only strand of hope that she held for Mary was the fact that the ex-preacher was out on probation and it probably wouldn't take much to get him returned if he tried anything. "Do you really think he's changed, Mary?"

There was a pause on the other end of the line, and Livia heard her friend's breathing, as if she had been running, then, "I don't know. I don't want to go back to him. I just need to see him…this last time."

"If you don't want to go back to him, Mary, then you do not *need* to see him!" Livia had burst out, despite her attempts to remain calm.

"I need to face him," Mary said. "I need to tell him that I've left him for good."

"But must you do it face-to-face?"

Again the pause and the shallow breathing. "I ain't laid eyes on him since the day I brought him home from the hospital. I ain't exorcised his demons, Livia, and the Lord says be not afraid."

Livia felt her own calm beginning to bubble around the edges, her own breathing becoming shallow. Whenever Mary resorted to her southern hillbilly language and peppered it with religious phrases, Livia knew she was having great difficulty.

Livia was familiar with that, as well, having many times in her own life with her husband, resorted to biblical rhetoric when she felt overwhelmed. The hold that religion had, especially on the wife of a preacher, could be strong. She knew what Mary was up against.

"Where is Mr. Conger?"

"He's got that trailer. We owned that 'n that lot next to the ch'uch."

Livia felt Mary slipping away, but at least she knew where she would be. If she didn't hear from her, she knew where to look. "Why don't you make him go to the Lamplight, Mary? At least there, you'll have people around."

But Mary had insisted that she would be all right and had hung up.

Now, as the graduation ceremonies were drawing to a close, and people had begun to stir in the audience, she hoped Mary would be all right. She intended to call her at home as soon as she could get to a pay phone.

*   *   *

Clara felt Margaret's presence beside her, as though her pride for Sharon Minninger was radiating outward, touching and warming her and the rest of those in the classroom. But Clara was warm enough, as it was, as she watched Sharon cross the room to get her diploma. *Such a beautiful woman!* She thought. She leaned toward Margaret and said so in a whisper.

Margaret nodded, holding her hands clasped together and her eyes glistening with tears. She whispered back: "I feel as if she's my own daughter. I'm so proud of her. And to think that only a little over a year ago, she was as innocent and ignorant as a child."

Clara nodded and returned her attention to the rest of the ceremonies. In the few months that she had known Margaret and Sharon and their most beautiful gay friends, Tom and Joel, she had marveled at the ignorance, not of the people in this small town, but of those in Chicago or, say, New York, whose conscious awareness of anything outside the eastern states was telling. She marveled at it, because people on the east coast, and no doubt the west coast, thought of themselves as sophisticated. Yet she had learned that even a small dot on the map like Common and the surrounding communities were just smaller versions of big cities. She had been amazed, once she had got to know

Margaret and her small circle of friends, that they were every bit as interesting and much more sociable than those she had said good-bye to back in Chicago.

But most of all, she had found a true calling, here, not only at the children's hospice, taking over Albert Hossley's heavy load of children and other patients, but in working with some of the women she had met.

She looked down the row, taking in the smiling and intense faces of JoAnna Hoffins, Eva Reece and Livia Allen. Including Margaret, all of these women were what people now called *liberated*; though she doubted that some of her more liberated female friends in Chicago would look at them twice, or find them admirable. When she thought of Eva and JoAnna, Clara realized that even married women could be liberated in the truest sense. They were, because of their strong independence and their down-to-earth ways of dealing with other women in the community. She had worked closely over the last few months with Livia and JoAnna Hoffins. Livia made her home a sort of refuge for some of the women who had come forward about their own abuse in the church run by Billy Conger. To Clara, such openness and generosity for the battered women of the small community was admirable.

Like Livia, she was also worried about Mary and glanced at her own watch every now and then as the graduation ceremonies came to a close, since she also knew that Mary had gone to meet her husband.

When everyone began clapping and standing as the dozen graduates stood and faced them, smiling and holding their diplomas, Clara slipped out of the row and went around to the other side, to stand next to Livia.

"Why don't we find a phone and give Mary a call?"

Livia let out a breath, as if she had been holding it for the last half-hour. "I was thinking the same thing." Then she told Tom where they were going. "Clara and I will be over at Margaret's in a little while, dear. You'll tell everyone?"

Tom nodded. "Okay, Mother, but don't be too late. We've got to get Shara home."

*   *   *

Across town behind the John the Baptist Calvary Mission in Billy Conger's travel trailer, Mary Conger was fighting for her life. Her lips were bleeding, her scalp was bleeding where locks of hair had been yanked out. Billy was screaming at her, and spittle flew into her face in what she knew was a mock and mocking infusion of the Holy Spirit. "Woman brought the first sin! Woman is shame! Did you think to forsake me?!" His eyes were on fire as he held her pinned against a bookshelf, where books had fallen around them. Still conscious, Mary deliberately fell limp, hoping to wear him out as he sought to hold her up. She kept sliding down, scraping her back against the rough shelving, and he kept pulling her up, fifty pounds heavier and a head taller.

She tasted the salt of blood on her mouth, felt it trickling down into her eyes. Her arms and legs were burning, her stomach churned, and she bit into her cheek to keep herself conscious. She pulled downward with her weight, and Billy had to release her wrists, attempting to get his hands under her arm pits.

In one movement, she slammed her knee into his groin—a self-defensive move Clara Tyler had taught her and some of the other abused wives—and then shoved him with both arms, using her position against the shelving to gain support.

He fell backwards, surprise and pain showing on his face. As he lost balance, doing a backward summersault over the chair, his head crashed into the desk.

Mary knew if she didn't get away, now, she would not leave the trailer alive. She staggered toward the door, peering through stinging eyes lined with blood, gripping the handle with slick hands. Then she pushed and fell down the three wooden steps, landing on her left shoulder; pain shot through like knives into the base of her skull, almost knocking her unconscious.

*   *   *

Margaret had made a cake and decorated it with a cap and gown, and it was sitting in the middle of the dining room table. Around it, Margaret had set out silverware and napkins, and had made a bowl of punch, with clear demitasse cups hanging off the punch bowl on silver hooks. As people came in carrying their gifts, she indicated a side-board in the living room. Eva took everyone's coats and took them down the hall to the first bedroom, where they had begun to pile up.

But Tom was uneasy, looking around at the guests who had arrived, realizing that his mother had left the graduation over an hour before with Clara Tyler. He had seen them in the hallway at the high school, next to the gymnasium at a pay phone. She had covered the mouthpiece, with a worried expression on her face.

"She's not there, honey," she had said to Tom. "Clara and I need to check on her."

He knew they were talking about Mary Conger, because she had mentioned her as they were going into the high school. She had told him about the ex-preacher having gotten out of jail on probation and that Mary intended to visit with him.

He also knew what Conger was capable of, and still cringed every time he recalled what he had done to his mother, and recalled Mary Conger's face with the faint bruises around her eyes.

But he had had to help Margaret set up for Sharon's party. She had to have her special moment, he thought, and he did not want it spoiled by that nasty preacher. He didn't even think of stopping his mother and Dr. Tyler from trying to find out if Mary Conger was all right. He hoped that she was.

Still, it was getting late, and he was relieved that people had been delayed, many of them having to go home after the graduation ceremony to change into dressier clothes.

When Margaret had decided that she would give a party for Sharon, she wanted to make it something the young woman would never forget. On specially engraved invitations, she had specified evening wear. Tom was certain that some of the people Margaret invited would come just to get a look at the old lady's house, because she had never thrown a party in the many years she had been in Common.

As many times as he had been in Margaret's house in the evenings, he noted that she liked bright lights. The living room was lit brightly this evening from a large chandelier hanging from the high ceiling. Even the fireplace was lit, and on the mantle, instead of a the single rose in the vase for her mate, Margaret had filled it with yellow roses, save for a single red rose in their midst.

The antiques from an era long past had been polished to a bright sheen, from the side-board where the presents were collecting, to the marble-topped chests and tables. It was a matter of some surprise that Tom discovered furnishings in Margaret's living room he'd never noticed before, and everywhere he looked, the dark, rich furniture gleamed.

Terrance Lawton's father and his wife had come in just a few minutes before, shaking hands with Eva and Douglas, who were standing at the door to greet people. Pete Thompson's father, the jeweler, and his wife had even been invited, and Tom nudged Joel when they came in, both sharing the knowledge that it hadn't been too many years since they had bought their wedding rings from him over his objections. Joel just smiled. He was holding Shara, who was wearing a little yellow dress with white ruffles Margaret had given her, asking that she wear it to Sharon's party. Her dark hair was brushed and her bright little eyes were taking in the laughter and talk. They had waited to change her until the last minute, since she was teething and tended to drool. Both he and Joel were wearing suits they had bought just a couple of years before and hardly ever wore.

Sharon, however, had still not made her entrance; Tom knew she was nervous. When she was leaving the high school, she had stopped to talk with him and Joel, taking a moment to hold the baby; then she was off in her new car with JoAnna, who was going to help her get ready.

Tom looked at his watch. It was almost eight-thirty.

*   *   *

Mary tried to stand, but it was as though her husband's entire weight was on her, only she knew it was not, because she could feel the cold air scald the bloody gashes on her back. She lay at the bottom of the steps of the trailer. She rolled sideways, moving beneath the trailer, gasping for breath, listening for him.

Off in the distance, somewhere in the neighborhood, a dog began howling, and other dogs joined in, until it seemed there were a pack of wolves coming in her direction, having smelled her blood and fear.

She rolled farther beneath the trailer, knowing she couldn't stand or run away, and pulled herself into a fetal position. Above her, inside the trailer, she heard scraping as her husband roused himself. She knew that weight, had felt it upon her in the night a thousand times.

"Mary! You ansa' me darlin!"

She tried to still her breathing.

"Why, Mary?!"

She heard his voice now at the door above her. Then his weight settled on the first step, and tears began to flow out of her eyes, stinging and hot.

Then she heard a scrape as his weight settled on the second step. "Mary! You know you gotta be punished!"

Then off in the distance like the wailing of a child she heard a high-pitched screaming.

But it wasn't a child. It was a siren, wailing.

"M-a-a-ry!" came Billy's voice, and his foot landed on the third step. She saw the heel of his work boot through the gap between the steps, and she rolled farther beneath the trailer, almost crying out at the pain that shot through her arms.

Closer came the wail of the siren. Then lights played off the walls of the church, and she was suddenly blinded by a spot light as a police cruiser pulled into the church lot, bumping over the ground, its siren still wailing.

Her husband landed with a bounce onto the bare ground, walking toward the lights of the cruiser, more of him becoming visible, until she could see him from behind, one arm up, shielding the light from his face.

"Evenin' officers! What seems to be the trouble?"

It was then that Mary screamed at the top of her lungs.

*   *   *

When the telephone rang at Margaret's house, Sharon was in the middle of opening her gifts, and she was crying, while everyone else smiled at her.

The telephone rang again, and Margaret tore herself away from Sharon's side.

Tom watched Margaret at the doorway to the kitchen, as her face went from a smile to a frown, then she caught his eye and motioned for him. He was holding Shara, who had finally fallen asleep. He hated to move, but the look on Margaret's face told him he had to. Eva was sitting next to him on the sofa and he slid Shara into her lap.

"Be right back," he said, and went to the kitchen.

"It's your mother, Tom. She's at the hospital with Clara. Mary Conger has just been admitted. Looks like that husband of hers tried to kill her." Then she handed him the phone.

Tom listened to his mother's explanation of why she and Clara had not made it to Sharon's party, then to the list of injuries Mary had sustained as a result of her husband's beating, and his stomach churned with the grisly details, from the patches of hair and scalp that had been pulled out to bleeding from an ear, broken teeth, cracked ribs, and a dislocated shoulder.

The poor woman's suffering was in direct contrast to the enjoyment the women were having at the party. He was standing in the kitchen doorway, looking out on the guests, from the elegant and quite lovely Mrs. Lawton, to JoAnna, who was dressed in a thin-looking white gown that she had worn, despite the cold December night, to Eva Reece, dressed in an uncharacteristically feminine black gown, with matching high heels, with her granddaughter on her lap, in her little frilly dress.

Margaret had worn a dress from what era, he had no idea, but in its black velvety, high-necked design, with her hair done in a perky style, he could picture her when she was much younger, perhaps even as a woman in her thirties. He had seen photographs of Rose and could imagine Margaret and Rose together at some party.

Free women, he thought. He spoke into the telephone. "Mother, I understand. I'm sorry you missed this party, but I think it's best you stay there with Mary." Then he said good-bye, thinking of his mother, who had in her own way been abused, and Mary, who had been abused and now lay in the hospital with injuries that would take months to heal. He recalled Edna Stroud, the poor mother of the twins and Henry and Sally, and the many times he had seen her at church, barely able to disguise the bruises and swollen lips her husband had given her. It was to the cause of helping women that his own mother had apparently decided to turn her life, now without his father, whose body she had simply shipped back to Texas—a simple and neat way of being rid of him.

As he made his way back into the living room amid all the bright lights and people smiling and laughing, Tom realized that women were often treated as gay people were, as a group to be beat on, silenced into subservience, many times with the blessing of society.

Then he studied Sharon. She was the most beautiful woman in the room, dressed in a green gown that fairly flowed over her body. Her blonde hair was pinned up and her face, without makeup of any sort, shone with a radiance that made him smile. So different from the girl he and Joel had found on the streets of Nuevo Casas Grandes, dressed in drab grays and looking lost; now, she was about to leave them and enter UC Berkeley. In a few short months, it seemed to Tom, Sharon had come out of a cocoon and was now a raving beauty, whose wings were poised to fly. How far she would go, he could only anticipate. She was perhaps the most free of them all. He felt warm and happy, despite what he'd just heard on the phone with his mother.

When he settled back down next to Joel, he took his hand, right there in front of everyone, but no one noticed, except Joel, who gripped his hand and squeezed hard.

CHAPTER 28

THE GATHERING, 1971

They both looked forward to Shara's first Christmas. She was already nine months old and, Tom thought, showing Joel's strength. Joel had once told Tom that his parents had named him Joel *Hale* Reece, meaning hale and hardy. Shara was like that as she moved around on the floor on knees and hands slapping the floor in front of her. By nine months, she was already pulling herself up, usually on their pants' legs, always interested in getting between them and looking from one to the other as they sat on the couch in the evenings.

"Dada?" she would say to either of them and sometimes "Mama?"

"No, baby," Joel or Tom would say, "Sharon is your mama."

When Sharon came to visit, as she did quite often now that she had her own car and was no longer in night school, she would hug them both and then look around for Shara. Shara slept less and less and, in the evenings, once she'd been fed, they would keep her up until after the Red Rooster closed, and tell her: "Your mama's coming, Shara!"

Sharon would usually find her daughter in the living room on the floor and, as soon as Shara heard her mother's voice, she would do her hand-slap, crawl thing, with her head down heading toward her mother like a charging bull, then Sharon would scoop her up.

"Dada?"

"No, I'm 'mama,'" Sharon would laugh.

This morning, Tom was working in the kitchen. He had already put a turkey in the oven for his part of the Christmas Eve dinner. As the turkey began to cook, the aroma filled the kitchen. On the counter next to a sink full of dishes, pumpkin pies were cooling. Shara was in her high chair at the table, with a bib, a spoon, and a bowl of pabulum, only part of which was actually making it to her mouth.

Joel was at his parents, to have breakfast with his two sisters and their families. They had got in late the night before and were staying for the holidays. It was bright and cold outdoors, and a blanket of snow shined with diamonds of ice in the bright, clear morning.

They had taken Shara outdoors the morning after they woke up to the fresh snow and she had seemed to realize that things were different. Even though her little breath showed in the air, she seemed to ignore the cold in her excitement, pointing with one finger "da no?"

Everything was 'da no' to her, Tom thought, recalling her surprise when they held her over the snow and allowed her to stick her hands in a drift of it on the porch railing. She had not just touched it, but plowed her hands through it, gasping, "Oooh! Da no!"

Tom laughed, watching as she pushed the food around in the bowl with the spoon, while reaching into it with the other hand, which immediately went to her hair.

"Oh, baby," Tom said, getting a warm cloth and wiping her face and hair. "Your Aunt Kathleen and Tricia are going to be here any minute."

Shara was used to getting her face washed, her nose wiped, and she had a habit of sticking out her tongue to taste the cloth.

Then he pulled her from the high chair. "I better get you changed, so you can be pretty."

"Da no?"

"Yes. Right now."

He was in the nursery, pulling on a little denim jumper when he heard Joel in the living room, talking excitedly. Tom knew it must be his sisters. Kathleen and her husband Carl had two children, aged seven and eight which, when they came to visit thrilled both Henry and Sally, since the oldest of their two children was a boy and the youngest was a girl. Tricia and her husband Justin also had two children, though they were much younger and, if it had been as it was the last time they were in Common visiting, they would be trying to tag along with the other four. The twins had come back home a few days before, and the first thing they did was take Sharon out with Terrance.

As Tom was struggling with the last shoe, which Shara had decided didn't need to be on her foot, Joel came into the room with his sisters, and Tom stood aside holding the shoe as Kathleen and Tricia moved up next to him.

Kathleen picked Shara up, making faces, which Shara returned with "Da no?" and an intense concentration as she looked at her aunt.

"Oh guys!" Kathleen said. "She's beautiful!" Then as everyone did, Kathleen studied Shara's face, looking from Tom to Joel. "What do you think, Trish?"

Like Joel, Tricia had blonde hair, while Kathleen had unmistakably Irish red hair like Eva's. Tricia took the baby and everyone walked back into the living room. Tom glanced at Joel's proud expression, smiling to himself. Even though it didn't matter to either of them, he and Tom sat together on the other couch, while Kathleen and Tricia studied Shara to see who Shara favored most. Tricia sat Shara in her lap and took the remaining shoe from Tom, expertly pushing the baby's foot into it and tying the strings.

"She has your hair, Tom," Kathleen said.

"Your eyes, though," Tricia said, looking from Shara to Joel.

"But we haven't seen the mother, yet," Kathleen said to her sister, then looked at Joel, smiling. "You boys do know, don't you, that it can't be both of you?"

Tom watched Joel's expression, and the way he was a little more subdued beneath his sisters' scrutiny. While they treated him as an adult, Tom thought there was still the slightest kid-brother habit in the way Joel grinned. "We know," he said. "It doesn't matter to us."

But it mattered to Shara. She wasn't much in favor of this interesting detail, and with an emphatic movement, she indicated she wanted down. Tricia hugged her close and kissed her cheek, and then Kathleen kissed her as well.

Tricia stood her up next to the couch and, for a moment, Shara was standing alone, though a little wobbly. She knew as well as did her fathers that this was a big thing. She shrieked and took a step, then hit bottom, rolled expertly onto knees and hands, and crawled over to Joel, pulling herself up on his pants leg.

"So, what do you think?" Joel asked, patting Shara's head.

Tom watched Kathleen and Tricia. While they definitely had their parents' features, they were both taller than Eva and slightly taller than Joel. Still they were petit women. He knew they lived near each other in Phoenix, and both of them had married professional men. While they had led what Tom knew to be conventional lives, attending church regularly with their husbands, who had come from more devout Presbyterian backgrounds than their own parents, they had not been exceptionally judgmental—no more than Douglas had, and less than Eva had, once the shock dissipated of finding out that their kid brother was gay. Nor had their husbands reacted negatively—unless of course their reactions had been filtered through Joel's sisters.

Tricia looked most like Joel and, to Joel's vague question, she smiled, with a bit of a twinkle in her eye. "You know you thrilled Mom to death, don't you,

Joel, once she found out she was going to be a grandmother? She grieved about that when she found out about you and Tom."

Kathleen frowned at her sister, then smiled at Joel, as well. "She didn't grieve that long, Joel, because she loves Tom, as well."

Tom smiled at a memory of the first Christmas he had met Joel's sisters, when they and their families had come from Phoenix to spend the holidays. They ate Christmas Eve dinner with Tom and Joel. Kathleen had helped Tom wash dishes that night, and while they were putting them away, she set a plate down and hugged him. Over his shoulder, she said, "*Carl and I really like you, Tom.*" Then she pulled away and smiled. "*I've been watching my kid brother with you tonight, and I can't imagine him with anyone else—man or woman. When we were kids, Tricia and I couldn't wait to get away from here. But Joel never seemed to want anything he didn't already have, and we thought he was retarded or something. But I know what it was. He was different, in a way that made him love everything—maybe too much. And he's in love with you like that—like everything he's ever touched and liked the feel of. I'm glad he's got you, Tom. I hope you're ready to grow old with him.*" She picked up the plate and placed it in the cabinet, then looked at him with a kind of smile that often infused Joel's face and said, "*That sounds silly, I know. It's hard to put.*"

"But what do we think?" Kathleen said, repeating Joel's question. "I think it's great, though I'm really sorry for her mother." She nodded toward Shara. "Are you really sure she's all right with this? I know I couldn't do it, under any circumstances."

"I couldn't either," Tricia added. "You are going to allow her into your lives, aren't you?"

This time, Joel didn't have the kid-brother grin. He picked Shara up and sat her on his lap. She turned and put her hand on his chin. Absently, Joel kissed at her fingers. "Of course we are. We want her to be here when Shara starts school, and whenever else. But you'll have to meet Sharon to know why we don't feel bad about things, the way they are." He looked at Tom. "Won't they?"

Tom agreed. He remained vague about how he and Joel had met Sharon. "We weren't really looking at her to be the mother of our child. It wasn't until a few weeks later that she called us and offered to carry the child, although she knew we were looking."

"But you were hoping to find some woman who would do that, right?" Tricia asked.

Tom nodded. "Yeah. But I don't think either of us saw Sharon like that. We just really liked her, because she was so…" he trailed off, then looked to Joel.

"She had run away from this really strict religious family in Montana," Joel said, repeating what Tom knew was the "story" they were to tell people. "We met her through a friend of ours, here in town."

"She wants things she would have never had a chance at, coming from her background," Tom added. "At first, we just liked her as a friend—and still do."

Both Joel's sisters nodded, but Kathleen looked serious. "You still surprised us, Joel," she said.

"You'd think I couldn't do that any more," he said. "I mean, you know, after me and Tom got together."

Both of them laughed. "I'm sure you'll find a way. And if not you, then your daughter will," Kathleen said.

A little later, Joel and Tricia took Shara to the main house, so that his brothers-in-law could meet the baby, and Tom and Kathleen worked in the kitchen, storing the food in plastic containers to take to the main house for the dinner to be held later that evening.

Tom felt a special connection with Joel's oldest sister, but didn't tell her that; rather, he enjoyed talking with her about Joel and, now, the baby. Several times, he had even thought about telling Kathleen Sharon's real story, but decided against it. It wouldn't be fair to Sharon, nor would it show the kind of trust Eva had in him and Joel to tell Kathleen and not Eva. It was a history of Sharon's Mennonite heritage that would remain only between him and Joel and Sharon and Margaret.

Of course, Tom reminded himself, as he worked with Kathleen, that no one could look far enough into the future to say exactly what might eventually be discovered.

He told Kathleen of his own mother's return and the death of his father. A few years before, he had told Kathleen that they had disowned him, never dreaming that his mother would one day return to Common. Now, he was happy with the story he related to her.

"She's even helping other women," he said, telling her of the business that had happened within the Calvary Mission church, telling about the subsequent jail time the preacher had been serving, and finally how he had attempted to kill his wife, the same day he got out on probation.

Kathleen's eyes shone with tears as he related Mary Conger's injuries. "Of course, she's not able to work, now, so Mother has taken her into her home."

"I hope the husband is back in jail," Kathleen said, still horrified.

Tom smiled wanly. "The sheriff saw to that, and the same D.A. who oversaw the first trial added attempted murder to the new one that'll be coming up."

Kathleen just nodded. "How's your mother handling things with Mrs. Conger living there?"

"Mother has really blossomed," he said. "This thing she has with abused women is really making her a tough woman. Just what she needed." He was pouring coffee for both of them. They had just finished drying the dishes and were ready to load the pickup with the food to take to the main house.

"I'm glad for you, Tom," Kathleen said. "Especially now that your mother is back in your life. It may have been hard on our own mother for Joel to turn out to be gay, but they have to be the wisest people I know. They raised all three of us to think independently, to trust our feelings; and you know it's difficult to know how they did that."

"What do you mean?" Tom said. "I saw the same thing in Joel, and I learned to trust my feelings, as you say, because I saw how confident and strong he was."

"My son, Doug, is turning eight in February. But he's shy and is a follower."

Again, Tom asked what she meant.

"Not like Joel, at all. Not the way Dad and Mom raised us. We've tried, you know, to instill self-confidence in him; but he finds it easier to like what his friends like, to want what they want."

"And Joel, of course," Tom said, "is the kind of person who knows what he wants, regardless of how other people see it."

"Exactly!" Kathleen said. "I know it's got its drawbacks, and he sure has gone after some…surprising things in his life. But I'd rather Doug be like that. Sometimes it frightens me that he's so…fluid in what he thinks he wants. In a big city like Phoenix, kids get into serious trouble all the time and get talked into doing things they shouldn't. There are so many runaways living on the streets in Phoenix or headed for California. We've got to keep a close eye on Doug. I just cringe when I think what he's going to be like as a teenager."

Tom nodded, feeling suddenly apprehensive. "I know what you mean, Kathy, because I've already felt afraid for Shara, not even a year old. It's…" he trailed off, taking a sip of coffee. "Joel and I have already talked about our fear for the way she's going to be received at school. You know, with her having two fathers."

Kathleen covered his hand with her own. "I'm glad you have been thinking about that," she said. "You will have to deal with it. It'll surprise you how astute kids are, how quick they prick up their ears to precisely what you don't want them to hear. They'll repeat things you weren't even aware you said in front of them—the wrong things."

Tom felt even more apprehensive, but Kathleen laughed. "Don't be quite so afraid, Tom. You will also have years of enjoyment from her. I can tell Joel is head over heels in love with his daughter."

Tom laughed, then, too. "Yeah. He is. I think you're going to like Shara's mother, too. If Shara turns out like her, she's going to take this town by storm."

         ✶   ✶   ✶

There were times, when Joel was a kid, when he remembered relatives coming to stay for a weekend, and his aunts and uncles brought children his age to play with. Sometimes more than one set of aunts and uncles came and brought all their kids, and there would be a whole house full of children and adults. But the times between were long enough that, with each visit, Joel and his two sisters had to get to know their cousins all over again.

When he came into the house with Shara and Tricia, and looked around at the wreck of last night's arrival still evident in the living room, where pallets had been made for Kathleen and Tricia's four children, and pallets for Henry and Sally (so the adults could have their beds), Joel was reminded of relatives' visits. The pallets had been rolled up and were stashed along the wall out of the way. Carl and Justin and Douglas and Eva were now visiting, and somewhere in the back of the house, Joel heard the ruckus Henry and Sally and the other four children were making, but no one seemed to mind. The twins were apparently already off somewhere, and he shrugged off the disappointment that they weren't there with the rest of the family.

As soon as Joel walked into the room with Shara, Eva got up and greeted her granddaughter, taking her from Joel and introducing her to her two uncles. They both stood up and held her little hands while Eva told them her name. Then they both smiled at Joel, but Joel saw the subtle, appraising look that passed over their faces, though neither of them seemed as outright curious as his sisters about who the baby favored.

Eva didn't notice a thing. "Come on, Shara," she said. "Let's go find your cousins."

"Maybe I should check on the kids, too," Tricia said, following Eva down the hall.

Joel sat down on one of the chairs next to a sofa. His two brothers-in-law were on the sofa with Douglas. Carl was olive complexioned with dark hair like Tom's and was rather muscular. Joel had never seen him in anything but denim, but knew he was a lawyer. Justin, Tricia's husband, was an accountant for a different law firm, and was pale, and he had never worn anything but slacks and loafers when he came to visit. But both men had always taken an interest in the Reece farm, and Justin wasn't as fussy as he might have appeared; when Douglas took them around to look at the crops, both men seemed to enjoy getting their hands dirty now and then. Joel had always liked them and, even after Tom had come to live with him and he and Joel had moved into the old Bracero house, they were just as amenable to spending an evening with them as they were in visiting with Douglas and Eva.

As the conversation began to pick up, both Carl and Justin asked about Tom and confessed they were both surprised that they had decided to have a child.

"You'll really like Sharon," Joel said. He turned to his father. "Sharon and Margaret are going to be here tonight. Did Mom tell you?"

Douglas nodded. "They better be," he said. "I've been telling these two about Sharon, myself."

It was all so odd to Joel how, within the span of just six years, now, his and Tom's relationship with the rest of the family had settled in so comfortably— excluding perhaps the more religious faction of the family in the Sacramento Mountains near Cloudcroft. He recalled that, shortly after Tom had moved in with him, his sisters' first visit was without their husbands, and he had been too hesitant to ask them what they thought.

He was glad they were sensitive enough at his hesitancy to tell him that both Carl and Justin had said essentially the same thing: "He's still the same kid we always knew, so it's no big deal."

Further, considering what he and Tom and Sharon had just gone through with the birth of their baby and the scandal within the small town, Joel was glad that within his own family, among all those he loved and respected, there had been an openness to accepting him, even if they could not completely understand it. The introduction of his daughter had gone just as well, though he could tell that his brothers-in-law might still be curious, but hesitant them- selves to ask for the details of how he and Tom had decided to do it. They were probably even more curious to meet Shara's mother.

*   *   *

Sharon took a long time getting dressed. Margaret was helping her, and they were both laughing. It was dark out, but only a little past six. When the twins had called, inviting both her and Margaret to Christmas Eve dinner at the Reeces, Sharon was glad but was expecting to do it anyway, and she was plan- ning on wearing something nice. But then they had said that Terrance was going to be there, too, and Sharon had gotten weak in the knees. She knew he liked her, and she liked him. Even though she had gone to the movies with him and the twins just a couple of days before, this was different, though she didn't know exactly why.

"Joel's sisters and their families will be there, too," Patrick had told her. "Everyone is dying to meet you," Detrick had added.

And so now, she and Margaret were basically dressed, but they were contemplating something that before now Sharon had never done.

"My dear," Margaret teased, "if you put on just a touch of makeup—say, just a bit of lipstick and just a hint of color to your cheeks and eyes, you'll really stand out beneath the chandelier in the Reece dining room."

At first Sharon did not want to. True she had made many changes in her life since coming from Mexico, from the way she dressed, to the way she talked, even to holding her head high, but she had always stopped short of wearing paint on her face.

"But will they not think of me with less…um…respect? Think of me as trying to be something that perhaps I am not?"

"No, of course not, dear!" Margaret had assured her.

Still, when they had applied the first hint of lipstick to her lips, and Sharon tasted it, she could not go any further, until she had studied herself in the mirror.

But now, Margaret was frowning through her laughter. "Look at me, child," Margaret said and studied her. "I fear I need another person's opinion. One who is better at these things than I am."

And so they were laughing together waiting for Livia Allen to get there. She had agreed immediately to give Sharon a hand, and to Sharon's question about the appropriateness of wearing any makeup at all, Livia assured her that it would be fine. "I'm only surprised you've never done it before."

But Margaret explained to Livia about Sharon's strict upbringing in Montana. To which Livia had responded with encouragement. "I understand your reticence, dear. But even some of the more conservative churches I've been in do not object to bits of color."

*   *   *

Eva was in her element, as the dinner hour approached for what she could only think of as "the gathering" of her family. Her daughters were home with their husbands and children, an all-too-rare occasion in itself. In fact, she had not had everyone together at once for almost three years. The house was filling up quickly, tonight, since Tom and Joel were there with their daughter, and the twins had brought their friend Terrance Lawton.

She smiled at this, as she and her two daughters were putting the finishing touches on the dinner. Terrance had come, no doubt, to see Sharon, who had not yet arrived. She and Margaret and Livia were coming in Sharon's new car. They had just called and said they would be there within twenty minutes, so it was with a bit of haste that Eva was making sure everything was set up.

Douglas had just put in the three leaves to the dining room table and it would comfortably seat twelve people, although she needed to squeeze two other people in at the table, plus Shara's high chair, making fifteen in the dining room, leaving the six children—Kathleen's two, Tricia's two, and Henry and Sally—in the breakfast room.

"Gosh, Mom," Tricia said to her as they were putting down the pads on the dining room table, "don't you feel a bit overwhelmed?"

Eva just laughed.

"I mean, how many people are coming?"

Eva aligned the various pieces of the pad, then pulled the cloth liner out of the china cabinet, unfolding it and handing Tricia the other end. Together they held it over the table and lowered it, then Eva began smoothing it out. "Just about everyone I love and care about," she said, smiling at her daughter.

Then she pulled out the lace table cloth, holding it under the light, fingering the edges. She showed it to Tricia. "I've never used this. I bought it one year when Douglas and I took a vacation in Dallas. I told the sales lady at Nieman Marcus I wanted the largest table cloth she had." They unfolded it and laid it over the liner. "And look, it's just barely going to hang right."

She looked up. Tricia was smiling at her.

"What?"

Tricia shrugged. "If you could've, I bet you would have given birth to a dozen children, yourself!"

"I didn't have to, since we adopted four of Edna Stroud's, then had the three of you, and Tom is like a son to us, as well."

"And Sharon?"

Eva smiled at her daughter. They hadn't had a chance to talk about that, nor about what Tom and Joel had done. "Just wait until you meet her. Honey, she's a beautiful girl!"

"You don't sound the least bit…ah…reserved, Mom. Aren't you, at all?"

They smoothed out the table cloth and from the china cabinet, began getting out the plates. "I'll have to use the Limoges and the Spode," Eva said, "since I only have twelve settings of either."

Kathleen was coming into the dining room with freshly washed glasses. "Oh, no you don't, Mom. The children can use the Franciscan plates. There's no need"—

"Oh yes, there is," Eva said, smiling at her oldest daughter's frown. "We haven't had a family gathering like this in a long time." Both her daughters rolled their eyes, but she continued to smile, hugging one of the Limoges plates to her breast. She recalled many times when it was only the three of her children at home and both girls had always watched out for her china, and she appreciated it. But tonight was going to be special.

*   *   *

Joel, Douglas, and his sons-in-law were in the living room with the twins and their friend Terrance, trying to keep the children under control. Douglas was holding Shara, and she was looking up at him with what had to be Joel's eyes. Like Eva, he couldn't have been more happy. The boys, Henry and Doug (Carl's son) and the little one, Tim (Tricia's youngest) were wrestling on one of the pallets they would be sleeping in later, while the three girls, Sally, little Trish, and little Eva were fussing with the Christmas tree, which had been set up just that morning. The angel and the lights and bulbs had already been put on the tree, but the girls were rearranging whatever they thought the boys had done, and Douglas smiled about that. Kids never changed, and even at their young ages, the war between the sexes raged on, both the girls and boys claiming that the other camp couldn't do anything right.

When Joel plugged in the Christmas lights and turned off the ceiling lights, Shara's little face lit up with awe as she stared at the tree. She was pointing with one little finger. "Da! Dada!"

Both Tom and Joel looked over at her. "Did you hear that, Dad?" Joel said. "She's already learning to talk."

"Translate for us," Douglas said in return, getting up from the sofa and setting Shara down on the floor. He stood her up and took her little hands, straddling her so she could "walk" toward the lights.

"She said 'come on, Grandpa, let's go see what that is,'" Joel said.

Shara pumped her little legs, leaning forward without fear, pulling her grandfather along, and it was all he could do to keep from laughing. She was Joel all over again, he thought—at least in the way she never seemed to be cranky or afraid. Though she did have Tom's hair color, and he bet she was going to be taller than Joel as an adult.

When the doorbell rang, the twins and Terrance jumped up from where they were sitting, and Douglas' heart raced just a little. He was interested to see what Justin and Carl thought about Sharon. Privately, when he had taken them around the fields, and showed them the other farms he had bought up, he told them about the arrangement that Sharon and Tom and Joel had made with each other. They had both said they couldn't imagine how a mother could give up her own child, and Douglas had not argued with them about it. They would just have to meet her, to hear of her plans to attend college, to realize that she was too bright to tie herself down to a child; she needed to get a few skills and an education under her belt.

Douglas, like Eva, had also noted what appeared to be a blossoming thing between the twins' friend Terrance and Sharon, and he enjoyed watching them together, as he had on a couple of occasions. Besides, he didn't think Sharon was going to be out of her child's life; and if he had anything to say about it, she would always have a place in the family.

*   *   *

This was the first time Margaret had met Joel's sisters and their husbands, and to tell the truth, she was a bit nervous, not so much for herself, but for Sharon. She felt, once again, that Sharon was like her own daughter, and she was making her debut to one of Common's most important families—this night, the entire family. Further, that nice young man, Terrance Lawton, was there, and she meant to see if he and Sharon did seem to have that special spark.

Margaret was wearing a charcoal gray pantsuit, and a special pin she had had the jeweler Thompson make, a rather large gold pennant rose stem and leaves, with an inset of rubies for the rose pedals. It contrasted so well against the charcoal of her jacket, that it stood out—her way of bringing Rose with her to this event. As everyone greeted her and Sharon and Livia just inside the living room, Margaret thought how much Rose would have enjoyed herself.

Sharon was dressed in a wool suit that JoAnna had helped her pick out the day after she graduated. It was amazingly light, but warm, and its light gray color contrasted beautifully with her blonde hair. In the subdued light of the living room, with the Christmas tree lights burning at the opposite end of the room, everyone's faces were lit as if by candles, which brought out such beauty in the children's faces, Margaret thought, and smoothed out the wrinkles in the older adults. But in fact, two people's faces glowed the rosiest—that of Sharon and Terrance Lawton. He was wearing a rather nice suit for the occasion, but Margaret thought that, like Sharon, he had probably dressed up for someone's special benefit. The first thing Sharon did, however, was hold Shara Margaret for a few minutes, not caring at all that her daughter's hands went straight for her face and hair; then reluctantly, it seemed, she relinquished the baby to Livia.

Douglas came up to her, then, and stood her at arms' length and complimented her. "You can't be the same girl who just graduated a week ago," he teased. "You're just as beautiful as a model." Then he hugged her and introduced her to his two sons-in-law, and Margaret could tell he did so with genuine pride.

Then Eva hugged Sharon and introduced her and Margaret and Livia to her daughters Kathleen and Patricia. She nodded at Margaret.

"Margaret's been like a second mother to Sharon," she said, looking from Margaret to her daughters. "I suspect you've been responsible for Sharon's remarkable progress. When I first met Sharon, she was as shy as little Doug."

"Working in the café has introduced me to many people," Sharon said, laughing, "but it is true, Mrs. Reece. I was terribly shy, though I still am."

Margaret turned her attention to the twins and Terrance. They had stood back until all the adults had been introduced, and Margaret saw the attention Terrance had been paying to everyone, his eyes, however, fixed on Sharon. Margaret smiled to herself. He was smitten as badly as any young man she'd ever seen.

When the introductions were finally over, and everyone moved into the dining room and were finally seated at an elegantly set table and the children were seated in the breakfast room, Douglas Reece stood up from his end with a wine glass in his hand.

He made a short toast, looking a bit awkward, Margaret thought, but knew that she could do no better. Margaret noted, first that Shara was enthralled with all the people at the table, and her little eyes were bright with wonder, then Tom held a cracker out to her and she began munching it.

Margaret was seated near Eva, who sat at one end of the table. Livia sat to Margaret's left followed by Eva's oldest daughter, Kathleen and her husband Carl; and next to them were Patricia and Justin. Douglas sat at the head of the table at the other end. To his left was Sharon and, as if by design, Terrance, then the twins, Tom and, in a high chair, Shara; then Joel, who smiled across the table at Margaret.

She winked at him, then studied Sharon, who was currently involved in a conversation with Douglas. Margaret felt she had been right. The touch of makeup Livia had helped her to apply had accented Sharon's beauty. This was not lost on Terrance. He could not take his eyes off her, until Patrick nudged him, laughing.

And so the dinner proceeded. *Ah, Rose*, Margaret thought, as she ate and talked with Livia and Eva and looked at Sharon and Shara and all the rest. *The years, how they pass without you, how our friends change and grow. Too short our years, too short my moment here with Sharon. You would have loved her so.*

          *   *   *

Livia listened much more than she talked, glancing around the table, but time and again turning her attention to her granddaughter in the high chair between her son and Joel. They were almost totally absorbed in their baby, both of them feeding her, both wiping her mouth and hands, and looking at each other over her.

If, until now, she still had misgivings about them, she felt all her doubts melt away. She thought of her husband for the first time in weeks, and sighed quietly. *Milton, you were such a fool!*

Then she turned to Eva. "I want to thank you, Eva, for inviting me this evening."

Eva looked surprised. "Why, there's no need to thank me, Livia. Our little gathering wouldn't have been complete without you."

CHAPTER 29

DADDIES' GIRL

The spring winds of 1972 abated early in the season, and people were invoking the old saying "in like a lion and out like a lamb," to describe it, though it confused Sharon, and she asked Joel and Tom what it meant one morning when they were in having breakfast. It was a bright clear Saturday in early April, which had begun cold, but by nine o'clock, had begun to warm up, and most people had shed their jackets, smiling to each other where they met. "Beautiful day, ain't it?" "Gonna be a hot summer, though."

They had been seated not more than five minutes and Sharon had already taken their orders and was back at the table. Shara was loaded into a high chair and was already ripping through a box of corn flakes, which Sharon had given her, with just the top sliced off, so that she could discover (and put into her mouth) the contents. Sharon had also delivered a plate of eggs and bacon to an old man at a table next to the window display of a mother hen and baby chicks, and then she sat down with Tom and Joel and asked them what the old saying meant.

"When March comes in like a lion," Tom said, "then"—

"And what is this 'lion?'"

"Windy and dusty." Joel said, smiling at Sharon and turning his attention back to Shara, who was not the least interested in lions or anything else, except for the way the corn flakes could become stuck to her hand, which then required licking.

"Then, the old saying goes that March will go out like a lamb," Tom said.

Sharon nodded. "I see," she said, still looking a little confused, causing Tom and Joel both to smile. Then she brightened. "Then, one assumes that if March comes in like a lamb, it will go out roaring?"

"That's it," Tom said. This was just a simple exchange like those more complicated ones they had with Sharon all the time, and he recalled when they had first met, that every little detail fascinated her, but especially the use of language. She had a knack for picking up accents and could parrot back with amusing accuracy the twang of some local biddy complaining about her cold food or the occasional traveler with a foreign accent. Now, her speech no longer made people wonder where she might be from.

Shara appeared to have the same fascination with language, Tom thought, and both he and Joel were amazed that, at just a little over a year old, she listened to them and pronounced letters they were sure other children of similar age could not. But of course, they could not get her to perform her feats of linguistic skill when they wanted to show her off. One had to wait for her to decide when it was time to speak.

"Corn fake, dood," she said, now, holding out a little hand to her mother with a pulverized mass of them in her palm, and Sharon looked at her with a smile.

Side-by-side as they were, Tom saw the unmistakable resemblance between mother and daughter. But he also saw the resemblance between Shara and Joel. Though her cheeks were round with baby fat, he saw Joel's strong jaw in her; Joel contended, however, that Shara was beginning to favor him more and more.

As always, it didn't matter, Tom thought, as the four of them sat at the table. All of them enjoyed what little time they had left with each other. Sharon rarely commented on it, but he and Joel discussed it frequently, knowing that Shara was going to miss her mother, and so they made an effort to spend as much time with Sharon as they could.

Today, however, once they had finished breakfast, they had to run a few more errands. It was a rare free day, now that the fields were plowed and row beds were being watered for the planting. Douglas had said that he and Henry could watch the water, but the irrigation went long into the night. So it was with a sense of sadness that, as soon as breakfast was over, they had to leave.

It showed in Sharon's face when they were finished eating. So she took Shara out of the high chair, hugging her, and taking her in the office where Margaret was working on the books for the tax accountant. Then only a few minutes later, she came back out carrying Shara. When she handed her to Joel, Sharon smiled sadly. "Guys, she's growing so fast. Every day I see her she feels as if she has gained a pound."

"Come out when you can," Joel said. "She's beginning to walk more and more."

Although Sharon had been out for dinner a few days before on one of her rare days off, she had been spending time at a typing class in Deming a few nights a week. That night she had watched Shara get up from the floor by herself, walking to her on wobbly legs and shrieking with delight. "She will be walking everywhere, soon, then," she had said.

Now, she kissed Shara. "You be a good girl for mama, okay?"

Shara held up a hand and, in the way she had been taught, waived. "O'tay. Bye bye!"

*   *   *

Tom was apprehensive as they took Shara into the Farmer's Association, where Jeannie Lynn worked. They had promised Eva that they would pick up a few staples. Even though her garden provided them with all the vegetables they ever ate, and the chickens, pigs, and cows provided meat, they needed baby formula and baby food, as well as other groceries, so they took Shara through the aisles, with Shara riding in the shopping cart. People they knew stopped to talk with them and to look at the baby. Some looked at Shara, smiling and talking to them both, asking the usual, cooing at the baby's pretty face; but others looked from Shara to them and back, and Tom knew what they were doing. Still, most people were as friendly to them as they might be to a young heterosexual couple with a baby.

When they got up to the check out line, they deliberately chose Jeannie's counter. Tom was used to Joel's insistence that they not avoid her. But he agreed. When she looked up from her last customer, her eyes narrowed, then she said hello, and smiled at the baby, looking from Joel to Tom. They had seen Jeannie several times after the incident at the Angus Iron, when Detrick had slapped her face for her remarks about Sharon, and Jeannie had chosen not to mention it.

She began keying the items in on her register, moving them from the cart to the end of the counter, where a bag boy was stuffing them into paper bags. She was wearing the store's apron and, beneath it, a sleeveless top and jeans. Her blonde hair was full and shiny and Tom thought it was a shame that she could not be as nice on the inside as she looked on the outside, though he realized he didn't know what sort of life she had beyond clerking at Farmer's. At least she stuck to her job. She had been clerking here ever since she had graduated from high school.

"You're baby's cute," Jeannie said, without her usual cutting manner.

"Thanks," Joel said, smiling. "She's already walking a little."

At this, Jeannie actually smiled, and Tom was surprised. But he didn't entertain the idea that she was softening up.

When Jeannie had totaled the bill and told them how much it was, she looked at the baby, then at Tom, and then at Joel. "It's amazing, Joel," she said in a normal voice, "I really can't tell who she looks most like, and I know it's impossible that it's both of you."

"That's how we want to keep it, Jeannie," Joel said, handing her a hundred-dollar bill.

"But do *you* know, which one of you…?" Jeannie persisted.

Joel grinned at her. "If you promise not to make a big deal out of it, I'll tell you the truth."

Tom was surprised at him and was about to open his mouth to object, when Jeannie laughed. Even her laugh was not the usual fire-alarm laughter that drew attention to her. "I promise…as a fr—as a past friend."

"We have no idea," Joel said, "and that's the truth."

"Then there's not much to tell, is there?" Jeannie said, digging the change out of a drawer and counting it back to him. "She's real pretty, though. Just like her mother."

Again, Joel said, "Thank you."

A moment later they were pushing the cart through the doors, and Tom glanced back over his shoulder, expecting to see Jeannie leaning into the next customer and laughing about her exchange with them, but she was busily entering numbers on the register and was not involved in a conversation.

Still, as they got into the pickup, he decided that Jeannie must have been having a bad day, or she would have come up with some cutting remark to leave them with.

✶   ✶   ✶

They stopped by for a quick visit with Tom's mother, and were surprised to find that Mary was no longer living with her.

"She's finally gone back to work," Livia told them. She had taken Shara and was holding her on her lap. Even Livia had toys for Shara to play with, since she had been babysitting occasionally, and now she was squeaking a little tiger, and Shara was grinning up at her grandmother, then grabbing the tiger and squeezing it mercilessly, trying to get it to squeak like grandmother did.

"Doesn't her shoulder still bother her?" Tom asked, meaning Mary.

"Not so much now that the weather's warming up a little," Livia said. Then she sighed. "I think she's finally beginning to get over feeling guilty about her husband. That awful man!"

"How long is he going to be in jail?" Joel asked. "I lost track of the trial."

"We don't know, though I think he's already been shipped out of state. He got prison this time." Livia squeaked the tiger again, then set Shara down on the floor with it. But Shara wasn't interested in sitting and she got up and walked to the chair Joel was sitting in.

"Oh! Will you look at that!" Livia said. "When did she start that?"

Tom smiled at the surprise and delight on his mother's face. "Just a couple of weeks ago, just a few steps at a time. We were hoping she'd perform for you, but you can't get her to do it, if you tell people she can walk."

"Shara?" Livia said, "Come to Grandmother." She clapped her hands and Shara turned around at the sound; then, as requested, she walked back, carrying the tiger out in front of her with one hand. Midway through, she dropped to her knees and crawled the rest of the way.

"Queek tiga?"

Again Livia was surprised. She laughed. "Listen to you! Grandmother needs to see you more often! You'll be reading before I realize it!"

She followed them out to the pickup, carrying Shara, then reluctantly handing her to Tom. "Bye bye, honey."

Shara waved and said, "Bye Ganmutha!" which left Livia with her hand on her mouth and tears in her eyes.

Tom watched as his mother turned and made her way back into the house, tears stinging in his own eyes, glad that she was back in Common, glad for so many things. He positioned Shara in his lap and settled back in the seat. "You made Grandmother Livia very happy, Shara, did you know that?"

"Happy!" Shara said.

*   *   *

Joel drove home by the quickest route, since they'd stopped at Livia's and some of the food needed refrigerating. He was proud of Shara, today, and kept glancing over at her. Tom's hands were around her, holding her tight, even though she was squirming.

"You're daddies' girl, aren't you Shara?" Joel said, glancing from the road at her. She looked at him with her gray eyes, sitting back into Tom's chest.

"Dada. Dirl," she said.

They were heading down Eighth Street, passing by the trailer parks that had sprung up, then free of them, began to pass by the freshly cultivated fields where other farmers had their water running, and Joel thought back to when he and Tom were kids in high school, and he was taking Tom out to the farm for the weekend. Joel would be telling Tom what crops were coming up and just beginning to show a green haze against the brown of the moist earth.

Before they had realized their love for each other, Tom would have been sitting on the far side of the pickup, much like he was doing now. It was not out of a sense of distance from each other, but a way to keep their daughter out of the way when Joel had to shift gears.

Tom glanced over at Joel. "Could you believe how nice Jeannie Lynn was today?"

Joel knew what he meant, since she had never said anything to them in the last few years that wasn't designed to be a dig. He had wondered at it, too. "Maybe she's finally cooling it," he said. "You know, tired of the same old thing."

"The big test will be if we hear anything in the next few days about whose baby Shara is," Tom said. "She seemed awfully interested in your answer to that."

Joel just smiled at Tom. "She didn't get much of an answer, though. But she's right, Tom. It really isn't easy to decide who Shara favors the most."

Tom kissed Shara on the head. "Maybe she defies science and really is both of ours. What do you think?"

Joel knew Tom was joking. "Yeah, you're probably right."

CHAPTER 30

SO SOON

It had taken months, but the time finally came when Joel and Tom took Sharon to see a little bit more of New Mexico. She had never asked them about it, having had what turned out to be a very busy life, since coming into the United States. But one morning in June, almost two years to the day, when they had driven across the border and she had seen the same desert landscape on the U.S. side of the border as she had grown up in near Nuevo Casas Grandes, the three of them, and their baby, Shara, got into Sharon's car outside Margaret's house. Margaret was already at the café, but she had given Sharon the weekend off, telling her that she would have to get used to running the café without her, anyway, so to enjoy herself. They had also decided that this was a trip they were going to take by themselves, as a kind of last time to be together before Sharon went away to college.

Sharon said she wanted Joel to drive, and she got into the passenger side in the front seat, while Tom and Shara got into the back seat. Shara was now fifteen months old and had begun to string words together into short sentences, and when all four of them were in the car and Joel was heading west toward Deming on Interstate 10, Shara seemed pleased about something and insisted that she stand on Tom's thighs.

"Me see!" Shara said. "Daddy, me see!"

Sharon turned around to look at Shara. "What do you see, honey?"

"Dada, Daddy, Mama."

With that simple declaration, Tom realized that she had given each of them a different name. Either he had not noticed before, or she had not articulated the distinction in such a way. So Tom experimented to see if Shara's naming of them was as distinct as it sounded.

"Where's Dada?" he asked.

Shara was now standing on his thighs, and he was holding her around the waist with both arms, so that if Joel had to suddenly slam on the brakes, she would not go flying. "Dada dwive."

"Where's Daddy?" he asked.

Shara thought his question was funny and she laughed. "You Daddy."

"I'm not Dada?"

"Dada Zoel," she said, still having difficulty with her "j" sounds, as when she went down the front porch steps at the house, she sang out "Zump! Zump! Zump!" as she landed on each one.

"Where's Mama?" Sharon asked, peeking at Shara through her fingers.

"Mama gone, gone!" Shara said.

Although everyone laughed, it hit Tom that it was true. Mama would be gone gone, so soon.

While they had been playing this game, they had quickly come to Deming, then headed toward the town of Silver City, New Mexico, some sixty miles north.

Sharon looked around at the desert; but ahead the mountains seemed closer and, though she did not have a name for the mountains, she saw Cook's Peak, which dominated the northern horizon.

Joel began telling her about the small settlements nestled in the mountains to the north, about the copper mining that had been going on since the last century. As they drove steadily northward, the land began to rise, and now it went from bare desert with mesquite and yucca plants to taller and more lush, yellow gramma grasses.

"This is so much like Nuevo Casas Grandes!" Sharon said. "It is so beautiful!"

Tom heard a touch of homesickness in her voice and wondered if she missed Mexico.

It was mid-morning. The sky was an azure against the rolling away yellow hills of the prairie, and up ahead, the blue of the mountains began to take on deeper colors. They continued to climb, and Sharon turned around in the seat, looking back toward Common.

"The view is…magnificent," she said.

Tom turned in the seat and stood Shara up so she could look out the back window. "Nifent!" Shara said, her little voice rising higher, and Tom wondered what she was looking at—surely not the sweeping away view with the now distant Florida Mountains.

The highway began to curve northwest, and Cook's Peak, which had been almost due north, was now off to the right. As the terrain continued to change, hills and mountains rose up on either side of the highway.

The small mining town of Hurley came up on the east side of the highway, and Shara, who had been looking around, began pointing excitedly. "Big cigette, Dada! Big cigette, Mama. See?" and with a tiny forefinger she pointed at the tall smokestacks.

"They do look like giant cigarettes!" Sharon laughed.

"But where on earth did she learn about cigarettes?" Joel asked, glancing back at Shara, though no one could answer.

Within a few moments, as the road continued to curve toward the northwest, the big cigarettes were blocked out by a close hill. A little while later, as the highway rose and fell over the undulating terrain, Piñon pines and juniper bushes began to dot the fields of gramma grass, and they passed through the town of Cobre/Bayard.

When they entered the outskirts of Silver City, Joel turned off onto Highway 15 that ran due north. "This is where we leave the desert, for sure," Joel said.

Sharon continued to look around as did her daughter, though Shara was becoming less and less active. Tom and Sharon smiled at each other about their daughter when their eyes met and, again, Tom thought of Sharon's leaving for college within a few weeks.

As he understood it, Terrance was going to leave his car in Common and he and Patrick were going to take turns riding with Sharon on their trip to California. Since they were all heading to Berkeley, the three of them had decided it would be fun and easy on Sharon if they drove back together. Once back in school none of them would have an excessive need for a car, and the three of them could share rides when it was necessary. Tom suspected that Terrance and Sharon would be seeing quite a bit of each other.

But neither he nor Joel felt too comfortable talking to Sharon about it; she never offered any information on her own about her friendship with Terrance. The only two who did talk to them about Terrance and Sharon were, of course, Patrick and Detrick.

Although Tom thought Detrick might feel jealous or left out, since Patrick and Sharon would be together in Berkeley, while he was down in Texas, Tom had never seen any evidence that this was so. Then he shrugged off such thoughts as they began heading into the mountain range itself and the road began curving through pine trees.

Joel's window was down and the air coming in was cool, rather than the hot air of the desert.

"Told you," Joel said, glancing at Sharon. "We're barely fifty miles from Common and, look. Forest. What do you think?"

"I have never seen a forest, Joel," she said. "It is so beautiful! Are there forests in California?"

There it was again, Tom thought. Hanging over all their heads.

Joel nodded at her question. "Old growth redwood forests north of San Francisco. Trees so big there's this one that they've cut through the trunk, and put a road through it."

Sharon laughed. "You're teasing me, of course. No tree could be that big!"

But Joel glanced over at her, smiling. "Honest, Sharon. There's a picture of it in the *National Geographic*, I think. I'm sure it's not much wider than your car, but I've seen the picture."

"Then I hope to see it," Sharon said, settling back into the seat and looking out the window. "There is so much, so very much to see and learn," she said, though not speaking directly to anyone in particular. Then she turned in the seat, so that she could look at both Tom and Joel. Though she was smiling, her bottom lip quivered a little.

"Do you both mind, terribly? Please be truthful."

"What?" Joel said, glancing at her. From what Tom saw of his profile, he could see that Joel was serious, as well, now.

They both waited.

Sharon took a deep breath, trying to smile, but her lip quivered nonetheless and, as a tear fell on her cheek, she quickly wiped it away. "That I am leaving my daughter behind, while I attend school."

Joel started to answer, but Sharon put a hand on his shoulder. "People will say, how can a mother do this. And I would have said the same thing a few years before now, before I knew that my life would be so different from what it was."

"But that's what we agreed on," Joel said. "Sharon, you have nothing to feel guilty about."

Sharon reached over the back seat and took her daughter's hand. Shara was almost asleep, but when Sharon took her hand her little eyes blinked open, then fell shut. She squeezed her hand then let it go.

"Still," Sharon said, "I am unsure. I did this for the two of you, so that you might have a child. But now I see her and, at night, I miss her, and I think that she will miss me."

"But you need to get an education," Tom said, wondering how Joel was feeling about Sharon's guilt and, something else—seeming not to want to give her daughter up.

Sharon smiled. "Yes, I know. I must get an education. I must see the world, so to speak. And yes, I must allow my daughter to grow up with her two fathers."

"We don't want you to think that you have to give up Shara," Joel said. "Maybe that's how we thought about it when we all agreed what we were doing that night. But I am sure that Tom will agree that Shara will need you in her life. A child needs a mother. At least that's what I've learned in the last couple of years."

Tom was surprised and, in a way, pleased that Joel had put it as he did. "Joel is right, Sharon," he said. "If you want to come back to Common after you graduate and share our daughter with us, isn't that what her name means, after all?"

Sharon smiled then. "Then it is not terrible of me to do this?"

"No!" both Tom and Joel said together.

All three of them laughed then, and Tom thought it was something they had needed to discuss, and probably would have to talk about again once she had graduated. What if she decided to stay in Berkeley, or took a job on the east coast and, yet, wanted Shara with her? But he did not mention those thoughts as they continued on into the village of Pinos Altos, which Sharon translated as "tall pines."

*   *   *

The town of Pinos Altos looked to Sharon like something she had seen in a John Wayne western on Margaret's television. They came into the small village from the south. Small dirt roads led off in different directions, where people's houses sat among the juniper and grass, and farther away, the pines stood magnificently over the town. The main street was paved. On one side, just like in the movies, was a saloon and old split-rail posts where a cowboy could dismount and tie his horse. Even the sidewalk in front of the saloon was made of raw lumber, and the only thing that ruined the effect of being back in the last century were the cars parked here and there. Most of them were parked at the Buckhorn Saloon.

It was around noon, and Sharon realized that she was hungry, now that they had arrived in the small town. Smoke from a chimney filled the cool air over the saloon, and she smelled what had to be cooking meat.

She could not put into words what she was seeing as she stepped out of the car and stretched her legs. It was if she had been transported into a different world. The air was chilly, and she was glad Joel had suggested she bring a sweater. She gratefully put it on, smiling as she did so, looking around. She read the hand-painted signs above the saloon, as well as the one that said "Opera House, Circa 1860," above the adjacent building.

They ate lunch at the Buckhorn Saloon, and Sharon was as interested in the waitresses working among the crowd that had gathered there as she was in the decorations. Shara was bright-eyed and jabbering at the team of horses drawing a wagon full of barrels on one of the beer signs, and the glitter of the wine glasses hanging by their stems above the bar, where people sat drinking and watching a television behind the counter.

In the room where they were sitting to eat, a large fireplace had been lit, and Joel suggested they order a bottle of wine.

"I'd like to celebrate our friendship," he said, to which Sharon and Tom agreed, and when they each had a glass of wine, and Shara a glass of water, they clinked their glasses, each of them touching Shara's glass, as well, and smiling at her. She was sitting in a high chair the waitress had brought for her and grinned back, showing what was quickly becoming a mouth full of teeth.

Sharon saw others looking their way and smiling. But inside, Sharon suddenly felt like crying, for this was not the beginning of something, but the end. It was all too soon, she thought, as the waitress served their meals, and yet, she knew this too was as it should be. Joel and Tom had each other; yet she was like Shara, a child, just starting out in life.

She thought for a moment about Terrance Lawton, a small thrill coursing through her. But she knew she could not let it go beyond a friendship with him, for a long while. She had too much to do in the next few years to consider marrying someone.

Later, they drove out of Pinos Altos, again continuing north and spent a long, beautiful day, driving along winding roads, with pine trees growing on this side and that, and meadows full of wild flowers suddenly appearing around a bend. In places, the earth dropped away, and far below ran the Gila river, and they stood on the side of the road and looked down where it ran far below them.

Still later as they returned to Pinos Altos, they rented a cabin with a fire place and two bedrooms upstairs. It reminded her of her parents' house, in a way, from the stone fireplace, dominating the living room, to the small windows, though these did not have curtains. The walls were raw wood with pictures of bears and the forest, and even one of a meadow with a stream running through it. In the center of the room, two couches of thick fabric sat on a hook rug, and this too reminded her of home, though of course the house on the community farm was much more well furnished, and she supposed this cabin was more like a motel. There was a kitchen, divided from the living room, where they had brought out the cooler and made sandwiches and opened cans of Coca Cola for themselves and made a bottle for Shara and fed her mashed potatoes, which Tom and Joel had brought.

Then long after Shara had been put to bed, she and her two saviors, whom she now counted as her greatest friends, talked long into the night. Their faces were lit and rosy from the fire's glow, and she thought of their night in Casas Grandes. They were much more at ease, now. Tom and Joel sat on one couch, close together, as they always sat, and Sharon sat on the other couch, feeling both full and, somehow empty. They talked until the fire in the fireplace became glowing embers and a chill settled into the room.

Later, when Sharon lay in the bed with Shara, she looked out the window at the night sky full of stars, and this too reminded her of home, which only seemed so many years ago. But she did not shut her eyes to dream of what might be; instead, pulling her sleeping daughter close and hugging her, she gazed at the night sky, watching as falling stars shot silently across the sky and were gone in an instant.

I have come so far, she thought. *I love so many people!* And she felt loved, as well. Yet too soon, she would once again be leaving all those she loved. This time, however, she would not be leaving in sorrow, as she had left Neuvo Casas Grandes. This time, she knew she could always come back home to Common.

CHAPTER 31

LEAVING

On the day that Sharon Minninger left for college, Margaret did not open the café; nor did she drive out to the Reece farm to say good-bye. Instead, she had had Sharon all to herself the night before, and Margaret had told her so many things that had been left unsaid during the two years she had known her.

She had talked mostly about her relationship with Rose Crutcher, whom she had met at a girl's finishing school in Boston in 1918. She told her how they had recognized their kinship with one another and how, when they had matriculated from the finishing school, she had taken Rose home to Montana. "It was there," Margaret said, "that Rose and I confessed our love for each other. But when my father divined the relationship that we had, after trying to marry me off to one of his business associates, whom I spurned, Rose and I set off on our own."

Sharon had listened. They had sat on the couch in their nightgowns, drinking hot tea, despite the muggy evening, and Sharon had cried for the breakup with her father, while crying with happiness for Margaret's long relationship with her beloved Rose.

"You do not mind," Margaret had asked, "that I have not told you so much of myself these past two years? I did not want you to think"—

Sharon had only touched Margaret on the shoulder. "I have learned many things, Margaret, from you and my friends, Tom and Joel. I shall always love you as a friend and as a mother. I have learned to figure many things out and to reason that you are a wonderful and good person. So, I do not mind."

Margaret had not wanted to cry in front of her, but she did. Then she had told her how much she would miss her, once she was away at school. "You will write to me, dear, won't you?"

Sharon promised that she would. "But I shall also come home and stay with you for the holidays and during the summers between semesters. So it is not such a bad thing, is it?"

Margaret wiped the tears away. "It is a very good thing that you will get an education and, even though you may feel obligated in a way to return here to Common after you graduate, I would like to advise you to see as much of this great country as you can, as well as to develop a career. There is so little, here, in this small town for young people."

Sharon had just nodded, though looking a little sad for a moment. "That, I will have to see about," she said. "At this moment, tonight, however, I feel that Common is my home, and I should be sad to stay away too long. For my daughter is also here."

Margaret understood. And so, when Sharon got up the next morning, and had packed her belongings in the car, except for those things she would leave in her room, they had hugged and cried, and she watched Sharon drive expertly down the street, turning a corner, and disappearing. Margaret returned to the house and wept, speaking to Rose, as if she were there on the couch with her.

*   *   *

Livia called the Reece home as early as she thought would be appropriate, speaking to Sharon and wishing her luck on her trip. "We'll take good care of your daughter for you, Sharon," she said, and then she confessed something that she asked her not to tell her son or anyone else.

Sharon promised that she would not.

"You are precisely the kind of girl I had always dreamed that my son would marry; and even though I know this is not to be, I want you to know I will always consider you like a kind of daughter-in-law to me. I hope you do not mind."

"Of course, I don't, Livia," Sharon assured her. "You should know that you have made Tom very happy, to have come back to Common to be his mother, again. So I will consider you my mother-in-law, too."

Livia hung up a moment later, fighting back tears. And, again, she thought of her dead husband and what a fool he had been.

*   *   *

Eva Reece kept herself busy to avoid thinking too much about how empty the house would be once the twins were gone. She had spent the day before helping the boys with their laundry, and going through the clothes they were taking with them. She didn't try to dissuade Patrick from taking those awful tie-dyed shirts and bell-bottoms, though she insisted that he throw in one of his suits, along with ties, dress shirts, and nice shoes.

"With Sharon, there, I'm sure you boys will want to take her out to a nice dinner once in a while. And you've seen how nice she dresses."

Patrick had smiled at her, accepting whatever it was she insisted that he take. "We will, Mom. Take her out, that is. Though really, people in Berkeley dress a lot more casual than you'd think."

Despite that, Eva didn't back down. She stayed up late into the night, baking and packing containers for both Patrick and Detrick. But especially for Detrick, she doubled up on the brownies and cookies, knowing that he was probably hanging out with a much different crowd of cowboys down in West Texas. She didn't insist that he take many dress clothes, either, since the kinds of clothes he wore were much more conservative than those that Patrick apparently dressed in when he was at Berkeley.

Then she got up the next morning and continued baking and cooking breakfast. The dining room and kitchen were buzzing with the boys rushing in and out, packing stuff, and when Terrance arrived, she fed him breakfast, too.

Henry and Sally were in the thick of the buzz, talking and pulling on their older brothers' sleeves for a little attention. Eva noticed that Douglas wasn't out doing chores, either, but helped the twins pack their vehicles.

Then, when Sharon drove up shortly after the sun had burst over the Florida Mountains, the whole timbre of the busy-ness changed. The twins and Terrance wanted to go through all the stuff she had packed, making sure that she had her paperwork and supplies. Eva wanted a few minutes alone with her before she and the boys left. Once everyone was seated at the breakfast table, with the breakfast out of the way and they were drinking coffee, Eva asked if Sharon would follow her for a moment.

Sharon was wearing Levi's and a man's shirt. Her blonde hair was done up in a pony-tail, and Eva was glad to see that she was wearing a pair of sensible shoes. "It's going to be a long trip, so you look like you're going to be comfortable," she said, when they were in the living room.

Douglas came in, as well, and gave Sharon a hug. "It's always hard on me and Eva when the twins pack up and leave for college, but this time, it's going to be worse, since we're losing you, too."

Sharon smiled, and there were just the slightest glimmer of tears in her eyes. "It is going to be difficult for me, as well, Douglas." She looked from him to Eva. "I am going to miss you both."

"Well, then," Eva said, pulling an envelope from her apron pocket and handing it to Sharon. "Douglas and I want you to have this. You tuck it into your purse. It's a little something from us. You'll need it when you get an apartment. There's so much you'll have to buy to get started, and you'll need a little for emergencies and what not."

Sharon looked at the envelope and Eva saw that the tears were really beginning to pool in her eyes. "I do not know what to say. I—everyone has been so good to me."

Eva hugged her then. "You have brought joy into everyone's lives, here, and your daughter is so precious to us."

"Speaking of Shara," Douglas said, "Where are Tom and Joel?"

As if in answer to his question, Shara came from the dining room walking with her little legs as fast as she could go, and Sharon scooped her up, hugging her.

Shara was dressed in little pants and a T-shirt. Her face was freshly washed, and her hair had been combed, Eva saw, and one of the boys had attempted to put a beret in her hair, where it usually stuck up or out.

"How's my baby?" Douglas asked, taking Shara's hand.

"I dood, gampa!" Shara said in a high voice. "Mama go tool?" she asked, then, touching Sharon's face with her hand.

Eva was surprised at the baby's question, realizing that Tom or Joel had been trying to explain to her what was about to happen.

"I'm going on a trip, honey," Sharon said, then hugged Shara close. "You'll be a good girl for your daddies?"

"Shara be dood," she said.

A few minutes later, the inevitable leave-taking got under way. Everyone followed the twins, Terrance, and Sharon out to their cars. Detrick got into his pickup and started it up, waving to his twin. "Take good care of Sharon for me guys! Take good care of little Shara, Joel! Make him write, Tom!" As everyone waived, Detrick put his pickup into gear and drove down the driveway and out the gate.

Then Patrick got into his car, and Terrance and Sharon got into her car. Eva waived, then quickly walked back into the house, feeling her own tears welling up. In a few days, things would be back to normal, and in a few months, the twins and Sharon would be home for Christmas.

Douglas came into the house a few minutes later. "Well. Here we are again, Eva. Guess I better get back to work."

*　　　　　　　*　　　　　　　*

Joel knew Shara couldn't understand that it would be a long while before she saw her mother again. He figured that even the four months of a school semester to her would be like a year to him and Tom. As they walked back to their own house with Shara between them, each holding one of her little hands, Joel could not help but recall the night they had spent with Sharon in the hotel in Casas Grandes.

They had their child, now, and he vowed to himself, while looking over at Tom, that in the years to come, their little family would be as happy as any family could be. But it hadn't turned out quite as he had at first thought he wanted it.

Out there in the world was one of the most wonderful women he'd ever known; he hoped that what she had done for them would not bring her too many tears.

AFTERWORD

The series of novels, of which *The Blind Season* is a part, has been my attempt to represent common experiences that real-life gay men and women have always shared. The series, consisting of four books, is entitled "Common Threads in the Life." There could be a dozen books in this series, however, and there would still be common threads to be included.

Common Sons, the first book in the series, is basically a coming-out story, and even though some book editors have decided that "coming out stories are old hat" or that there have been enough of them, I cheerfully and wholeheartedly disagree. Coming out before Stonewall was decidedly different than coming out in this new millennium. Even though violence against gays and lesbians and transgendered people is far more prevalent today than it was forty years ago, in a way, gay youth have an easier time "coming out" now than they did before Stonewall. People in general are more apt to be aware of gay men and women and questioning youth, more apt to know of resources and groups to recommend to someone who is struggling with this identity. And gay people themselves have at their fingertips the internet and email through which they can learn about gay issues. I deliberately set *Common Sons* in a place and time where the characters would have to discover for themselves what their homosexuality meant, far from the jet-stream of any gay subculture.

Further, one of the common threads all gay men and women experience is either the acceptance or rejection of their families; or, in many cases, accepting or rejecting their families when they come out. *Common Sons* also explores these issues.

In *The Blind Season*, the second book in the series, the characters deal with another important thread—whether to have children by adoption, artificial insemination, some sort of surrogate relationship, or by raising the children they might have had through a previous heterosexual marriage. Again, as in

Common Sons, I set the characters in a time and place distant from today, because I wanted them to have to come to terms with the issues of gay parenting themselves. Although it is probably less likely in the early 1970s that gay people dealt with gay parenting, I do not doubt that it occurred. *The Blind Season* also deals with other issues of family life that gay men and women must deal with on a daily basis. And that is how much to involve their families in the raising of their children with their aunts and uncles, grandparents and cousins.

Another common thread that the vast majority of gay men and women experience is the way in which the religion they grew up in relates to them, or the way they relate to their religion. In the coming-out process, gay people either struggle with their religion, trying to find a way to retain it in their lives, or struggle with a way to reject it as being too alien or repressive. So in both *Common Sons* and *The Salvation Mongers* (the third book in the series), I introduced characters who would explore this common thread. Before Stonewall, before Anita Bryant and her "Save Our Children" campaign—and even before the Metropolitan Community Church movement—gay people had very uneasy alliances with their religious upbringing. *The Salvation Mongers* explores common threads of religious experience most gay people have shared in one form or another. The ex-gay movement is only a formalized process of what many have put themselves through. They have all too often tried to become heterosexual through some sort of religious conversion (or other magic bullet) and, in most cases, have come out on the other end of the process in tact and a little wiser. For some gay men and women, however, this is a struggle that wastes lives, either in the years' long self-loathing that results, or in the literal loss of life through suicide.

In *The Gathering*, the fourth book in the series (to be published in 2003), a whole host of other common threads will be explored, including how children of gay parents deal with having same-sex parents, how same-sex parents deal with raising children; how gay people deal with aging parents of their own; how they deal with the loss of friends with AIDS; even how gay people deal with hate crimes. Set on the cusp of the coming new millennium, the characters in this final book of the series are, like all of us glbt people, poised on the edge of an abyss—our spotted and stained history at our backs and before us a future at once bright with possibilities and fraught with dangers from those who continue to act against us.

Although my work is not autobiographical in any real sense (I'm neither Joel Reece nor Tom Allen), I've drawn extensively from my own parallel experiences of coming out of the closet in the middle of nowhere, of struggling with the expectations of society and religion (being in a heterosexual marriage, fathering a child), alternately feeling rejected by my family and rejecting them, to slowly, inexorably finding my way back home.

And so it is that I've spent over a decade immersing myself in the writing of this series.

—Ronald L. Donaghe, Las Cruces, New Mexico

ABOUT THE AUTHOR

Born before the widespread use of plastics but after atomic bombs had been used in warfare and the cold war had begun, Ronald L. Donaghe was aware that the world could be a dangerous place at a much too young age. He recalls the 1950s, when the United States was the undisputed world leader economically and militarily, yet was almost like a police-state during the era of the "Red Scare" and the McCarthy Senate hearings, when blacklisting occurred frequently, especially of those in the entertainment industry and all it took for a career to be ruined was innuendo and frequent (if unproven) accusations that someone was a "card-carrying member of the Communist Party." He recalls the nuclear bomb drills in grade school and the advice from the government to build fallout shelters.

Still, growing up on a family farm in southwestern New Mexico was a relatively safe place from all that. He recalls the clear night skies, frothy with stars, the way the water in the irrigation pond would be warm at night, perfect for swimming in after a day working in the fields. The oldest son of a family of six children, Donaghe enjoyed the visits from aunts and uncles, and cousins, playing "Kick the Can" and "Red Rover" when the sun set in the west and dusk seemed to last for hours.

Donaghe discovered the Russian literature of Tolstoy and Dostoevsky when he was a freshman in high school; the French existentialists when he entered college, and the highly charged and entertaining gay fiction of Gordon Merrick and, later, Patricia Nell Warren. Wanting to be a novelist at an early age, Donaghe filled many spiral notebooks with stories and, later, filled such notebooks with journal entries.

He took every course in poetry and creative writing offered at New Mexico State University and Southwest Texas State University, where he received his bachelor's in literature and philosophy. He majored in history and English in graduate school at SWTSU and majored in technical writing and computer science in graduate school at NMSU. After working as a technical writer for the military defense and communications industries in Washington, DC, Dallas, Texas, and elsewhere, he returned to New Mexico where he settled into a job as technical editor at New Mexico State University and continued to pursue his other career as a novelist.

Although he has lived in big cities from Texas to the east coast, he prefers the climate, people, cultures, and clear atmosphere of the desert southwest.

**If you enjoyed this book,
check out these iUniverse authors:**

Mark Roeder
A Better Place
A Better Place is the story of two boys from two completely different worlds struggling to find themselves amongst a
whirlwind of confusion. The unlikely pair struggle through
friendship and heartbreaks, betrayal and hardships, to find
the deepest desire of their hearts.

Josh Thomas
Murder at Willow Slough
A gay reporter, a straight cop and thirteen dead men: will
the good guys get the killers, or will the killers get them?
Murder at Willow Slough is simultaneously terrifying, tough
and tender, as two very different men stare down danger
and discover the truth: the only defense against evil is people who care for each other.

Mark Kendrick
Into This World We're Thrown
New challenges face the boys when they come out to
family and friends in the sequel to **Desert Sons**.
As their relationship becomes public, Scott and Ryan deal
with heartache and jealousy.

**Buy these books through your local bookstore
or at www.iuniverse.com.**

iUniverse™
Star

0-595-18976-8

Printed in the United States
149952LV00001B/278/A

9 780595 189762